Dear Reader,

Okay, I'll admit it—authors have favorite books. I know, I know, books are like children and we don't always want to admit to liking one better than another, but it's true. The Goddess Summoning books are my favorite children.

As with my bestselling young adult series, the House of Night, my Goddess Summoning books celebrate the independence, intelligence, and unique beauty of modern women. My heroes all have one thing in common: they appreciate powerful women and are wise enough to value brains as well as beauty. Isn't respect and appreciation an excellent aphrodisiac?

Delving into mythology and reworking ancient myths is fun! In Goddess of the Sea *I retell the story of the mermaid Undine—who switches places with a female U.S. Air Force sergeant who needs to do some escaping of her own. In* Goddess of Spring, *I turn my attention to the Persephone/Hades myth and send a modern woman to hell! Who knew hell and its brooding god would be hot in so many wonderful, seductive ways?*

From there we take a lovely vacation in Las Vegas with the divine twins, Apollo and Artemis, in Goddess of Light. *Finally we come to what is my favorite of all fairy tales, "Beauty and the Beast."* *In* Goddess of the Rose *I created my own version of this beloved tale, building a magical realm from whence dreams originate—good and bad—and bringing to life a beast who absolutely took my breath away.*

I hope you enjoy my worlds, and my wish for you is that you discover a spark of goddess magic of your own!

P. C. Cast

Praise for *Goddess of the Sea*

"Suspense, fantasy, time travel, all topped off with a very healthy dollop of romance . . . The good news is that this is just the beginning."

—*Romance Reviews Today*

"Captivating—poignant, funny, erotic! Lovely characters, wonderful romance, constant action and a truly whimsical fantasy . . . Delightful. A great read."

—*The Best Reviews*

"A fun combination of myth, girl power and sweet romance [with] a bit of suspense. A must-read . . . A romance that celebrates the magic of being a woman."

—*Affaire de Coeur*

"[An] adult fairy tale . . . the audience will cherish."

—*Midwest Book Review*

"Vivid and colorful . . . Splendid blend of fantasy, history, intrigue and passion . . . Outstanding. Watch out for this author."

—*Rendezvous*

"Most innovative . . . From beginning to end, the surprises in P. C. Cast's new page-turner never stopped. Its poignancy resonates with both whimsy and fantasy . . . I loved it!"

—*New York Times* **bestselling author Sharon Sala**

"Sweet and funny."

—*Huntress Reviews*

Goddess of Spring

"One of the top romantic fantasy mythologists today."

—*Midwest Book Review*

"As always, there's a dash of humor and lots of meltingly hot sex."

—*Affaire de Coeur*

"Enchanting . . . Lovely."

—*The Romance Readers Connection*

"A veritable feast for readers who just can't get enough fantasy dished up with their romance. Mythology has never been so fun!"

—*Romance Reviews Today*

Goddess of Light

"A charmer . . . Cast continues her unique brand of delightfully mixing a modern-day romance with a mythological legend . . . Creative."

—*Midwest Book Review*

"Pure enjoyment . . . Anything can [happen] when gods and mortals mix."

—*Rendezvous*

"A fanciful mix of mythology and romance with a dash of humor for good measure . . . Engages and entertains . . . Lovely." —*Romance Reviews Today*

Goddess of the Rose

"P. C. Cast [is] well-known for her blending of mythological tales and romance . . . [A] beautiful adult fairy tale . . . Readers will be enchanted."

—*The Best Reviews*

"Outstanding . . . Magic, myth and romance with a decidedly modern twist. Her imagination and storytelling abilities are true gifts to the genre."

—*Romantic Times*

Goddess of Love

"Sexy, charming and fun, *Goddess of Love* is the fantasy romance of the year! You will fall in love with this book. (I did!)"

—*New York Times* **bestselling author Susan Grant**

"Touching, clever, and an excellent heiress to the Goddess Summoning series. Cast's ability to subvert misogynistic mythology . . . and reaffirm what makes women wonderful, is always worth celebrating . . . I bestow my snarky blessings on this book." —*Smart Bitches Trashy Books*

"Scorchingly sensual, utterly delicious! P. C. Cast is a true master of her craft."

—*New York Times* **bestselling author Gena Showalter**

Sensation Titles by P. C. Cast

The Goddess Summoning Series

GODDESS OF THE SEA
GODDESS OF SPRING
GODDESS OF LIGHT
GODDESS OF THE ROSE
GODDESS OF LOVE
WARRIOR RISING

Anthologies

MYSTERIA
(with MaryJanice Davidson, Susan Grant, and Gena Showalter)
MYSTERIA LANE
(with MaryJanice Davidson, Susan Grant, and Gena Showalter)

Goddess

OF THE

P. C. Cast

BERKLEY SENSATION, NEW YORK

THE BERKLEY PUBLISHING GROUP
Published by the Penguin Group
Penguin Group (USA) Inc.
375 Hudson Street, New York, New York 10014, USA
Penguin Group (Canada), 90 Eglinton Avenue East, Suite 700, Toronto, Ontario M4P 2Y3, Canada
(a division of Pearson Penguin Canada Inc.)
Penguin Books Ltd., 80 Strand, London WC2R 0RL, England
Penguin Group Ireland, 25 St. Stephen's Green, Dublin 2, Ireland (a division of Penguin Books Ltd.)
Penguin Group (Australia), 250 Camberwell Road, Camberwell, Victoria 3124, Australia
(a division of Pearson Australia Group Pty. Ltd.)
Penguin Books India Pvt. Ltd., 11 Community Centre, Panchsheel Park, New Delhi—110 017, India
Penguin Group (NZ), 67 Apollo Drive, Rosedale, North Shore 0632, New Zealand
(a division of Pearson New Zealand Ltd.)
Penguin Books (South Africa) (Pty.) Ltd., 24 Sturdee Avenue, Rosebank, Johannesburg 2196,
South Africa

Penguin Books Ltd., Registered Offices: 80 Strand, London WC2R 0RL, England

Cover art by Don Sipley.
Cover design by George Long.
Interior text design by Tiffany Estreicher.

Berkley trade paperback ISBN: 978-0-425-22688-9.

PRINTING HISTORY
Berkley Sensation mass-market edition / October 2003
Berkley Sensation trade paperback edition / October 2008

The Library of Congress has cataloged a prior edition under LCCN: 2004572953.

PRINTED IN THE UNITED STATES OF AMERICA

10 9 8 7 6 5 4

For Kim Doner,
muse and friend.
Thank you for being the perfect problem solver.

Acknowledgments

Thank you, Meredith Bernstein, for being a wonderful agent. Your support and belief in me are priceless.

Christine Zika, you are a pleasure to work with. Your insight is invaluable; you truly are the Goddess Editor.

Thanks, Mom, for letting me borrow your maiden name.

Rachael Ryan, thank you for your enthusiasm, you're a great first reader.

And a special thank-you to the students in my second-hour Creative Writing II class for the helpful brainstorming. Hope you like your cameos!

The Valley Spirit never dies.
It is named the Mysterious Feminine.
And the doorway of the Mysterious Feminine
Is the base from which Heaven and Earth sprang.
It is there within us all the while.
Draw upon it as you will, it never runs dry . . .

FROM THE TAO TE CHING

Part One

Chapter One

Arms filled with groceries, CC struggled to pull her key from the lock and push the door shut behind her with her foot. Automatically, she glanced up at the clock in the foyer of her spacious apartment. Seven thirty already. It had taken her an eternity to finish things up at the Communication Center and then stop by the package store and the commissary. After that, fighting the traffic from Tinker Air Force Base had been like driving through axle-deep mud. To add to her frustration, she had tried to take a shortcut home and had ended up taking a wrong turn. Soon she was hopelessly lost. A kind soul at a Quick Trip had given her directions, and she had felt compelled to explain to him that she was lost only because she had been stationed at Tinker for just three months, and she hadn't had time to learn her way around yet.

The man had patted her shoulder like she was a puppy and asked, "What is a young little thing like you doing in the air force?" CC had treated the question rhetorically, thanked him and driven away, face hot with embarrassment.

Understandably, her already harried nerves jumped at the insistent sound of her ringing phone.

"Hang on! I'm coming!" she yelled and rushed into the kitchen, plopping the bags unceremoniously onto the spotless counter and lunging for the phone.

"Hello," she panted into the dead sound of a dial tone that was broken only by the rhythmic bleat of her answering machine. "Well, at least they left a message." CC sighed and carried the phone with her back to the kitchen, punching in her message retrieval code. With one hand she held the phone to her ear, and with the other, she extracted twin bottles of champagne from one of the bags.

"You have two new messages," the mechanical voice proclaimed. "First new message, sent at five thirty P.M."

CC listened attentively as she picked at the metallic casing that covered the wire-imprisoned champagne cork.

"Hello, Christine, it's your parents!" Her mom's recorded voice, sounding a little unnatural and tinny, chirped through the phone.

"Hi there, Christine!" More distant, but similarly cheerful, Dad's voice echoed from an extension.

CC smiled indulgently. Of course it was her parents—they were the only two people on this earth who still insisted on calling her by her given name.

"Just wanted to say we didn't actually forget your big day."

Here her mom paused, and she could hear her dad chuckling in the background. Forget her birthday? She hadn't thought they had—until then.

Her mom's breathy voice continued. *"We've just been running ourselves ragged getting ready for our next cruise! You know how long it takes your father to pack."* This said in a conspiratorial whisper. *"But don't worry, honey, even though we didn't get your box off, we did manage to fix up a little surprise for our favorite twenty-five year old."*

"Twenty-five?" Her dad sounded honestly surprised. *"Well, good Lord. I thought she was only twenty-two."*

"Time sure flies, dear," Mom said sagely.

"Damn straight, honey," Dad agreed. *"That's one reason I told you we should spend more time traveling—but only one reason."* Dad chuckled suggestively.

"You certainly were right about that *reason, dear."* Mom kidded back breathlessly, suddenly sounding decades younger.

"They're flirting with each other on my message," CC sputtered. "And they really did forget my birthday!"

"Anyway, we're getting ready to leave for the airport—"

Dad's voice, even more distant, broke in. *"Elinor! Say good-bye, the airport limo is here."*

"Well, have to go, Birthday Girl! Oh, and you have a nice time on your little air force trip. Aren't you leaving in a couple of days?"

Her little air force trip?! CC rolled her eyes. Her ninety-day deployment as noncommissioned officer in charge of Quality Control at the Communications Center at Riyadh Air Base in Saudi Arabia to support the war on terrorism was just a "little air force trip?"

"And, honey, don't you worry about flying wherever it is you're going. You're old enough to be over that silly fear by now. And, my goodness, you did join the air force!"

CC shuddered, wishing her mother hadn't mentioned her phobia—airplanes—since she would soon be flying halfway around the world over oceans of water. It was the only part of the air force she didn't like.

"We love you! Bye now."

The message ended and CC, still shaking her head, hit the Off button and put the phone on the counter.

"I can't believe you guys forgot my birthday! You've always said that it's impossible to forget my birthday because I was born right before midnight on Halloween." She berated the phone while she reached into a cabinet for a champagne flute. "You didn't even remember my box." She continued to glare at the phone as she wrestled with the champagne cork.

For the seven years CC had been on active duty service in the United States Air Force, her parents had never forgotten her birthday box. Until now. Her twenty-fifth birthday—she had lived one-fourth a century. It really was a landmark year, and she was going to celebrate it with no birthday box from home.

"It's a family tradition!" she sputtered, popping the cork and holding the foaming bottle over the sink.

CC sighed and felt an unexpected twinge of homesickness.

No, she reminded herself sternly, she liked her life in the air force and had never been sorry for her impetuous decision to join the service right out of high school. After all, it had certainly gotten her away from her nice, ordinary, quiet, small town life. No, she hadn't exactly "seen the world," as the ads had promised. But she had lived in Texas, Mississippi, Nebraska, Colorado and now Oklahoma, which were five states more than the majority of the complacent people in her hometown of Homer, Illinois, would ever live in, or even visit.

"Apparently that doesn't include my parents!" CC poured the glass of champagne, sipped it and tapped her foot—still glaring at the phone. It seemed that during the past year her parents had gone on more Silver Adventure Tours than was humanly possible. "They must be trying to set some sort of record." CC remembered the flirty banter in their voices and closed her eyes quickly at that particular visual image.

Her eyes snapped back open, and her gaze fastened again on the phone.

"But Mom, none of your homemade chocolate chip cookies?" She sipped the champagne and discovered she needed a refill. "How am I supposed to cover all the food groups without my birthday box?" She reached into the other bag and pulled out the bucket of Kentucky Fried Chicken, original recipe, of course. Pointing from the chicken to the champagne, she continued her one-sided discourse. "I have the meat group—KFC—mixed with the all important grease group for proper digestion. Then I have the fruit group, champagne, my personal favorite. How am I supposed to complete the culinary birthday ensemble without the dairy/chocolate/sugar group?" She gestured in disgust at the phone.

Lifting the lid off the KFC, she snagged a drumstick and bit into it. Then, using it to punctuate her hand gestures, she continued.

"You know that you guys always send something totally useless that makes me laugh and remember home. No matter where I am. Like the year before last when you sent me the frog rain gauge. And I don't have a yard! And how about the GOD BLESS THIS HOUSE stepping stone, which I have to hang on the *wall* of my *apartment*, because I have no house!" CC's disgruntled look was broken by a smile as she recounted her parents' silly gifts.

"I suppose you're trying to tell me to get married, or at the very least, to become a homeowner."

She chewed thoughtfully and sighed again, a little annoyed to realize that she probably sounded fifteen instead of twenty-five. Then she brightened.

"Hey! I forgot about my *other* message," she told the phone as she scooped it back up, dialed her messages, and skipped past her parents' voices.

"Next new message. Sent at 6:32 P.M."

CC grinned around a mouth full of chicken. It was probably Sandy, her oldest friend—actually she was the only high school friend CC still kept in touch with. Sandy had known her since first grade, and she rarely forgot anything, let alone a birthday. The two of them loved to laugh long distance about how they had managed to "escape" small town Homer. Sandy had landed an excellent job working for a large hospital in the fun and fabulous city of Chicago. Her official title was Physician Affairs Liaison, which actually meant she was in charge of recruiting new doctors for the hospital, but she and Sandy loved the totally unrealistic, risqué-sounding title. It was especially amusing because Sandy had been happily and faithfully married for three years.

"Hi there, CC. Long time no call, girl!"

Instead of Sandy's familiar Midwestern accent, the voice had a long, fluid Southern drawl. *"It's me, Halley. Your favorite Georgia peach! Oh, my—I had such a hard time getting your new phone number. Naughty you forgot to give it to me when you shipped out."*

CC's grin slipped off her face like wax from a candle. Halley was one of the few things she hadn't missed about her last duty station.

"Just have a quick second to talk. I'm calling to remind you that my thirtieth birthday is just a month and a half away—December fifteenth, to be exact—and I want you to mark your little ol' calendar."

CC listened with disbelief. "This is like a train wreck. It just keeps getting worse and worse."

"I'm having the Party to End All Parties, and I expect your attendance. So put in for leave ASAP. I'll send the formal invite in a week or so. And,

yes, presents are acceptable." Halley giggled like a Southern Barbie doll. *"See y'all soon. Bye-bye for now!"*

"I don't believe it." CC punched the Off button with decidedly more force than was necessary. "First my parents forget my birthday. Then not only does it look like my oldest friend has forgotten it, too, but I get a call from an annoying non-friend inviting me to *her* party!" She dropped the phone back on the counter. "A month and a half in advance!"

CC shoved the unopened bottle of champagne into the fridge.

"Consider yourself on-deck," she told it grimly. Then she grabbed the open bottle of champagne, her half-empty glass, the bucket of KFC and marched purposefully to the living room where she spread out her feast on the coffee table before returning to the kitchen for a handful of napkins. Passing the deceptively silent phone she halted and spun around.

"Oh, no. I'm not done with you; you're coming with me." She tossed the phone next to her on the couch. "Just sit there. I'm keeping an eye on you."

CC picked out another piece of delightfully greasy chicken and clicked on the TV—and groaned. The screen was nothing but static.

"Oh, no! The cable!" Because she would be out of the country for three months, she had decided to have the cable temporarily disconnected and had been proud of herself for being so money conscious. "Not tonight! I told them effective the first of November, not the thirty-first of October." She glanced at the silent phone. "You probably had something to do with this."

And she started to laugh, semihysterically.

"I'm talking to the telephone." She poured herself another glass of champagne, noting the bottle was now half empty. Sipping the bubbly liquid thoughtfully, CC spoke aloud, pointedly ignoring the phone. "This obviously calls for emergency measures. Time to break out the Favorite Girl Movies."

Clutching the chicken thigh between her teeth, she wiped her hands on the paper towel before opening the video cabinet that stood next to her television set. Through a full mouth she mumbled the titles as she scanned her stash.

"*Dirty Dancing, Shadowlands, West Side Story, Gone With the Wind.*" She paused and chewed, considering. "Nope, too long—and it's really not birthday material. Humm . . ." She kept reading. "*Superman, Pride and Prejudice, Last of the Mohicans, The Accidental Tourist, The Color Purple, The Witches of Eastwick.*" She stopped.

"This is exactly what I need. Some Girl Power." She plunked the video in the VCR. "No," she corrected herself. "This is better than Girl Power—it's Women Power!" CC raised her glass to the screen, toasting each of the vibrant movie goddesses as they appeared. They were unique and fabulous.

Cher was mysterious and exotic, with a full, perfect mouth and a wealth of seductive ringlets that framed her face like the mane of a wild, dark lioness.

CC sighed. She couldn't really do anything about her own little lips—if she did, they would look like a science experiment. But everything else about her was so small. Maybe it was time to rethink her short, boyish haircut.

Michelle Pfeiffer—now there was a gorgeous woman. Even playing the role of Ms. Fertile Mom, she was still undeniably ethereal in her blond beauty.

No one would ever call *her* cute.

And Susan Sarandon. She couldn't look frumpy even when she was dressed like an old schoolmarm music teacher. She oozed sexuality.

No guy would ever think of her as *just a friend*. At least no heterosexual guy.

"To three amazing women who are everything I wish I could be!" She couldn't believe her glass was empty—and the bottle, too.

"It's a darn good thing we have another." She patted the phone affectionately before rescuing the other champagne bottle from a life of loneliness in the fridge.

Ignoring the fact that her steps seemed a little unsteady, she settled back, grabbed a fourth piece of chicken and slanted a glance at the ever-silent phone. "Bet it shocks you that someone who's so little can eat so much."

It answered with a shrill ring.

CC jumped, almost choking on the half-chewed piece of chicken. "Good Lord, you scared the bejeezes out of me!"

The phone bleated again.

"CC, it's a phone. Get it together, Sarg." She shook her head at her own foolishness.

The thing rang again before she had her hands wiped and her nerves settled enough to answer it.

"H-hello?" she said tentatively.

"May I speak with Christine Canady, please?" The woman's voice was unfamiliar, but pleasant sounding.

"This is she." CC clicked the remote and paused *The Witches of Eastwick.*

"Miss Canady, this is Jess Brown from Woodland Hills Resort in Branson, Missouri. I'm calling to tell you that your parents, Elinor and Herb, have given you a weekend in Branson at our beautiful resort for your twenty-second birthday! Happy Birthday, Miss Canady!" CC could almost see Jess Brown beaming in delight all the way from Branson. Wherever that was.

"Twenty-fifth," was all she could make her mouth say.

"Pardon?"

"It's my twenty-fifth birthday, not my twenty-second."

"No." Through the phone came the sound of papers being frantically rustled. "No, it says right here—Christine Canady, twenty-second birthday."

"But I'm not."

"Not Christine Canady?" Jess sounded worried.

"Not twenty-two!" CC eyed the newly opened second bottle of champagne. Maybe she was drunk and hallucinating.

"But you are Christine Canady?"

"Yes."

"And your parents are Elinor and Herb Canady?"

"Yes."

"Well, as long as you're really you, I suppose the rest doesn't matter." Jess was obviously relieved.

"I guess not." CC shrugged helplessly. She decided she might as well join the madness.

"Good!" Jess's perkiness was back in place. "Now, just a few little details you should know. You can plan your weekend anytime in the next year, but you will need to call to reserve your cabin . . ."

Cabin? CC's mind whirred. What had they done?

". . . at least one month ahead of time or we cannot guarantee availability. And, of course, this gift is just for your personal use, but if you would like to bring a friend, the resort would be willing to allow him or her to join you for a nominal fee—*or* for totally free if he or she would be willing to attend a short informational meeting about our time-share facility."

CC closed her eyes and rubbed her right temple where the echo of a headache was just beginning.

"And along with your wonderful Woodland weekend," Jess Brown alliterated, "your parents have generously reserved a ticket for you to the Andy Williams Moon River Theater, one of the most popular and long-running shows in Branson!"

CC couldn't stop the bleak groan that escaped her lips.

"Oh, I can well understand your excitement!" Jess gushed. "We'll be sending you the official information packet in the mail. Just let me double-check your address . . ."

CC heard herself woodenly confirming her address.

"Okay! I think that's all the information we need. You have a lovely evening, Miss Canady, and a very happy twenty-second birthday!" Jess Brown cheerfully clicked off the line.

"But where *is* Branson?" CC asked the dial tone.

Chapter Two

"THAT'S right!" CC shouted at the TV, sloshing champagne onto the carpet as she raised her glass dramatically. "Click him off, girlfriends! Jack Nicholson wasn't cute, anyway—it was the three of you who really had the magic the whole time."

CC hardly noticed her unsteadiness as she got to her feet to dance the Woman's Magic Victory Dance while the movie credits rolled.

"Mr. Phone." She took a break from her Victory Dance to catch her breath. Fleetingly, she wondered just who had eaten all that KFC.

Mr. Phone seemed to be smiling at her from his place on the couch.

"Do you know that women have all the magic?"

He didn't answer.

"Of course you don't—you're a phone!" CC giggled. "You didn't even know I was twenty-five instead of twenty-two." She laughed until she snorted. "But you do now. And after watching that most excellent movie, you should know that women have magic, too."

Mr. Phone seemed skeptical.

"It's true! Didn't Cher and Michelle and Susan just prove it?" CC wobbled, but only a little. "Oh, I see what you mean. You think *they* have magic, but you don't really believe that an *ordinary* woman, like me, could have magic."

CC couldn't be entirely sure, but he appeared to be willing to listen.

"Okay. You may be right, but what if you're not? What if women really do have something within them, and we just have to find it? Like they did." CC felt the spark of an idea, and her brow wrinkled in an attempt at concentration. "They didn't believe it at first, either, but that didn't stop it from working. Maybe it doesn't matter if you're ordinary-looking, or if you're new somewhere and you don't have any friends yet." Or, CC's mind added, if your birthday has been forgotten. "Maybe all it takes is a leap of faith."

And a milky light flashed in the corner of her left eye, breaking her concentration.

What the . . . ? A little shiver of trepidation fingered its way down the nape of her neck.

The light was coming from behind the closed drapes that shrouded the patio doors leading to her balcony.

CC checked the VCR clock. The digital numbers read 10:05 P.M.

"Must be the streetlights," she told Mr. Phone, but her eyes remained riveted on the captivating glimpse of brightness. The sliver of light she could see had an odd quality, totally unlike the sterile brightness of streetlights.

"Could be headlights from a parked car." But as she said it she knew it couldn't be true. Not in her top floor apartment. Car headlights didn't shine *up*. They also didn't have a quality of warmth that made her want to bathe herself in them.

CC's feet took her to the drapes before she consciously told them to move.

"You asked for some magic," she whispered. Slowly, like she was moving through the sweet twilight between awake and asleep, she reached up and parted the curtains.

"Ohhhh . . ." The word came out on a breath. "It *is* magic."

The full moon hung perfect and luminous above her as if the goddess Diana herself had placed it there as a birthday offering. It bathed the riot of potted plants that crowded the balcony in a warm, opal-like glow. She quickly unlatched the glass doors and stepped out into the gentle warmth of a late October night.

CC's balcony was large, and it looked out on a greenbelt that divided the apartment complex and an upscale neighborhood. The amazing balcony was the reason she had decided to stretch her budget and afford the rent for the pricey apartment. She loved to sit there and let the comforting sounds of the greenery melt away the tension that relentlessly clung to her from work and could even stubbornly stay with her through her kick-boxing class and the warm bubble bath soak she so often took after class. She had spent many evenings there, as was evident by the comfortable wicker rocking chair and the matching whatnot table that was just the right size to hold a book and a glass of something cold. Nestled in the middle of the lush plants was her favorite piece of balcony furniture, a mini version of a chimenea.

Tonight the creamy color of the chimenea caught the moon's caress and reflected its light like moonlight off the sands of an exotic beach.

Suddenly, she tilted her head back and spread her arms, as if she could embrace the night. The full moon filled her vision and she felt her body flush, like she was being saturated in the light of another world.

And her head snapped up.

"It is true," she said to the listening night. "It must be true."

And an idea was born, conceived of champagne and moonlight. CC grinned and whirled back through the open glass doors. Practically skipping, she rushed to her bedroom, already unbuttoning her air force uniform. The dark blue skirt and light blue blouse pooled with her pantyhose and bra.

"Step one."

Naked, CC pulled open her pajama drawer and pawed through it until she found the long, silk nightgown that lay at the bottom, ignored for her more practical cotton nightshirts. A uniform is good for work, but not for magic, she told herself and pulled the pale gown over her head, loving the erotic feel of it as it slid down her naked body.

"I will wear this more often," she promised aloud.

"Step two." She moved resolutely to her spare room, which she had recently begun to set up as an office. So far she had only had the time and money to buy a computer desk and chair for her five-year-old computer. Her books were stacked neatly on the floor, waiting for the bookshelves that she had promised them. She flicked on the overhead light and started searching through the piles of old textbooks, accumulated over the past seven years while she haphazardly took college classes, never sure which field she wanted to major in. CC combed through texts that ranged from Anatomy and Physiology lab guides to Basic Business Accounting 101

"Here you are!" She pulled out the medium-sized text that had been hidden under an enormous Humanities tome. It was entitled, *The Matriarchal Era—Myth and Legend*. CC fondly remembered her semester of Women's Studies and the witty Professor Teresa Miller who had made that class one of her all-time favorites. She could still hear Ms. Miller's expressive voice reading aloud words that had been authored in an ancient time when women had been revered and even worshipped.

"Where is it?" she mumbled to herself as she scanned the index, her finger lightly going down each row of names, finally stopping near the beginning of the *G*'s.

"Gaea!"

She sat back on her heels, turned to page eighty-six, and read aloud: "Gaea, or Gaia, was an Earth goddess, the Great Mother, known as the oldest of the divinities. She ruled magic, prophecy and motherhood. Although Zeus and other male gods took over her shrines during the emergence of the patriarchal insurgence, the gods swore all their oaths in her name, thus ultimately remaining subjected to her law."

CC nodded her head. This was exactly what she had been looking for. Gaea was the Mother of Magic. Flipping back to the index she turned pages till she found the *R*'s.

"Rituals! Earth Ritual page one-fifty-two." She shuffled through the slick, white pages and made a victorious exclamation when she found it. "Ha! I knew it!" Silently she read the ancient invocation, tugging on her bottom lip in concentration. When she had finished reading, she took the book to her desk and sat quietly for a moment, then with a satisfied smile she wrote a single sentence in blue ink on a piece of plain white Xerox paper and folded it once. Bending the page to mark her place in the text, she headed back to the living room, book and paper in hand.

This time when she stepped onto the balcony she brought with her the book, the piece of paper, a clean champagne flute filled with cold water, a box of long-handled matches and a determination that showed clearly in the square set of her shoulders.

The chimenea was just big enough to hold one block of fragrant pinyon wood. Deftly, she fed its small mouth and lit the dry pinyon. Then she moved to a long, thin planter that was hooked to the wrought iron balcony railing. She caressed the velvety leaves and bent to inhale the tangy fragrance of mint.

"It's a lucky thing that I have such a green thumb." She smiled.

Choosing carefully, she snapped off the tops of several of the larger plants.

The spicy scent of burning pinyon rose from the chimenea like mist. The smoke hovered around the balcony. Clearly visible in the moonlight, it twisted and lifted in the warm breeze like ocean waves. CC's breath caught in excitement as she hurried to position herself in front of the chimenea. She placed the cut mint on the little table next to the glass of water and the piece of paper, then she opened the book to the turned-down page. With a growing sense of excitement she cleared her throat and began to read.

"Great Mother, Gaea, ripe creatress of all that exists, I call upon you to be here with me now."

As she fell into the rhythm of the ancient ritual, the tentative quality left her voice and she felt an unexpected rush of feeling pass over the hair on her bare arms, almost like a spark of static electricity.

"I need your guidance as I strive for spiritual knowledge and growth. Help me also with . . ." CC paused. Here in the text there were the parenthesized words *priestess states her purpose.* She took a deep breath and closed her eyes, concentrating with all of her heart and soul, then she repeated, "Help me also with creating magic in my life."

Reopening her eyes, she continued to read. "I wish with all my heart to accomplish my desires in a positive way. Reveal to me the direction to take. I await your guidance and aid."

A breath of air touched the pages of the open book and for a moment it quivered and felt alive in her hands.

CC shivered in response. The night was hushed, like a lover waiting for her beloved's next words.

"I give my desires and dreams into your keeping."

With one hand she held open the book. She used her other hand to fan her fingers slowly through the drifting pinyon smoke.

"By air, I create the seed." The smoke swirled in lazy, dancing circles.

With the same hand she reached for the piece of folded paper, on which was written a single sentence in CC's compact cursive hand, "*I want magic in my life*." The wish filled her mind . . . Oh, please, she prayed.

"By fire, I warm it."

The paper went into the fire and caught instantly ablaze with a fierce, green flame.

Through her mind brushed the thought that it shouldn't have done that—it was just a simple piece of copy paper. Nothing about it could have made a wild green flame. CC's heartbeat increased erratically, but she forced her hand to be steady as she took the crystal glass filled with cold, clear water, and with delicate flicks of her fingers she scattered it in a small circle around the chimenea.

"By water, I nourish it."

CC stepped within the newly made circle. It glistened in the moonlight like lacework made of mercury. She bent back to the table and gathered the sprigs of mint in her hand.

"By Earth, I cause it to grow."

She tossed the delicate plants into the fire where they sizzled and glowed. She watched as they began to dissolve. For an instant CC thought they looked like some kind of exotic seaweed, and she could actually smell the salty tang of the ocean.

"From spirit, I draw the power to make all things possible as I join in the power of the goddess." With a burst of emotion CC dropped the text to the table and completed the words of the ritual as if they were written upon her heart. "Thank you, Gaea, Great Mother Goddess!"

As if in response to her invocation, the breeze shifted and cooled. The pinyon smoke spiraled up, diaphanous and glowing with the light of aquamarines. Transfixed, CC watched it disappear into the moon-drenched sky.

The breeze continued to increase, and CC impulsively raised her hands over her head, fingers outstretched as if she could capture the moon within them. Slowly she began to sway, letting the wind move her in time to the symphony of the night. Her bare feet found their own dance as they followed the circumference of the damp circle. The wind licked her body, drawing the silk of her nightgown against the warmth of her skin.

CC looked down at her body, and felt her eyes widen in surprise. Usually she thought of herself as too petite to be considered sexy, but tonight the moonlight mingled with silk, casting a spell on her body. Through the thin fabric her breasts were clearly visible and her small, perfect nipples felt sensitive and tight as they puckered against its softness. She swung her leg forward in a graceful dance step that had lain dormant within her since grade-school ballet lessons. The nightgown molded itself to her thighs, making her feel like she had just stepped from the canvas of a voluptuous Maxfield Parrish painting. The moonlight caught the ripples and folds of silk, giving life to the pale color and turning it into frothing sea foam. She laughed aloud at her unexpected beauty and twirled on feet that had wings.

"I have magic!" she proclaimed to the night.

Shadows flitted across the balcony, and she looked up to see wisps of clouds, like half-formed thoughts, beginning to obscure the face of the attendant moon. The wind increased, and CC's dance kept time with it, mirroring the tempo of the swaying trees.

The deafening crack of thunder should have frightened her, but instead CC felt like the coming storm had originated within her body. When the blue-white shard of lightning pierced the sky, it only fueled her appetite for the night, and she whooped, adding her own voice to the tempest.

Like a ripened fruit the sky burst apart, sending a rush of whimsical rain to join in her celebration. CC spun and twirled and laughed aloud. She reveled in every instant. She noticed how her plants seemed to move their leaves with her, and how the falling rain glistened amidst them like faceted jewels. Her eyes were drawn to the mundane stretch of blacktop parking lot below her, and she was amazed at how the rain had transformed it into the glasslike surface of a mysterious, shadow-covered ocean.

CC lifted her arms and pirouetted as the rain swathed her in damp majesty. She laughed aloud and believed she clearly heard the sound of another woman's musical laughter—and for a magically suspended moment their voices merged, filling the balcony with joy and love.

Then the sky exploded with another flash of light, and the rain roped down in a torrent. CC realized that her drapes were billowing wildly within her apartment and rain was drenching her living room carpet. Still laughing, she scrambled wetly through the open patio doors and pulled them securely closed behind her.

Shivering a little in a puddle of sopped carpet she should have felt melted; instead she felt invigorated. CC held her arms away from her body and watched as drops of water, sparkling like diamonds, slid down the soaked cloth of her nightgown.

"I have never been this alive." She was compelled to speak the words aloud. She shook her head, letting the water float around her, and ran her fingers through her short curls.

"I will let it grow," she promised.

And she realized her hair wasn't all she was ready to change. She was going to break her own mold.

Walking lightly, she made her way back to her bathroom and pulled a thick towel from the linen shelf. On the short dresser next to her bed she lit a candle that she had bought from a quaint little boutique aptly named the Secret Garden. She breathed deeply, filling herself with the candle's delicious vanilla-rum fragrance. The sweet scent drifted around her as she flicked the thin, damp straps of the gown from her shoulders and let the fabric slither from her body. Standing in the candlelit room she began to towel-dry, rubbing her already sensitized skin with light, circular strokes. Her hair was almost dry when she slid naked between the coolness of the clean sheets. With fingertips that were on fire, she caressed herself. Closing her eyes she moaned and arched into her hand, delighted and surprised by the exquisitely electric sensations that cascaded through her body.

As velvet sleep swept her away, CC was sure she heard a woman's laughter, the same magical laughter she had heard while she danced in the rain on her balcony. CC's lips curved into a smile, and she slept.

And while she slept, CC dreamed that a man's voice called to her in deep, seductive tones. Her dreaming body responded to that call and strained forward, but she felt unusually sluggish. In her dream she opened her eyes. She was surrounded by a veil of liquid blue. I'm underwater, her sleeping mind acknowledged.

Come to me, my love.

The rich voice sounded within her mind, and CC's pulse jumped.

Yes! She tried to yell her answer, but in her dream she was mute.

A light shimmered over her head and she peered up, squinting into the brightness. Just above the surface of the water a shape appeared. CC floated up, and the shape took on form and became a man. He was dark and exotic. His hair fell around his wide, bronzed shoulders in a black wave and his eyes laughed down at her. Through the ripples of the crystal waves she could see his easy smile as his outstretched hand beckoned to her.

She tried to reach up and take his hand, but her arm felt leaden. It would not obey her desire to respond.

The man's handsome face saddened. He looked lost and the voice inside her head was filled with longing.

Please come to me . . .

Chapter Three

A DIFFERENT kind of light played crimson shadows across her closed eyelids. What an odd dream, CC thought as she stretched luxuriously. The smooth feel of fresh sheets against her naked body mixed with the poignant, unfulfilled seduction of the dream. She still felt super-sensitized and her naked body tingled.

Naked?

She never slept in the nude. Why the heck was she naked? She flung her eyes open and cringed at the brightness of her bedroom, then quickly closed them again. It couldn't be later than 0730. Could it? Hadn't she set her alarm? Was she late for work? Her heart pounded.

Memories of the night came flooding back—the two bottles of champagne, the movie, the sudden brainstorm that led to the idea that led to the ritual. Here she cringed and tried to burrow down into her sheets, but her memory was relentless.

"You'd think I'd had enough champagne that I would have blacked it all out," she groaned.

She peeked over the side of the bed. The vanilla-rum candle had burned out. Well, at least she could be thankful she hadn't set her apartment on fire. She glanced down. Her nightgown made a rumpled, pale spot on her cream-colored carpet.

She shook her head and sighed. Two bottles of champagne—what had she been thinking?

"I forgot," she muttered. "The process of rational thought stops after bottle number one."

No wonder she'd had the weird dream; she'd been in a drunken stupor.

She glanced back at the nightstand and squinted at her bedside alarm clock, which read 11:42 A.M. CC's eyes widened. Panic banished the dream, and she sat bolt upright.

"It's almost noon!" She yelped, scrambling to her closet to frantically pull out a fresh uniform before she remembered that she didn't have to report for duty that day. She was flying out tomorrow, which meant that today would be dedicated to packing and tying up the loose ends being gone for three months created.

She took a shaky breath and ran her hand through her hair. Actually, the only reason she had to go on base at all that day was to stop by the orderly room and pick up her new set of dog tags. (She was still chagrined that she'd lost her old set during the move from Colorado.) Besides that, she just needed to buy some last minute toiletries for the trip, come back to the apartment and move her plants from the balcony to her living room so that her neighbor, Mrs. Runyan, could water them and finish her packing. And, of course, she had to remember to drop her key off with Mrs. Runyan before she left for the airport the next morning.

CC took a deep breath. What was wrong with her? She was usually so organized and logical about a deployment. She had planned to get up early that morning and finish her business on base, and then get her plants taken care of and her packing completed early so that she could spend the rest of the day relaxing. The trip to Saudi would be long and exhausting, and CC definitely was not looking forward to it—and that's not even considering how much she hated flying.

She shook her head. Instead she'd chosen to send herself off with an enormous hangover. CC marched into the bathroom and flipped on the shower. As the warm, soothing mist began to rise, she started searching through the cabinet for some aspirin for her tremendous headache. But before she found it, she stopped herself.

Headache? No, now that her heart wasn't yammering a mile a minute, and she wasn't afraid she'd been AWOL for half a day, she realized her head didn't actually hurt. At all. Actually, she felt fine. She closed the cabinet door and studied herself in the mirror.

Instead of the sallow, hollow-eyed look of a morning-after hangover, CC's chestnut-colored eyes were clear and bright. Her gaze traveled down her naked body. Her skin was healthy and vibrant; she glowed with a lovely pinkish flush. It was almost like she had spent the night being pampered in an exclusive spa instead of drinking two bottles of champagne, eating a ton of KFC and getting caught in a thunderstorm while she danced in the moonlight.

"Maybe . . ." she whispered to her reflection.

A thrill of delight traveled the length of her nakedness as she remembered the moonlight and the electric passion it had fueled within her body. She could almost feel the night against her skin again.

The warm mist from the shower crept around her in thick, lazy waves.

"Like the pinyon smoke," she gasped, and her heart leapt. "Remember," she told her reflection. "You promised to break your mold."

Tentatively, she raised her arms, trying to mimic her movements of the previous night and turned slowly in a sleepy pirouette. The fog swirled around her, licking her naked skin with a liquid warmth that reminded her of her sensuous, bittersweet dream. Thinking about the handsome stranger her sleeping mind had conjured, CC continued to spin, catching quick glimpses of herself in the mist-veiled mirror. Her petite body looked lithe and mysterious, as if she had trapped some of the moonlit magic within herself.

"You believed last night; believe today, too." As she spoke something deep within her seemed to move, like smooth water over river pebbles.

"Magic . . ." CC whispered.

Maybe the night and the dream had been signs of things to come—things that would change—in her life. Maybe she just had to be open to change and answer when it called.

"Magic . . ." CC repeated.

She danced and laughed her way into the shower, loving the warm fingers of water that rippled down her body.

She didn't stop smiling the entire time she dressed and applied just a touch of makeup. The feeling wouldn't go away. It was like someone had taken a key and opened up something inside her, and now that it was open, it refused to be locked away again.

She stepped into her favorite pair of button-up 501 jeans. After listening to the decidedly cooler weather forecast, she pulled on her thick gray sweatshirt with AIR FORCE written in block lettering across her chest. Her feet felt light as she grabbed a V8 Splash from the fridge and hurried out of her apartment.

The stairs that spiraled gracefully from her top-floor apartment were still damp from last night's storm, which made CC's smile widen. Everything looked preternaturally clear and beautiful. Her car was parked almost directly below her balcony, and as she unlocked it, she glanced up. Her lips rounded in a wordless *O* of delight. The light of the midday sun formed a halo over the rich green foliage that still sparkled with beads of rain, making her balcony appear more like something submerged in an ocean than something on land.

Magic is happening. The thought sprang unbidden into her mind, and instead of questioning it, CC took a deep breath and let the enticing idea settle.

The gate guard at Tinker's North Entrance was checking military IDs, and when her turn came, CC rolled down her window and beamed a cheery "Good morning!" to the serious-looking young airman.

The granite set of his face softened, and he returned her grin with an endearingly lopsided smile. "It's afternoon, ma'am," he corrected gently.

"Oops!" She grinned. "Well, everything's so bright and clear that it still seems like morning."

"Hadn't thought about it till now, but I guess you're right. It is real pretty today." He looked honestly surprised at the discovery. "You have a good day, ma'am." He waved her through the gate, but his eyes stayed fixed on her car and the lopsided smile was still painted on his face long after she'd disappeared.

The Communications Squadron's orderly room was located in the Personnel Building. It was a typical military structure, large and square and made of nondescript red brick. CC was pleased to see that a front row parking space was open. Usually the parking lot was ridiculously crowded, and she had to park far away down the street. The lawn surrounding the building and the hedges that bordered the entrance were meticulously manicured. The sense of obsessive neatness carried through to the interior of the building as well.

CC pulled open the door and was greeted by the familiar smell of military clean. Yes, ma'am. You *could* eat off the floors, walls, ceilings and desks . . . literally. Directly in front of her a full-length mirror showed CC her reflection. She automatically read the words printed across the top of the mirror: DOES YOUR APPEARANCE REFLECT YOUR PROFESSIONALISM? CC started to grin sheepishly at her jeans and sweatshirt, then she did a fast double take.

Had her eyes ever looked so big? Entranced, she stepped closer to the mirror's slick surface. Her mother had always described her eyes as "cute" or "doelike." CC usually didn't give them much thought beyond being glad that she had twenty-twenty vision. But today they seemed to fill her face. Their ordinary hazel color sparkled with—

"May I help you, ma'am?"

The rough voice caused CC to jump guiltily. Her cheeks felt warm as she turned around to face a weathered-looking chief master sergeant.

"Uh, yeah. Can you tell me where I'd go to pick up my dog tags?"

"Sure can." As soon as she'd started speaking his gruff appearance softened, and he smiled warmly at her. "The office for tags and military IDs is on the third floor. You can take the elevator that's down this hall." He gestured to the right.

"Thank you, Chief," CC said and bolted to the elevator, face blazing.

The old chief stood for a moment looking after her.

"Now there's a pretty girl," he pronounced to the empty air.

The ID office wasn't hard to find—it was the busiest office in the building. CC sighed as she took a number and found a seat along the wall. Orderly rooms were always ultra-busy during the lunch hour. She should have known better. Trying to find an interesting article in an old *Air Force Times* newspaper, she wished she had remembered to bring a book with her.

The room was almost empty and the black hands of the government issue clock told her forty-five minutes had passed when her number was finally called and she retrieved her new set of dog tags. Finally! CC felt like she'd been set free. She punched the Down button on the elevator, and as the door glided open she ticked off her "To Do" list on her fingers.

One: go to the Base Exchange and get a few toiletries. Two: pick up some plant food—her stomach growled. And three: some people food. She'd eaten most of the KFC last night, and anyway she couldn't handle KFC two nights in a row. Or at least she shouldn't.

She had just begun to step forward into the elevator when a woman's commanding voice spoke a single word.

"Wait!"

CC hesitated and turned. The woman standing behind her was breathtakingly lovely.

"What?" CC asked stupidly, stunned by the woman's beauty. She was tall—she seemed to tower over CC's petite five foot one inch frame. And her hair was amazing; CC had never seen anything so beautiful. It was the color of rich earth and it cascaded to the curve of her waist. Her face was regal and her cheekbones were high and well formed. But it was her eyes that captured CC in their liquid blue depths.

"Wait, Daughter." The woman smiled, and CC felt the warmth of that smile envelop her. She wanted to ask why she should wait, and why the incredibly gorgeous woman would call her daughter, but her mouth didn't seem to want to work. All she could do was to stand there and grin inanely back at the woman like a nervous kindergarten child meeting her teacher.

"WAIT, MA'AM!"

The shout came from the far end of the hall, and she turned her head just in time to see a man dressed in a firefighter's uniform launching himself at her. The tackle carried them several feet from the elevator's open doors. As soon as they slid to a halt the firefighter jumped up.

"Are you okay, ma'am?" He was trying to help her to her feet while he brushed nonexistent dirt off her jeans.

CC couldn't believe it. The wind had been knocked out of her, so all she could do was gasp for air and glare at the man.

"Sorry, ma'am. Didn't mean to be so rough, but I had to stop you from getting in that elevator," he said.

"W-what," CC sucked air and wiped her tearing eyes, "are you t-talking about?"

"Well, the elevator, ma'am." He pointed at the still-open doors.

The doors must be stuck, CC concluded.

"You knocked me over because the doors were sticking?" Thankfully she was regaining her ability to breathe and speak at the same time.

"No, ma'am. Not 'cause the doors are stuck." As if on cue the doors closed. "Because the elevator is stuck." He paused, letting CC absorb his words. "On the first floor."

"That can't be," CC spoke woodenly. "I just rode it up here."

The firefighter made a scoffing sound. "Sure, and an hour ago it was working. It just stuck 'bout five minutes ago. We were running an exercise next door for some new recruits when the First Shirt asked us to give him a hand in posting the warning tape and being sure that everyone on this floor knew about the problem."

For the first time CC noticed that clutched in one hand he had a roll of yellow warning ribbon much like the tape civilian police used to secure crime scenes.

"I don't believe it," she said.

"Take a look for yourself. Just be careful." He stepped out of her way.

CC approached the elevator and pressed the down button, just like she had only minutes before. The doors swung smoothly open and CC peered down into a dark shaft of nothingness. She felt dizzy.

"Good thing I saw you. I'd hate to think what would have happened if I'd been a second later." The firefighter shook his head and pursed his lips.

"But it wasn't you," CC said shakily. "I *was* getting ready to step into the elevator." CC looked wildly around the hall, ashamed it had taken her so long to acknowledge the woman. "It was the woman standing behind me. She warned me—that's why I hadn't already walked into the elevator."

CC felt a wave of nausea. She hadn't been paying attention to her surroundings; she'd been too busy tallying errands.

"Uh, ma'am," the firefighter said gently. "Are you sure you're feeling okay?"

"Of course. I'm fine." CC was still looking down the hallway, trying to catch a glimpse of the beautiful woman.

"Maybe you should sit down for a while."

"What are you talking about?" CC snapped. First the guy tackled her, then he was trying to analyze her. She checked the stripes on his arm. Yep. She even outranked him. "I just want to find the woman who warned me so that I can thank her."

"That's what I mean, ma'am. There was no one else in the hall with you."

A chill shivered through CC's body. She shook her head in disbelief. "Yes there was. She was standing right behind me. I was talking to her when you knocked me over."

"Ma'am," he took her arm and eased her down the hall away from the open shaft. "You weren't talking to anyone. You were just standing there getting ready to step into the elevator."

"She was right behind me," CC repeated.

"No one was there. No one is here now." His gesture took in the rest of the hall. "There's only one way out besides the elevator, and that's the stairwell, right there." He pointed at the doorway from which he had emerged. "She would have had to walk past me to get there, and she didn't."

"You didn't see her?" CC asked numbly.

"No, ma'am," he said quietly. "And people don't just appear and disappear like magic."

Magic . . . The word echoed in CC's head and she had to struggle to pay attention to the rest of what he was saying.

"Maybe you hit your head. You know you could have blacked out for a second. I knocked you down pretty hard. Our guys can take you to sick call at the clinic and have you checked out."

"No!" CC swallowed, regaining her wits. "See, I'm fine." She ran her fingers through her close-cropped curls and around her head, pushing and prodding without cringing to show there was no tenderness.

The door to the stairwell opened and another fireman appeared and yelled down the hall. "Hey, Steve! Got that tape run yet?"

"I'm working on it," CC's fireman answered.

"Well, hurry it up. We don't have all day to play with pretty girls." He smiled and tipped his helmet to CC.

Steve's face colored, and CC took the opportunity to make her retreat.

"I'll let you get back to work." She headed quickly for the door, which the second fireman held wide open for her. "And I do appreciate you saving me from a nasty fall."

She ducked into the stairwell and Steve's "Don't mention it, ma'am" drifted after her, but CC hardly heard him. She was too busy repeating a single sentence that she could see clearly in her memory. It was written in her concise cursive on blue ink against plain white paper.

I want magic in my life.

Chapter Four

CC drove quickly to the Base Exchange, glad it was situated between the Personnel Building and the base's north exit. She could run in, grab what she needed and get right out—and then she could hurry back to her apartment. She needed to be alone to sit and think about what had just happened.

She hadn't imagined the woman; she was certain of that. But that was all she was certain of.

She pulled into the crowded Base Exchange parking lot, and as she drove by the main entrance she noticed an empty parking spot—the closest spot to the front doors that wasn't reserved for high-ranking officers. CC parked with a growing sense of wonder.

"I am having some seriously good parking luck today," she murmured.

The Base Exchange, known by military personnel as the BX, reminded CC of a weird cross between an upscale department store and a flea market. Tinker's BX was no exception. Just inside the front doors, but before she entered the body of the Exchange itself, was scattered booth after booth of sales people hawking everything from deli sandwiches to "designer" handbags and jewelry. CC hurried past the colorful area and impatiently let the BX worker check her ID. She almost sprinted to the section of the store that sold toiletries and haphazardly chose the necessary travel items. Then she had to stop herself from screaming with impatience as the cashier seemed to take forever to ring up her purchases.

Rushing back out the door, the scent of food and the insistent growling in her stomach made her pause. Why not get something for dinner right there? That meant she wouldn't have to stop again on the way home. She followed her nose down the row of kiosks until she located the deli sandwich stand and ordered a hot Italian sub.

While she was waiting for her order to be filled, the back of her neck began to itch. Like someone was staring a hole into it. Brow wrinkled in irritation, CC turned to find the woman at the jewelry stand directly across from the sandwich booth smiling graciously at her. She was wearing a flowing dress made of sapphire velvet. She raised a well-manicured, bejeweled hand and gestured for CC to join her.

"Come!" she said.

CC opened her mouth to decline the odd invitation, but the woman spoke again.

"No. Do not think. Just come." Her thick accent rolled the words.

"That'll be five dollars," the sandwich man said.

CC paid him, and then she did something unusual, something outside her mold. Without thinking, she let her feet carry her across the aisle to the jewelry stand.

"Ah," the woman said, taking CC's right hand in both of hers and turning it over so she could study her palm. "I knew it. She has touched you."

"She?" CC asked.

"The Great Mother." The woman didn't look up from CC's palm, but kept speaking matter-of-factly in her richly accented voice. "Yes, I saw it in your aura, and I see it clearly here. You are beloved by her."

"How—" CC started to ask, but the woman wasn't finished.

"But your journey will be long and arduous." She squinted at CC's palm like she saw something disturbing there.

"Well, I am leaving for a ninety-day TDY to Saudi Arabia tomorrow," CC said.

The woman's gaze lifted from CC's palm.

"No, little daughter, I do not mean a journey of distance. I mean a journey of spirit." CC was struck by a sense of familiarity as their eyes met. Then the woman abruptly dropped her hand and turned.

"Where is it?" The woman muttered to herself as she searched through a nest of hanging necklaces. "Ah, here you are." Triumphantly she held the necklace out to CC.

It was lovely. The silver chain was long and delicate, and suspended from it by a latticework of silver ivy was a glistening cinnamon-colored stone. It was about the size of CC's thumb and shaped like a perfect teardrop.

"Amber," the woman said. "It was formed by resin fossilized in the bosom of the earth."

"I've never had any amber," CC said. "But I've always thought it beautiful."

"This piece is the same color as your eyes." The woman smiled.

CC thought she was doing one heck of a sales job. "How much is it?" CC asked, returning the exotic woman's smile.

"This necklace is not for sale."

CC frowned. Was the woman trying to get her to look at a more expensive piece?

"This necklace is a gift." In one motion the woman placed it over CC's head.

"But, I can't accept this!" CC sputtered.

"You must. It is meant to be yours," she said simply. "And I sense that there has been a recent event for which a gift is appropriate. No?"

"Well, it was my birthday yesterday," CC admitted.

"Ah, a Samhain child. How appropriate. So you see, it is already yours. Take it with you on your journey. Wear it always. Amber is an earth stone. Know that it has the power to absorb negative energy and turn it to positive." The woman's eyes were dark and serious. "You may have need of it, little daughter." Then her eyes lightened and she hugged CC. "Now go home and prepare." She cocked her head like she was listening to something and added, "Your plants are calling you."

"Thank you," CC said. Blinking in surprise, she let the woman turn her and give her a gentle push toward the front doors. The amber drop nestled heavy and warm between her breasts. CC touched the stone and her face broke into an amazed grin.

Chapter Five

Dear Mrs. Runyan,

Thank you for taking care of my plants while I'm gone. I put the plant food next to the watering can in the kitchen. Please remember to feed them every two weeks. And it would be really nice if you'd talk to them a little, too. I know it sounds silly, but I think they like it. Enclosed you'll find my key and a gift certificate to Luby's Cafeteria. I hope you and your girlfriends have fun. I'll be home in ninety days. If anything goes wrong you have the number of my first sergeant on Tinker.

Again, thank you so much.

CC

P.S. Yes, you can borrow any of my videos! Enjoy!

CC slipped the letter into the envelope with her key and the Luby's gift certificate, then she slid it under Mrs. Runyan's apartment door. Mrs. Runyan was sweet and about a thousand years old, and she flat refused to take any money for watering CC's plants and keeping an eye on her apartment while she was gone. But CC knew that she and her girlfriends loved to go to Luby's after church on Sundays—so she'd splurged on a one-hundred-dollar gift certificate for her. CC wished she didn't have to leave so early, and she could be there to see the expression on

Mrs. Runyan's kind face when she found the gift certificate. The thought made her smile in the predawn light while she struggled to carry her duffel bag, suitcase and carry-on bag down the three flights of winding steps and stuff them in the trunk of her car.

It was so early that the traffic to Tinker was unusually light, and CC's thoughts drifted back to the events of the past twenty-four hours. After she'd left the base and gone home, the rest of her day had been spent moving her horde of plants and finishing her packing.

There certainly hadn't been any magical happenings in any of that. That night she had even stood on the balcony trying to recapture the moonlit magic of the night before, but clouds had rolled in and there was no moonlight, nor any magic.

Could she have imagined the lady by the elevator yesterday? She didn't think so. The weight of the amber tear between her breasts told her the lady at the BX hadn't been a figment of her imagination either. And why should she question and try to poke holes into what had happened? She wanted it to be true; she wanted magic in her life.

One hand crept up to rub the amber drop with restless fingers, and CC nervously checked the car clock. It was 0530, and she was almost to the base. The shuttle that would take her from Tinker to Will Rogers Airport left the base at 0615. Her flight departed Will Rogers for Baltimore at 0825. At Baltimore she would board a military charter that would take her to the U.S. Air Base in Italy. From there she would travel via an Air Force C-130 cargo plane to Riyadh, Saudi Arabia. The whole trip would total just over twenty-four hours, with about twenty of those hours spent in the air.

And she really didn't like to fly. Right now the sour feeling in her stomach was a silent testament to how much she was not looking forward to the long trip.

If her mom had been here she would berate her, for the thousandth time, for joining the *air* force.

"Well, honey," she would say, "why in the blue blazes would you join the flying branch of our armed forces when you're afraid to fly?"

CC's answer was always the same. "I researched it, Mom. The air force was the branch of the service that had the best overall package. And there are a lot of jobs in the air force that have nothing to do with flying. Mine, for one example."

Her mother would make a scoffing sound and shake her head. CC had to wonder if her parents really understood that her military job was much like a civilian position in a big multi-media corporation. She was in charge of quality assessment for the Base Communications Center. Did they think she was covertly flying fighter planes?

She usually had only one or two temporary duty assignments each year, and, yes, she had to fly to them, but that would be no different than what her schedule would be like if she had worked her way up in a civilian company. Many jobs required their employees to travel periodically.

Well, CC smiled to herself, civilian jobs didn't typically require their employees to travel periodically into war zones. Her smile tightened. She was good at her job, and she was well trained. And she believed in what she was doing. She didn't think of it as being a hero or particularly patriotic; she had simply chosen a career that gave her the opportunity to serve her country in a very visible way. And, she admitted to herself, she liked the adventure of the air force. There were always new people to meet and new places to go. CC thrived on change—she'd had enough stagnation in the first eighteen years of her small town life to last for the next fifty-eight.

She breathed deeply, trying to quiet her nerves. Actually, she realized that she was feeling more than the normal amount of her preflight jitters. Right now she'd rather face several members of the Taliban than a long airplane flight. Weird, she told herself, noting again the sick feeling in her stomach. Maybe she was having some kind of premonition of danger? Could she be ultranervous because her sixth sense was trying to tell her something?

Her stomach growled, startling her, then making her smile. No, it was more likely that her upset stomach had been caused by the fact that she had been in too much of a hurry to eat breakfast. She'd have to try and get something to eat on the plane. She laughed out loud. Now there was something really terrifying—airline food. . . .

CC reminded herself of that while her stomach continued to roll nervously as she made her way across America. The layover in Baltimore was brief, and she had to scramble to catch her shuttle to the military charter, which was actually a huge commercial 747 stuffed with military personnel of varying ranks. CC stuck her face in a book and tried desperately to ignore the fact that they were hurling forward at an obscene rate of speed entirely too far above the earth.

The captain of the flight announced via the intercom that they would be landing at the air base in Italy in twenty minutes. He informed them proudly that the weather was a beautiful seventy-five degrees, with clear skies and a local time of almost 10:00 A.M., even though CC's internal clock insisted it was almost 2:00 A.M. instead. She ran her fingers through her tousled hair and rubbed her sand-filled eyes, wishing desperately that she could have relaxed enough to sleep during the long flight.

Just one more leg of this trip, she told herself. CC took the file that held her orders and her itinerary out of her carry-on. Yes, she'd remembered correctly. She had a little over an hour and a half layover in Italy. Unfortunately, it was not enough time to see any of the country, but it would give her time to grab something to eat and to change from the civilian clothes she had been traveling in, to the desert cammo fatigues that were the accepted uniform for the last leg of her trip on the C-130.

The thought of the military cargo plane made her shudder and almost forget that the plane she was on was landing, the second most dangerous time in a flight—takeoff being the most dangerous time. CC had flown in a C-130 twice before; both times had been extremely uncomfortable. C-130s were huge cargo transport vehicles with bigger-than-human sized propellers, no real passenger seats and rough, loud rides. That's why they were called C-130s. The *C* stood for cargo, which is what they were built to carry, not passengers.

CC thought that it would probably be a futile quest to try and find a nice bottle of chilled champagne at 10:00 A.M. anywhere on the air base within walking distance of the flight line, but she decided that as soon as she changed clothes she would make the attempt. Food could wait. Champagne should be a travel necessity.

"SARG! Wake up, we're boarding now." A rotund master sergeant shook her shoulder.

CC looked blearily around and tried to remember where she was.

"Let's go—everyone else is already on board and we're closin' up the tail." The master sergeant continued. "Should be airborne in no time."

Reality caught up with CC, and she scrambled to follow the master sergeant out of the passenger waiting area and onto the flight line proper. She rubbed her fingers through her hair and struggled to wake up. She couldn't believe she'd fallen into such a deep sleep. Her mouth tasted stale and her mind was fuzzy, but she quickly pieced together the past hour and a half. She had changed out of her jeans and sweater into her desert fatigues, then she'd gone in search of libations. No, she hadn't found any champagne, just a semihot roast beef sandwich and a semicold beer. She guessed she should have never had that beer—it certainly hadn't agreed with her like champagne did.

And then all thoughts of food and drink scattered out of her head as she approached the C-130. The enormous plane crouched on the runway like a mutated insect. It was painted the typical military green, which did nothing to dispel its buglike appearance. Its opened tail end was facing her, and she could glimpse enough of the inside of the thing to see that it was crammed full of huge, plastic-draped pallets of cargo. CC mentally shook her head in disgust. It looked like some horrible bug that was getting ready to poop. The metallic sound of hydraulics being engaged clicked on, and CC watched the tail section begin to close.

The master sergeant motioned at her to catch up with him. "Don't worry about the butt end being closed. You can board through the door in the front."

He pointed to a tall, narrow open area in front of and below the left wing. Stairs were pulled down from somewhere within the plane, and it was just a few short steps up into the aircraft. CC walked a wide circle around the silent, evil-looking set of propellers that were on that side of the plane, all the while sending them nervous glances.

The master sergeant noticed her discomfort and laughed. "Hell, they can't hurt you when they're not turned on."

"But they are getting ready to be turned on, aren't they?" she responded.

"Right you are, Sarg. So you better get aboard." He took her elbow to steady her on the steps. "Watch your head," he added.

"Ouch!" Too late, CC thought, grabbing her forehead where she had smacked it into a ledge of low-hanging equipment that protruded from the ceiling just inside the entrance.

Rubbing her head, she turned to the right and stepped up into the cargo/passenger area of the plane. Her eyes were watering with pain, and she could already feel a knot swelling under her fingers. She sincerely wished she was better at cussing; this was certainly the proper time to let loose with several choice words.

"Well, that's a darn stupid place to put a—" CC stopped and blushed furiously.

Six male faces were turned in her direction. They belonged to men clad in traditional sand-colored desert-issue flight suits. Each man wore the same distinctive patches and wings that clearly identified him as an F-16 Viper pilot.

"Hey, Sleeping Beauty," called out one of the pilots, a young lieutenant with a face that looked like it should have been on the cover of an air force recruiting poster. "Nice of you to wake up and join us."

CC felt her blush deepen. She was exhausted. Her face was greasy. She had sleep-head hair, and she was wearing desert cammos that on the best of days made her look about twelve years old. Needless to say, that moment was far from the best of days. Her eyes were bloodshot and her breath had to smell like the bottom of a birdcage. And she had just walked into a whole group of handsome fighter pilots after smacking herself on the head like an idiot right in front of them. Not to mention she was inside of a plane that was getting ready to take off.

She was probably in hell.

"Ignore him Sergeant . . ." said a colonel with just enough gray in his thick hair to make him look dignified. He hesitated as he read her nametag. ". . . Sergeant Canady. He's just pissed because he doesn't look as cute as you do when he sleeps."

"Yeah," a lanky-looking captain added. "He drools."

That got a laugh from the group, and CC hurried into the cargo bay, settling into the first seat that was available. She stowed her carry-on under her feet and busied herself with securely fastening her seat belt, which was the same red color as her fold-down seat and the meshed webbing that served as a backrest. CC wondered, as she did each time she flew in a C-130, why the seats and webbing were all bright red, when everything else about the plane was either military green or metallic gray. It made her feel vaguely uncomfortable, as did the open view of aircraft equipment and pipes and wires and such. At least civilian airplanes had all the "stuff" covered by smooth, white walls. Here the guts of the plane were showing.

Lashed to the floor at intervals of about six feet were the pallets of cargo CC had caught sight of from outside the plane. They filled the body of the cargo bay. Hesitantly, CC let her eyes travel to the other occupied seats, and she breathed a sigh of relief when she realized that she could only see three of the six pilots. The cargo blocked her view of the others. CC sighed. As usual the plane was outfitted with little thought to human comfort. Hers appeared to be the last available seat—the rest were either folded up or already occupied. A young captain was seated a little way to her right. He was listening to a CD through headphones, and he had his head propped comfortably back on a pillow, but nodded a brief hello to her. Across from her and about three folded seats to the left she could see the colonel, who was obviously the pilots' ranking officer. He was deep in a discussion with someone sitting to his right, but CC couldn't see him because a stack of plastic-covered equipment blocked her view.

The only other pilot she had a clear view of was sitting across the aisle from her and to her right. She glanced at him and caught him staring at her, and then was astounded to see a bright crimson blush rise into his well-defined cheeks.

Good Lord, she thought. Why is *he* blushing? The man looked like a gorgeous statue come to life. She quickly looked away, but the sound of his voice made her eyes snap back to his.

"Um, hello," he said. His voice was deep, but he didn't boom it at her like so many military men seemed to think they needed to. His eyes traveled up to the knot on her forehead.

Great. No wonder he was blushing. He had obviously seen her bonk her head like a moron, and he was probably embarrassed for her.

"I did the same thing on the way in," he said and pointed to his own head, where a faint pink splotch painted a raised bump in the middle of his forehead.

CC couldn't have been more surprised if he had sprouted wings and laid an egg.

"And I don't even have the excuse that I'd just woken up and was still groggy. Mine, Sergeant Canady, was the result of plain clumsiness."

CC felt a genuine giggle bubble from her lips. The handsome pilot echoed her laugh.

"Please," she said. "Call me CC."

"Okay CC. I'm Sean."

CC's grin sobered. "Don't you think I better call you Captain something?" It was fine for an officer to call an enlisted person by his or her first name, but the other way around was considered too familiar—and the air force sincerely frowned on too much familiarity between officers and sergeants. Even if the officers looked like living statues, CC thought regretfully.

But Sean's grin didn't fade. "Actually, no. Like the rest of these guys, I'm stationed at the Air National Guard Unit in Tulsa, Oklahoma." He leaned forward and glanced around like they were sharing a secret. "We do things a little differently in the Guard. So just plain Sean is okay with me."

CC didn't know what to say. Of course she knew there was an Air Guard Fighter Unit in Tulsa—her Comm Center had sent and received messages from them several times during the past three months. But she'd never met any of the pilots. Actually, the only fighter pilots she'd ever met had been stationed at her last duty assignment, Peterson AFB, Colorado. They had been arrogant and conceited and had not impressed CC or her girlfriends at all. She couldn't imagine any of them insisting she call them by their first names, at least not in daylight. Thankfully, she was saved from answering Sean by the appearance of the master sergeant who had herded her on to the plane.

"Okay gentlemen," he said, glancing at CC and adding, "and ladies. We're fixin' to get underway. I shouldn't have to tell such a distinguished group to buckle up and stow your carry-ons, but I thought I'd better remind you since you're not used to riding in the back seats." He chuckled at his lame joke as he made his way slowly through the cargo bay, checking the security of the pallets and the pilots. The pilots paid him about as much attention as did the pallets.

CC sighed as the numbing noise of the giant, rotating propellers started to vibrate through the plane. The sound made her realize that she had left her earplugs in her carry-on. CC unsnapped her seat belt and crouched down to pull her carry-on out from underneath the seat, and as she was feeling around in the side pocket her eyes traveled to the wall behind her seat. Her brow furrowed in confusion. That was odd; she hadn't noticed before that framing her seat were two thick, red stripes painted on the inside wall of the plane. Between these stripes were stenciled in bright red the words DANGER and PROPELLER, over and over.

"Sarg, you need to stow that and take your seat." The master sergeant had made his way over to her.

CC grabbed her earplugs, shoved the bag back and regained her seat. But when the master sergeant tried to walk on down the bay, she called him back.

"Sergeant," she almost had to yell to be heard over the propeller noise. "What do those red lines and words mean?" She pointed over her shoulder.

"That's marking where the propeller would come through the aircraft if we was to throw one." He grinned, showing her a wealth of yellow teeth. "But that don't happen very often." He laughed and moved on.

CC wasn't sure if she should cry or scream—but her body had suddenly frozen solid, so she found she was only able to sit there, ramrod straight and perfectly still.

Across the aisle Sean had overheard the whole exchange. He grimaced to himself as he watched the little sergeant's face turn a ghostly shade of white, which only made her big amber eyes look more fawn-like and appealing. She was such a small, young thing. She'd already looked a little scared when she'd bumped her head and stumbled into the plane, and now she looked practically terrified. Something inside of him lurched insistently.

"CC," he called to her.

She didn't respond.

"CC," he repeated, noting the glazed look in her eyes when they finally met his. "Would you trade seats with me? I hate flying on this side of the plane." He thought for a second, then added. "It's one of those weird pilot superstitions." He shrugged helplessly, like he was ashamed to admit it.

"Trade seats with you?" she asked as if she hadn't heard him correctly.

"Yep. I'd sure appreciate it." He beamed his best nice-guy smile at her.

"I suppose so," she said slowly. "If you really want to."

"I really want to," he said.

"Okay then."

He unbuckled his seat belt and grabbed his flight bag from under the seat. Before she could get her own carry-on, he crossed the ten feet or so that separated them.

"I'll get that for you," he said, taking the bag from her.

CC looked up at him. This close he was even more gorgeous. And just how tall was he? His muscular body seemed to stretch on forever. His short, military cut hair was a medium shade of blond, shot with glistening streaks that looked like they had been dipped in the sun. Actually, his whole body, or at least what could be seen peeking out of his flight suit, looked like he had been blessed by the god of the sun. Unlike so many blonds, he wasn't washed-out looking. Instead he was an irresistible shade of golden tan. His face was made of strong, square lines, and his lips . . . CC felt herself staring and she jerked her gaze from those amazing lips to his soft, brown eyes, which were smiling down at her.

"Thank you," she managed to stammer.

"Not a problem. Actually, you're doing me a favor." He took her elbow and guided her to his seat.

"Always the gentleman, ain't ya, Apollo." The master sergeant scoffed as he passed back by the two of them. "Just get her in that seat, then get yourself into yours. We're ready to get the hell outta here."

CC hurried to sit down, then she sent a questioning glance up at Sean.

"Apollo?" she asked.

"That's my call sign." He made a dismissive gesture with his hand. "Believe me, it wasn't my idea."

"Oh," was all CC could make her mouth say. It might not have been his idea, but it was certainly appropriate. The man oozed Greek god.

"Don't forget to fasten your seat belt," he said before turning to cross to his new seat.

CC's eyes had a will of their own, and they definitely enjoyed Apollo's rear view. He was one spectacularly handsome man. Of course, when he turned around and took his seat, she made sure she was very busy checking her seat belt, trying to find a comfortable place in the webbing, doing anything but gawking at him. And anyway, why was she getting all moon-eyed over him? Men who looked like that, especially fighter pilot men who looked like that, weren't interested in little, ordinary-looking staff sergeants. Unless maybe they had some kind of kid sister complex.

That was probably it, she told herself. He probably had a younger sister at home and that was why he was paying attention to her.

The propeller noise grew to a deafening level, and CC put in her earplugs. Then the C-130 lurched forward. It moved slowly at first, but soon picked up speed as it made its way down the flight line to their designated runway. CC felt her palms begin to moisten and her stomach knot. She closed her eyes and repeated over and over to herself: *military flights rarely crash; military flights rarely crash; military flights rarely crash.*

Too soon they were poised at the end of the runway, propellers gyrating at a crazed speed, plane quivering with the need to take off. Or, CC thought desperately, with the need to smack itself into the ground and engulf them in a ball of flame right *after* takeoff. She felt the brakes release, and the C-130 began its acceleration down the runway. CC's eyes popped open. She didn't want to die with her eyes closed.

A movement caught her panicked gaze and drew her eyes across the aisle to Sean. His long body was sprawled comfortably in its new location. He was giving her a thumb's-up sign, and he looked relaxed and calm. Sean grinned boyishly at her and mouthed the words, "Not a problem." Then he gave her a flirty wink.

Well! CC felt a rush of pleasure. She certainly didn't think he'd give a little sister a wink like that. And the way he continued to smile and stare at her . . . it just didn't look like the way a man looked at a woman he was only interested in because she reminded him of a little sister. Stunned, CC realized the butterflies in her stomach had nothing to do with her fear of flying.

When the plane lifted off a few seconds later, CC thought that she might have just experienced the most graceful, effortless takeoff in the history of the United States Air Force.

Actually, once the plane became airborne, CC's nervous stomach had completely disappeared. It was like the whole flight seemed to be charmed. They climbed to their cruising altitude so smoothly that CC found herself totally relaxing against the soft webbing, and she was surprised to feel her eyelids growing heavy. Struggling to stay awake, she glanced at Sean. He was reading a book, but the moment her eyes touched him he looked up. He studied her for a second, then an astounding thing happened. CC could hardly believe it when he mouthed the words, "Sleep—I'll keep watch." Then he gave her that flirtatious wink again.

CC felt a little thrill travel down her spine. He was going to stay awake and keep watch. Over her. And that wink said he wasn't thinking of her as a kid sister. CC's eyelids fluttered shut as her sleepy mind whispered that Sean's presence was certainly going to make the deployment more interesting.

Sean watched her as she fell asleep, a contented smile curving her sexy lips. He rubbed a hand over his brow and smiled quizzically at himself. What was it about that girl? Ever since he'd caught sight of her curled up in the waiting area sound asleep, he couldn't stop looking at her or thinking about her. It was totally unlike him. Women usually threw themselves at him because of how he looked, and while he didn't complain about that, he certainly didn't have to seek them out, or change seats with them because they looked scared, or reassure them because they were afraid of—of all things—flying. He rubbed his brow again and tried to force his attention to the novel in his hands, but instead of black words on white paper, he kept seeing amber eyes framed by thick, sandy-colored lashes.

CC dreamed that she was swaying gently in a hammock that hung between two giant palm trees on the shore of a crystalline ocean. Warm tropical breezes tickled her skin and kept the hammock moving hypnotically back and forth. Then, the wind shifted and icy gusts started blowing toward land over the white-capped waves. They reached her hammock, and it started to shake and pitch and . . .

CC's eyes flew open. She was instantly awake. It was no dream. The C-130 was shaking violently, like it was in the jaws of a giant animal. She swallowed a scream and her eyes immediately found Sean. His face was flat and expressionless, but CC could sense the tension that he was trying to mask. She began fumbling with the safety latch of her seat belt, her only thought that she needed to be next to him.

"No!" He shook his head.

She tore the earplugs from her ears.

"Don't get up. It's too dangerous." He shouted against the horribly sick sound of the engines.

"What's happening?!" she yelled.

Before he could answer, the shaking increased dramatically. CC couldn't believe the plane was still in one piece; it felt like it had to be shaking itself apart. Then everything happened very quickly. Over the noise of the engines came the shriek of a metallic scream. While CC watched in horror, a deadly blur sliced through the skin of the plane just a few feet to her right and arrowed its way directly across the aisle. Like an invisible missile, the broken propeller blade splintered and struck Sean before tearing through the skin on his side of the plane. Time suspended as the left side of Sean's head exploded in a spray of crimson and he slumped silently forward.

CC's scream was swallowed by the deafening sound of the plane decompressing, and she grasped on to the webbing, desperately trying to find an anchor in a world gone mad. Everything that wasn't strapped down went flying through the plane in a maelstrom of noise. CC couldn't get a clear sight of Sean—there was too much debris in the air between them. But she could see the widening trail of blood and fluids that blanketed the area around his seat.

His seat? It should have been her seat. CC felt a sob catch in the back of her throat.

Gradually, the debris settled, but the shaking was still violent, and the roar of the air rushing through the gaping holes in the sides of the airplane was deafening. With an amazing effort, the young captain who was sitting to Sean's right unbuckled his seat belt and crawled to his friend's still body. The captain had a square white piece of cloth in his hand, and as he wrapped it around Sean's head, CC realized that it must be the pillowcase off his pillow. With precise motions he unlatched the folded seat next to Sean. He loosened Sean's seat belt enough so that he could swivel his legs around and lay his torso horizontally along the seats. Then he managed to secure another belt around Sean's chest.

CC couldn't take her eyes from the pillowcase and the grotesque scarlet stain that was soaking methodically through it to pool against the matching red of the seat.

Suddenly, above the din CC could hear short bursts of a clanging bell. She counted six times. The next thing she knew the colonel had his seat belt unbuckled, and he lurched his way to her side, where he quickly pulled down a seat and resecured himself.

"They're ditching the plane," he yelled into her ear.

Her eyes widened. She didn't have to be a pilot to know that meant they were crashing into the ocean.

"It's okay. We're going to make it." He gave her a smile meant to reassure her. "The water's warm. Good thing we're in the Mediterranean and not the Atlantic."

CC wanted desperately to believe that.

"What do I do?" she shouted.

Before he answered her he twisted around and pulled two life vests free of their holding place behind the webbing. CC noticed the captain across the aisle had done the same and was struggling to strap one on Sean's unresponsive body.

"Put this on. You'll need to brace yourself and hold on. Everything will be thrown forward when we hit. Be ready to get out of here. Don't know how long this thing will stay afloat."

"Sean?" she asked.

The colonel's face was grim as he shook his head. CC's eyes filled with tears.

"He's beyond our help; worry about yourself now," he said gruffly. The plane dipped sickeningly forward. The colonel pointed toward the rear of the cargo bay. "Remember where the tail opens up?"

CC nodded.

"There are two escape doors on either side of the plane. That's where we'll exit. Life rafts are in slots up there." He pointed to an area above the wings.

CC hoped that he wasn't explaining those things to her because he planned on being dead. Just then the master sergeant burst from the crew door at the front of the plane.

"We're goin' down!" he yelled as he strapped himself into a seat to the right of CC and the colonel. "Be ready to get your feet wet!"

CC couldn't believe it, but he almost sounded gleeful.

The nose of the plane sank again, and the colonel squeezed her shoulder.

"Ready?" he yelled.

Over the past seven years CC had researched and prepared herself for an airplane emergency. She had watched PBS specials on airline safety. She always dressed sensibly when she flew—jeans and sneakers, never heels and bare legs. She counted the seatbacks to her nearest exit, and she paid attention to the flight attendants when they gave their safety spiels.

But she knew she wasn't ready. She was numb with terror. CC nodded at the colonel and tried to give him a brave smile. Through the ragged tears in the C-130's skin CC could see the bright blue of a clear morning. She closed her eyes and tried to pray, but her mind was a whirlwind of fear. All she could think of was how much she didn't want to die.

Then from between her breasts she felt a sudden warmth. Her first thought was that something must have struck her, and she was bleeding. She opened her eyes and frantically felt down the front of her uniform top. No, no rips and definitely no blood. Just a hard lump.

Oh! She realized the lump she was feeling was made by the amber teardrop that dangled from around her neck, just below her dog tags. On an impulse she had decided to keep wearing it, even after she had changed into her uniform, but of course wearing dangly jewelry wasn't within military regulations, and she had had to keep it hidden under her top. Now it felt warm, and that warmth was spreading throughout her chest.

If ever there was a perfect time for magic, she thought, it was now.

"Brace yourself!" the colonel yelled.

CC just had time to wrap her hands into the netting and brace her feet firmly against the floor when the world exploded. The plane slammed into the ocean with an obscene metallic scream, as if it knew its life were coming to an end. The white froth of ocean spray could be seen through the holes in the sides of the plane. But the C-130 didn't stay down. CC could feel it lift, a temporary respite, before they met the ocean again with an even worse grating jar. They skipped several times over the surface of the water, like a broken, bloated stone. Each time the plane met the ocean, passengers and cargo were flung forward. CC saw a major get hurled against the front bulkhead when his seat belt snapped loose. She watched as one of the huge cargo pallets pulled free at the same time and came crashing against him, pinning him to the metal wall.

CC glanced over at Sean and then looked quickly away. Rag doll-like, his body was still strapped against the seats. Like a puppet whose strings had been cut, his limbs flailed in limp response to the jarring of the plane.

Something sharp hit her left shoulder. She didn't feel any pain, but when she looked down she saw that her flesh gapped open and a line of blood had started to spill down her arm. Then there was a final wrenching, and the plane settled and did not rise again. CC could see the bright blue of ocean water through the holes in the plane.

The colonel was the first to react, but CC could see that all of the pilots except Sean and the major were struggling to their feet.

"Out! Out! Let's go!" he barked, making his way quickly to the area over the wings. Then he started shouting orders.

"Ace, T-Man, Kaz, get those rear doors open!" The two captains and one lieutenant scrambled around the loose cargo, hurrying to the rear of the plane.

"Sarg!" the colonel yelled at her. "Out—now!"

With shaking hands, CC unbuckled her own seat belt, amazed that she was able to stand. She noticed that already the plane was tilting down at the head.

"The major is dead!" the master sergeant yelled from the front of the bay. He was kneeling by the bloody body of the major, still trapped against the bulkhead.

"Leave him," the colonel said as he lifted a slot and pulled out a neatly folded bright orange thing that CC guessed must be a life raft.

"The door to the cockpit is blocked!" The master sergeant had moved from the major's body to the area that should open to the front-most area of the plane. But another cargo pallet was wedged within the opening, effectively blocking the door.

"There's an exit they can use in the cockpit," said the colonel. He motioned for the master sergeant to get to the back of the plane, then he caught sight of CC still standing there. "Move, Sergeant!" He turned and headed to the rear of the plane, expecting CC to follow him.

CC meant to go to the rear of the plane and toward safety, but instead she found herself climbing over equipment and cargo until she was standing next to Sean's body. CC swallowed, trying hard not to be sick. There was blood everywhere. The two seat belts had kept his body from being hurled forward by the impact, and the pillowcase, now totally soaked with blood, was still wrapped securely around his head. His face was turned away from her, and all she could see was the strong line of his chin and neck. His skin was no longer golden brown. It had turned the chalky color of ash. CC forced herself to place two fingers against the spot where his jugular vein was. No pulse. His skin was already cool beneath her fingertips.

The plane heaved even farther down at the head. Now CC could see that the ocean was lapping around the gaps in the side of the plane.

"Sergeant!" the colonel's voice bellowed from the rear of the plane. "Where the hell are you?"

"Here, colonel!" she answered, crawling on top of a mound of cargo so she could be seen. The rear of the plane appeared to be raised up, and CC could see that the officers had one of the doors open. While she watched, one of the captains attached a tether to the deflated life raft, pulled a cord on it and threw it out of the door. With a *whooshing* noise the raft inflated.

"Get over here, now! This thing is sinking fast."

She looked back at Sean's body. It should have been her. Because of his kindness, he had taken her place and now he was going to be entombed in a lonely, watery grave. The thought was unbearable.

"We have to take Sean with us," she called back to the men.

"No time. The boy's dead. There's nothing to be done for him," said the colonel. At a signal from him, the master sergeant jumped out of the plane.

"I'm not going without him," CC said, surprised at the calm sound of her voice. Her heart was pounding, and she felt her hands trembling, but knew with a certainty that defied logic that she had made the right decision.

"Get up here, Sergeant. That's an order."

"No, sir. I'm not leaving him here."

Suddenly there was the sound of metal ripping, and CC felt sun on her face. She looked up to see a clean tear slicing a gap in the ceiling almost directly above her. The nose dipped farther forward, and CC had to struggle to stay on her feet.

"Goddamnit! Damnit all to hell!" CC could hear the colonel approaching before she saw him. He was cussing like crazy and yelling orders. "Unbelt the boy and get ready to get the fuck out of here!"

CC rushed to get Sean's seat belts undone and had just finished when the colonel climbed around the last of the debris. Without looking at her, he grabbed Sean's body and hauled it across one shoulder in the traditional fireman's carry.

"Keep up with me!" he yelled at her. CC was only too happy to comply with that particular order.

They were almost to the door when the entire front section of the plane tore free and sank with amazing speed. The tail area had been high above the water, but now that the rear of the plane was freed of the dragging weight of the flooded front, it flopped heavily down to sea level. To CC it felt like she was standing in an elevator that had just dropped several stories. She and the colonel fell hard to the floor. Water started rushing in through the open door.

The colonel regained his feet quickly. He grabbed CC by the scruff of her uniform and Sean by his leg and pulled them to the door.

CC had no time to think. The colonel tossed her roughly out of the door. She hit the water and went under, but almost immediately her life vest brought her bobbing to the surface like a human cork. She sputtered and blinked, momentarily blinded by saltwater and sunlight. She heard two quick splashes next to her, and in another instant the colonel's head broke the surface not far from her, along with Sean's lifeless body.

"There." He pointed and CC could see the florescent orange of the life raft about forty feet in front of them. "Swim! We have to get away from the plane." He set off, sidestroking and kicking hard as he dragged Sean's body with him.

Wishing desperately that she was a better swimmer, CC kicked and began stroking awkwardly after him. A horrendous explosion burst behind her, and she spun around in the water in time to see a flash of light and flame. The plane was an enormous, gaping monster that seemed to be thrashing and fighting against its death. And she was too close to it.

Adrenaline rushed through her body, and CC began swimming with everything within her. She didn't look behind her again, she just swam.

Then she felt it. A piece of wreckage wrapped around her ankle like a mechanical tentacle. Terrified, she kicked and kicked, but it wouldn't come free. She tried to reach down to get it off, but she was pulled under the surface with such force that she thought her leg would wrench from its socket.

Water surrounded her and the pressure on her leg was unrelenting. She tried to fight against it, but it was impossible. Her ankle had been securely captured, and she was being pulled to the floor of the ocean by the weight of the sinking plane.

She was going to die.

Panic rippled through her and she reached both hands up towards the fading light of the surface, struggling to kick against the enormous weight dragging her to her death. She didn't want to die—not like this—not so young. In that moment, CC didn't see glimpses of her life passing before her eyes, she just felt the despair of knowing that she was dying too soon, before she had ever really lived. She would never know the love of a husband; she would never watch her children grow and marry. Her chest was burning, and she knew it was only seconds before she would be forced to breathe in the deadly water.

CC closed her eyes. Please help me, she prayed fervently. Someone please help me.

Miraculously, the weight that had been dragging her under evaporated, and she was filled with an indescribable peace. She opened her eyes to find herself floating in a bubble of soft blue light. And she wasn't alone in that bubble. Suspended in the water directly in front of her, so close CC had only to lift a hand to touch her, was an incredibly beautiful young woman. Her long hair floated around her like a shimmering veil. CC thought it would be the exact color of her mother's buttercups, if flowers could shine and sparkle. The woman's face was a study in perfection. She had sculpted cheekbones and lovely aquamarine eyes that looked somehow familiar to CC. Her skin had the flawless complexion of a china doll. CC's eyes traveled down the body of the woman, who was quite obviously naked from the waist up. CC could clearly see her large, well-formed breasts. But what was she wearing on the bottom half of her body? Whatever it was glistened like it had been beaded with glass and colored in iridescent shades of blue and turquoise and amethyst. It fit her shapely body snuggly and tapered down to . . . CC felt her own body jerk in surprise. A large set of fins! She was no woman; she was a mermaid!

CC stared at the incredible creature, knowing that what she was seeing, what she was feeling, couldn't possibly be real. Her lungs didn't burn anymore. But it wasn't that she was breathing, because she was still definitely underwater; it was more like she had been infused with oxygen. She decided she definitely must be dead, or so near death that she was experiencing some kind of amazing hallucination.

The mermaid smiled tentatively at her.

CC smiled back.

Do you desire to continue to live, no matter the cost? The words were spoken clearly into CC's mind. She knew they had to have come from the mermaid, but her sensuous lips had not moved.

Well, of course I do, CC thought automatically and nodded her head vigorously.

The mermaid's timid smile was gone, replaced by a dazzling look of relief and joy. Without hesitation, the creature reached out and wrapped her smooth arms around CC in an intimate embrace. CC didn't feel any desire to pull away. Instead of being frightened or repulsed, she was mesmerized. The mermaid pulled CC gently against her body, and CC could feel the creature's naked breasts press softly against her fatigue shirt. The mermaid's curtain of gossamer hair surrounded them, and her tail wrapped around CC's legs. CC had always been firmly heterosexual, so she surprised herself when she felt her body respond and her own arms wrap around the mermaid's bare shoulders.

Suddenly CC understood that what was happening to her wasn't anything as simple as a sexual experience; it was a magical infusion of the senses. Just as the moonlight had energized her on the night of her birthday, so now was this creature bringing her back to life. Every inch of CC's body felt flooded with electricity. She wanted to throw back her head and shout at the surge of fabulous sensations.

Then the mermaid began to lower her face to CC's. CC closed her eyes as their lips met in a deep, intimate kiss. A wave of vertigo crashed through CC, and when she finally reopened her eyes, she was looking directly into her own face.

Disorientated, CC blinked and shook her head, but the image of the petite, waterlogged sergeant didn't shift, it simply smiled back at her.

Back at her? How could that be? CC turned her head to look for the edges of a hidden mirror and noticed the wealth of blond hair that was floating around her. She reached up to stroke its slick mass.

We must part now.

The voice was back inside her head, and CC's fragmented attention refocused on her mirror image. CC watched as hands that should have been her own reached into the neck of her uniform top to pull the silver chain over her head. Then the CC look-alike draped it over "her" head.

Keep this. It is your talisman, a part of your magic, the internal voice said.

The woman that looked like CC raised her arms and tilted her head back so that she appeared to be reaching for the surface.

I wish you well. Blessed be, little sister.

The soft light that they had been floating within refracted into a fireworks of rebellious blue. The body that CC should have been inside of was bathed in an eerie aqua-white glow, and with an intense explosion of light it was propelled violently up to the waiting surface. Caught in a tremendous wave of backlash, CC felt herself hurl end over end away from the site of the plane wreck. Everything became confused and dreamlike. CC had no control over where she was being pulled. It felt like she had been caught in an underwater tornado. The whirlpool was pulling her farther and farther down into the depths of the ocean, and even though she was having no problem breathing, she was still terrified of the black nothingness beneath her. So she struggled, swimming around and through different levels of turbulent currents.

Finally she broke through the wall of swirling current and found herself in a tunnel of calm water. Exhausted, she allowed herself to float for a moment, trying to sift through her scattered thoughts. What had happened to her? Was she dead? What should she do next?

The water in her little tunnel of calm was comfortable, denim blue, but outside of it, the dark and tumultuous currents through which she had struggled still surrounded her. CC could see them seething and frothing dangerously. She peered behind her and saw nothing but darkness. Ahead, farther down the tunnel, there was a faint, flickering light. That way, she thought blearily and kicked hard to propel herself forward. Even as tired as she was, CC noted with surprise that she had never swam so strongly and effortlessly before—it was like she had been shot from a liquid cannon. The dark sides of her watery tunnel blurred as she streaked past.

Then the spot of light was just ahead of her and she burst up, breaking the surface to find herself in a luminous grotto. Her vision was blurred with fatigue, but she could just make out a ledge around which calm water lapped softly. She forced her leadened limbs to move, and with an effort that left her quivering and gasping, she hauled her body out of the water. Curling into a fetal position, CC finally gave into unconsciousness and slept.

Part Two

Chapter Six

The rhythmic sound of water lapping against rock woke her. CC opened her eyes slowly and was greeted by the sight of sparkling blue crystals. She shifted her body and stared around her, amazed at the beauty of the rocks. If laughter was a color, she thought, it would be this exact shade of blue. She reached out to touch the side of the cave with her perfectly shaped cream-colored hand . . . and stopped.

That wasn't her hand. Her gaze moved from her hand to her arm. It was long and graceful and looked like it had been carved from living marble. In shock, she sat up. A mass of luxurious blond hair was swept over one of her shoulders so that it cascaded down the front of her body, covering her torso like a silken shawl. She could just make out the mauve tips of her well-endowed breasts peeking through the blond curtain. With shaking hands, she pulled the gorgeous mane back out of her way and looked at the rest of "her" body.

The flawless skin tapered down to a voluptuously curved waist. Just where her hips started to swell, skin gave way to closely woven scales. Where legs and feet should have been, instead there was a tail that ended in an enormous, feathered fin.

"Holy fucking shit; I'm a fish!"

Unaccustomed to using such harsh language, CC's first impulse was to cover her mouth and look around frantically to make sure her mother hadn't heard her, but the jerky movement of her upper body caused her tail to flip in response. It felt kind of like she had just twitched her legs to keep her balance and they had responded—together.

"My language would be the least of the things I would have to explain if my mother was here," CC blurted. The sound of her voice wasn't even her own—instead it was perfect, complete with a sensuous accent and a soft, breathy tone. "And to think I've always wanted to be gorgeous like Marilyn Monroe." CC shook her head at the irony. "Now that I am, I'm a . . . I'm a . . ." Semihysterical giggles broke from her mouth.

Swallowing back her hysteria, she closed her eyes and forced herself to calm down. Breathe deeply, breathe deeply she told herself—it wouldn't help for her to loose it now. Another deep breath, then she reopened her eyes and looked at her body again. And she couldn't wrench her eyes from her tail. CC told her legs to kick, and the feathery fin lifted gracefully in response. The blue light of the grotto was reflected in the scales, and her tail glinted with a myriad of brilliant sequins. CC had to acknowledge that it really was very beautiful. With a shaking, hesitant hand she reached out and touched the shining surface of fishlike flesh and was instantly surprised by the soft warmth under her fingers. Now that she was touching it, she could tell that the tail wasn't actually made of fish scales at all, it was more like the skin of a dolphin, just colored with amazing shadings of blues and purples. She stroked herself, enjoying the slick smoothness of her new skin. It was like being wrapped in liquid silver, she thought, only instead of one color, it was countless fantastic colors.

And she felt incredibly powerful. She could actually feel the energy that simmered within her body. She cocked her head, as if listening to that newly found strength, and she realized that the water seemed to call to her. CC could almost hear its voice asking her to come frolic within its depths.

Maybe she was dreaming, or even dead, but the thought didn't hold any horror for her. Whatever had happened to her, she still had her own mind, and she most certainly was getting a bigger dose of magic than she could ever have imagined possible in her old life.

CC dipped the finned end of her tail down so that it broke the surface of the enticing water, and then with a ripple of muscle she flipped it up again. Warm seawater rained in a glistening arch around her; wherever it touched her body she felt it as a lover's caress.

Leaning forward, she gazed into the calm water of the grotto at her remarkably changed reflection. The only familiar thing she saw was the amber teardrop that dangled between her bare breasts.

"I'm her." The beautiful creature's lips moved as CC spoke. "Somehow I'm the mermaid now." She remembered watching her own body lift toward the faraway surface. "And she's me."

A tremor ran though her, and she raised a hand to touch the curve of one perfect cheek. Totally engrossed in studying her refection, CC didn't look up at the sound of a disturbance in the water.

"Undine, need I remind you of the lesson the gods taught Narcissus?"

A deep, mocking voice made CC gasp and jerk back in surprise. Not far from her ledge a huge man floated in the water. His torso was bare and he was powerfully built. His hair was so blond it was almost white, and it fell in a thick wave past his shoulders. He would have been handsome, had it not been for his sneering expression.

"But of course I must admit that you are truly spectacular." He dropped his voice to a seductive purr. Then, noting her expression, he added. "Are you surprised to see me, sister dear?" He floated a little nearer CC's ledge. His storm gray eyes were intense. "How could you doubt that I would pursue you?"

"Wh-what?" CC's lips felt numb, and she shrank back.

"Please, let us not play your tiresome games. Our father demands you return, and you know how angry Lir can get when his demands are not obeyed." Slowly he floated even closer to her.

CC was confused and frightened. What did this man want and who was Lir?

"When Lir noticed that you were missing again, I graciously volunteered to find you and bring you home."

He wasn't looking in her eyes, instead his gaze kept shifting from her breasts to the jointure in her tail at the place where her thighs would meet, if she had thighs. His hot stare made her feel intensely uncomfortable and completely naked. She scrambled back until she could go no farther and was pressed firmly against the side of the cave.

He reached CC's ledge and placed his hands on the edge of it. With a quick flex of his powerful arms, he raised himself partially out of the water, and CC gasped again.

His muscular torso tapered down to meet the glistening skin of a mer-creature. CC's eyes grew round with shock. Mer*man*, she amended as she watched the hard pulsing flesh surge from a slit in his tail where a human man's groin would be. This creature was quite obviously male.

"Now," his voice was low and ominous. "I am finished with chasing you. I have tried wooing you. I have tried reasoning with you. I have even tried begging you. Nothing works. You continue to spurn me. Your stubborn tricks have left me no choice. You force me to take what I desire."

His malevolent presence filled the cave. CC could feel her heart beating erratically. Her reaction was intense and immediate. He repulsed her.

"Stay away from me." CC was surprised by the power in her new voice.

"No, my darling. Not any more. I am finished with waiting." He reached forward and stroked a thick strand of hair that had fallen over her breast. "So lovely." His breathing deepened.

CC flinched from his touch, which enraged him.

"You will be mine!" he screamed in her face. Then, with an effort, he regained control of himself, shifting his tone to a more reasonable one. "Why do you pretend you do not understand? Our father is busy elsewhere, and he has grown weary of your little escapes. He is not listening for your cries." The merman grimaced. "And your landlocked goddess mother cannot hear you within my wonderful little cave; I made quite certain of that. Do you like the gift I created for you?" One powerful arm gestured to take in the grotto. "Be reasonable and this will be pleasant for us both. You must realize that Father will actually be pleased when we have mated. I believe he even plans on granting us a realm of our own."

CC's mind whirred. No wonder the beautiful mermaid had been so eager to exchange places with her! CC would much rather be a plain, ordinary human girl than a magical mermaid raped by her perverted brother.

The creature pulled himself all the way up on the ledge. His body was almost twice the size of CC's mermaid body. His chest and shoulders bulged, and his powerful tail was banded with thick stripes of crimson and dark green.

"Do you appreciate that I attempted to duplicate the color of your eyes in these crystals?" Again his voice was ingratiating and deceptively gentle. He leaned closer to her. "But nothing could match the beauty of your eyes."

He brushed the fall of hair off her chest, leaving her completely exposed. Then he reached forward and cupped her breasts in his huge hands, worrying her nipples painfully between his thumb and forefingers. Before CC could even attempt to push his hands away, his attention wavered.

"What is that thing?" he spat. "It reeks of human design." The merman freed her breasts to grasp the amber teardrop, which glowed softly where it dangled between them.

The instant his skin met amber, he shrieked in pain and dropped the pendant. Stunned, CC watched him curl over his hand, his entire body shaking violently. He was moaning and she could see spittle frothing around his lips.

The jewelry lady's words echoed through her mind. *Know that it has the power to absorb negative energy and turn it to positive. You may have need of it . . .*

She had to do something. The cave was a prison; she had to escape. CC heaved herself forward, squeezing around the merman's convulsed body and hurled herself headfirst into the water. As soon as she was immersed, she felt her panic subside. With an instinct of its own, her body took control and she dove swiftly down and away from the crystal prison.

Expecting to be caught in the swirling current of black water, she was surprised to see that tranquil blue surrounded her. There was no sign of the tunnel through which she had traveled. Still swimming with incredible swiftness, she glanced up and saw the lighter blue of daylight against the surface not far above her head. CC angled her body up, and with one powerful stroke of her tail propelled herself to the surface and broke through the liquid barrier.

She looked frantically around. On the horizon behind her she could see the dark outline of the grotto. She was amazed at how far she had traveled so quickly. In front of her, the ocean appeared to come to a halt. Confused, she rubbed her eyes clear and let herself drift forward. No, it wasn't that the ocean stopped. It was a huge coral shelf. On her side of it the water was the deep sapphire of the bottomless ocean. White-capped waves crashed against the barrier. CC flipped her tail and raised herself up farther out of the water. On the other side of the barrier she could see calm, turquoise water, which led to—her heart beat faster—a sandy shoreline.

That mer-creature had said that he was hiding from her "landlocked goddess mother." If he had felt the need to hide, then that must mean he was afraid. Could the mermaid's mother help her? If so, since she was "landlocked," perhaps she could be found near the shore.

A prickly feeling along her spine interrupted her thoughts. Her skin twitched somewhere on the back of her neck where it seemed eyes touched her.

She turned quickly, searching the ocean for signs of her pursuer. Nothing. As far as she could see the surface was disturbed by nothing except waves. Almost as if it was as natural a movement as stepping backwards, she waved her finned tail and submerged herself under the water. The blue depths were clear and visibility was good, but CC could see nothing more villainous than a drifting jellyfish. She resurfaced.

Maybe she had escaped and was safe for that moment, but one thing CC knew for sure, she couldn't just float there and wait for that creature to recapture her. Doing anything was better than that. With a powerful flick of her tail she leapt up and over the thick coral reef, splashing headfirst into the clear waters of the cove and straight into a school of huge, brightly-colored fish.

CC's first reaction was fear—they were really big fish—and she made shooing motions at them. But they refused to shoo. Instead they quivered and milled around her, a little like puppies. Curious, CC reached a hesitant hand out to touch one florescent-scaled side. The ecstatic fish went into very doglike spasms of glee. CC laughed, which caused the entire school to explode into joyous leaps of playful abandon.

She was just thinking that she didn't know how the day could get much weirder when she came face-to-face with a full-grown dolphin.

"Ah!" She jerked back, bubbles of surprise bursting from her mouth. The dolphin didn't look at all shocked by the appearance of a mermaid who was surrounded by a school of jubilant, silly-acting fish.

They have so little dignity.

The thought was placed gently within her mind. She stared at the dolphin. She had never seen a real one this close. Well, she had visited Sea World at San Antonio once, and there had been dolphins there that people could pay to swim with, but the price had been beyond her budget. And this creature was no tamed hothouse flower; it was stunning. Its sleek skin glowed with vitality and its expressive eyes telegraphed intelligence.

I ask you to forgive me, Princess Undine. I did not mean to startle you.

I, uh, just didn't expect you, CC thought automatically.

The dolphin dipped its head in graceful acknowledgment. *May I offer you my assistance, Princess?*

She could send her thoughts to this wonderful creature? What an incredible gift!

I need to find my mother. CC quickly decided it was worth a try to enlist all the help she could get. And the creatures seemed to know her—maybe they would know how to help her, too.

Of course, Princess Undine. CC was almost sure the dolphin grinned at her. *Gaea comes to these shores often, as you well know. It would be my honor.* The dolphin glanced at the school of waiting fish with what CC thought was an endearingly long-suffering look before adding, *And the honor of these small ones, to escort you to shore.*

Gaea! The goddess Gaea was the mermaid's mother! What a bizarre coincidence. CC thought about the elevator and the jewelry lady . . . perhaps coincidence was the wrong word.

She smiled her gratitude to the beautiful creature. *Yes, please take me to my mother!*

Together they swam through the clear, warm water. The ocean floor was not far below them, and CC could easily see hulks of coral clustered like mysterious rock castles against the white sand of the bottom. Brightly colored fish darted in and around delicate underwater fronds like autumn leaves in a windstorm. CC looked in wide-eyed wonder at the underwater world. She had never imagined such loveliness existed. Honestly, she had always been a little afraid of the water; she hadn't even ever snorkeled. Look at what I've been missing, she thought over and over to herself.

Just a few feet from the shoreline the dolphin surfaced beside a half-hollowed rock. Its flattened top jutted just above the waterline. As if she had done it so many times before, CC slid onto its smooth surface and studied the lush shore. Diamond waters lapped gently against the velvet sand of the beach so that land and ocean melted together harmoniously, like lovers embracing. Huge trees decorated with flowering vines surrounded the cove. A slight breeze brought to CC the sweet scent of flowers mixed with the tang of salt air. There was a definite aura of peacefulness about the cove. CC breathed deeply, enjoying the unexpected serenity. She felt like she could stay there forever, basking in the warm sun and the honey-scented air.

Princess? The dolphin was looking expectantly at her, returning her thoughts to her present situation.

And the terror of the merman's pursuit rushed back into her mind. Quickly she looked over her shoulder, but she could see nothing except the serenity of the ocean. But she didn't even know if he could be seen approaching. Except for the leap over the coral shelf, she'd traveled underwater to get there. She probably wouldn't know if he was streaking after her at that moment. She had been stupid to relax like she was on some kind of Caribbean vacation.

What was she supposed to do now?

She studied the land, this time not allowing herself to be distracted by its beauty. She certainly didn't see a goddess waiting anywhere. CC fiddled nervously with the amber pendent. This wasn't exactly like picking up the phone and calling her mom. But maybe moms everywhere had at least one common characteristic—they were accustomed to answering the cries of their children.

CC squared her shoulders and cleared her throat.

"Mother!" she shouted, enchanted by the way her melodic voice carried over the water. "Goddess Gaea! It's me. Your daughter, Undine." She looked nervously at the dolphin, who was floating quietly, still looking toward the shore. "I need your help." Please answer me, she prayed silently.

From the thickest nest of verdant ivy and hanging flowers a movement drew her gaze. CC's eyes widened in surprise. A beautiful woman was tucked gracefully amidst the vines. She was sitting on a makeshift swing made of living plant.

"Good morning, Daughter." The woman's voice rang over the water.

CC felt a shock of recognition. "You're the lady who saved me from the elevator!"

A familiar smile curved Gaea's lips. "Yes, I heard your unique call which you offered under the full moon. It pleased me, and I like to care for those who remember me." She paused and her smile widened. "Even if they are living in a far-off world." She pointed at the amber teardrop that dangled between CC's breasts. "I am pleased that you value my gift."

CC swallowed hard past the lump that had lodged in her throat, and her fingers wound themselves around the warm stone. She was speaking with a real goddess. Or she was dead. Either way, it was nerve-wracking.

"Yes, thank you. It's beautiful and magical." She cleared her throat. "Then you know that I'm not really Undine."

The Goddess's eyes filled with unshed tears, but her expression remained kind. "Of course I know it, young one. Undine is a daughter of my flesh. You, Christine Canady, staff sergeant in the United States Air Force, who prefers to be called CC, are a daughter of my spirit."

"How?" CC felt overwhelmed.

Gaea made a slight motion with one hand, and the vine swing dipped low enough to let her step down to the ground. Gracefully, she walked toward the waterline. CC couldn't take her eyes from the goddess. She realized that the glimpse she'd had of Gaea outside of the elevator had been just a shadow of the goddess's true visage. Today she was magnificent. Her hair was the deep brown of fertile earth, and it curled thickly around her waist. Woven within it were flowers and glistening jewels. CC thought her face looked like it could have served as a model for countless classic sculptures—which, she thought, it probably had. CC couldn't remember getting a clear view of what the goddess had been wearing when she had seen her that day at Tinker, but today her generous curves were draped in transparent green linen, which was the exact color of the ivy growing in profusion all around her.

"You're so beautiful!" CC embarrassed herself by blurting.

Gaea's laughter glittered between them. "Come, child," she said as she reached the water and sank to the sand, letting her bare feet play in the crystal surf. "Come closer to me."

The dolphin chattered joyfully, leaping around the cove as CC slid off the rock and swam to the goddess. Gaea was gazing steadily at her, and CC realized that the reason Undine's startlingly blue eyes had seemed familiar to her was that they were the exact image of the goddess's eyes. Awkwardly, she pulled herself up on the sandy shore until she rested within touching distance of the beautiful immortal.

CC ducked her head apologetically. "I'm sure Undine was much better than I am at navigating with this." She pointed at her tail.

"Do you dislike this body?" The goddess didn't sound judgmental or angry, only genuinely curious.

"Oh, no! I think it's amazing. It's just a lot different from having legs and feet," she said. "And she's so gorgeous, much more so than I am. Or was. Or . . ." CC trailed off, confused by the tenses as well as the situation.

"I think you underestimate yourself, little one. But I am glad you are pleased with this form." The goddess's expression became distant. "And I am sure that my daughter, Undine, is pleased with her new form as well."

"So she is me now?" CC asked, amazed at how easy it was to talk with Gaea.

"Yes. She has taken your place in that world."

"Am I dead?"

Gaea's laughter caused the tree boughs to sway in delighted response. "Oh, no. You are very much alive."

"Then I don't understand," CC said, feeling more lost than ever.

The goddess reached out and touched CC's cheek in a motherly caress. "This must be very difficult for you, poor child. I will try to explain. Undine is the child of my body, but she is also very much her father's daughter."

"Lir," CC said.

Gaea looked surprised at her knowledge, but nodded. "Yes."

"Um, who exactly is Lir?" she asked.

The goddess smiled. "Lir is the great God of the Seas. You might recognize him by one of his other titles. He has been known as Tethys, Pontos, Neptune, Barinthus, Enki, Poseidon and many others."

CC's eyes widened in surprise. "Poseidon is Undine's father?"

Gaea's eyes held a faraway expression as she gazed out at the waters. "We knew that the land and the sea were not meant to mate, but one day I was bathing here, in this very cove, and the Lord of the Sea cast his eyes upon me." Her face softened with remembrance. "For one brief night I allowed him to envelop me, and from that union Undine was conceived."

CC listened intently to the tale the goddess spun.

"Undine was born a mermaid, so it was destined that she live in her father's realm, but she was not content there. She longed for the land

and for her mother." Gaea's face was shadowed by sadness, and CC felt her own eyes fill with tears in response. "I tried to coax Lir to allow me to gift our daughter with a human form so that she could live with me on land, but he adored the child and refused to be parted from her."

Gaea took CC's hand and squeezed it. "Do not think him cruel. Lir loved his daughter. And she wasn't always unhappy. She adored her father and the creatures of his realm, and she came here many times, sitting where you are now, telling me fantastic stories of the underwater crystal castle in which she lived and the wonders of the seas."

"It was only recently that she changed." The goddess's expression was haunted. "Sometimes I would find her weeping, there on that rock. Ceaselessly she begged me to gift her with a human form."

CC shivered. She thought she knew why Undine had become so desperate. "Did she tell you what was wrong?"

Gaea shook her head sadly. "No. I asked her, but she said only that she longed to be with me always."

Tears spilled from the goddess's eyes, yet Gaea didn't seem to notice.

"I was afraid she would do harm to herself. I am a goddess, but her father is also an immortal, and I could not cause her form to shift without his consent, as he could not have taken her from me if she had been born in human form." Her eyes glinted with determination. "But I am also a mother, and I could not allow my child to suffer. I wove a spell for her, giving Undine the ability to attain a human body, but only if she could find a human being who would be willing to exchange lives with her." Gaea stared into CC's eyes. "And I knew you would have need of her aid, as she had need of yours, little daughter."

"I don't understand," CC said.

"Your Samhain ritual was heartfelt, and I still heed the call of my children in other worlds, even a world in which I have been forgotten. You pleased me that night, and I touched you."

CC blushed, remembering the passionate feel of the moonlight on her skin.

The goddess put one perfect finger under CC's chin and lifted her face. "Do not ever be ashamed of a gift from a goddess." Before CC could respond she continued. "I asked the Fates to show me your future, and I saw your life's thread end too soon in a watery grave." She sighed sadly. "There was little I could do to aid you, as there was little I could do to aid the daughter of my flesh, but together you could help one another. Thus you are here and she is there."

"Where is here?" was the first of many questions that leapt to CC's mind.

"Here is a world where gods and goddesses still live."

CC's expression was puzzled.

Gaea tried to explain. "This cove is of my making, so it is like nothing that would be familiar to you, but beyond here you would find a land your world would call medieval Cymru." Her arm swept in a gesture meant to include all of the land behind them.

CC felt her face pale. "You're not talking about somewhere in southern California, are you?"

Gaea smiled at her. "Actually, I believe your books would tell you it is the Land of the Britons, or more specifically, ancient Wales."

"You mean I'm smack in the middle of medieval Europe!"

Gaea patted her hand reassuringly. "There is much that historians left out of your world's texts." The goddess winked one large blue eye at CC. "Like magic, my daughter."

"And how do I—"

The angry chattering of the dolphin interrupted CC's question. She looked over her shoulder and her body went numb. The merman had surfaced in the middle of the cove.

"Silence you meddling beast!" he snarled at the dolphin.

Automatically, CC scooted closer to Gaea.

"Goddess Gaea, what an unexpected privilege it is to see you." His voice had shifted to silk.

"And why would it be unexpected, Sarpedon?" Gaea smiled graciously at him. "This is my cove; it is well known that I come here often."

"*Your* cove?" The merman's instant sarcasm shocked CC. "I thought the water realm belonged to Lir."

"That would be true, young Sarpedon, had your father not gifted me with all the waters within this cove." Gaea's eyes narrowed. "You would do well to remember that water must flow over land, and where you find land, there you will always find my realm."

"I beg your pardon, Goddess Gaea. I did not mean to offend," he said, suddenly contrite. "I come to *your* cove on an errand for Lir himself."

When Gaea didn't respond, Sarpedon hurried on, taking the opportunity to drift closer to the two of them. "My father asks that I escort my sister back to him. Undine has been absent so frequently of late that she has been greatly missed," he said, and his intense gaze shifted briefly to CC.

"No."

The word slipped from CC's lips as a whisper. She glanced up at the goddess, who was studying her carefully. Bolstered by Gaea's presence, CC cleared her throat and repeated the word in a loud, firm voice.

"No!"

"You must obey our father," Sarpedon said between clenched teeth.

"Must she?" The goddess broke into the exchange. Gaea's eyes were wise as she looked from the mermaid to the merman.

"Yes!" Sarpedon struggled to control the anger in his voice. "Goddess, you know that Lir misses his daughter."

"I know that Lir loves his daughter and would not see her harried," Gaea snapped.

"I want only to do our father's bidding." Sarpedon raised his hands, palms open in a gesture of helplessness. CC could clearly see the angry red welts that dotted one palm where his skin had touched her amulet.

CC's head was whirling. She knew that Undine must have been trying to escape from this creature, but she also knew that the mermaid had not confided in her mother about her problem. Well, maybe Undine had spent her life being bullied and hounded by her half brother, but CC had spent the past seven years in the male-dominated United States Air Force. Even before the goddess touched her she knew how to stand up for herself. If this was going to be her world, she might as well get the rules straight right away. And she sure wasn't going to play by Sarpedon's rules. She raised her chin and looked straight in his almond-shaped gray eyes.

"You are a liar," she said.

"You have been too long away from your home." He had moved to within only a few feet of CC. His face darkened dangerously. "You have forgotten yourself."

"Really?" CC said sardonically. "I think I could be gone a lifetime and still know rape when I see it."

With an abrupt movement, Gaea stood. She spoke with deadly softness. "You dared to touch my child against her will?"

"He tried, but your amulet protected me," she said before Sarpedon could respond. For the goddess's ears alone she whispered, "I think he's what Undine was so afraid of."

"Leave my presence, Sarpedon!" The goddess's voice was amplified until it filled the small cove. "And I warn you to keep far from my daughter."

But instead of being admonished, the merman rose out of the water, balancing on his powerful tail until he towered over CC. Automatically, she shrank back.

"I will have her!" Spittle flew from his lips and his eyes flashed wildly. "My father is Lord of the Seas—you hold no power over me, *Land Goddess*." He spat the title like it was an oath.

"Foolish creature. Even the Lord of the Seas knows not to evoke the wrath of a goddess!"

Gaea pointed one slim finger at the sandy earth under her feet and made a small, circular motion. The sand stirred. With a flick of her wrist she gestured to the merman. The sand whirlpooled from its damp bed and flung itself into Sarpedon's face, causing him to choke and rub frantically at his eyes. He fell back into deeper water, sputtering and cursing. Then she stretched out her arms, as if she would embrace the cove. When she spoke her voice was seductive and rich with authority.

"Winds that play over my body, which is the living Earth herself, come to me now and blow this usurper from my presence."

The goddess pursed her full lips and blew a light burst of air at Sarpedon. Then something amazing happened to that light, almost playful bit of air. It seemed that all the winds in the cove suddenly rushed to join it. The gust struck Sarpedon like a fist, lifting him from the water and hurling him to the coral reef barrier.

"Trespass upon my realm again, and I will destroy you." The power in Gaea's voice lifted the hairs on the back of CC's neck. *"So have I spoken; so shall it be."* The air around the goddess shimmered, making her promise a tangible thing.

Awestruck, CC could only stare at Gaea. Her mind could hardly grasp what she was witnessing. The goddess loomed huge and powerful, and CC was overwhelmed by her majesty.

But Sarpedon seemed oblivious to Gaea's power. "Do not forget that Undine is a creature of the seas! She must exist in my realm, Land Goddess!" He shrieked at her before leaping over the coral reef and disappearing into the blue depths.

CC stared after him, shivering with an ominous foreboding.

Chapter Seven

"You were very brave." Gaea's voice had returned to that of a mother praising her child.

"I don't feel very brave right now," she said hesitantly, still awed by Gaea's power.

The goddess bent and stroked CC's soft hair. "I am proud of you. There is a strength in you that was lacking in Undine."

CC felt a rush of pleasure at her words.

The dolphin surfaced, blowing water on the two women and chattering like an upset nursemaid. Laughing, Gaea wiped the drops of seawater from her gown.

"You had better comfort her; she will not leave us in peace until she is assured of your safety."

Feeling a little shaky at first, CC slid from the shore. Again, she felt that prickle at the nape of her neck that made her think she was being watched.

No, she told herself firmly, Sarpedon is gone. He cannot come within Gaea's grove. She was just being paranoid—and who could blame her? Thankfully, as soon as she was immersed in the water, her fears began to subside. She glided up to the distraught dolphin and stroked the creature's smooth sides.

"Hey, I'm fine," she said aloud. "Gaea got rid of him. He can't hurt me here."

We feared for you, Princess. The dolphin nuzzled CC, then turned and bowed its head reverently at Gaea. *Thank you, great goddess, for protecting our Princess.*

Solemnly, Gaea inclined her head and acknowledged the dolphin's adoration.

CC could see the shapes of the smaller fish timidly hiding around the clumps of bright coral.

You can come out now. She coaxed and was delighted to see them respond by wriggling up to her. With one arm draped over the back of the dolphin, she petted and soothed the frightened fish.

"Sarpedon was correct about one thing," Gaea said.

"What?" CC's attention had been focused on the delightful fish, but the goddess's words sent a chill through her body.

"I cannot protect you there." The goddess pointed to the seemingly limitless expanse of ocean. "And you cannot live forever in this cove."

"But what am I going to do?" CC knew the goddess was right. How could she live her life in this small cove? It was the equivalent of being trapped forever in an apartment. No matter how luxurious or wonderful, she would still be trapped.

"We will do what we must to keep you safe," Gaea said.

"Which means what?"

Gaea studied the girl who inhabited her daughter's body. She had strength, yes. And she was outspoken and brave. But did she also have wisdom? Perhaps the child had a kind of wisdom that was foreign to this world; but perhaps that was the kind of wisdom that would be needed for her to survive the tests that were sure to be ahead of her. The goddess made her decision.

"There is only one answer. I must take you from the sea."

CC eyes widened in surprise. "But I thought that was the problem. You couldn't take Undine from the sea without Lir's permission." Then an idea came to CC. "So why can't we get Lir's permission now? You said he loves Undine. Doesn't that mean that he wouldn't want her own brother to rape her?"

"Sarpedon is Lir's child, too." Gaea's expression was grim. "Perhaps Lir has given his permission for your mating."

"Ugh, that's disgusting—brother and sister mating." Just the thought made CC feel sick.

"Gods and goddesses do not view these things the way humans do," Gaea said simply.

"You think it's okay that he wants me?" CC was shocked.

"Never," Gaea said firmly. "But only because you have rejected him; thus, he has no right to you. Understand that relationships are different between the gods."

"I'll take your word for it," CC muttered. "So we can't go to Lir. How do I get away from Sarpedon?"

"There is a way, but it may prove difficult."

"Is it worse than being raped by Sarpedon?" CC asked.

"Only you can answer that question, little one." The goddess began pacing back and forth along the shore as she explained to CC. "I can gift you with a human form, but it will not be permanent. You will still be tied to the seas." She gave CC an apologetic look. "Your body will long to return to the water; it may even be painful for you. And you must return to the waters and your mermaid form once each third night, or else you will sicken and die."

"Well, I suppose that's better than being trapped in this cove forever," CC said doubtfully.

The goddess stopped pacing and spoke earnestly to her. "But there is a way to make your human form permanent. You must find a man to love you and to accept with a full heart that you are a daughter of the sea, as well as that of the land. Then even Lir cannot break the bond of true love, and you will be gifted with your human form permanently."

"Oh, Gaea," CC groaned. "I'm not very experienced with men. Actually, they treat me like I'm a little sister." Then she added quickly, "And where I come from that didn't mean they wanted anything romantic to do with me."

"The handsome young pilot on your transport desired you."

Gaea's words cut into CC. Her eyes filled with tears as she remembered Sean's sweetness. "Yeah, and look what happened to him."

"He was living his destiny, child." Gaea's tone was soothing. "It was not your fault; he was fated to die on that journey. He did so heroically. You should honor his memory."

"He was going to die anyway?" CC asked.

"Yes. You did not cause his death. His life's thread had run out."

At Gaea's words CC felt a weight of guilt lift from her. She closed her eyes and said a silent prayer of thanksgiving for Sean's bravery. When she opened her eyes she met the Goddess's gaze with a clear conscience.

"Tell me what I need to do."

"I will cast the spell. You must simply find the man who can accept and love you."

"Wait! Shouldn't that be easy in this world? You said gods and goddesses live here. Aren't people used to magical things?" CC asked.

"At one time, perhaps." Gaea hesitated, as if weighing her words. "You have priests in your world."

Gaea hadn't made it sound like a question, but CC nodded anyway.

"They are here, too. And many of them are good men who serve their God with love and devotion." She paused, and when she spoke again her voice sounded disgusted. "But not all of them are honorable. There has begun a new sect of priest that has infected parts of their religion. They preach that all magic is evil, and that there is only one way to believe—their way. They believe beauty, especially that of the female body, is sinful and evil." Gaea's laugh was dry and humorless. "They are fools, afraid of their own desires. But of course they want people shut away from beauty. It is easier to control people who lack hope." She shook her head sadly. "Unfortunately, too many listen to their poison."

"I wouldn't want to be with a man who believed that anyway," CC said.

"Do not judge too harshly. Even good men can be misled. Be wise in your choice and all will be well in the end."

"Ha! My choice? I haven't even had a date in six months." CC felt her cheeks color at that admission.

"My daughter," the goddess smiled indulgently. "I promise you that men will desire you."

CC glanced down at her sexy curves. "Oh! I get to keep *her* body?"

Gaea's laughter rang throughout the cove. "What was hers is yours, *Undine.*"

"Ooooh." CC's mouth rounded in wonder. She was going to be beautiful. Incredibly, amazingly, as-gorgeous-as-Marilyn-Monroe beautiful.

"You must appear to be a princess who has survived a shipwreck." Gaea's words were coming quickly now that the decision was made.

"But—"

Gaea held up her hand, cutting off CC's question. "I am afraid I must create a storm." She looked narrowly at CC. "You can swim?"

"Yes, but not very—"

Again, the goddess cut her off.

"Good." Gaea paced while she spoke to CC in a matter-of-fact, instructional tone. "Feign loss of memory. You should even appear desperate to find your family . . ."

CC wanted to ask how she was supposed to find true love based on lies, and amnesia, but there was no interrupting the goddess.

". . . that desperation is why you must insist on staying near the ocean—so that messages can be more easily sent and received. And I will be certain that you come to shore in a place surrounded by water." Gaea's gaze was piercing. "But do not forget that in truth you must stay near the water or you will perish." Then the goddess softened. "But you will already know that, child. You will ache for the water. Just be wise when you change your form. Do not let yourself be seen, and always stay close to the shore where you will be under my protection. If Sarpedon traps you away from my shores, I cannot aid you."

"But you will be with me when I'm on the land?" CC's voice sounded panicky.

"I will be watching you." The goddess smiled softly. "Remember to wear your amulet. I will always be there when you truly have need of me, but you must choose your own path, Undine. Be sure to choose wisely."

Before doubts could overwhelm her, CC said, "I'll try my best."

"Are you ready, Undine?" The goddess asked.

CC fought back the nervousness that threatened to overwhelm her. She almost changed her mind and begged the goddess to let her stay in the protected cove where she knew she would be safe and loved. But she wasn't a fish in a bowl, and she'd already left one life that had been too small to contain her when she joined the air force. Was this really so different?

"I'm ready, Mother," she said resolutely.

"Then know my blessing as well as my love goes with you."

The goddess stepped away from the water and walked back to the greenery that lined the sandy shore. Once surrounded in living plants, she turned and faced the ocean. Lifting her arms over her head she began to speak, and CC shivered as the power of the goddess's words filled the cove.

"I call upon the elements I command. Air—that blows over and through me, ever present and ever blessed. Fire—that is fed and brought to life by me, a true partner and respected friend. And Earth—my body and soul. It is through you that my child was born, and to you she shall someday return."

As the air around Gaea started to glow, CC could feel the lower half of her body begin to tingle.

"With this Earth spell I protect my own. I command that only true love will complete it—and only death can break it. So have I spoken; so shall it be."

The glow that had been surrounding Gaea exploded, hurling its brightness outward and directly at CC. She closed her eyes and threw her hands over her face just before she was enveloped in a blinding flash of color and sensation. She could tell she was being pulled into the air, and her body felt as if it was on fire. CC could see nothing and she was deafened by a cacophony of shrieking wind.

Time had no meaning. She tried to scream Gaea's name, but the words were ripped from her mouth, lost in an unnatural gale of noise and light.

And then she was plunged back into the water. Only her body didn't obey her with the awesome power of a mermaid. This time she could feel her human legs kicking feebly against the angry current as she struggled for the surface. She couldn't breathe and her lungs screamed. Finally, she broke through the surface and gulped air.

The sky was black and bruised looking. Waves crashed over her head making her sputter and choke. The peaceful cove was nowhere in sight, nor was her dolphin friend or the goddess. She could see an unfamiliar shoreline a daunting distance away from her. Trying to keep a growing sense of panic at bay, she started swimming for land.

The skies opened and rain began to pelt her. A white-capped wave hit her, and CC was slammed under the water. She clawed for the surface and realized that in the liquid blackness she couldn't tell which direction was up. All rational thought fled her mind and panic surged through her as she flailed helplessly in the drowning darkness.

Strong hands gripped her by the waist and lifted her, holding her above the seething water so that she could suck air into her burning lungs. She coughed and gagged, vomiting the seawater she had been unable to keep herself from swallowing. Her body shook uncontrollably. She could feel hands holding her waist securely. Her naked back was pressed firmly against the hard muscles of a man's chest—she could feel his deep, even breathing. She thought that he had to be standing on firm ground to be able to support her so well. With shaking hands she rubbed her eyes clear of saltwater, expecting to see the shore close before her. Instead, it was still a too distant line of darkness.

Confused, CC twisted around to find that she was being held in the arms of an oddly familiar stranger. His wild black hair hung in runnels around his shoulders. He didn't speak, but his sable-colored eyes were fixed intently on her.

Questions surged through CC's mind. How could he look familiar to her? Hadn't Gaea sent her to a medieval world? Had the goddess made a mistake?

And then realization hit her with a rush of dizzy wonder. He looked familiar because he reminded her of the man from her dream! The one who had called to her so desperately the night she had summoned the goddess and danced in the rain.

Fascinated, CC stared at him. His broad chest was bare and smooth and felt hard and warm against her naked breasts. The corded muscles of his arms flexed with the effort of holding her above the surface. But instead of being able to feel the muscles of a man's legs against her own bare legs, the lower half of her body was pressed firmly against a single expanse of slick, warm flesh that flexed and beat steadily against the current. She glanced down. Even through the swirling water she could see the orange and gold brilliance of his thick, banded tail.

Chapter Eight

CC gasped with shock. The thought that flooded her mind was that she had to escape, and she pushed violently against his chest, kicking her way free of his arms. Instantly another wave battered her, pulling her under the water again. When she felt his hands on her, she forced herself to be calm and to quell the overwhelming urge to fight. She allowed him to lift her back to the surface.

This time, instead of holding her securely against his chest, he grasped her waist and held his arms straight out from his body, keeping her as far from him as he could. CC could see his thick tail beating hard against the water below, keeping them afloat.

"If you do not allow me to help you, you will drown." His deep voice sounded surprisingly gentle. "Your new body cannot breathe under the water."

"Who are you?" she asked breathlessly, pulling her water-soaked hair forward to cover her naked breasts.

"I am called Dylan."

"I won't go back to Sarpedon."

The merman's brows came together, and he shook his head. "I am no friend to the son of Lir."

"He didn't send you here?" She couldn't stop shivering.

"No." The word was clipped.

"Did Gaea?"

He shook his head.

"How—" she started to ask, but he broke in urgently.

"Undine, I must get you to land." He paused and looked deeply into her eyes. "It would be best if you would put your arms around my shoulders. I . . ." He hesitated again, trying to catch his breath, then he continued with an apologetic shrug. "I do not have the strength to carry you to shore as I am holding you now."

And he obviously didn't. His breath was coming in gasps, and the muscles in his arms were tight and quivering. CC could see the effort it was costing him to keep them afloat in the choppy waters. She looked at him more carefully. If he had been human, he would have been a tall man. The merman's torso was well defined; his arms were powerful and his flat abdomen rippled with strength. But he didn't have the bulky cords of muscles that had packed Sarpedon's frame, nor did he have the other merman's overwhelming size. Obviously, mer-creatures came in different shapes and strengths, just like people.

"I give you my oath that I will not harm you, Undine." Dylan spoke the words slowly and clearly, enunciating carefully around his ragged breathing. "Look—" He shifted one hand from her waist, causing her to slip a little way down in the water. He grasped her arm, still keeping her head and shoulders above the water, and with his other hand, he reached toward her breasts.

"Stop!" CC jerked back.

"You misunderstand," he assured her quickly. "I wish only to touch the amulet of the goddess. If it does not burn me, you will see that I have no desire to harm you."

CC held very still as the merman's hand moved slowly between her breasts. He cupped the amber teardrop in his palm.

Nothing happened. Dylan let the amulet fall from his hand and held his palm open for her inspection. It was unmarked.

"Do you believe me now, Princess Undine?" he asked.

She nodded. "What do you want me to do?"

"Hold onto my shoulders and rest your body against my back. Then I can swim under the water while you remain above the surface."

"Okay," she said, fighting back her fear.

"Come, then."

Still holding her securely by the arm, he pulled her toward him and turned so that she was facing his broad back. His skin was tan and flawless. His hair fell thick and heavy past his shoulders. It was wet and it glistened like a raven's wing. He slipped down in the water so that she could easily reach his shoulders.

She hesitated, afraid to touch him. He's just trying to help me, she told herself and forced her hands to grasp the rounded tops of his shoulders.

"You must hold tightly." He turned his head and spoke over his shoulder.

"I'm trying," CC said. Her hands felt numb and they didn't seem to want to obey her. Her lips were cold and the skin on her arms looked unnaturally pale.

Dylan reached around and with his forearm held her firmly against him. The length of CC's naked body was pressed to the back of the merman. She could feel his muscles tensing against her. His breathing was rough, and his skin felt incredibly warm against her chilled flesh. He turned his head again and their eyes met. Hers were wide with shock; his were dark with unspoken emotion.

"You have nothing to fear. I will not let you fall," he said simply.

A strong thrust of his tail sent the merman forward. He ducked his head under the water and began swimming just below the surface. CC clung to his back, struggling to breathe as waves slapped her face. Against her body she could feel the rhythmic beat of the merman's tail as it propelled them toward the shoreline.

As they neared the shore, the rain stopped. The sky began to clear and the waves quieted. Within minutes it was as if there had never been a raging storm. Dylan swam around jutting clumps of coral and rocks until CC could see that the shoreline was just a few yards from them. With a graceful flick of his tail he lifted his torso out of the water. CC still clung, gasping, to his back. Hesitantly, as if he didn't want to stop touching her, he unwrapped his arm from around CC. Her feet found the sandy bottom, and she let go of his shoulders.

The instant her feet met land, she felt an electric tingling throughout her body, and there was a burst of incredible light. Threads of brightness obscured her vision, like she had been trapped in a glowing spider's web. Then, as abruptly as it had begun, the light show ended.

CC was standing in water that came just below her breasts, and her body felt somehow different. She looked down at herself and gasped. She was clothed in layers upon layers of cloth that created a beautiful dress, which sparkled and shimmered with the exact colors that had been in her mermaid's tail. The fabric was heavy and wet, but CC could still see the intricate needlework that covered almost every inch of it. Her fingers and wrists were covered with rings and bracelets. She shook her head in wonder and felt dangling earrings brush against her neck. Her hair, too, felt unnaturally heavy, and CC raised a hand to touch strands of jewels that had been magically woven within it and draped around her slender neck.

"The Goddess Gaea cares for her own," Dylan said. The merman's tail was curled under him so that it appeared that he was standing beside her. He had drifted a step away from her, as if to give the magic room to work, but he didn't seem surprised by the sudden manifestation of CC's new wardrobe.

"Thank you, Gaea," CC said aloud. She studied the thickly leafed trees lining the beach, but she didn't see any sign of the goddess. Then her gaze returned to the merman.

"And thank you," she said. "I think I owe you my life." The sun had come out and its rays were already warming her. She was exhausted and her body felt like it was made of lead, but her uncontrollable shivering had stopped, and now that she was dressed, she didn't feel nearly as helpless.

He shook off her thanks. "No, Undine. There is no debt between us. I only offered aid when it was needed."

"Well, thank you anyway." Automatically, she offered her hand to him, and with only a slight hesitation he took it. But instead of shaking it he lifted it slowly to his mouth and pressed it to his lips. CC stopped breathing. Dylan's lips were warm—and that warmth traveled through her body, making the fine hairs on her arm rise in response. His eyes met hers, and CC realized how darkly handsome he was.

She found herself wanting to whisper *I think I dreamed about you*, but his gaze mesmerized her into silent breathlessness.

He continued holding her hand in his, and she felt him stroke it gently with his thumb. Her skin tingled under his caress, and her breath came back in a rush. The smile on his full lips was reflected in his dark, expressive eyes. When he spoke his voice was rough with emotion.

"Undine, you are most wel—"

A shout from the shore startled them. In one blink, Dylan dropped her hand and plunged headfirst, disappearing instantly beneath the waves.

CC turned to the shore in time to see, surging from the line of trees, a man riding a huge black horse. She took a step forward and her feet became tangled in the thick skirts of her dress. She fell face first into the water, where she struggled and floundered impotently against the weight of her clothes. Before she could regain her feet she was pulled roughly to the surface, swept up into the man's arms and carried to the beach like a child. She coughed and wiped water from her eyes, thinking how extraordinarily tired she was of swallowing seawater.

"You are safe now, my lady," the man said earnestly. Placing her gently on the sand, he kneeled beside her.

"Th-thank you." CC coughed. She looked up at him and couldn't help staring. He was dressed like she imagined an ancient knight would have been dressed. He wore a pointed helmet made of silver metal that left most of his face open, except for a studded nosepiece. A long tunic of gray chain mail covered him from torso to knees, leaving his thickly muscled legs bare. He had a huge sword strapped to his waist and the scarlet cape that was tossed over his shoulders was held in place by a large pewter brooch in the shape of a roaring lion. Blond hair escaped from under the helmet and curled around his shoulders. He looked like a young war god.

But he wasn't looking at her. His attention was focused on the water. "My lady, were there no other survivors from your vessel?"

"No," she said quickly. Then she remembered Gaea's words and pressed her hand to her forehead, leaning heavily back as if she was on the edge of fainting. "I-I don't know. I can't remember." She felt her body quiver with shock and the sob that escaped her lips was suddenly very real. "I can't remember anything."

He turned his attention back to her and his eyes widened as his senses registered the beauty he held within his arms. "Forgive me, lady," he said hastily, patting her shoulder awkwardly. "You have been through a horrible ordeal. It is just that for a moment I thought I saw someone in the water with you."

Two men on horseback burst through the tree line. The warrior shouted orders to them.

"Marten, Gilbert—search the shore and the waters for other survivors. This lady is injured. I must get her to shelter."

The two men saluted him and instantly obeyed his orders, but CC couldn't help noticing the way their eyes kept snaking back to her. The way they looked at her made her feel like she was still naked. The man kneeling beside her seemed to notice their looks, too, because he shifted his body to block her from their view.

"Can you ride?" he asked gently.

CC glanced at the gigantic black beast and gulped. Slung over its odd-looking, curved pommel was a large silver shield that looked a little like a monstrous kite. The creature pawed dangerously. The only horse she'd ever ridden had been attached to a carousel, and that had been many years ago.

"Not without help." She definitely wasn't pretending when her voice shook.

In one motion he scooped her from the sand and strode to the waiting horse, who snorted and shied at the waterlogged body in his master's arms. Without any warning, he tossed CC into the saddle, then grabbed a handful of the stallion's thick, dark mane and vaulted up behind her. Leaning forward he gathered the reins, kicked his heels into the horse's sides and the stallion leapt forward.

"Wait!" CC felt a stab of panic as they headed into the forest and away from the ocean. Something inside of her wrenched, and a wave of dizziness washed over her. "Where are you taking me?"

"Do not fear, my lady. There is a monastery not far from here. The good monks will give you aid."

"But I can't leave the ocean," she said frantically. "My family—" she broke off with a frightened sob.

His arms tightened around her protectively as he thought of her lovely helplessness. He was unaccustomed to having a woman touch his emotions, but it felt as though this young woman's beauty had already cast a spell upon him. She most assuredly shook him. When he spoke his voice was gruff, making his words sound harsh.

"We are not leaving the ocean. Caldei Monastery is but a short distance up this coast." He forced himself to add a smile to his voice, trying to reassure her. "And it would be impossible for us ride away from the ocean. Caldei Monastery is built on the island of Caldei. We are surrounded by the ocean."

The man's words didn't seem to register to her battered brain. She couldn't stop her body from shaking. What had she gotten herself into? Where was Gaea?

They broke through the trees onto a dirt-packed road and the warrior pointed his horse to the right. Clearing his throat and forcing himself to speak in a more soothing tone, he said, "My name is Sir Andras Ap Caer Llion, eldest son of the great Lord Caerleon. I am pleased to be of service to you, and I pledge that I will not allow any harm to befall you." His warm breath touched the side of her face. "May I be honored with your name?"

CC forced her eyes from the snatches of blue that she glimpsed through the trees. Her mind was in turmoil. She wanted nothing more than to shake free from the cage of the knight's arms and to hurl herself back into the ocean.

You will ache for the waters. Gaea's words drifted through her memory as she struggled against the primitive urge that engulfed her.

"Your name, lady?" the knight prompted.

CC breathed deeply, forcing herself to relax in his arms. The sun glinted through the trees that lined the dirt road, and as the stallion galloped forward, the play of light and shadow danced alluringly over the knight's silver helmet and golden hair. CC felt another wave of overwhelming emotion. She had been rescued first by a creature from her dreams and then by an authentic knight in shining armor.

And through it all, her body ached and cried for the sea.

"I am the Princess Undine, and I cannot leave the water," she whispered, closing her eyes and allowing her head to rest against the strength of his shoulder.

A safe distance from shore Dylan watched as the human man carried Undine away. His hands balled into fists, and he clenched his jaw until it ached. It didn't matter that he knew this was what she had always wanted. It didn't even matter that he knew the soul inside her body wasn't that of his childhood playmate, Undine. He still felt drawn to her. He remembered the look in her eyes when he had kissed her hand, and the hope that had filled him at her unexpected response to his touch. Watching her ride away, he felt like a piece of his body had been hacked from him.

Through the trees he could see that the horse had turned and was traveling parallel to the ocean. Ignoring his despair, he glided through the water, careful to keep her always within his sight.

She may still have need of him. He had failed her at the grotto; he would not fail her again.

Chapter Nine

"This princess has been shipwrecked!" The warrior shouted at the robed man standing nervously behind the barred doors. "I am Andras, son of Caerleon. I demand entrance and sanctuary for this lady."

"I must get the abbot." The little man scuttled quickly out of sight.

Andras made a derisive sound though his nose, and the black stallion pawed restlessly. CC closed her eyes on a wave of nausea. She could no longer see the ocean. The monastery had been built on the top of a cliff that dropped steeply to a rugged shoreline. Although out of sight, she could hear the waves crashing against the rocks below, and if she focused hard enough on the sound, it soothed her frayed nerves.

"Not much longer, Princess," Andras said. "Abbot William and my family are well acquainted. We will be admitted."

CC wanted to say that she thought monks were supposed to help people, whether they knew their families or not, but she couldn't summon the energy to speak. She wanted to get her drenched clothes off and sleep for days—and not necessarily in that order.

But most of all she wanted the sea to quit calling to her.

"Andras! Is that you, my son?" A soft voice with an accent that sounded vaguely British called from within the walls of the monastery.

"Yes, Father. I am in need of your aid."

"Of course, of course," the voice said hastily. "Brother, unlock this gate and allow our friend entrance."

Rusty hinges complained as the gate swung open. CC tried to sit straighter, ashamed of her bedraggled appearance. But before she could even smooth her hair, Andras slid from the horse's back and pulled her down beside him. CC was horrified to realize that she couldn't stand on her own. Her vision was blurred and everything went cloudy and gray as her knees buckled. Instantly the warrior lifted her into his arms.

"The princess needs rest and care. I found her washed ashore not far from here."

"Brother Peter, have the guest quarters readied for this lady and have one of the sculleries attend to her." CC could hear the scuffle of robes as the man hurried to do the abbot's bidding.

"Are there other survivors to follow, my son?"

CC could feel the warrior shaking his head.

"Poor child," the priest spoke quietly, but he made no attempt to mask the obvious curiosity in his voice. "And you say she is a princess?"

"She remembered her name, but I am afraid she has not been able to say much else," Andras said.

"What is her name?"

"She is the Princess Undine."

Silence greeted the knight's words, and CC wanted desperately to open her eyes and see the abbot's expression. But common sense warned her that it was best to keep up the pretense that she had fainted and was still unconscious.

"Undine?" The man enunciated the name carefully. "Are you quite certain she said Undine?"

"I believe so," Andras answered. "Yes, I am certain she told me her name was the Princess Undine. Do you recognize that name, Father?"

"I only know that in some tongues an *undine* is a spirit from the sea. How very odd."

"Abbot William." The first monk hurried back to them. "The guest room is ready for the lady and the scullery awaits."

"Let us get her safely within," Andras said. "There will be time to question names and such when she has recovered." CC could feel the warrior's eyes on her and when he spoke his lips were close to her ear.

"Look at her, Abbot. It is most certain that she is a princess." Andras's arms tightened possessively around her.

"Let us not be deceived by beauty, my son." The abbot's voice was condescending. "But you are correct, she must rest before we can expect her to speak. Follow me to the guest quarters."

CC rested her head against Andras's shoulder, slitting her eyes to try and catch a glimpse of her surroundings. She saw the green of the grass as they crossed some kind of courtyard, and she was surprised to note the fading light. It was obviously dusk, but it had seemed like only minutes had passed since she had been pulled ashore by the merman. Her hand twitched in remembrance. Surely that wasn't his kiss that she still felt warming her skin?

When they entered the monastery, the heels of Andras's shoes rang against the stone of the floor, and all CC could see through her half-closed eyes was the gray of the stone walls in a dark, narrow corridor.

"Through that door, my son," the priest instructed. "Leave her on the bed. The maid will care for her."

Andras put her gently on a hard, cotlike bed and reluctantly released his hold on her. CC curled onto her side, careful to keep her eyes closed.

"Isabel!" Abbot William's voice was hard and cold when he addressed the maid. "Get her some water with which to wash and one of the good Brother's robes to wear until her own clothing can be cleaned and dried. If she can take sustenance, offer her some broth and watered wine. Then come report her progress to me."

"Yes, Abbot." CC could hear the rustle of the servant's skirts as she curtseyed and rushed out of the room.

"Let us have our own dinner, my son. There will be ample time to speak with the child tomorrow." The priest's voice lost its hard edge when he spoke to the knight. "Your princess is in excellent hands, and as you said, she must rest."

The door closed securely behind them. CC breathed a sigh of relief and opened her eyes. The room was small and barren. The walls were made of thick gray stone. CC hugged herself, feeling a chill that the newly lit fire did little to dispel. The room held only a small, hard bed that was covered with a scratchy brown blanket and a narrow dresser on which was placed a large, plain bowl made of brown pottery. Over the head of the bed hung the only decoration in the room—a wooden crucifix which was bare except for pointed splinters of wood resembling nails that had been driven into it where Christ's hands and feet would have hung.

She squinted and stepped closer to the crucifix. During her years in the air force she had attended church services on several bases for many different denominations, everything from Baptist to Methodist, Protestant to Catholic, but she had never seen anything like that nail- decorated cross. Something about the barren crucifix made her feel very alone.

A breath of fresh air blew into the small room and ruffled her hair. CC breathed deeply, savoring a scent that was at once magical and familiar. She took another deep breath. The air was filled with salt and water and life. Desire flooded her. As if she followed the sound of an imaginary Pied Piper, her face turned to the wall farthest from the door. High up on that wall was cut a narrow window slit, probably less than three feet wide. CC's body went still as she breathed in the odors of the sea. She could hear the rush of the waves against the shore. She could almost feel the warm fingers of water against her body.

An image came to her of Dylan pressing her hand to his lips. She touched the back of that hand, remembering the jolt of feeling his caress had caused.

The door opened and CC jumped guiltily. A small, stooped woman wearing a dress made of rough, nondescript brown wool limped into the room. Her face was so heavily wrinkled that it almost looked deformed; CC thought that she had to be the ugliest woman she had ever seen. In one skeletal hand, she balanced a tray, which held a pitcher, a goblet and a bowl. In the other, she clutched a folded piece of material. Her body jerked in surprise when she saw that CC was awake and instantly dropped into a nervous, lopsided curtsey, sloshing some of the red liquid out of the goblet.

"Oh! I am so sorry, Princess." She lurched over to the dresser, pushing the tray onto the top of it. In her haste she almost knocked over the bowl that was already sitting there. "I am afraid you startled me. I thought you would still be asleep."

Her voice was low and whispery and creaked with age.

"It's me who should be sorry," CC said quickly, covering her shock at the woman's appearance. "I didn't mean to frighten you."

The old woman ducked her head and wouldn't meet her eyes. She curtseyed awkwardly again, then stood nervously plucking at her skirt with her free hand. CC waited for her to say something, but she just stood, looking like she couldn't decide if she wanted to faint or run.

CC cleared her throat and gestured at the goblet that was still on the tray. In a gentle voice she said, "I really am very thirsty."

"Yes, of course, my lady!" In a shaky motion, the woman yanked the goblet from the tray and held it out to CC, who took it with a grateful smile and drank deeply. It was wine watered with cool water, and it was sweet and delicious.

"If the princess will allow me to help her disrobe, I will take her garments to be cleaned and dried." She shook out the material with her gnarled hands and it became a towel-sized cloth and a long robe. "I will help you wash the saltwater from your body, then you can wear this robe until your clothes have dried."

CC looked down at her dress, which was really several dresses, each layered over the top of the other. Even wet the skirts hung gracefully and the long, full sleeves ended in embroidered points that almost dragged the floor. The outfit was certainly beautiful, but she didn't see one zipper or one hook. She had no idea how she would get out of it without the woman's help, and she was honestly too tired to care.

"Please," CC said gratefully. "I would appreciate your help."

CC's legs felt shaky as she stood. The old woman moved quickly behind her. CC could feel her tugging and pulling at laces and ties as she stripped several layers of damp clothing from her body. When CC was left with only a white shift, made of almost translucent linen, the woman averted her eyes hastily.

"I give you my word that I will not look upon my lady's body. I will just hold and rinse the washing cloth for you if my lady would like to clean under her chemise."

CC was baffled. Clean under her chemise? But the thing was wet, salty and just plain disgusting. CC's tired brain felt foggy. How was she supposed to clean herself with her clothes on?

"I need to take this wet thing off, *then* I can clean myself and put the robe on," CC said, feeling stupid for having to say the obvious aloud.

The woman sounded shocked. "You would wear the robe with no underclothing?"

CC ran her hand down the front of the shift, where it was beginning to dry and crinkle with sea brine.

"What is your name?" CC asked.

The old woman gave her an owlish look, and her eyes almost disappeared in the wrinkled folds. "Isabel."

"Isabel," CC said calmly. "This shift needs to be cleaned. I need to be cleaned. Both things can't happen together. Now, we're both women, so it's fine with me if you see me naked." CC gave her a weary smile. "I really do appreciate your help, and I don't mean to offend you, but I'm afraid if I don't get this wet thing off and sit down pretty soon, I'm going to fall down."

Isabel's eyes widened even farther, and with jerky movements she turned around, poured the water from the pitcher into the bowl, dunked the cloth in the water and then, without looking at CC, she handed her the dripping cloth.

"Thank you," CC said.

What a ridiculous attitude, CC thought as she washed herself. The woman had literally looked horrified at the thought of seeing another woman's naked body. CC remembered the silky green gown the goddess had been wearing. It had done little to hide Gaea's erotic, voluptuous curves. And Undine's mermaid form had only been clothed in skin. What was it the goddess had said? Something about some priests being afraid of beauty. CC pulled over her head the robe of rough, undyed wool the color of parchment and grimaced as it scraped against her bare breasts. She looked down at her own lush body, now engulfed and almost completely sexless within the enshrouding robe. A sliver of unease pierced her. Didn't she remember reading in one of her college Humanities texts something about medieval people believing that the naked body, especially the naked female body, was sinful and inherently evil?

"Are you covered, my lady?" Isabel asked.

"Yes, completely," CC said, trying to keep the worry out of her voice.

Isabel turned around and studied her. "Shall I dress your hair back, Princess? It is most unseemly that it is left all"—here she paused and gestured helplessly with wizened hands to her own hair that was pulled severely back and covered with a plain white headdress— "free."

Automatically CC reached up, letting her hand skim through the thick length of the heavy tresses that reached to her waist. She could feel the jewels Gaea had magically twined throughout her hair. The thought of hiding that wondrous hair and the generous gifts from her goddess mother made CC's stomach tighten.

"No," she said. "I think I'll leave it as it is tonight."

Isabel gave her a dark look and opened her mouth to argue. Before she could speak, CC smiled sweetly at the old woman. "It is the way of my people for maidens to wear their hair free."

Now where had that come from? CC thought. But she was glad she had said it, even if the effort it had taken to stand up to Isabel had sapped all of her remaining strength. Her knees felt wobbly, and, all of a sudden, she found herself sitting down hard on the bed while the room spun around her.

"My lady," Isabel's voice was back to being kind and subservient. "You are exhausted. Here, this broth will help you to regain your strength."

Isabel put the bowl in her hands, and CC sipped the warm liquid, surprised at how wonderful it tasted.

When the bowl was empty, Isabel took it from her and gathered CC's damp clothing.

"Sleep now, my lady. You will feel better in the morning."

Without another word, the maid shuffled out. CC thought she heard a bolt being drawn on the door, but she was too tired to care. She fell asleep listening to the soothing sound of waves lapping against the distant shore.

Chapter Ten

THE clean scent of the sea teased her awake. Without opening her eyes, she breathed deeply. The room was very quiet. Somewhere in the distance CC could hear the bleating of sheep punctuated with the call of gulls and the crash of waves on rock. She felt her body tremble with need. That's where she should be. That's where she wanted to be. The ache was lodged deep within her, like an unbearable secret. She opened her eyes and her gaze was instantly drawn to the window. She rose unsteadily, as if her legs weren't exactly sure how they should work, and tottered to stand under the high, open window. Even with the height of her new body stretched as tall as it could, she couldn't quite see out.

CC looked around the barren room. There was a large chamber pot that had been placed next to the bed. Thankfully, it was empty. She dragged it over to the window and turned it upside-down. Grasping the window ledge for balance, she stepped up.

The wall of her room made up part of the outside wall of the monastery, and it faced directly out to the ocean. The view was breathtaking. Under her window there was only a few feet of open ground, then it looked like the earth fell away and a steep cliff dropped to give way to the majesty of the ocean. CC could see the rocky shoreline below and the frothy caps of the playful waves. Her knuckles whitened as she clung to the window ledge, forcing herself to ignore her body's insistent longing.

Two quick knocks against the door forced her attention away from the window, and she hurried clumsily to put the chamber pot back in its place.

"Yes?" she called as she sat on the bed.

"It is Isabel, my lady." The door opened slowly, and the woman limped into the room, giving CC a tentative smile. "I see you look well rested."

"I feel much better." CC was happy to see that Isabel carried a bundle of her newly cleaned and dried clothing.

"Abbot William asks that you join him for the evening meal if you are recovered enough."

CC's stomach growled, and she realized suddenly that she was starving. "Do I have to wait for evening to eat?"

Isabel looked surprised. "It is evening now."

CC felt a rush of foreboding. "How long have I been asleep?"

"You have slept for two nights and into evening of the second day," Isabel answered. "If you allow me to help you dress, you can join the abbot immediately."

Almost as if she was detached from her body, CC let Isabel help her into the gown. No wonder her body ached so badly. This was the third night. She had to find a way to get to the water tonight so she could change back into her mermaid form. Just the thought of that transformation made her heart hammer against her chest.

"There, my lady," Isabel said as she tied the last of the laces. "Please follow me."

They left the room and turned down the long, dark corridor that CC had glimpsed between half-closed eyes two days before. She was relieved that the more she walked, the stronger her legs felt, because even though Isabel moved with remarkable agility for an old, lame woman, CC had to struggle to keep up with her. They stepped out of the hall and headed across a grassy courtyard, at the far side of which was the closed gate through which CC had arrived. Directly in the middle of the courtyard was a large, round well, made of the same ponderous gray stone as was the rest of the monastery. As they walked by it, CC felt a rush of cold air, and she was overcome with dizziness.

"Princess Undine!" Isabel called in alarm when she noticed her charge was no longer beside her.

CC rubbed a hand over her eyes. "I feel strange."

Isabel's arm went around CC's waist. "You are still weak from your ordeal. Let me help you." The two women stumbled forward together.

After a few steps the dizziness passed and CC was able to walk on her own again. She thought she must be so hungry her glucose levels were messing with her equilibrium, and she sniffed the air hopefully, trying to catch a whiff of something cooking.

They left the courtyard through a low, arched doorway and entered a room that was filled with long wooden picnic tables. Seated at the tables were monks, all dressed in the same drab cream colored woolen robes belted with huge wooden rosary beads. CC quickly estimated that there were probably twenty or thirty monks in the room, but it was unnaturally silent for a room filled with that many people. The only sound of conversation came from the head table, at which sat a slightly built man whose robes were brilliant crimson instead of cream, two monks in the more typical lightly colored robes, and the knight, Sir Andras.

The instant the knight saw her, he leapt to his feet and hurried to her side. CC was struck anew by his strong masculine features and his easy charm.

"Princess Undine," he said, taking her hand and kissing it gallantly. "I am pleased to see you looking so well." He linked her hand through his arm and led her to his table. "Princess, I am honored to present you to an old family friend, Abbot William. Caldei is his monastery."

Instead of greeting CC, the abbot ignored her and smiled warmly at Andras. "Sir Andras, truly Caldei belongs to you as well as to me. It was your great father who gifted it to our Holy Order. I would be pleased if you thought of Caldei as your home while you visit us." Finally, his gaze shifted to CC and all traces of warmth instantly died.

Something about the coolness of the man's expression told CC not to offer him her hand. Instead, she decided it would be best to drop into a quick, impromptu curtsey.

"I'm pleased to meet you, Abbot William. Thank you so much for your hospitality."

The abbot was a short, slender man with well-defined features and a severely receding hairline. His hands were very white, small and soft looking, and CC noticed that he liked to use them to punctuate his gestures when he spoke. He wore a large, square ring on the middle finger of his right hand, which he tended to hold solicitously straight, like he was afraid it might slip off. The square, rust-colored stone that was set in the middle of the ring caught the dim light in the dining room and winked with a fierce brilliance. But the priest's most striking feature was his eyes, which were an unusual shade of brilliant blue. CC thought that he would have been considered a nice-looking man, had his expression not been so pinched and hard-looking.

"The pleasure is mine." The priest's smile was tight. "Please, join us." He gestured at an empty place setting across from him. "You must be hungry."

Andras returned to his seat next to Abbot William. The other two monks sitting at the table nodded briefly at her and then returned to their meal. An old woman hurried up and ladled a generous portion of aromatic stew onto CC's plate. When she smiled her thanks at her, the woman shot her a surprised look before she rushed away.

"There have been no other survivors found, Princess."

Abbot William's voice was soft and seemed gentle, but when CC met his eyes, his expression was flat and guarded. She forced herself to take a bite of the stew and chewed carefully, buying time as she tried to choose how best to respond to this intimidating-looking stranger.

She had never been a very good liar, and her seven years in the air force had only reinforced her dislike for lies. Dishonesty led to problems—usually career-ending problems. She had decided early on that it was better to tell the truth and deal with the consequences than to be a dishonorable person. Unfortunately, she thought, that lesson was not much help in her current situation. She glanced at Abbot William. She had a feeling that telling him the truth would probably get her burned at the stake.

The next best choice was to stick as close to the truth as she could.

Swallowing, she said, "I am sorry to hear that, Abbot. I was hoping another survivor could help me remember more about my past."

"Then you still have not regained your memory?" Sir Andras asked. Leaning forward he reached across the table and took her hand.

At Andras's gesture, CC saw a dark flicker in the priest's eyes. Now there was definitely a man who had issues with women—major issues. CC didn't want to antagonize the priest, but Gaea had made it clear to her that she had to find a man to love her. Right now Andras was her best, if not only, chance at that. And, she admitted to herself, the knight was certainly handsome and obviously interested in her.

In the back of her mind the memory of the merman's kiss lingered enticingly, but she pushed it away. Gaea had said *man*, not *merman*. And beside that, Dylan was long gone somewhere out at sea and could be of no help to her. Trying her best to ignore Abbot William's hateful look, she smiled warmly at the warrior and squeezed his hand before releasing it.

CC squinted, like she was trying hard to think. "No. I remember my name, but I can't remember much else." She bit her bottom lip. "I don't even know what year it is." She blinked innocently at them while her heart raced.

"It is the year of our Lord, one thousand and fourteen. You are on the island of Caldei near the mainland of Cymru." The abbot's voice was as hard as his eyes.

CC gulped. Trying not to show her shock at hearing it confirmed that she was, indeed, smack in the middle of the European Dark Age. She flashed the abbot a grateful smile. "Thank you. The more I know, the more I might be able to remember." She paused. "I do also remember a terrible storm and a giant wind." She let her eyes widen. "It picked me up and dropped me into the ocean. I remember I was drowning,"

CC said truthfully and reached for a goblet of wine with shaking hands.

"After such a horrible ordeal it is understandable that your memory has fled," Andras said quickly.

"Can you remember nothing more about your journey, Princess Undine?" Abbot William enunciated her name carefully. "Or perhaps why you were so near our island?"

CC could feel his eyes studying her, and she forced herself to meet them, while she shook her head sadly.

"No. I wish I could."

"And you can remember nothing about your family nor your home country?"

CC couldn't tell which irritated her more, his fluttery hand gestures or the cruel edge to his condescending tone. The modern woman in her wanted to snap at him to stop being such a jerk, but she quickly squelched that impulse. She wasn't in the modern world; she was in ancient Wales, and this man was providing her sanctuary. And wasn't it perfectly natural for him to be wary of her? She had literally washed up at his doorstep; he really knew nothing about her.

She met his cold blue eyes with a sweet, apologetic smile.

"I remember my name and that my parents love me very much. I truly wish I could remember more." Then she added, "I am sure that my family will be looking for me, and that they will reward anyone who has helped me."

The priest pressed his lips together. Their edges turned up in a parody of a smile. "Those of us who have chosen the priesthood seek a reward that cannot be found in this world."

"Of course not, Abbot," CC agreed quickly, stung again at the man's cold, disdainful tone. "I didn't mean to imply anything except that I'm sure my family will be very grateful to you for helping me."

"I will send inquiries to the nearby ports on the mainland. Perhaps there will be word of your family there," the knight said.

"You won't leave, will you?" CC asked. She definitely didn't want to be left alone with the abbot.

Sir Andras took her hand again and smiled. "I have pledged to be your protector. If you would have me stay, I will send my men in my stead."

Not looking at the priest, CC nodded. "I would like that."

"Yes," Abbot William's tone was ingratiating. "I would welcome your visit. I get so little news from inland. And you haven't told me, what brought you to our island?"

Andras shrugged nonchalantly. "My father was holding Tournament and, as a boon to a friend, I agreed to complete a quest to the sea." Then he smiled warmly at the abbot. "When my quest took me near Caldei, I knew I could not continue until I had ferried here and greeted my old teacher." Then he turned his gaze to CC. "And how was I to know that my sea quest would yield such a treasure?"

"Ah, the Caer Llion Tournament." Abbot William's eyes sparkled, and he pointedly ignored Andras's last comment. "How well I remember those fine games. You must tell me of all who attended."

While the priest monopolized Andras's conversation, CC concentrated on eating, glad that for the moment she didn't have to fabricate any more answers. As often as she could, without seeming ridiculously obvious, she sneaked looks at the warrior. He was definitely a gorgeous man. Today he wasn't wearing the chain mail or the silver helmet. Instead, a plain brown tunic made of fine linen draped over his strong body and belted at his waist. CC had a hard time stopping herself from staring. She just wasn't used to seeing such a blatant display of male muscles and strength. Yes, there were handsome, well-built men in the military, but they didn't just sit around partially bare and bulging, unless they were working out at the base gym. And this certainly wasn't a gym.

She also wasn't used to the way Andras kept looking at her. If she had been having a hard time remembering that the body in which her soul resided was a beautiful stranger's, this handsome knight's blatantly appreciative glances were all the reminder she needed. Their eyes met, and CC felt color heat her cheeks as she realized he had been speaking to her and she didn't have any idea what he was saying.

"I'm sorry, Sir Andras, my mind was elsewhere. What did you say?"

"I asked if you would consent to take a short walk with me before retiring to your chamber."

"Do you think that is wise?" Abbot William asked in a voice that CC thought was just a little too tinged with sarcasm to be considered concerned for her welfare. "The princess has yet to recover from her ordeal."

CC wiped her mouth on her napkin and stood. "Thank you for your concern, Abbot, but I think a walk would do me good. I believe in exercise."

"Does that mean that you are remembering more about your life, Princess?" the priest shot back.

"No," CC said, smiling energetically into his frozen eyes. "It means I'm healthy." Placing her hand on the arm Andras held out to her, she inclined her head graciously to the priest. "Thank you for the lovely meal." In a swirl of skirts, CC allowed the warrior to lead her from the dining room.

"Shall we walk around the courtyard, Princess?" Andras asked.

CC looked across the green expanse to the closed iron gate. The perfect lawn was broken only by the large stone well which sat in the middle of the courtyard. A breeze stirred the air around them, and CC breathed in the alluring scent of saltwater.

"Actually, Sir Andras, I would like to see the view." She looked determinedly toward the gate.

"Oh," he sounded surprised, but recovered quickly. "Certainly, Princess."

"I would like it if you called me Undine," CC said as they started across the courtyard.

"I would be honored, Undine." He looked intimately into her eyes as he repeated her name. "And it would please me if you did not address me formally, but simply called me by my Christian name, Andras."

"Then I will." They smiled at one another.

They were walking by the well when a sharp chill passed through CC. It was so intense that it was painful, and she felt the blood drain from her face. Her knees felt weak, and she tripped. If it hadn't been for Andras's strong arm she would have fallen.

"Undine! What is it?"

"I just need fresh air," she managed to whisper, and the knight helped her over to the gate.

After walking a few feet, the chill left her and she could feel the color coming back into her face. What was wrong with her? Was this part of her body longing for its true form? CC didn't think so. This feeling was different from the ache that seemed planted permanently within her.

"Perhaps Abbot William was right, you are not recovered enough for our walk." Andras's eyes were bright with worry.

"No, I'm better now. I was just feeling a little dizzy. I want to walk; the exercise will be good for me. And if I keep a hold of you, I'm sure I'll be fine." She smiled and squeezed his arm.

He placed a warm hand over hers. "Then I will simply have to be certain you do not release your hold on me."

Trying to shake off the creepy feeling that seemed to have rooted itself in her spine, she walked forward. Andras unbolted and opened the gate for her.

The road that led to the front gate was lined with tall, exotic-looking pines, and it looked vaguely familiar, like CC had visited it in a dream. But it wasn't the road or the trees that interested her. Like a homing pigeon, her feet found a little path that hugged the side of the monastery's outer wall. She pulled Andras with her.

"Undine, this path can be dangerous. It leads to the face of the cliff. The drop to the ocean is treacherous."

"I'll be careful," she promised breathlessly. She had to force herself to walk slowly when everything within her wanted to rush around the bend in the path and drink in the sight of the ocean.

Finally, they turned the corner and CC felt a thrill of pleasure. The endless ocean was swallowing a huge, shimmering sun, which painted the waters with gold and amber. Like giant teeth, rocks peppered the rugged shoreline, and even in the fading light CC could see the foamy caps of the crashing waves. She wanted to climb down the steep side of the cliff and let the water carry her body away. Then the never-ending aching inside of her would stop—she would be where she belonged.

"It is so beautiful," CC said, unable to hide the longing in her voice.

"Yes, I have never seen anything as beautiful."

Andras's voice had deepened, and she pulled her eyes from the ocean to see that he was staring intently at her. Something moved within his eyes, and his gaze flared with a heat that took CC completely by surprise. With a choked moan, he grasped the hand that she had wrapped through his arm and lifted it to his lips. Closing his eyes, he kissed her hand as if he was dying of thirst and her skin was water.

His lips were warm and soft, and CC appreciated the passion he was demonstrating. She studied the strong lines of his handsome face and enjoyed the way his chest flexed as his breathing deepened. But that was it. His touch awakened nothing inside of her except a detached appreciation for his masculine beauty.

Andras raised his face from her hand and his eyes captured hers. Lust flared so blatantly there that for a moment they glowed with an unnatural light. It even seemed his features shifted and darkened. His breath came in ragged gasps. CC felt a tremor of foreboding. This man wasn't the chivalrous knight who had rescued her and pledged his protection. He was a powerful stranger whose expression was filled with barely controlled lust. CC gasped at the change in him.

Instantly, a shadow lifted from the knight's eyes. He dropped CC's hand and took a step away from her, blinking in confusion.

"Forgive me, Princess," he said, mopping a hand across his brow like he had been sweating profusely. "I did not mean to take advantage of you."

"You didn't take advantage of me, you just kissed my hand," CC said nervously, trying to keep her tone light.

"If I frightened you—" he started to say, but CC interrupted him.

"No, you just surprised me." She was relieved that he appeared to be himself again, but she continued to watch him carefully. He looked dazed, like he had just awakened from a bad dream. Again, CC felt a tremor of warning shiver through her stomach.

"You are not angry with me?" the knight asked.

"No, I am not angry."

"Then you will forgive me? I assure you that my behavior is not usually so dishonorable."

"There is nothing to forgive. You only kissed my hand." But even as she said it, a part of her mind whispered that there had been more to the knight's actions than an impulsive kiss.

"Thank you, my Lady," Andras said, inclining his head in a small bow. "Would you care to continue our walk?" he asked hesitantly.

CC glanced down the path and then back at the knight. She really did need to continue their walk. It was the third night; she had to study the land around the monastery and figure out how she was going to get to the ocean. The knight appeared to be his normal, gallant self again, his eyes had quit flashing, and his breathing was back to normal. Maybe she had overreacted. After all, she hadn't had very many men react so passionately to her. Okay, she admitted, she had *never* had a man react so passionately to her.

And wasn't she supposed to be finding true love? How the heck was she going to do that if she ran from a man's desire? Get a grip on yourself, Sarg! CC took a deep, steadying breath.

"Yes, I would very much like to continue our walk."

Almost reluctantly, he offered her his arm and they continued walking down the path, which curved gently until they came to an area where the cliffside dropped away almost directly under their feet. CC halted there, staring out at the beckoning sea.

Andras didn't speak, and CC pretended to watch the sunset, the knight's presence almost forgotten as her mind raced with possibilities. Behind them the monastery sat dark and silent. The view from where she was standing was familiar enough that CC was sure that one of the windows on the nearby wall must be the window to her room. Rocks and fallen logs rested against the side of the monastery. Climbing in and out of her window would not be impossible. She studied the face of the rocky cliff. From her room, it had looked too sheer and imposing to scale, but now that she was closer, she could see that it was riddled with little trails that crisscrossed down to the ocean. In the distance she could hear the ever-present sound of bleating sheep and silently thanked them for liking to climb rocky cliffs. If she was careful, she could use the trails to get down to the water. As if echoing her thoughts, in a last burst of light, the sun sank into the ocean.

"We should return, Undine," Andras said.

CC nodded reluctantly and let him lead her back the way they had come. She was so busy considering all that she would need to do that night that she was surprised when she and Andras had stopped in front of the door to her room.

"Thank you for the honor of your company this evening, Undine."

His motions were formal as he bowed to her. He turned to leave so quickly that she had to reach out and grab his arm to stop him. At her touch he stiffened, but he turned back to her.

"I haven't thanked you for saving me." She stretched up on her toes so that she could kiss his cheek softly. "Thank you."

His frozen look thawed a little, and he smiled at her. "I am only glad my actions have brought you into my life."

CC knew that then would be the right time to say something encouraging to the knight, but the memory of the change that had come over him earlier still seemed to hang in the air between them. When she spoke, all that she could make herself say was, "Good night, Andras. Could you please send Isabel to me? I am very tired."

"Of course. You must rest and regain your strength. I will see you tomorrow." This time his bow was accompanied by a warm smile. "Rest well, Undine."

"Thank you, Andras. You are very kind," she said before entering her room. She closed the door and leaned against it. What was wrong with her? Andras was handsome, sweet and obviously interested in her. Yes, for a moment he had been a little scary, but couldn't it have been her own inexperience that frightened her?

"But I didn't feel anything when he kissed me," she whispered. "At least nothing good." His kiss had been a little like visiting a museum and admiring a lovely statue. It had been nice enough to look at, but she certainly didn't want to get in bed with it.

"Well, Gaea didn't say anything about me having to love the man back. Maybe the spell will work if he just falls in love with me," CC said to the silent room, but she was afraid that it was a futile wish. Gaea had said Lir wouldn't break the bond of true love, and CC didn't think "true love" and "one-sided, infatuated lust" were anywhere near synonymous.

I'll try harder to care about him, she promised herself. *Next time he kisses me, I'll make sure it's on my lips and not my hand. And I won't let his passion scare me.* She shook her head at herself. She wasn't a skittish teenager. She was a sergeant in the United States Air Force, and she certainly wasn't afraid of men.

Unbidden, the memory of the merman's kiss burned through her mind. Just the memory caused her body to tingle in response.

Chapter Eleven

This time Isabel didn't argue with her about her hair. She seemed mollified that CC was willing to wear her shift under the coarse night robe, and CC solved the bathing problem by saying she was too tired to wash that night—she would do it in the morning. Isabel had even appeared concerned at CC's obvious exhaustion and nagged her good-naturedly about doing too much too soon. CC agreed readily with her and asked only that Isabel make sure she wasn't disturbed so that she could get a good night's rest. Isabel limped out, humming happily as her charge pretended to fall asleep before the scullery had finished folding her clothes and banking the fire.

As soon as the door was closed CC leapt out of bed, pulled the scratchy robe off and put on her shoes. The clank of her many bracelets sounded like alarm bells ringing in the quiet room, and she quickly took off all her jewelry, except, of course, Gaea's amulet, leaving the bangles and rings in a sparkling puddle in the center of her cot. Pressing her ear against the door, she listened intently. She could hear nothing—not even the sound of the monks' swooshing robes.

"They're probably all in church or something," CC muttered to herself.

She went to the narrow dresser and set the pitcher and bowl carefully on the floor. Then, very slowly, so that she didn't make any noise, she dragged the heavy piece of furniture over to the window. Using the bottom drawers as ladder rungs, she climbed to its smooth top. CC breathed a sigh of relief. It was the perfect height. All she had to do was sit in the narrow window frame and let her legs dangle down until she found a toehold. And she'd noticed on her walk that there was a lot of debris outside against the wall. She shouldn't have any trouble piling enough up so that she could easily climb back through the window.

She peered into the night. The moon had just risen. It was almost full, and it glistened off the waiting ocean like a beacon. When she looked at the water, the ache in her body twisted unbearably. Nothing moved outside her window. She slid onto the windowsill. With her soft, moccasin-like slippers, it was easy for her to find a toehold, balance and then drop quietly to the grassy ground. Her feet felt light as she picked her way carefully down the side of the cliff, following the well-worn sheep path. She could hear her own heartbeat echo the sound of the waves.

Then her feet sank into sand, and she was standing on the shore, quivering with need.

What am I supposed to do? CC's mind screamed. She was panting, and she felt disoriented.

"Simply call your true body to you, Daughter."

Smiling graciously at her, Gaea was sitting near the beach leaning comfortably against the trunk of an ancient tree.

"I don't know how," CC gasped.

"Your body does. Listen to it," the goddess reassured her.

CC tried to listen, but all she could hear was the call of the water.

"Then follow that call," Gaea said, as if she could read her mind.

CC started to walk forward, but paused when the goddess called, "Take off your chemise. You do not want them to have any evidence of where you have been."

Without any hesitation, CC pulled off her shift. Naked except for the goddess's sparkling amulet, she walked into the ocean's embrace. Stretching her arms over her head, she dove into the surf. *I want my true body back*, she thought desperately. The tingling began at her waist and spread quickly down her body, exploding in a burst of energy out through the feathered fins that replaced her feet. Her powerful tail sliced through the water, propelling her forward. Then, with a simple flick she changed directions and shot up through the surface with a joyous shout. CC shook the water from her head and looked for the goddess, but she had disappeared.

She was about to call a thank-you, or a good-bye, or something, after the absent goddess, when she felt the skin on the back of her neck twitch. Just like it felt at the cove, she thought. Someone had to be watching her.

A familiar chattering behind CC made her jump, but she turned with a happy cry of welcome.

"It is you! I'm so glad to see you." CC swam over to the dolphin and stroked her slick side.

I have missed you, Princess. The dolphin nuzzled her.

"I've missed you, too," CC said. "Swim with me—I want to be surrounded by the water."

Of course, Princess!

The dolphin butted CC playfully, then dove under the waves. Laughing, CC followed. Surprisingly, it wasn't dark under the moonlit surface. The crystal waters seemed to capture the light of the moon and the underwater world was illuminated with a silver glow. CC was thrilled by how easily she caught the dolphin and she reveled in the power of her body as the two of them played tag, swimming around the rocks that dotted the shallows, then over and through colorful masses of coral that grew in deeper water. CC wanted to swim on forever. The deeper within the water she swam, the more she wanted to immerse herself in the silken depths and never leave.

A strong hand grabbed her arm and jerked her to a stop. CC whirled, at once frightened and angry. Dylan floated in front of her, worry creasing his brow.

The goddess told you that you must stay near the shore. The words bored into her mind.

A shudder passed through CC. How could she have forgotten about Sarpedon? She looked frantically around.

Sarpedon is not here tonight, but he does search the waters for you, so you must have care where you go.

How do you know all of this? CC thought to him.

Come near the shore, and I will explain.

The dolphin swam back between them, clicking and whistling restlessly. CC watched the merman's face soften as he gently touched the creature's blue-gray side.

I will care for the princess now, faithful one.

The dolphin ducked her head, nuzzled briefly against CC's side and then disappeared into the depths.

Dylan gestured towards the shore, and CC nodded. She followed the merman, noticing how in the moonlit water the orange and gold of his tail glistened like it glowed magically from within.

They surfaced next to one of the huge rocks that lined the shallows. CC faced the merman. Tonight his thick dark hair was tied back. He floated next to her with his shoulders and most of his chest exposed above the water. The moonlight touched his bare chest and clearly illuminated muscular ridges and hollows. CC still felt a little uneasy at her own body's nakedness, and she was glad that her mass of hair covered her breasts.

"Okay, now tell me how you know so much," CC demanded, covering her nervousness with a no-nonsense military tone of voice.

"I followed you."

"After you just happened to be there to rescue me and bring me to shore?" CC shook her head. "That doesn't explain enough. You were there when I was drowning, and now you're here again tonight. Seems too coincidental for me."

"I followed you from the grotto," he admitted, looking away from her with a pained expression. "I did not know Sarpedon had you trapped in the cave. I knew something was very wrong when I could not find you for the length of an entire day. It was only after you escaped from him that I found you again. I followed you to the goddess's cove, and I watched your transformation. That is how I knew to help you when you were drowning."

"So you know that I'm not really Undine?"

"I know that the soul of another lives in Undine's body," he answered simply.

"You say that so easily, like it's a normal thing. You obviously knew Undine before. Doesn't this surprise you, or upset you, or make you angry? Why are you willing to help me when you know that I'm not her?"

"Undine and I were childhood playmates. We spent many years together," he explained, choosing his words carefully. "But she was not happy here. She longed for the land even before Sarpedon desired her."

"Did you love her?" CC asked, suddenly understanding the strained expression on the merman's face.

Dylan's jaw tightened, but he nodded his head. "Yes, but she would not allow herself to love a creature of the seas."

"But she was a mermaid—and that is definitely a creature of the sea."

"When you are on the land, your body is human, is it not?" Dylan asked.

"Yes, of course."

"But do you not long continually for the water?"

CC's memory of that horrible, empty ache was sharp. "Yes, constantly."

Dylan's smile was sad. "That is how Undine felt. I am glad for her. She has finally been granted her wish and her longing has ended."

"Then you're helping me out of love for her." CC was ashamed of the twinge of jealousy she felt.

"I could not very well let you drown." Dylan's sudden grin was boyishly endearing. He reached out to pluck a long piece of seaweed from CC's hair. "And you know nothing of how to be a creature of the sea."

CC surprised herself by batting playfully at his hand. "And you're going to teach me?"

He raised one eyebrow at her rakishly. "That I will, my princess."

CC's heart did a little skip beat at his expression. Did his words have a double meaning, or was she being too sensitive?

CC told herself firmly not to be ridiculous. He was being kind to her because he was in love with Undine. Well, she could certainly allow herself the pleasure of his company—and she truly had a lot to learn about his world. She spread her arms, meaning to encompass the entire ocean. "Good! I want to know everything."

"Everything?" He crossed his arms. CC thought if he'd had feet, he would have tapped one of them at her.

"How about everything in this little area around here—for starters."

"That can be easily accomplished." He held his hand out to her, enchanted by her innocent enthusiasm. "Come with me; I will show you the wonders of our world."

CC put her hand in his. At his touch, she felt a shiver of excitement, but she didn't have time to dwell on her reaction because immediately he dove, tugging her under the surface with him.

Hand-in-hand they swam around the shallows. Dylan seemed to know just where the most unusual fish were playing and where the most colorful coral grew. He showed CC long, orange tubes, bright red fans and purple rectangles—all of which he explained were types of sponges. He pointed out a large, flabby-nosed octopus that rested sedately on the sandy bed; CC laughed and thought it looked like a wrinkled old man. The octopus seemed to take offense and swam off in a jet of dark ink, which made both of them laugh. Like underwater angels, jellyfish floated silently past them, ethereal and translucent. Huge, bloblike sea anemones enchanted CC with their lilac coloring, and she was intrigued by their friends, the brightly colored clown fish.

And Dylan was intrigued by this new Undine. It had been true that at first he had watched over her because she had taken the form of the mermaid he had known and loved all his life, but her physical form was where any similarity between them ended. The mermaid Undine had been a beautiful, ethereal creature who was kind, but aloof. She had been his friend, but she had always yearned to be something else, somewhere else. This new Undine was so very different. She seemed to be bursting with energy and curiosity. She embraced the sea as if she couldn't get enough of it. Her endless questions were laced with humor and a sweetness that moved the merman more than he wanted to admit.

She, too, was a creature of the land, he reminded himself. She belonged there; he belonged to the seas.

Dylan had been so patient with her many questions that CC had thought that he was actually enjoying himself, so she was a little surprised when he pulled her away from a cluster of feathery starfish and back to the surface.

"What—" she started to ask, but the predawn lightening of the morning sky was explanation enough. "Oh. I hadn't realized so much time had passed."

"It is almost dawn," he said. His face, which had been so expressive and animated all night, was now neutral. "You must return to the land."

CC nodded, biting her lower lip. "You were the perfect teacher. Thank you."

His quick smiled warmed her. "In the oceans we say that the teacher is only as good as the student."

"Well, isn't that a coincidence?" CC grinned back at him. "We say the same thing on land."

Dylan's laughter, rich and deep, surrounded them. They were still holding hands, and she used her free hand to splash water at him.

"It's not very dignified for a teacher to laugh at his student."

Dylan tried to compose his face, but his eyes sparkled with good humor as he teasingly bowed his head to her. "Forgive me, my princess. It has been an honor to be your teacher."

Dylan lifted her hand, meaning only to give it a gallant, playful kiss, but when his lips met her skin all thoughts of jesting with her fled his brain. He breathed deeply, and her delicate, feminine scent filled him. Her skin was unbearably soft, and he couldn't stop himself from turning her hand over and pressing his lips to the pulse point at her wrist. He felt her tremble, and he lifted his face slowly, afraid he would see rejection in her eyes. She was staring at him, and in her eyes he thought he read passion, not disgust. His mind registered her expression, and even though he knew he should not touch her, should not allow himself to love her, he could not stop. The way she looked at him made him feel as if his heart would break from happiness.

"When you touch me," CC said softly, "you make me tremble."

Still holding her hand, Dylan drifted closer to her until their bodies almost touched. "Is that because I frighten you?" he asked. Maybe he had misread her eyes. His heart stopped beating as he waited for her answer.

"No," her voice sounded breathless.

Slowly, she reached up and touched the side of his face. She let her fingers trail down his neck and shoulder until they finally came to rest against his chest. He quivered under her caress.

"Is that because I frighten you?" she whispered his words back to him.

"No," he said quickly. Then he captured her eyes with his. "What is your name?"

The question surprised her, and, not knowing what he meant, she hesitated to answer him.

"I want to know your true name," he explained. "I do not want you to think I care for you only because I wish to be with Undine."

CC could feel her cheeks coloring. She hadn't been thinking that; she hadn't been thinking about anything except the way it felt when he touched her.

"My real name is Christine Canady, but almost everyone calls me by my initials, CC."

He raised one brow at her. "Almost? Who does not call you by these initials?"

"My family."

"Then I ask that I be awarded that privilege. May I call you Christine?"

"Yes." She thought her name had never sounded so beautiful.

"Christine, when will you return to the water?" Again, he tried to keep his face neutral, but she heard the longing in his voice.

"I have to come back every third night." Under the palm she still had pressed against his chest she could feel his heartbeat. "Will you be here?"

He was caressing her hand softly with his thumb, just like he had done on the day they had met.

"I will be here every third night until the end of eternity."

At his words her heart lurched, but the thought instantly went through her mind that even though she didn't want to leave the water or him, she didn't have a choice. She wasn't safe in the water. Dylan had said Sarpedon was searching for her—it was only a matter of time until he found her again. Could Dylan protect her? She remembered Sarpedon's size and incredible strength and blocked that thought from her mind. She wouldn't put Dylan in danger.

"I have to change back," she said aloud. As soon as she had spoken the words, she felt the already familiar tingling begin around her waist. Heat shot down her body and an instant later she was kicking her legs feebly and clutching Dylan's chest to keep from slipping under the water.

"I'm sorry," she said. "I didn't know it would be that easy to change back."

His strong arms wrapped around her waist and he held her securely against him.

His smile was sad. "I understand. You must go." But neither of them moved.

"I wish you would kiss me," CC said the words quickly, before she could take them back.

With a moan, he bent his head to hers and their lips touched, gently at first. CC shivered in response.

Against her lips Dylan again asked one last time, "Not frightened?"

For her answer CC lifted her chin and recaptured his lips. Winding her hands around his neck, she pressed herself against his body and opened her mouth to accept him. His hands caressed her back and then slid to her sides and up, so that his thumbs rubbed erotic circles across the edges of her breasts. CC was lost in the taste of him, which was salty and wild. Her body was on fire and his mouth consumed her.

The tolling of the bell that called the monks to early Mass splintered their world. Dylan broke the kiss and for a moment he rested his forehead against hers while he forced his breathing under control.

"I will take you to the shore."

He leaned back, pulling her up on his chest so that she lay more securely in his arms. With strong strokes of his tail, he swam slowly backwards, with CC nestled against him. When the water was shallow enough to allow her to stand, Dylan loosened his grip and she slid out of his arms.

"I want to kiss you again," he told her. "But I am afraid if I do so, I will never be able to let you go."

CC felt a silent cry burning in her throat and she nodded, not trusting herself to speak. She walked out of the water and back to where she'd left her crumpled shift and shoes. She couldn't look at the water. She didn't want to see him disappearing under the waves. Without looking back, CC pulled on her clothes and started toward the path.

"Christine," Dylan's voice carried easily over the water.

She turned. He was floating exactly where she'd left him.

"Remember that I will be here," he said resolutely. "For an eternity, Christine. I would wait for you for an eternity."

She nodded again and turned to begin her trip up the side of the cliff. This time the path wasn't obscured by darkness, but by her tears.

Dylan watched her go, keeping his eyes on her until she was only a light-colored smudge that climbed up and over the side of the cliff. His heart ached as she disappeared. Why was he doing this to himself? He raked his hand through his hair. Like his mother before him, was he forever fated to love the unattainable?

He could still feel the softness of her lips against his. He clenched his jaw. He wanted her, and not because she wore Undine's body. He wanted Christine, her sweet humor and her exuberance.

He thought about the innocent trust she had shown him as she had rested in his arms, and her passionate response to his touch. His heart made the decision for him. If he could only have her every third night, then so be it. He would love her, and, just perhaps, this time he would break the cycle and be loved in return.

Chapter Twelve

CC awoke thinking about him. The internal ache that throbbed with its incessant reminder that her human body was only a borrowed shell mingled with her desire to see Dylan again until she couldn't tell where one began and the other ended. Just tonight, then tomorrow night—then she would be able to go to the water and to him. She sighed and touched her lips. They felt wonderfully bruised and sensitive.

She had dreamed of him. Somehow in another world, in another time, he had called to her, and now she wanted nothing more than to return to the ocean and answer his call.

Two quick knocks on the door made her jump. She cleared the sleep from her throat.

"Yes, I'm awake."

Isabel limped quickly into the room. CC was beginning to wonder if the woman ever slowed down.

"Good morning, Princess," she said in her raspy voice, exchanging the old pitcher of water for a new one. "Sir Andras has asked that you break your fast with him. I believe he has something special planned."

"Something special?" CC sat up and swept the hair back from her face.

"Yes, my lady. Here, let me help you into your dress." Isabel shook her head and clucked what was probably meant as a mild rebuke when she noticed what CC was, or rather wasn't, wearing. "It is unseemly for you to sleep only in that light chemise."

"Why?" She couldn't stop herself from asking as she stepped into the layers of soft fabric that made up her wonderful gown. "That other robe is hot and the material scratches. And the only person who could possibly see me in it is you."

Isabel worked the intricate laces, and her voice took on the tone of a schoolroom lecturer. "It is proper that the coarse fabric of the robe remind us of our sins, which we carry with us eternally, so that we are constantly aware of our need for absolution. To surround ourselves with luxuries is to give in to the temptation of the corporeal world."

CC felt suddenly very sad for Isabel. Had the old woman spent her entire life being deprived of beauty out of fear of damnation? CC was careful to keep her voice light and curious when she asked, "And from whom do we need absolution?"

"The good abbot, of course." Isabel sounded surprised that she should have to ask.

"Isabel, what if the beauty around us is meant as a reminder of the many gifts we have been given, and our need to give thanks for them?" CC asked slowly, as if she had just considered the idea herself.

Isabel made a scoffing noise in her throat, but when CC turned and their eyes met, the old woman was studying her with an openly curious expression.

"It was just a thought," CC said, smiling brightly at Isabel while she put on the jewelry that was a gift from a goddess. Isabel averted her eyes at the show of opulence. CC could only imagine what the old woman's reaction would be if she knew where the jewels really came from.

"Sir Andras is waiting in the dining hall. I can take you there in just a moment," Isabel said as she started to make the bed.

"There's no need—I remember the way. You go ahead and do whatever you need to do, Isabel. I know you must be very busy. Thank you for your help with my dress."

Ignoring Isabel's sullen expression, CC smiled cheerfully and walked quickly out of the room. Having Isabel around was like being shadowed by a brooding schoolmarm. The woman seemed to dislike her on sight. CC sighed. And no wonder. CC glanced down at her lush, richly clad body. Isabel had been raised to believe beauty and luxury were dangerous and sinful.

"To her I must be the embodiment of everything she's been taught is bad," CC muttered.

She realized the old woman's dislike really bothered her. People usually liked CC—a lot. Maybe not with the passionate response that Undine's body evoked, but CC had never had any problem making friends. Well, she was still the same person; she was just shelled in a different body. CC made a mental note to make sure she got up early enough the next day to make her own bed. She would show Isabel that she wasn't a spoiled, pampered princess. Sexy, incredible body or not, Christine Canady would win the old woman's friendship.

The hallway abruptly emptied out into the courtyard. The sun beaming into the open space was such a contrast to the dim interior that CC had to hold a hand up to shade her eyes from the sudden brightness. Squinting, she stepped out into the well-manicured lawn, heading toward the arched doorway that led to the dining hall. A movement at the well caught her eye, and she felt a shudder of fear pass through her body. Hovering over the middle of the open well was a dark shape, easily noticed in the otherwise brightly lit courtyard. The form was in the shape of a man's torso, but it was insubstantial. CC could clearly see the far wall of the courtyard through it. Its back was to CC, and there was something horribly familiar in the massive breath of shoulder and in the thick length of ghostly hair that floated around the apparition as if it was underwater.

As she watched, it rotated slowly and shifted its glowing gaze until CC was staring into the spectral eyes of Sarpedon. The creature saw her, and his triumphant smile was terrible. She couldn't stop the scream that ripped from her throat.

Andras burst from the arched doorway and into the courtyard, followed closely by Abbot William. The moment the two men appeared, the image of Sarpedon wavered and dissipated back into the liquid depths of the well.

Andras rushed to her side. "Undine! What has happened? Are you ill?"

"I-I saw something." She pointed. "There, over the well."

Both men turned to look at the offending structure. Abbot William walked over to it. CC flinched as he bent over its open mouth and peered down.

"There is nothing here now," he called over his shoulder.

"Come." Andras put a strong arm around her waist. "Let me help you into the dining room and out of the sun."

Abbot William gave the well one last look before following them.

"Bring the princess some wine!" Andras ordered one of the servants, helping CC onto a bench.

The servant reappeared almost immediately. CC's hands were shaking so badly that she spilled some of the wine. Drinking deeply, she tried to steady herself, while she wondered how much, if anything, she could dare tell the two men.

"What exactly did you see?" Abbot William asked. He was studying her with an expression that verged on gleeful.

CC felt a tremor of foreboding. It was like he reveled in her fear. "I'm not sure," she said slowly. "I had just stepped into the courtyard, and I glanced at the well. There was something there, floating over the top of it. The figure was dark, like a shadow, but it seemed to be in the shape of a man."

"Could it not have been the shadow of an oddly shaped cloud?" Andras said. "The day is bright and you had just entered the courtyard. Perhaps your eyes misjudged."

CC summoned up a relieved laugh, glad the knight had given her an acceptable answer. "You're probably right, Andras. It just startled me. I think fear and my imagination must have temporarily caused me to see something."

"Of course." Andras patted her back awkwardly.

CC could still feel the priest's eyes on her, but he remained silent.

"I had planned a small surprise for you, Princess," Andras said. "You so enjoyed the view last night that I had a few things packed into a basket for us. I thought we could break our fast outside, near the ocean you find so intriguing. But perhaps now would not be a good time for such exertion."

"No!" she reassured him quickly. "I'm feeling much better. It was ridiculous of me to be so frightened of a little shadow. Fresh air and a view sound wonderful." Just the thought of being near the water again made CC's heart race—and if Sarpedon was close by, surely she would be safest away from the monastery's enclosing walls and near the lush land that was the domain of the goddess.

"If you are sure." Andras's face brightened at the prospect. "I will take care not to overtax your strength."

He called for the servant to bring a basket that had already been prepared, but before they could leave the dining hall, Abbot William spoke with a sly sharpness.

"Princess Undine, before you go, I must ask you about the interesting design that decorates your gown. Do you know what those symbols represent?"

CC looked down at the fabulous dress. It was made up of several layers of material that felt like an intriguing mixture of silk and gauze. She smiled at the familiar coloring that so accurately represented her mermaid's tail. The topmost layer of material was covered with silver needlework. CC had noticed the intricate embroidery before. It was a repeating pattern of symbols interwoven with birds and flowers. Now that she studied it, she could see that amidst the land creatures and symbols Gaea had woven dolphins and starfish. She ran a finger reverently down one long, silver-threaded sleeve.

"No, I don't know what they represent. I just know that they are beautiful."

"Let us not forget that beauty can hide many things," the priest said cryptically.

CC beamed a smile at him. "Well, wouldn't you say this dress hides much less than your robes?" She laughed and pointed at his voluminous skirts. "I think you could probably hide a small person under there."

"Undine!" Andras's voice had a hard edge to it CC had not heard before. "It is unseemly to say such a thing to Abbot William."

CC didn't allow her smile to falter, but as she studied Andras's handsome face, she felt a twinge of unease. For a moment she had forgotten where she was, which was definitely not twenty-first century America. Women in medieval Europe didn't kid around with uptight abbots, or if they did they probably ended up flayed or boiled or . . . She bit her lip.

"Oh, Andras, you're right. I guess I'm still a little nervous about what I thought I saw in the courtyard." She turned her set smile on the priest. "I do apologize, Abbot William; I certainly didn't mean to offend you."

Abbot William waved his hands dismissively. "There is no need to apologize, Princess. I understand that young women sometimes say things that are fraught with several meanings, even if they are unaware of it."

CC's eyes widened at the abbot's rudeness, but her smile didn't waver. "That is such an interesting observation, because I've noticed that men sometimes read double meanings into things that women say, even when none are intended. I think that could be why there seems to be such confusion between the sexes. I'll have to be more careful in the future so that there are no such misunderstandings between us." She turned back to Andras and took his arm. "Are you ready? All this excitement has made me very hungry."

Andras smiled and patted her hand. His façade of good-guy-boyfriend was securely back in place. "Of course, Undine." He bowed his head reverently to Abbot William. "I look forward to our evening game of chess, Father."

"I, too, my son," the priest said. Then he added, as if it was an afterthought, "Princess Undine, about the symbols on your gown. They remind me of runes that I have seen on pagan shrines." He made a dry sound in his throat that CC assumed was supposed to be a chuckle. "But, as you said, you would know nothing of that."

"That's correct," CC said truthfully. "I know nothing about runes or pagan shrines."

"Then you would have no objection to joining us for vespers this evening?" His eyes were bright, and he watched her reaction closely.

"I'm sure the princess would be happy to attend evening mass," Andras said quickly.

CC had to grit her teeth to keep from telling the knight that she preferred to speak for herself. Instead, she met the priest's probing gaze evenly. "That would be lovely; thank you for inviting me."

"I shall look forward to seeing you there," Abbot William said.

Chapter Thirteen

Andras didn't choose the path they had taken the evening before; instead he followed the road. It angled steeply down, then took a sharp, right-handed turn before it wound back toward the sea. All the while they walked he talked about the history of the island and how there had been a monastery on this site for more than four hundred years. CC struggled to listen to him. Most of her attention was focused on the nearness of the sea and the call it had on her body. She did try to look attentive when he explained that he was so well acquainted with the monastery and Abbot William because the land had belonged to his mother's family for centuries. When his mother married his father, the land had passed to the Lord of Caer Llion, and, naturally, the most senior priest from his father's barony had to take over the running of Caldei Monastery.

"Oh, that's why you and the Abbot know each other so well," CC said, trying to appear interested.

"The Abbot taught me how to read and write. He is an exceptional teacher, unrelenting in his desire to instruct," Andras said with a definite tone of hero worship.

CC thought about the way Abbot William looked at Andras, and she wondered cynically if he would have been such an exceptional teacher if Andras had been less rich and handsome.

"It's nice that you had such a dedicated teacher," was all she said aloud.

Andras grinned at her. She couldn't help smiling back at him. He really was endearing in a chauvinistic, clichéd kind of a way.

Once they were at sea level, several small paths branched off from the main road. Andras turned onto one that led through a thick grove of tall, fragrant pine trees and spilled out onto the pristine sand of well-shaded beach.

The ocean was heartbreak blue that morning, and CC trembled at its beauty. She wanted to rip off her clothes and dive into the frothy waves.

"Do you like it?" Andras asked in a smug voice. "I chose this spot especially with you in mind."

CC tore her eyes from the allure of the waves and gave him a compulsory smile as she tried to cover the rush of resentment she suddenly felt towards the knight. He knew nothing about the ocean or about her.

"I hope it pleases you."

At her hesitation, Andras's voice had lost its smug edge, and he was once again only a man trying his best to impress a woman. CC sighed. It wasn't that he was doing anything wrong, she realized. It was just that he wasn't Dylan.

"It's perfect," she said, warming her smile. "I love the ocean. I feel at home when I'm near it."

He gave her an odd look and said, "I find that rather surprising, Undine. I would think that in light of your recent experience you would be frightened of it."

"I'm not frightened of it—or at least I'm not anymore." The water pulled her gaze, and her expression became dreamy. She wondered where Dylan was at that moment. He said he would stay there as long as she was there, too. Actually, she thought back, he had said he would wait for her for an eternity. But that didn't mean he was keeping a constant lookout for her; he wasn't expecting her to return to the ocean until the third night. Could he be out there, watching her now? She shivered at the thought of his possible closeness.

"Did I not tell you that you must be frightened?" Andras had unfolded a blanket that had been packed in the basket, and he paused to glance at her as he unloaded their brunch. "You are trembling."

He was bent over the basket and his shapely rear end was all too easy to see. She had a sudden, mischievous urge to lift her leg and kick him squarely in that oh-so-perfect butt, watch him fall flat on his oh-so-perfect face and then tell him that where she was from women didn't need men to think for them.

"I just shivered because the ocean and my recent accident remind me of the frailty of the human body—that no matter how strong or how wise humans think they are, the might of the ocean is even greater."

Andras gave her an appraising look, like she could possibly be more intelligent than he had originally anticipated, but the look was fleeting, and soon he went back to unpacking their food.

CC watched Andras unload their brunch. She understood that he really couldn't help his archaic attitude towards women—after all, he truly was archaic. And he wasn't a bad man, actually he was quite charming. It wasn't his fault that he was trying to woo a modern woman with his ancient ideals. He had hauled her from the water, she reminded herself, and he had pledged to protect her. For that he deserved to be treated courteously. She glanced at his handsome profile. Maybe they could even be friends.

She sat on the edge of the blanket. Picking up a hard-boiled egg and the leg of a grilled bird, she started eating both with genuine gusto. As close as she could figure, she had only slept for just a few hours, and she should have been very tired, but instead of fatigue she felt exhilarated, like she had exercised all day and slept soundly all night, and her body was demanding that she feed it. She finished the egg and started on a thick slice of tangy yellow cheese.

"This is really very good," she said through healthy bites.

"You seem to be enjoying it. I have rarely witnessed a lady eating with such vigor." His tone said that ladies either shouldn't eat with such *vigor*, or if they did, they should do so only when not in the company of gentlemen. How very Old South of him, she thought, and almost giggled.

"Where I come from, ladies enjoy their food," she said, thinking that sometimes they even eat entire buckets of fried chicken—especially when it's their birthday and they're under the influence of too much champagne.

"Undine, are you remembering more about your homeland?" Andras asked eagerly.

Oops—CC took another big bite of meat, forcing him to wait while she chewed and thought up an appropriate answer.

"Sometimes I remember little things during the course of conversations—and then I wonder, *Now how did I know that?* because then I can remember no more." She moved her shoulders. "Like when Isabel tried to pull my hair back and I told her, no, that maidens from my land wear their hair down. I remembered the fact that maidens in my land can let their hair be free, but nothing else." She chewed thoughtfully and hoped he'd be satisfied with her vague answer.

Reaching across the space that separated them, he captured one of her glistening locks and wrapped it around his finger.

"I am pleased that you remembered this custom of your people. I would not have your hair bound."

CC realized that she didn't need to be worried about him questioning her too much. Unlike Abbot William, Andras wasn't bent on interrogation; his interests were obviously elsewhere. CC pulled the strand of hair out of his finger and laughed with what she hoped was maidenly nervousness.

"Isn't memory a funny thing?" She clapped her hands together, then made a show of searching through the food. "Did you bring anything to drink? All this eating is making me very thirsty."

"Of course. I brought a wine skin we can share." Andras uncorked a floppy baglike thing before passing it to her. He let his fingers linger just a moment longer than was strictly necessary on hers before releasing it to her.

CC stifled the urge to slap him away like a mosquito. Courtesy, she reminded herself firmly. Treat him like he's a superior officer who is acting fresh.

"Thank you," she said, and smiled through a mouthful of food. His quick grimace at her unladylike behavior was worth the breach in manners. She felt the tension in her shoulders relax as he withdrew out of her personal space. The wine was thick and delicious, and she felt a satisfying warmth begin to build in the pit of her stomach.

They ate in silence, and CC took the opportunity to absorb the sight of the ocean. She had to admit that Andras had chosen well. That particular area of the shore was much tamer than the breakers below the monastery had been. Here the waves were still white-capped, but they met the beach with lazy strokes, rather than the violent crashing of water against rock. And the sea appeared more shallow, too. The water that lined the beach was turquoise, rather than the sapphire of deeper seas. There were a few bunches of coral that clustered here and there. Her full lips curved up in remembrance. Last night Dylan had introduced her to many of the colorful fish that made coral their home.

"You are so beautiful when you smile like that." Andras's voice broke into her daydream. "What are you thinking?"

"I was thinking about creatures of the sea and their beauty," she said.

Abruptly, he reached out and snatched her hand that was temporarily emptied of food. She jerked back in surprise, but he kept a firm hold on her.

"No beast of the sea could ever hope to match your beauty," he said fervently. He lifted her hand to his lips and kissed it passionately, leaving a wet spot in the middle of her skin.

CC's stomach jolted in a fluttery brush of fear, and she looked closely at his well-defined face, afraid she would see the frightening lust that had blanketed his features the first time he had kissed her. She drew in a shaky breath of relief when all she read in his expression was earnest and open adoration. Unfortunately for the knight, she felt nothing in response except an embarrassed sense of unease. The only urge she had to touch him was to pat his cheek and apologize for her lack of romantic interest.

"Andras," she said carefully. "I don't think it's proper for you to—"

A loud chattering interrupted her, and Andras dropped her hand in surprise. CC's attention swiveled to the water, and with a joyous laugh she jumped to her feet. Lifting her skirts, she ran to the edge of the shore.

"Hello, pretty girl," she called to the dolphin, who continued chattering while leaping and whirling in jubilant welcome. "Isn't this a beautiful day?" CC laughed again, and without thinking she did a little dance step and twirled around, loving the feel of her skirts twining around her legs.

The thunk of stone against flesh came hard and sharp, jarring CC's happiness. The dolphin's shrill cry of pain pierced the air, and the animal dove quickly beneath the waves and disappeared. CC spun around to see Andras testing the weight of another rock in his hand.

"What are you doing?" CC's voice had the sharp edge of command seven years in the air force had honed.

Andras blinked in surprise. "It is a wild beast; it could have caused you harm."

"Don't you know that wild is not synonymous with evil?" She forced her voice to be even. He had thought he was protecting her. "The dolphin wasn't going to hurt me. She was just a beautiful creature enjoying her freedom."

"Abbot William would remind us that many things are not as innocent as they appear, Undine, and that excessive beauty must be guarded against, for it can hide prurient intent," he countered.

CC could hardly believe she had heard him correctly. Prurient intent? A dolphin? She took a deep, cleansing breath and counted to ten before she spoke again.

"Andras, I really do appreciate the help you and the abbot have given me, and I don't mean to sound disrespectful, but did you ever consider that some people get power by convincing others they should constantly be fearful?" she asked.

"Abbot William gets his power from God," Andras said as if he was reciting a Sunday School lesson.

"I'm not saying that he doesn't; I'm only saying that just because something is beautiful or exotic or even wild, doesn't mean that it's dangerous or sinful," she said, forcing the knight to meet her gaze. He looked away quickly.

"I think you have become fatigued, and it is time we return," Andras said stonily. He was already busy repacking their leftovers.

"I think you're right. I am ready to return," CC said.

She stood looking out at sea like a breathing statue, ignoring the sounds the knight was making as he tossed their leftovers haphazardly into the basket. She felt displaced and alone. Her entire being ached to be a part of the waves. For an instant she thought she saw the glint of orange and gold, barely visible offshore just below the crystal surface, and she had to close her eyes. If she really saw him would she be able to stop herself from going to him? Then what would happen to them?

With her eyes still closed, she concentrated on sending two words out into the ocean. *I'm sorry*, she thought desperately. She wasn't sure if she was sending the message to the dolphin or to Dylan.

As she wearily accepted Andras's offered arm and trudged away from the water yet again, one thought was foremost in her mind. She had to talk to Gaea.

Chapter Fourteen

"Shall I escort you back to your room? You just have time for a refreshing nap before evening vespers and dinner."

Andras turned to face her as they entered the front courtyard. They hadn't spoken on the walk back to the monastery, and the stiffness in the knight's voice matched his body language. CC knew that her behavior must baffle him, and she felt sorry for the tension between them, but her head was throbbing. She wanted relief from the stress of having to continually watch her words and actions around Andras, but she didn't want to be closed up in her little room.

"No, I think I'd rather explore the monastery." Andras opened his mouth and CC hurried on before he could insist on accompanying her. "And I think I need to spend some time alone in, uh, prayerful meditation before evening mass." She blinked innocently up at him.

"Of course. I would not want to intrude upon your need for prayer." His voice was smooth, but his eyes had hardened. CC was unexpectedly reminded of Abbot William.

"Didn't I see another courtyard and some gardens out past the dining room?" she asked.

"Yes. The entrance is through the hall on the other side of the monastery. You may enter it through the dining chamber. I need to take our basket back to the kitchens, so I can escort you to the entrance myself." He smiled at her, satisfied that she could not immediately escape him.

CC tried not to sigh when she took his arm. She knew the knight was well meaning, but she could feel the pulse in her right temple beat in time with her headache. She truly needed some time alone. As they walked past the well, she was careful to keep Andras between it and her, but nothing unusual happened. She slanted a gaze at the silent rock structure. It looked innocent and mundane. Surely she hadn't imagined the image of Sarpedon?

The dining room was empty and Andras strode across it, leading her into another dimly lit hallway. At the far end of that hall there was an arched exit that opened to a large courtyard-like area. Andras pointed at the exit.

"Through there are the gardens and a pond. At the far end is the chapel." His gaze was searing as he raised her hand and pressed it firmly to his lips. "I look forward to escorting you to evening mass."

She pulled her hand free. "Thank you for lunch. I'm going to attend to my prayers now," she reminded him in case he was having second thoughts about letting her go. Then she beat a hasty retreat.

CC stepped briskly into the garden area and glanced around to make sure there was no one nearby. Without conscious thought, she wiped Andras's lip print off her hand. She needed to talk to Gaea. Perhaps tonight she should sneak out into the woods. Maybe she would be able to find the goddess there. Absently, she continued to rub the back of her hand. She sighed, wishing she had a couple of Tylenols.

CC began to walk slowly down a little trail that curved and looped through the monastery gardens. Ornamental trees and trellises laced with fragrant flowers dotted the area. Everything was meticulously cared for—not a leaf was out of place or a branch unpruned.

"No wildness, that's for sure," CC mumbled to herself.

Stone benches were arranged strategically amidst the greenery so that one could sit and meditate with the optimum of privacy. CC thought it felt wrong—too contrived, too well planned. Somehow its controlled beauty came across as stilted and forced.

A delicate breeze brought the tinkle of running water to her, and automatically she followed the sound, choosing a left-handed fork in the path that turned in the direction of the outer monastery wall. The path brought her all the way to the wall, which was lined with oaks that were decidedly older than those in the rest of the garden. CC smiled up at them. These were obviously too big for the monks to cut and reshape into their idea of proper foliage. Actually, that whole area looked more natural than the rest of the gardens. Wildflowers painted the grasses with splashes of orange, violet and lace, and honeysuckle vines covered the wall, filling the air with sweetness. A little brook ran along the wall, too. It bubbled noisily over smooth rocks, pooling in a rounded area before disappearing under the wall and out into the forest. There was no orchestrated sitting area, so CC brushed off the top of a large rock that rested near the pool and sat down. She watched a frog leap from the bank to a lily pad and let the sound of running water ease away her headache.

"What am I going to do?" she whispered.

"About what, Daughter?"

CC pressed a hand against her chest like she was trying to hold down her leaping heart. The clear, beautiful voice of the goddess came from above her. CC looked up to see Gaea reclining regally along a thick branch of the largest oak. Today her transparent robes were the color of bark, except that the browns and grays in the material shimmered magically like they had been sprinkled with gold dust.

"You're going to give me a heart attack someday," CC said.

Gaea's laughter made the water reeds and grasses sway in response. CC looked around quickly, worry creasing her brow.

"Do not worry, Undine," Gaea reassured her. "I choose who can see and hear me." A brief grimace marred her lovely face. "And none here will be allowed to hear me but you."

"I'm a little surprised to see you." CC gestured around at the monastery. "In here, anyway."

The corners of Gaea's eyes crinkled with her smile. "You might be surprised, Daughter, to learn that even here I have not been completely forgotten. But that is not why I have come." She sat up. The sparkling fabric of her gown drifted sensuously around her. "You look thirsty, Daughter." She clapped her manicured hands together and ordered, "Wine, please!"

Immediately a pewter goblet, decorated with vines and flowers, appeared in her hand. CC blinked in surprise and the goddess pointed to a spot on the ground in front of CC, where an identical goblet had appeared.

"I think you will enjoy the taste. Cernunnos gifted me with this particular vintage during the last fertility festival." She sipped and sighed happily. "He certainly knows wine."

CC took the goblet and lifted it to her lips. The wine was golden in color and so cold it hurt her teeth. As she took a drink the bubbles that broke the surface tickled her nose, and she almost sneezed. Then her eyes opened wide in amazement.

"It's champagne! The most delicious champagne I've ever tasted!" She grinned up at the goddess. "After the day I'm having, I can sure use some of this."

"I thought you would appreciate it. Now, child, tell me what has troubled you."

CC sipped and talked. "Andras can't be the one."

"Andras is that tall, handsome warrior who pulled you from the water?" Gaea inquired with a purr in her voice.

CC nodded and rolled her eyes. "Yeah, but he's not Mr. Hero. As a matter of fact, the more time I spend with him, the more he reminds me of Abbot William."

Gaea's face twisted in a frown. "Abbot William! That silly child. He is terrified of everything he cannot control or understand, which means he is filled with bitterness and rage, especially towards women. He is a eunuch." The goddess looked like she wanted to say more, but instead she took a deep drink from her goblet. Shaking her head as if to free her thoughts, she asked. "Are you certain the warrior and he are the same?"

"Well, I don't think Andras is exactly like him; actually sometimes he can be very charming. And I understand that it's a different world with different beliefs, but he sure doesn't respect women, and I've spent the last seven years working hard at being respected—so that's a major strike against him. The truth is, I'm just not interested in him, even if he is the classic knight in shining armor and I should swoon at the thought of him sweeping me off my feet." CC sighed and took another drink of the delicious champagne. "Is Abbot William really a eunuch?"

Gaea made a scoffing noise in the back of her throat. "Not physically—I refer to the way he has chosen to live his life. He hides behind the robes of priesthood and uses his position for selfish reasons. He is not fit to serve any God. Be wary of him. He is a desperate, lonely man, and he should be pitied, but always remember that unacknowledged despair can make men dangerous."

"I'll be careful. It was pretty easy to see that he didn't like me. And it's not that I think that Andras is the same kind of man as he is, it's just that the knight seems to parrot Abbot William's beliefs without thinking for himself."

Gaea's eyes narrowed thoughtfully. "I do not like the sound of that."

"So, does it have to be him?" CC blurted.

"Explain *it*," the goddess said.

"You know, that whole my true love thing. Does it have to be Andras—or if it does, is it enough for him to love me without me loving him back?"

The goddess tossed back her hair and laughed again, and even though she had assured CC that no one else could hear her, CC's eyes restlessly searched the clearing for listeners.

"Daughter, how you make me laugh! True love is not a potion one person can swallow and another refuse to drink. It happens only when the souls of two join together to form one."

"Well, I don't think I'm going to be joining my soul with Andras's. I don't even like it when he kisses my hand," CC said.

"That does not bode well for true love," the goddess agreed.

They drank together in thoughtful silence.

CC cleared her throat and glanced up at Gaea. "Um, speaking of kissing, do you know anything about a merman named Dylan?"

Gaea studied the young woman who inhabited her daughter's body. She was truly coming to care for this child and not just because she felt obligated to watch over her. She was special, this young one—curious and outspoken and witty. It would be a lovely thing, to have this remarkable child live beside her as her daughter forever. But Gaea recognized the longing the girl was trying hard to mask. The goddess smiled sadly at the irony. She finally had a daughter who could be gifted with the ability to exist on land, and the child was falling in love with the sea. Sometimes life was surprising, even for a goddess.

"I know Dylan well. He was Undine's playmate of old." Gaea raised her delicate eyebrows at the girl. "What is this about kissing?"

CC felt her cheeks warm. "Well, it's just that I feel different when Dylan kisses me." Now her cheeks were practically on fire. She never could talk to her mother about sex—apparently that meant *any* mother, even if she was a goddess.

"So, the merman has kissed you?"

CC could hear the smile in Gaea's voice, but she didn't look up at the goddess. Instead she busied herself with drinking the last drop of champagne.

"Too bad that's gone," she said, trying to avoid the kissing subject she had bumbled into. "It was delicious."

Gaea snapped her fingers and suddenly the goblet had refilled itself.

"Thank you!" CC took another long drink. This time she did sneeze at the bubbles.

"The merman kissed you?" Gaea repeated insistently.

CC nodded.

"And you found pleasure in his touch?" Gaea asked.

CC nodded again.

Lost in thought, the goddess remained silent until CC couldn't stand it any longer.

"Is that a bad thing?" she blurted, looking desperately up at Gaea.

"No, child," Gaea said. "But you must understand that Dylan is a lesser creature than Sarpedon."

The goddess held up her hand, silencing CC when she would have defended Dylan.

"I do not mean that Sarpedon is more honorable than Dylan—that is obviously not true. What I mean is Sarpedon holds a position of much greater power than Dylan. Sarpedon's father, as you know, is the great God, Lir. His mother is Morrigan, the Goddess of Battle. Dylan's mother was a simple water nymph named Okynos. Unfortunately, she committed suicide after her human lover, Dylan's father, rejected her." The goddess held her hand out to CC in a sympathetic gesture. "Dylan does not have the protection of a mother, or of a father. He is not helpless, but his gifts are much less than those of Lir's son. Dylan exists peacefully within the waters only because Lir is generous and because Sarpedon ignores him."

"But if Sarpedon thought I loved Dylan, he would destroy him," CC finished the unspoken thought.

Gaea's eyes were sharp. "Do you love him?"

CC considered the question while she stared into the little pond. She had never been in love before. She was technically not a virgin, but it was hard to count that one time, right after basic training when she had come home on leave and her high school boyfriend, Jerry Burton, had groped her in the back seat of his Impala. He had penetrated her. She vividly remembered the flash of pain, but it was over soon and everything had ended up on her inner thigh. The event had been awkward and unsatisfying—not an experience CC had been in a hurry to repeat—so she hadn't.

Since Jerry, she hadn't even come close to having a lover, let alone being in love. She thought about Dylan, and the way he made her smile. He had been so patient with her silly questions. And when he touched her he made the world dissolve into a pool of throbbing feelings.

But did that mean she loved him?

"I don't know," she told the goddess honestly. "I need to spend more time with him. I think I might, but it's just too soon to know for sure."

"A wise answer from one so young."

Gaea's look was tender and motherly, and CC felt a sudden rush of homesickness for her own mom.

"Then spend time with him, Daughter. Find the truth of your feelings," the goddess added. "But be kind to the warrior, too. Allow yourself the luxury of learning more about both males. Do not let lust make decisions of the heart. Do not mistake desire for true love. And remember, right now the seas are only safe for you if you stay near the shore and under my protection. Even if you decide you love the merman, you have to stay in your human body until I find a permanent solution for the problem of Sarpedon. That mer-creature is even more dangerous than the childish priest."

"Sarpedon!" CC slapped her forehead. "How could I have forgotten? I think I saw him, or at least some kind of ghostly vision of him today."

The goddess's eyes widened at CC's words, but a shout kept her from responding.

"Princess Undine!" Isabel sounded out of breath as she limped up to CC. The instant the servant appeared both the goblet of delectable champagne and the goddess disappeared. "Well, there you are! I have been searching and searching these gardens. Sir Andras sent me to find you. Evening mass is beginning; you must come at once."

CC reluctantly allowed the maid to help her to her feet.

"Sir Andras does applaud your piety, but you certainly cannot miss vespers, even for prayerful meditation." Isabel looked sharply at CC. "At least you must not miss it *again*."

"I suppose I did get carried away with my prayers," CC said, following the old woman as she hurried down the path which would take them through the garden to the chapel that stood at its far end.

"I am sure you were in need of much prayer," Isabel rasped over her shoulder.

"If you only knew," CC muttered under her breath.

Isabel chose the most direct path across the garden area, which led to the wooden doors of a modest chapel. It was made with the same gray rock as was the rest of the monastery, but on this building the stones were carved into intricate renditions. CC squinted at the carvings and then her eyes opened in shock. All of the scenes were horrible. Horned demons were eating naked, writhing people. Stone flames burned full-fleshed women. Men who were half goat whipped human men, who were chained to each other, their tortured mouths open, frozen in eternally silent screams. CC shuddered and was glad that Isabel literally pulled her through the doors and into the dimly lit chapel.

The first thing CC noticed was the incense. It was thick and pungent and it curled in waves over the carved stone pews, which were filled with monks who were already kneeling and chanting in a dirge-like litany. Their cream-colored robes made them appear like spirits hovering in the dim, smoky light.

CC sneezed. At the sound, several of the heads turned briefly in her direction. One tall, blond-headed figure stood and moved quickly down the aisle and to her side. Andras took one look at her and shook his head like she had just flunked some kind of test.

"Why are you not prepared for mass?" he asked in a strained tone, making an obvious effort to keep his voice low.

CC blinked at him in confusion. She was here, wasn't she?

But before she could ask what he meant, Isabel sighed and gave her a severe look. "Princess, I am shocked that you did not think to bring a covering for your head." Clucking and shaking her head, Isabel dug into the depths of her apron pocket. "It is fortuitous that I thought to bring an extra scarf, although it is not so grand as the Princess is accustomed to, I am sure."

Isabel handed CC an ivory-colored scarf made of plain, serviceable linen. Her own head was already covered with a similar cloth.

"Thank you," CC said, draping the fabric over her head.

"It was very kind of you to think of the princess," Andras said formally.

"I only wish to serve. Sometimes those who are very young and very beautiful can also be very forgetful," Isabel said nonchalantly, but CC was sure she heard the hurt that hid in the old woman's gravely voice. Then the servant melted her way silently into a rear pew.

CC watched sadly as she disappeared into the gloom. She certainly wasn't making much headway in her quest to win Isabel over.

"I waited for you and was disturbed that you did not come," Andras whispered fiercely to her.

CC allowed her face to assume a shocked expression. "I was praying, Andras. Time seemed unimportant."

She watched as he brought his anger under control. "Of course. I was just concerned over your absence."

Oh, right, CC thought. That's why he looks like he'd love to shake me to death.

"Come, we are seated near the front. It is a great honor."

With a sigh CC followed him into the heart of the chapel, pausing briefly at the stone edifice that held the shallow pool of holy water. And she'd thought that those Sundays on base when she had mistakenly shown up for Catholic instead of Methodist services had just been pleasant little ceremonies she'd accidentally sat through. Without fear of making a fool of herself, she followed the correct motions of dipping her fingers in the holy water and genuflecting.

She had to hurry to catch up with Andras, who led her to the second row of pews. (The first row was unoccupied.) He motioned for her to go before him, and she slid down the empty pew, trying not to grimace at the coldness of the stone bench.

Evening mass was already under way, and CC was pretty sure that Abbot William had shot her a quick, contemptuous look, but it was so dark in the chapel that it was hard to be certain. His voice droned on and on, soft and rhythmic, in a language that CC decided must be Latin. The priest stood behind an ornately carved wooden table at the chapel's nave. The table was filled with gilded relics that glittered and sparkled, even in the dim light. There was an enormous golden chalice and a matching platter, which held a loaf of bread. Huge candelabrum stood on either end of the table, but even the light of their many candles did little to dispel the gloom of the chapel.

Suspended almost directly over Abbot William's head was a life-sized golden crucifix. CC squinted, trying to get a better look at it. As on the cross in her room, the only sign of Christ were the shards of wooden nails that pierced the cross where his hands and feet would have been. This time drops of blood were painted on the gold, the color of which reminded CC of Abbot William's robes, and she had to suppress a shudder of revulsion.

What had happened to Christ? Why was he conspicuously left off of the crucifix? The omission both saddened and angered CC.

The cross was suspended between two thick gray columns. At the base of each column were lit dozens of tall, white candles. Their soft flames seemed to be swallowed within the cross's shadow.

CC followed Andras's lead, kneeling and genuflecting when appropriate. She even managed to whisper what she thought were correct responses to the small portion of the service that was in an understandable language.

CC had just begun to think that her knees had fallen asleep when Abbot William turned his back to the congregation and raised the chalice to the bleeding cross, asking for the blessing on the wine. As he returned the chalice to the table and lifted the bread to be blessed similarly, a flickering movement to her left caught CC's gaze. The shadows that ringed the pews were thick, but she was sure she saw something in an alcove off to the side of the sanctuary. She concentrated, peering into the murky darkness, and an image formed out of the haze. Her breath caught and her heartbeat quickened.

"We will take communion next," Andras's voice spoke in her ear.

She looked around, startled at his words. The monks who had been seated in the row of pews directly across from them were standing and making their way slowly and reverently to take the blood and the flesh from Abbot William's hands.

CC's decision was quickly made. When Andras stood, she stood with him, but instead of following him like a good little lamb, she patted his hand and whispered, "Please excuse me, Andras. There is something I must do."

As she slipped out from the other side of the pew, the knight's face tightened in anger, but instead of following her, he moved out of the opposite end of their row and stood obediently in line behind the cream-robed monks. She ignored his irritation and headed with unerring certainty to a forgotten alcove in the side of the chapel.

The figure of the Virgin Mary was carved within the chapel wall. An arch made of ivory marble framed her. Intrigued, CC stepped closer. The statue was filthy, completely covered with dirt and spider webs, but an area around the base of the figure was worn smooth, as if hundreds upon hundreds of velvet knees had once rested there. CC's eyes traveled up the exquisite figure. Mary's robes swirled in graceful simplicity around her sandaled feet. Her hands were open and beckoning; CC found something very comforting in the gesture. CC's eyes continued up, and she sucked a breath in shock.

Mary's face! It was ethereal in its serene beauty and astonishingly familiar.

"Gaea!" CC gasped.

The statue had the goddess's face. Gaea's words came back to her: *You might be surprised, Daughter, to learn that even here I have not been completely forgotten.*

The shuffling of the monks to communion invaded her thoughts, drawing her attention back to the nave. The profusion of candles winked at her. Moving with swift silence, she tiptoed, sneaking through the foglike shadows to grab a lit candle in each hand and carry them back to the statue. She set them at Mary's feet, pleased that the flames seemed to burn suddenly brighter.

On impulse, she sank to her knees, clasped her hands and bowed her head.

"Great Mother," she prayed aloud. "Help me to be wise." She glanced up at the face she knew as that of the goddess, smiled brightly and let her voice drop to a whisper. "Please keep me safe from Sarpedon—I think I can handle the rest of this mess. Him, I'm not too sure about, though."

CC was so surprised when an answer rang in her head that she let out a little yip of shock.

Sarpedon is near and dangerous, but stay close to my realm, Daughter, and the merman cannot possess you. My blessings go with you . . .

"Undine! What are you—" The warrior's angry voice trailed off as he recognized the statue she was kneeling before.

CC closed her eyes tightly, gritting her teeth. Deliberately ignoring him, she kept her head bowed. Her lips moved silently as she recited to herself as much of the rosary as she knew. What she didn't know she ad-libbed, sending a silent plea for forgiveness to the Virgin/goddess for the unintentional blasphemy. She took her time finishing, before genuflecting deliberately and slowly. Then she glanced up at the knight who was still standing at her side and blinked her eyes in pretended surprise.

"Oh, Andras!" She held out her hand and automatically he helped her to her feet. "I'm sorry. I was so lost in prayer that I didn't even know you were there." She looked around at the empty chapel and painted a concerned frown on her face. "Is mass over? I wish I hadn't missed the end of it, but when I noticed this wonderful statue of the Virgin Mother, I felt compelled to come to her."

Andras's expression said he was torn between his desire to reprimand her for once again doing the unexpected and his pleasure at her decidedly Catholic piety.

"I am just surprised. I have never before noticed this statue of the Virgin."

"No wonder." CC didn't hide the irritation in her voice. "She looks like she's been abandoned!" CC leaned forward and pulled a cobweb from Mary's head. "It is disgraceful that the Blessed Mother is in such a state! I intend to speak with Abbot William about it."

Andras seemed to be having trouble forming his thoughts into words, but he finally cleared his throat and asked, "May I escort you to dinner, Princess?"

CC took his offered arm. "That would be nice. Thank you, Sir Andras."

Chapter Fifteen

DINNER was already being served when CC and Andras entered the dining room. CC tried to ignore the frowning looks the monks shot her, but she felt a little like an errant Catholic schoolgirl who was being sent to the headmaster's office. Obviously, she was in trouble for missing communion.

CC struggled to keep her expression neutral as Abbot William stood and greeted Andras with effusive warmth, offering the knight his ring, which Andras kissed without hesitation. Although he ignored her, CC curtseyed respectfully to the priest before taking her seat.

A servant hustled over and filled her plate with a steaming lamb stew that made CC's mouth water. Another servant topped off her goblet with sweet white wine. CC drank deeply, enjoying the cool liquid.

"I noticed you refused to take Holy Communion, Princess Undine." The priest's voice was a whip.

CC furrowed her brow in confusion. "Refused? Why would I refuse Holy Communion, Abbot?" She shook her head. "I'm sorry you misunderstand. I discovered a beautiful statue of the Holy Mother, and I was simply overcome with emotion when I noticed its state of disrepair." CC met his cold gaze evenly, and she made sure her voice carried. "I know how busy you must be, Abbot, so I am sure you had no idea that the Mother of God was being neglected."

The priest's face darkened, and his jaw clenched.

CC squeezed Andras's arm and smiled up at him. "I knew the abbot didn't realize the awful state of that statue."

"It was indeed fortuitous that you noticed it," Andras said.

CC brightened her face and laughed girlishly. "I have an idea! I will take special charge of the Blessed Mother's statue. While I'm here, it will be lovingly tended and restored to its original glory."

When Abbot William started to speak, her brilliant smile silenced him.

"There is no need to thank me." She beamed. Then CC deliberately mimicked the words he'd spoken to her the day before. "For this I seek a reward that cannot be found in this world."

The priest's eyes narrowed, but his lips smiled. "Of course, Princess. That is very"—he hesitated as if choosing his words carefully—"generous of you."

"I have noticed that there aren't many women here, so I suppose it's not surprising that the Holy Mother has been accidentally neglected." She looked at Andras and widened her eyes. "Maybe that's my purpose in coming here. Maybe the Holy Mother guided me to this shore, not just to save me, but to save her statue." And, she added silently, maybe if the knight believed she had been specially blessed by the Virgin, he would be less inclined to seduction and more inclined to respect.

Andras looked impressed. "Yes, Undine. I am quite certain the Holy Mother is watching over you."

The priest's voice sliced across the table. "It is good for a person to know one's purpose."

CC studied him over her goblet. "I agree completely with you, Abbot William."

The look the priest sent her was clearly adversarial. She met it with a forced smile.

"Father, I have been considering the move that lead to my checkmate last evening . . ." Andras began, oblivious to the tension between his old teacher and the woman at his side.

As the abbot's attention shifted from her, CC suppressed a sigh of relief and concentrated on her second helping of stew. She needed food to ground her and to stop her head from reeling. So many things had happened in such a short amount of time. Despite the confidence Gaea showed in her, she felt a little like the Dutch boy who'd tried to stop the leak in the dike with his finger. And her medieval dike was feeling very, very leaky. Little wonder she was overwhelmed. She'd traveled a thousand years into a mythical past, exchanged bodies with a sea creature, met a goddess, kissed a merman . . . CC's stomach butterflied at the thought and she had to remind herself to chew.

Now she had to deal with the obvious hatred of a powerful abbot and the amorous attentions of an incredibly handsome, macho knight. And, of course, there was Sarpedon. CC thought about the goddess's words that day in the garden and again scolded herself that she hadn't thought to mention Sarpedon's manifestation earlier in their conversation. But she had received her answer in the chapel. Sarpedon couldn't possess her as long as she was under Gaea's protection. With one hand she absently fingered the amber amulet. She must be careful to stay near land, even when she reverted to her mermaid body, no matter how alluringly the sea called.

Her quiet contemplation was broken by the noisy clanging of boots against the floor of the dining hall. CC looked up to see one of Andras's men quickly approaching their table. He stopped and bowed sharply to the knight.

"Forgive me for interrupting you, Sir Andras."

"Gilbert, have you news of Princess Undine's family?" Andras asked.

CC held her breath.

"No, Sir Andras." The squire glanced around the room and lowered his voice, obviously reluctant to speak further. "I do have a message for you from the mainland."

Andras looked apologetically at Abbot William and CC.

"I regret I must ask you to excuse me."

"Of course, my son, we would not think of keeping you from your rightful duties." The abbot fluttered his fingers in the direction of the exit.

"I should not be long detained." Andras stood and bowed to them. He and the squire hurried from the room.

The knight's absence left a definite hole in the conversation, which the abbot filled with chilly indifference. Except for an occasional disdainful glance, he pretended CC didn't exist.

CC kept her eyes averted from him and tried to focus on finishing the delicious mutton stew. She wouldn't allow him the pleasure of seeing her bolt through her meal and rush from the room like a terrified child. She remembered his reaction to her fear when she had seen the specter of Sarpedon. Fear fed the priest.

She chewed slowly and sipped her wine. She had been in difficult situations before. Like the time she was a young two-striper and the noncommissioned officer in charge of the Comm Center had come down with a violent stomach flu, thirty minutes before he was to give an instructional briefing on changing procedures for their newly installed computer system. Between dry heaves he had ordered CC to give the briefing. Two hundred people had filled the base briefing room that day, and she was pretty sure that one hundred and ninety-seven of them had outranked her. She'd done fine. No, she'd done better than fine; she'd been awarded a commendation for her ability to perform under pressure.

She wasn't a shrinking flower easily intimidated by powerful men. She wouldn't let him see her fear. No, as before, she'd do better than that. She wouldn't let one mean-spirited priest intimidate her. Gaea had told her that he should be pitied, and it was ridiculous to be intimidated by someone she should feel sorry for.

Eventually her stew bowl was empty and her stomach was pleasantly full, and CC couldn't stifle a yawn. This time when she felt the priest's censoring gaze she met it.

"I'm going to have to ask you to excuse me, Abbot William. The day has exhausted me, and I'm afraid I won't be able to wait for Sir Andras to return. Could you please give him my apology and tell Isabel that there is no need for her to come to me until morning? I know how busy she is."

If CC could run a complex military communications system, she could certainly figure out how to untie the lacings of her dress herself, and she really didn't want to keep appearing to Isabel as selfish and bothersome.

"It is understandable that you are fatigued. Women were made as weaker vessels." His voice was laced with undisguised hostility, and his smile was a patronizing façade. "I will await the knight. I can assure you that he will not be concerned with your absence. He does so enjoy our chess matches."

Good lord, he made it sound like the two of them were rivals.

"I'm glad he does. I hope you two have a nice evening," CC said with as genuine a smile as she could force on her tired lips. "Good night, and, again, thank you for your hospitality." CC curtseyed and hurried from the room, aware that the priest's reptilian gaze followed her unblinkingly.

She paused under the arched exit. It was late evening, and high, winglike clouds obscured the fading light, casting the little courtyard that separated the dining hall and her wing of the monastery into shadowed darkness. CC stepped onto the soft grass and rolled her shoulders, determined to relax now that she was away from the priest's oppressive presence. She inhaled deeply the cool, moist air. It smelled like rain. The thought of water, even if it just came from the sky, lightened her spirits. She yawned and stretched, wishing she had a book she could curl up with for a little while before falling asleep.

She was halfway across the courtyard when a noise startled her. It was the deep sound of a man's chuckle, but it held no humor. Instead it vibrated with sarcasm. CC stopped. Blinking, she peered through the darkness, unable to distinguish between shadows and shapes.

"Undine."

"Is that you, Andras?"

One of the shadows moved and became a man. He was standing near the well. As he spoke, he walked towards her.

"Did you think you could hide from me?" His voice had an unnaturally hollow sound, as if he were speaking to her from a great distance instead of mere feet.

Something was very wrong. Fear curled taut in her chest, and she had trouble breathing.

"Why would I hide from you?" She tried to keep her voice calm and matter-of-fact. "I just asked Father William to make my apologies to you. I'm afraid he was right about me doing too much too soon. I am very tired."

The knight stood directly in front of her; they were almost touching. His eyes flashed with the same eerie, silver light that she had seen within them the first time he had kissed her hand. Transfixed by a paralyzing sense of horror, she watched while his face seemed to shift, as if his well-defined features had suddenly become fluid and mutable. Power radiated from him with a palpable force. His lips twisted into an obscene leer.

"You will belong to me!" he snarled and lunged forward, grabbing her arms in an iron grip. He crushed her against his body, and CC could feel his huge erection pulsing though the silky layers of her gown.

Then a blast of heat shot with electric speed from her chest as the amulet of the goddess came into contact with the knight's body. His shriek was deafening, and he flung CC away from him so violently that she fell to the ground with a jarring thud.

"What is the meaning of this?" the abbot's voice cut through the night.

The breath knocked out of her, CC could only look up and gasp for air. The priest was silhouetted in the dining room doorway. Like a nest of baby birds, several shocked monks peered at her from behind him. How long had they been watching? She tried desperately to catch her breath and glanced at Andras. He stood near her, rubbing his chest and looking dazed.

"The well . . ." Andras began, sounding shaky. "There was something in the well." The knight was breathing hard, and CC could see that a sheen of sweat covered his pale face.

"Yes! It was scary!" CC's breath came back in a rush of words. She gave a jittery laugh and held out her hand. After only a slight hesitation Andras took it and helped her to her feet.

"What of the well?" the abbot asked sharply, striding into the courtyard and approaching Andras.

The knight hunched his shoulders and struggled to speak. His eyes were glassy and blank.

CC wasn't similarly confused. She knew who had emerged from the well. She also knew that it would be disastrous if the abbot realized what had really happened.

"Bats!" CC said suddenly and added a shiver she didn't have to fake. "I'd just begun to cross the courtyard when I noticed Andras standing by the well. He said he'd seen something, and after my experience earlier today he had, of course, felt the need to take a closer look." Thinking quickly she wove the fabrication. "All of a sudden a huge bat came flying up out of the well. It knocked Andras in the chest and then came straight at me. I screamed and fell to the ground." She shivered again and puckered her face. "I hate bats."

"That must have been what you saw this morning," Andras said slowly. The confusion was clearing from his face and he appeared willing to accept CC's story.

Relieved, CC nodded enthusiastically. "I think the well mystery has been solved. I feel like such a fool making a big fuss over nothing. Abbot William, please forgive me for interrupting you again."

The abbot's blue eyes narrowed at her, but he gave her a brief nod.

"We must speak, Father," Andras said suddenly. CC was pleased that he sounded coherent and in control once more. "I have had news from the mainland that is of concern to Caldei." As an afterthought, Andras turned to CC. "Undine, I—"

CC waved her hand. "I wouldn't think of taking you away from important business with the abbot. I'm fine now and can easily find my way to my room. Goodnight Andras, Abbot William."

"Come, my son. Let us retire to my chamber where we may speak in peace."

Without another glance at her, the Abbot and the knight hurried from the courtyard, and the monks returned to the dining hall. CC was left alone with the silent well.

She ran a shaking hand across her face. Her knees wobbled and she felt the sharp bite of bile in the back of her throat. Sarpedon had followed her, and he had found a way to reach beyond his realm. The thought of being trapped within the walls of the monastery with the merman's malevolent spirit overwhelmed her. She needed space. No, she acknowledged grimly to herself—she needed the ocean. She ached for its comfort and the sense of belonging she felt whenever she was submerged in its liquid embrace.

And Dylan, her heart reminded her. She needed Dylan. Could he be out there in the soothing water, waiting for her?

CC hesitated, chewing her bottom lip. Yes, the ocean was Sarpedon's realm, and she was vulnerable to him there, but apparently that vulnerability now extended to the monastery. CC felt a surge of anger. What right did he have to stalk her?

The gate to the monastery was open, and it was much easier to walk through it than it would have been to climb out of her window. She would only be gone a little while, she promised herself. She'd be back before anyone would notice her absence. Squaring her shoulders stubbornly, she followed the sound of the calling waves through the gate and out of the monastery.

Picking up her skirts, she jogged down the path that led around the outside wall of the monastery to the edge of the cliff. The sun was low in the sky, and blushing colors of mauve and saffron lit the sea. On the horizon cumulus clouds billowed like giant dust bunnies that had been dyed the colors of evening. Carefully, she chose the winding path she had followed the night before, forcing herself to slow down so that her dress wouldn't catch and rip on the scrubby brush that lined the little trail.

Unexpectedly, fog began to form over the water. CC watched it spread, surprised at the ease with which it covered the rich colors of the evening sky. Like the cloak of a giant, it billowed up the side of the cliff. Within just a few steps CC was totally surrounded and had to slow her descent even more, picking her way down a path that seemed to dissolve into fairylike mist. She waved her hand in front of her body and was intrigued at the way the tendrils of wetness curled around her. She had never seen fog like that before—it shimmered with a strange iridescence, as if it was made of opals and pearls. She probably should have been frightened; instead the soupy fog made her feel hidden and secure.

Her shoes sank into sand at the moment a small section of mist shifted and parted, allowing Gaea to step through its diaphanous curtain. Tonight her robes were the color of smoke sprinkled with starlight and diamonds.

"Good evening, Daughter." The goddess embraced CC, holding her within the maternal comfort of her arms. "I thought you would desire to be free of the monastery this evening."

CC stood with her head resting on the goddess's shoulder. Gaea smelled like summer grass and lilacs.

"It was Sarpedon, wasn't it?"

"Yes. He possessed the knight." Gaea stroked her hair.

"I was so scared!" CC sobbed, feeling her body begin to tremble again.

Keeping one arm around her daughter, Gaea motioned to a large moss-covered rock behind them, inviting her to sit.

"Sarpedon only intensified the desires which already exist within the young man." Gaea's lips tightened. "The knight is honorable, but Lir's son is very powerful. It is a simple thing for him to manipulate Andras's lust. The knight has no defenses against Sarpedon, and you cannot warn him. Andras is a man who has been fashioned to despise the supernatural and the unknown."

"He didn't seem to remember any of it. He just accepted the explanation I made up."

"No doubt Andras has only a vague, dreamlike memory of his actions while he is under Sarpedon's influence. He is not the kind of man who would admit weakness, and a loss of memory, or of control, would be something that he would refuse to acknowledge, so consciously he will cling to any excuse offered him. It is only unconsciously that he will be in tumult. The knight's will and soul are as a kingdom in civil war, and he does not have the ability to reach beyond what he has been taught to seek aid."

"Then what can I do?"

"I do not mean for you to fear Sarpedon, but I do want you to be wise. Right now he enjoys toying with Andras. It amuses him to use the warrior's desire while he searches for a way to possess you." The goddess's tone was businesslike, which was as much a comfort to CC as was her presence. "But as long as you stay under my protection he cannot possess you directly, nor do I believe he can force the knight to act so against his nature as to actually do you harm, even if that was his intention."

CC gave the goddess a dubious look.

"Remember, Sarpedon does not want you injured; he simply wants you returned to him." Gaea's frown was a gentle chide. "Do you not trust me, Daughter?"

"Of course I trust you," CC said quickly, feeling her fear begin to thaw.

"There . . ." Gaea cupped her daughter's chin in her hand. "All will be well, do not doubt it." The goddess kissed her forehead gently. "Now, I hear the waters calling to you. I know they will soothe you even better than I."

"Isn't Sarpedon still looking for me?" CC asked.

"My fog will hide you from his eyes tonight. And I believe you need to conduct a search of your own." Gaea raised her beautifully arched brows suggestively and nodded towards the sound of the waves. "Find what is in your own heart, Daughter."

"Is Dylan out there?" CC's voice had dropped almost to a whisper.

"Did he not say he would be waiting for you?"

"He thinks I won't be here until I need to change back to my mermaid form, and that's not for two more nights." CC brushed a hand through her heavy hair. "Can I even change tonight?" She felt the call of the water, as always, but it wasn't as intense as it had been the night before. Instead of an overwhelming desire, it was just an itch somewhere under her skin.

"You must wait for the third night to change into your mermaid form—if you change more often than that, you may not be able to overcome your desire to remain a creature of the water."

"And then Sarpedon would get me." And he would kill Dylan, CC added silently to herself.

"Do not concern yourself with Sarpedon tonight. Concentrate instead on knowing your heart."

"But if I can't change back into a mermaid . . ."

"If Dylan is your true love, he must accept the part of you that is human."

CC gestured at her layers of skirts. "I'm not exactly dressed for swimming."

Gaea's smile was mischievous. "I have always believed one should not be dressed at all when one finds herself embraced by the ocean." With a slender finger she touched the intricate laces at CC's back. Instantly they fell open and the cloth slipped from her shoulders as if twenty nimble-fingered servants had assisted her.

CC stood to step out of the dress and smoothed it across the rock. Before she pulled off the shift, she glanced at Gaea. "How am I going to get back into that thing?"

Gaea's smile widened, and she passed her elegantly shaped hand over the dress, speaking softly to it.

"When she wills, your braids rebuild. So have I spoken; so shall it be." The air around the dress stirred, and CC could feel the spark of Gaea's magic.

CC grinned at the goddess. "Thank you." Then she lifted the chemise over her head and kicked off her shoes. Almost automatically she pulled her long hair forward, obscuring the view of her bare breasts.

"Are you ashamed of your body, Daughter?" Gaea asked.

"No. I think it's beautiful."

"Then perhaps living at the monastery has convinced you that beauty is something to be feared and hidden?" The smile in Gaea's voice softened the reprimand.

"Absolutely not," CC said firmly. In one quick motion she swept her hair back, leaving her breasts totally bared. Then, naked except for her jewelry, she started walking toward the sound of waves. But soon her steps faltered and she was suddenly unsure of herself.

"Call to him." Gaea's voice came from behind her.

"Just call?" CC asked, looking over her shoulder at the goddess.

"He will hear you." The mist started to close and thicken around Gaea, so that her last words were disembodied. "You cannot remain long tonight. There is a storm coming, and they will be looking for you. My blessing goes with you, Daughter."

"I'll remember," CC said to the mist before turning back to face the sound of water. She walked slowly forward, making her way carefully between the many rocks and shells that littered the sand. The fog surrounded her, brushing against her skin in a wet caress, forming tiny drops of dew which glistened to decorate her body like liquid jewels.

When her feet touched water she stopped, peering outward, but she could see nothing through the thick fog. Feeling a little foolish, she cupped her mouth with her hands and called to the merman.

"Dylan! Are you here?"

Only the sound of waves breaking against the rocky shore answered her. She sighed and cupped her mouth again.

"Dylan!"

CC felt him before she saw him. There was a tingling all along her skin that settled somewhere low in her stomach—and she knew he was there. Over the section of ocean that stretched in front of her the mist thinned.

Dylan broke the surface, sweeping his long dark hair from his sparkling eyes. His blood throbbed hot at the sight of her. She was so lovely, standing there in her exotic human body which was all soft curves and long, supple lines. Her beautiful face lit at the sight of him, and her full lips shaped a delighted grin that was solely Christine—his vibrant, joyous Christine.

There was laughter in his voice when he spoke. "You do not need to shout for me, Christine. You need only call me from here." He smiled and pointed to his own temple. "Simply send your thoughts to me, as we do under the water. I will hear you."

"Oh," CC said inanely. She was sure he could also hear the herd of butterflies that were pounding around in her stomach. "I didn't know. Gaea just told me you would come if I called."

His expression sobered. "Always, Christine. I will always answer your call." He glanced around at the fog. "Is this the doing of your goddess?"

CC nodded. "It seems Sarpedon is on the prowl. Gaea says he can't find me in this. And, anyway, I think he's busy at the monastery tonight."

"It almost makes me feel pity for the monks," Dylan said, trying to lighten his voice, but it was clear the mention of Sarpedon made the merman uncomfortable.

"Don't be too hasty with your sympathy. I think that monastery could use a little shaking up, or at least that abbot sure could." She dug her toes into the sand and looked down. She didn't want to tell Dylan about Sarpedon's possession of Andras. She could only imagine how it would make him feel—probably mad and jealous and frustrated that he couldn't do anything about it. And she didn't want the oppressive subject of Sarpedon to ruin her time with Dylan.

She glanced at the merman, and all thoughts of Sarpedon dissipated. Dylan's eyes were on her naked body. She could feel his gaze. It made her skin flush with a sensuous tingle.

He made her feel breathless and very nervous.

"I know it's not the third night, so I'm early, and, well, I can't *change* yet, but I'm glad you came."

He smiled at her. "I am glad you appeared early."

"Even if I can't, uh, be a mermaid tonight?" she stammered.

He raised one eyebrow, grinning at her boyishly. "Are you worried that I might let you drown?"

At his easy jest, CC felt her nerves loosen, and she smiled back at him. "Well, I do remember swallowing a lot of water the first time we met."

He laughed. "That is only because I was unprepared for your kicking and squirming." Drifting closer to shore he held one strong hand out to her and his voice deepened seductively. "Tonight I am prepared; come to me. I will not let you drown."

Without hesitation, CC walked into the water. When her feet no longer touched ground, she began to swim, but before she could finish a full stroke Dylan pulled her into his arms.

"I think it would be safer if you allowed me to do the swimming," he said with mock seriousness.

"And what will you do if I kick and squirm?" CC teased.

"I said that tonight I am prepared." His arms circled her naked body, pressing her firmly against his chest. CC could feel the rhythmic beat of his powerful tail as he tread water, easily keeping both of them afloat in the calm, fog-shrouded ocean. "I will simply hold you closer."

"That makes me want to kick and squirm," she said breathlessly, his touch making her feel a little light-headed.

"And I will be careful that you do not drown," Dylan murmured as he bent his head to her.

Their lips met in a rush of heat, and CC wrapped her arms around his shoulders, loving the mixture of hard muscle and slick, wet skin under her hands.

"Oh, Dylan," CC whispered against his lips. "I missed you today."

Dylan kissed her forehead softly. When he spoke his voice was rough with suppressed emotion. "I saw you."

CC blinked in surprise. "You mean when I came to the beach to eat brunch?"

"Yes. With the man."

CC touched his cheek gently, hating the haunted look in his eyes.

"I watched as he kissed you." The merman's jaw clenched. "I have never before wished to have legs, but today I wanted nothing more than to walk from the waters and take you from him."

A tingle of emotion flushed her body at his words. She took his face between her hands and looked into the deep brown of his eyes. "You need to know something." She felt him tense, as if readying himself for a blow, and she hurried on. "I'm not very good at this. I mean I'm not very experienced in relationships. I really haven't had much practice, so there's a lot I'm not sure about. But there is one thing I do know. I won't lie to you. I believe in truth and fidelity. And I'm giving you my word that I do not want Andras. He is not the man for me."

The tension in the merman's jaws relaxed under her hands, but his eyes were still shadowed.

"Man . . ." Dylan said, smiling sadly. "You say he is not the man for you, and I am glad of it. But I am also not a man."

"I didn't mean—"

Dylan's lips brushed gently against hers. "*Shssh.* I have something to show you."

Before CC could say more he flipped to his back, pulling her up so that she rested against him, safely out of the water. He propelled them backward, careful to keep her protected from the wash of waves while she lay securely within his arms.

"I did miss you," she whispered into his ear. He didn't answer her, but she felt him nod, and his hand caressed the curve of her back intimately.

After traveling down the shoreline, Dylan stopped in front of a large arrangement of stone and coral, part of which towered above the ground. It was vaguely cavelike, but the top was open to the sky. It was round and reminded CC of a corral.

"There is no other way to enter than from under the surface. You will have to hold your breath, but it will not be for long."

The sun had set, and it was almost totally dark, with the mist obscuring even the dim light left in the evening sky. CC looked nervously at the hulking structure that jutted imposingly out of the water. "Are you sure?"

Dylan smiled reassuringly at her. "Do you promise not to kick and squirm?"

"I'll be good," she said, trying to laugh off her trepidation.

Dylan kissed her forehead gently and cupped her chin with his hand. "I would never cause you harm."

His eyes were warm and she felt undeniably safe wrapped in his strong arms.

"I'm ready," she said.

Dylan shifted her so that she floated in front of him, then he turned her so that her back was to him. His hands cupped her waist, which left her own hands free.

"When you are ready, take a deep breath and dive. I will do the rest."

Before she could change her mind, she took a huge breath, nodded and stretching her arms over her head, she dove under the surface. Guiding and pushing her from behind, Dylan's power made CC feel slick and strong under the water—and she was almost disappointed at how quickly he angled them up so that their heads broke the surface together. CC shook the water from her face, laughing.

"Wow! That was almost like I had a tail of my own . . ." Her words trailed off as she registered the beauty that surrounded them.

They floated in the center of a ring of coral and rocks. As she had already observed from outside, the structure was open to the sky, and the circle formed a calm pool in the center, sheltering them from the rhythmic crashing of waves against rock. But that wasn't what was so spectacular about the structure. All around them hundreds, maybe even thousands, of phosphorescent blue fish the size of one of CC's thumbs, darted in schools of perfectly synchronized swimming. Their lights illuminated the ring of water with an otherworldly turquoise glow, giving their little section of the ocean the appearance of a swimming pool lit by magical, moving bulbs. It was an oasis of brilliance in their fog-shrouded world.

"Dylan," CC breathed. "I've never seen anything like this."

"That is not all." He pulled her with him to the side of the wall. Pointing down at a little pocket of coral under the water, he said, "Watch."

CC peered down into the clear, neon-lit water and gasped in wonder. Within the rocky pocket she could see two sea horses. The miniature equine replicas were about six inches long and colored mostly an amazing black-bronze, except for an area of their bodies that looked like waistcoats; there they were splashed with brilliant patches of pink, yellow, blue and white. As CC watched, the two creatures swam in delicate circles around each other, coming ever closer. Finally, they met in a trembling embrace, joining their bodies together.

"There are more." Dylan's lips moved against her ear and he pointed to another place within the coral wall. CC followed his gesture to see that another pair of sea horses were beginning their graceful mating dance.

CC leaned back against the merman, wrapping her arms around his. "I didn't know there was such beauty in the ocean. I never spent much time around it, and I didn't realize how incredible it could be." She turned fluidly in his arms. "You really are a wonderful teacher. Thank you for showing me."

"I cannot imagine you away from the water."

"It seems ridiculous now, but I used to be afraid of the water. As you may have noticed, I'm not even a very good swimmer."

"Then you did not know any of the mer-folk in your old world?" Dylan asked.

CC laughed. "There aren't any mermen or mermaids where I come from."

Dylan looked startled. "Are you certain?"

"Well, I'm pretty sure. They are considered mythological beings. People tell stories about them and draw pictures of them, but if they ever existed in my world they haven't been seen in more than a thousand years."

Dylan studied the woman in his arms with new eyes. He was struck by the realization that he loved a woman who was not simply a land creature, but from a strange world where none of his kind even existed. How could he hope to win her love in return? He knew she found him interesting and probably even exotic and appealing, but those were not emotions on which to base a lifetime of love—they were fleeting, transient and would vanish like mist with the rising sun of experience. He began to understand the despair that had destroyed his mother.

"I must seem very strange to you."

CC could hear the vulnerability in his voice and felt him pull away from her—not enough that she would be in danger of slipping under the surface, but the intimacy with which he had been holding her faltered, like he was suddenly afraid to be too close to her.

"Strange is not the word I would choose." She tightened her arms around him, so that he had to come back to her.

"Then what word would you choose?" Dylan asked, trying hard to keep his voice neutral and his tumultuous emotions controlled.

"Well, I don't think one word would do—I think I would have to use several." She kept one arm wrapped securely around his shoulder. With the other she let her hand trace a path down his face and over his chiseled cheekbone. "Beautiful," she said softly, moving her fingertips down the side of his neck and over the firm muscle of his shoulder. "Spectacular," she continued, stopping to caress his thick bicep before crossing over to his chest and continuing down. "Amazing." CC's hand moved over the side of his taut waist. When her fingers felt the flesh of his skin change from human to mer-being, she hesitated and her gaze shifted to his eyes. He was watching her intently, and his breathing had deepened.

"I have legs now and not a tail," CC said.

Her words made Dylan's lips curl up in a surprised ghost of a smile. "Yes, I did notice that," he said.

"Have you ever, uh, been with a human woman before?" she asked.

Now his surprise was complete. "No! I have never before known a human woman." He paused, trying to find the right words. ". . . in any way . . . What I mean is that I have not . . ."

CC nodded quickly. "So what you're telling me is that you've never been intimate with, or even known, a human woman, yet you don't seem to find me repulsive, even though right now my body is very definitely human."

"I could not find you repulsive," Dylan said as understanding lit his eyes. "Even though I have not known any other beings of your kind." *She* had been worried about *his* acceptance. She truly desired him! In part of his mind he allowed himself to begin to believe that perhaps he wasn't destined to repeat his mother's tragedy. Relief flooded his body and the ghost of a smile became real.

"Then I don't think you should worry about me not having known any other mermen. That is unless you want me to start worrying about you thinking my legs are disgusting."

CC could feel Dylan's body relax, and she floated easily against him once more. One of his hands traveled down her back and past her waist. CC sucked in a surprised breath when it skimmed over her butt to caress the length of her thigh.

"Your legs are soft and warm." His voice was deeply seductive. "And I admit to wanting to touch them—very much."

"I want to touch you, too," CC said, letting her hand move purposefully down from his waist to skim over the unique texture of the rest of him. She looked into his eyes. "But I would like to see you, too. A little more clearly. Do you mind?" She hurried on as his brow furrowed. "I mean, you've seen me—all of me—very naked. Just a little while ago I was standing on the shore with not much on except a smile. But, well, I haven't really been able to see . . ." She nodded her head toward the water and what shimmered gold and orange beneath it, "*you*."

Dylan made a muffled noise in the back of his throat, but he shook his head, holding her gaze with his own.

"No, I do not mind," he said.

Looking around the ring of rock, Dylan searched until he found what he needed. With CC still in his embrace, he floated them across the turquoise pool to a smooth ledge that protruded about a foot above the water. CC eyed it. It was easily seven or eight feet long, curving gently along the inside of the rocky corral. It looked wide enough that two people could lie next to each other on it, especially if they were lying on their sides and didn't mind being very close.

CC felt a thrill of nerves mixed with excitement as Dylan lifted her out of the water and sat her gently on the ledge. She moved to her side with her back against the rock and lay on one hip, watching him. In a powerful movement he grabbed the edge of the ledge and lifted himself out of the water, shifting his weight so that he lay on his side, too, facing CC.

The first thing CC noticed was his size—he seemed so much bigger out of the water. She felt dwarfed by him, even though Undine's human body was tall and voluptuous.

"You're really big," she blurted.

Dylan's chuckle helped to ease some of her tension. "Christine, I am the same as I was in the water."

His dark hair had fallen over his shoulder, and CC brushed it back from his face. He turned his head and caught her palm in a quick, playful kiss, making her smile.

Dylan's torso was strong and familiar, and CC let her hand rest briefly on his chest. Then, taking a deep breath, she looked down.

His bronze skin tapered to his well-muscled waist, where it joined with the merman's tail. The colors were unbelievable. What CC had thought was only orange banded with gold was really a convergence of many different shades of yellow and cream and rust and red, all combining to form a rainbow the color of sunlight and flames. The bands of gold were metallic in color, and they ran in thick horizontal stripes around his muscular tail, which ended in a huge feathered fin that glistened gold streaked with ebony.

CC leaned forward and let her fingers stroke the side of that amazing tail. As she had discovered with her own mer-body, the flesh wasn't actually scaled, it just caught the light in a swirling pattern that could be mistaken for scales. Under her fingers Dylan's flesh was warm and smooth. She let her hand explore him, enjoying the feel of the bunch and swell of his muscles as he quivered under her touch.

CC forced her gaze from his body to his eyes. "You are amazing, Dylan. I could explore you forever."

Dylan thought his heart would explode with joy. She was his! By some incredible miracle, she wanted him as he wanted her. With a moan he wrapped CC in his arms and crushed her against him. His lips met hers and began their own exploration as they tasted each other. Intoxicated by the feel of her, Dylan's hands moved over CC's body, cupping her butt and stroking her legs.

CC's breath caught in her throat when she felt his hardness press against the center of her body. She shut out the mental picture of

Sarpedon's throbbing maleness as it had emerged, engorged and demanding from his pelvic slit. No! She would not allow memories of Sarpedon to taint her. This was Dylan; she welcomed his touch—and he would never hurt her.

She slid her hand between their bodies and cupped him, wishing suddenly that she had more experience with men. He felt much like she had remembered Jerry feeling, with that wonderful combination of hardness wrapped in a shaft of velvet softness that she had found arousing, despite Jerry's awkward attempt at lovemaking.

Tentatively, at first, CC stroked him, allowing herself to become accustomed to him. He's just a man, she thought. Just a different, incredible type of man. Dylan's skin was hot and his body was becoming slick with sweat. The scent of him filled her senses with its uniqueness. He was sea and man melded together and she wanted to drown in him.

His breathing was ragged as he suddenly broke their kiss.

"Slowly, Christine." His hand shook when it brushed her cheek. "Your touch enflames me."

She pulled her hand abruptly from between their bodies. "I'm sorry. I told you I wasn't very experienced with men—or males—or . . ." she looked away, embarrassed.

He took her chin in his hand, forcing CC to meet his eyes. "You misunderstand. It is I who am having an experience," he raised one eyebrow and gave her his boyish grin, "or rather I should say, *control* problem. You are making it very right for me, but I would have it be so for you, too, my love."

"Oh, I didn't know," CC said, feeling a rush of joy at his endearment.

"Let me learn your wonderful human body. Perhaps I will find a way to give us both pleasure."

Then he began his own exploration. At first CC closed her eyes as his mouth moved from her lips to her neck, and on to kiss the swell of her breasts, where they lingered. But soon she found she preferred to keep her eyes open. She liked watching him as he bent over her, his eyes dark and his face taut with desire. His lips kissed the curve of her waist and his hand moved over her rounded hip to her legs. He bent one of her legs and kissed the inside of her knee. Lingering there he nuzzled and nipped gently.

"They are so soft that they cry for my touch," Dylan murmured, his lips still exploring her legs. He loved the distinctly female scent of her. The smooth heat of her body filled his senses, and he fought to control his desire to bury himself within her. He would not allow himself to rush. He inhaled deeply and let his tongue taste her thigh. "Your skin is a silk finer than any even your goddess could wear."

CC bit her bottom lip to stifle a moan.

"Do you like that, my love?" Dylan asked.

"I like it when you touch me," CC said breathlessly. "Anywhere—everywhere."

Dylan's hands caressed her inner thighs, moving toward her core. When he finally touched her wetness she couldn't stop herself from arching up into his hand and moaning aloud.

"Show me," he pleaded. "I want to know how to please you."

With trembling hands she guided his, until his fingers found the right rhythm. When she cried his name in release, he covered her mouth in fierce joy and held her against him, so that when the world stopped spinning she was lying on top of him. She could feel the tension in his muscles as his heart beat wildly against her bare breast. Sitting up, she moved his hands to her waist as she straddled his golden flesh. His eyes widened in surprise when she lifted herself and reached between them once again, this time guiding his hardness to the center of her.

She set her teeth against the pain she remembered experiencing with Jerry, and in one swift motion, sheathed him within her own slick heat. But instead of pain, she echoed his cry of pleasure as he fit perfectly within her.

Dylan spoke her name, murmuring wordless sounds of passion as he held her hips tightly while she arched her back and rocked against him. Now it was his turn to guide her and they moved together over and over, their rhythm increasing until the wave of pleasure crested and pulled first CC, then Dylan over into fulfillment. She collapsed against him, and they held onto each other while their bodies stopped trembling. CC fell asleep cradled within Dylan's arms.

THE sound of annoyed chattering woke her. She was snuggled securely against Dylan. His eyes were closed, but his lips were tilted up in a satisfied smile, and he was stroking her hair.

"She sounds angry with you," he said.

Lifting herself up on one elbow, CC peeked up over his shoulder at the fluorescent water. The dolphin's head bobbed in the middle of the calm pool.

The goddess sent me for you, Princess.

CC felt a stab of fear. "I didn't realize! How late is it?"

Do not worry. The dolphin soothed. *You have time.*

Dylan sat abruptly and pulled her into his lap. "What is it?"

"I have to get back. Gaea warned me not to be gone too long. She said they would be looking for me."

Dylan's jaw tightened, but he nodded and slid both of them easily into the waiting water. In an absentminded gesture of kindness, he reached out to stroke the squirming dolphin.

"Thank you, loyal one. Assure the goddess that I will return your princess to land now."

The dolphin chattered at him, nuzzled CC and disappeared under the surface.

Dylan kissed the side of CC's neck. "Are you ready?" he asked. "Just like before."

She nodded and took a deep breath, diving down with the power of her lover steering her to safety.

They didn't speak as Dylan backstroked to shore. CC clung to him, trying not to think about the separation that had to come next.

"You can stand now," the merman said reluctantly.

CC stood, but stayed close to him, still wrapped in his arms. She could hear the surf breaking against the nearby shoreline, but fog and darkness prevented her from seeing it.

"I have to go back," she said, not able to look at him.

"I know." His arms tightened around her. "Will you return tomorrow night?"

"I don't know," she said. "I'll try. But if not tomorrow, the next will be the third night, and I have to return and change back to mermaid form."

He loosened his grip on her so that he could look into her eyes. "I will be here. Always. You need only call me."

CC tapped her head, trying to smile. "In here?"

Dylan kissed her forehead. "Yes, and I will hear your call in here." He took her hand and placed it on his chest over his heart.

CC tilted her face to his and they came together with desperate urgency. The kiss was deep and frantic.

"You are a part of me now!" Dylan broke the kiss to grip her shoulders and force her to meet his gaze. "We belong together. There will be a way." Then he kissed her one last time.

Fighting back tears, she stepped away from him. He brought her hand to his lips before releasing her. She turned and forced herself to walk out of the water. As she stepped onto dry land, she glanced over her shoulder, but the fog had already hidden him from her view.

"Christine?" His disembodied voice found her.

"I'm still here," she said.

"You know how you feel when you are separated from the sea? How your body aches for it?"

"Yes. I know the feeling," she said to the fog.

"That is how I feel when you are not with me. If you ever doubt that I will be here, or doubt that I will wait for you, remember that feeling, and know that I can do nothing else. For an eternity, Christine. I will wait for you for an eternity . . ." His voice faded as he returned to the sea.

"I'll remember," she called after him, biting her bottom lip to keep from crying.

In front of her the fog thinned, and she could see the rock where she had left her clothes. Hurrying, she used the shift to dry herself, grimacing as she pulled the damp cloth over her head. Then she stepped into the layered gown. As soon as she put her arms within the sleeves, CC felt a tugging at her back and the intricate laces magically rebraided themselves together.

"Thank you, Gaea," she said to the silent, misty night.

This time the goddess didn't answer, but to her left the fog swirled and parted, providing a little pathway of clarity in the darkness. She followed it unquestioningly, trying to ignore the pang of loss she felt as each step took her farther from the water and from Dylan. Soon it was obvious that the path she was taking was not any of the ones that lead up the cliff. This one wrapped over and around rocks and sandy dunes, and at first it appeared to be taking her away from the monastery. Just as she was beginning to worry about where the goddess was leading her, the fog shifted and opened at a sudden right angle and CC found herself following a familiar trail, which she recognized as being the path she and Andras had taken earlier that day. It led up past tall trees and emptied into the well-packed road. CC turned to her right and sighed in relief when she saw the lights of the monastery glowing dimly in the murky distance. She hadn't realized before how exhausted she was, but two nights of very little sleep had caught up with her. She smiled grimly to herself. Even her hard, narrow bed would be welcome that night. She lifted up her skirts and tried to coax her tired feet to move more quickly.

"Let's get going, girls, before they send out a posse."

"To whom do you speak, Undine?"

CC let out a little shriek of surprise as the knight materialized out of the fog before her.

"Andras! You scared me." She felt like her heart might beat its way out of her chest.

But Andras wasn't looking at her. Instead he was walking a tight circle around her, obviously searching the area.

"To whom do you speak, Undine?" he repeated the question more forcefully.

"No one except my feet. I'm afraid you caught me talking to myself."

She smiled and fluttered her hand in front of her face like she was trying to fan away the heat of embarrassment, but her mouth went dry when he turned to her. Had Sarpedon possessed him again? She swallowed down her fear and studied him. His face was a mask of barely contained fury, but no manic silver light glowed from his eyes and his features remained his own. CC felt a surge of relief. She was just dealing with an angry man, not a malevolent spirit.

Automatically, CC took a little half step away from him, but the knight moved forward and roughly took her shoulders in his callused hands.

"Where have you been?" he demanded.

"Nowhere. I just went for a walk." CC forced herself to meet his furious gaze calmly.

"Alone, as night was falling? Why would you do such a thing?"

CC's thoughts raced as she fabricated an answer. "The bat that came out of the well scared me more than I realized." She allowed her voice to shake. "You were busy with the abbot, and I really didn't want to interrupt either of you again with my silly fears, but I couldn't stand to be in my room alone, so I thought I would go back to the beautiful beach you showed me today." She gestured with her head back down the road, and she saw the knight's eyes widen as he recognized the entrance to the path they had taken earlier. CC sent a quick, silent thank-you to Gaea for putting her in a place that lent itself to a ready excuse for being gone so long. "Then this fog came in and I got lost." She let a little half sob escape her lips. "And it got dark and I didn't think I would ever find my way back."

Andras studied her face, noticing for the first time the circles that darkened the area under her lovely eyes. She did look exhausted and disconcerted. The princess needed his protection—that was very apparent. And, of course, he wanted very much to protect her. He almost pulled her into his arms, until he noticed that her thick mass of hair was soaking wet, yet it seemed that under his hands her gown was dry. His eyes narrowed.

"How did your hair get so wet?"

Before his sentence was completed the darkened sky opened and a cold rain began to fall, effectively dissipating the fog.

"All of me is wet!" CC said, unable to keep the exasperation from her voice. "It's been a foggy, rainy night." She wiggled her shoulders. "Andras, you're hurting me."

Slowly, Andras dropped his hands from her shoulders.

CC hugged herself and shivered. "I'm cold and wet and tired. I've been lost and afraid most of the night, and my feet—who you already heard me talking to—are aching. Now would you like to escort me back to the monastery, or do I have to walk back by myself?"

Silently, the knight held his arm out for her. His look told her that he didn't like what she had said, or the tone in which she had said it, but as she took his arm he didn't comment on her rudeness or reprimand her. Instead he appeared to be deep in thought. CC was glad he wasn't questioning her, but she didn't like the idea of him thinking too much either—at least not about her or her fabrications.

It was raining steadily as they entered the deserted courtyard. CC was careful not to even glance at the well, but she didn't need to look at it to feel its ominous presence. They were almost to her room when the abbot stepped out of the shadows in the dimly lit hall.

"I see you found her, Andras." He smiled warmly at the knight, but when he turned to face CC, his expression changed to a sneer. "The good knight was worried about you, Princess, as well he should have been. I cannot imagine why you would choose to leave the monastery alone at night."

Courtesy, she reminded herself. She forced the annoyed sarcasm from her voice.

"I didn't think I was doing anything out of the ordinary. Maybe where I'm from women don't have to worry about being safe if they want to take a walk." Before either man could press the issue she added. "No! That does not mean that I've remembered anything else about where I'm from—unfortunately. Now if you will excuse me, I need sleep. Please have Isabel come help me get out of this wet dress."

She started to turn to open her door, but the abbot's voice stopped her.

"Isabel is already within. She is the reason we knew you were missing. When she came to your chamber to assist you, as you had requested, you were not there. She, too, was very worried, and she immediately reported your absence to me."

CC couldn't believe what she was hearing. She had specifically asked this jerk *not* to send for Isabel. Obviously, he was letting her know that he would be sure she was being watched, no matter what.

"I thought I asked that Isabel not be bothered to wait on me tonight. Perhaps it is because I'm so tired that my memory is not clear. I will apologize to Isabel for having worried her. I'm usually not so inconsiderate." She gave Andras a tight smile. "Goodnight, Andras. I am sorry that I worried you, too." Her gaze shifted to the abbot and hardened. "I will be more careful in the future."

This time she had the door partially open when the priest's question stopped her.

"Princess Undine, what does the name *Wyking* mean to you?"

Wearily, she looked over her shoulder at him. The priest's glittering eyes were locked on her, but CC noticed that Andras wasn't looking at her at all, instead he was staring at Abbot William, and his expression said that the priest's question had come as quite a shock.

The word he had said sounded very much like *Viking*—which made sense, she realized. This was an island and the Vikings had done a lot of raiding during the Middle Ages along the coast of Europe, or at least she thought she remembered that they had. She opened her mouth to quip a fast answer, denying any knowledge of anything, even if the word sounded familiar, but an idea came to her.

Slowly and distinctly CC raised her chin and squared her shoulders, forcing the weariness out of her stance and replacing it with what she hoped was the regal bearing of a princess. She smiled cordially at the priest and said, "If you mean *Viking*,"—she enunciated the word carefully—"to me it means tall, blond, vengeful warriors who do not like it when something that belongs to them is mistreated by another. Good night gentlemen. Even a princess can get tired of answering questions."

Tall and blond, she stepped gracefully into her room, closing the door securely behind her.

Chapter Sixteen

THE unrelenting ache in CC's body caused her to wake early the next morning. It started in the pit of her stomach and traveled through her in a wave of pain. The distant sounds of the ocean spilled through her window, enticing and tormenting her at the same time. She lay with her eyes closed, breathing deeply and trying to quell her internal torment. Just one more night, she told herself, then she could rest in her natural form—and she could be with Dylan again.

"Dylan," she whispered the merman's name. Just the sound of it made her stomach flutter.

Last night she hadn't had the opportunity to think about what had happened between them. After her confrontation with Andras and the abbot, she had only been able to keep her eyes open long enough to apologize to a silent, sulking Isabel, get undressed and fall into bed. She thought she might have been asleep before her head had hit the hard, narrow cot.

But this morning she was completely awake. The soft gray of dawn filled her room with a hazy, slate-colored light, reminding her of last night's fog. CC smiled and stretched like a cat, the ache in her body suddenly secondary to the memory of pleasure. She longed to be with him again and not just so that they could make love—although she admitted to herself that she was eager to do that again, too. She wanted to hear his deep, caring voice as he explained the fascinating world beneath the seas to her. And she wanted to make him laugh. She wanted *him*, all of him.

"I love him," she spoke the words quickly, then covered her mouth like she had betrayed a secret. "Oh, Gaea," she breathed. "What are we going to do?"

Sitting up, she kicked her legs free from the scratchy blanket. The air force had trained her to act when there was a problem to be solved, not to sit around and worry. That morning she said a silent thank-you for her early crises training. She needed Gaea's help, and a plan to get it was already forming in her military brain. Not wanting to wait until Isabel decided to assist her, she rejected the multi-layered gown. Instead, she pulled on the raw wool robe that Isabel had left in her room and took off all of her jewelry except for Gaea's amulet. Then she rolled up the sleeves of the robe and used one of several long-stranded pearl necklaces as a belt. Satisfied with the results, CC remembered to make her bed before she quietly pulled open the heavy wooden door.

Peering into the hall, she listened intently. Nothing was moving, and no one was making any noise. She tiptoed silently down the hall, glad the soles of her slippers were soft and soundless. When she came to the entrance to the courtyard, she hesitated. No, she thought sternly. She absolutely did not want to chance facing Sarpedon. But she needed to get to the kitchen, and the entrance to the kitchen was on the other side of the dining room, which was on the other side of the courtyard. She closed her eyes and visualized the dining room. There had been, she counted in her head, the entrance from the courtyard, the entrance the servants used that had to lead to and from the kitchen and two others. Opening her eyes she looked down the shadowy hall that led away from the courtyard. It was, after all, a main hallway. It must lead to something that would eventually take her to the kitchen, she decided quickly. She'd definitely rather get lost and bumble into some lecherous monk's bedroom than come face-to-face with Sarpedon.

When the hall came to a T, CC chose the left-handed fork and breathed a sigh of relief when the smell of hot porridge drifted to her. Ahead she could see that the hall turned to the left again, and she thought that from there it would probably empty out into somewhere near the area of the dining room. Happily, she picked up her robe, ready to rush ahead, when she heard the sound of two familiar voices. She slowed, creeping noiselessly forward until she could make out their words, then she stopped, listening intently.

"But a Wyking?" Andras sounded as shocked as he had looked the night before when the priest had mentioned the word. "I would not have thought so."

"After the news you received last night, how can you doubt it? The heathen have been raiding the shores of the mainland anew. It is simply too coincidental that she was discovered at the same time. She was quite possibly involved in the raiding herself. It is known that the Wykings educate their women, so why not involve them in their plundering, too?"

"It is so difficult for me to believe. Are you certain, Father? She attended mass. And look at her tie to the Blessed Mother—how could one of the heathen be touched so?"

"She is a princess. She could easily have been nursed by a slave who had been captured from our shores. The poor woman probably tried her best to instill within Undine the true religion. You must remember, though, that she refused to take Holy Communion," he said, self-satisfied and smug. "My son, it was her beauty that deceived you." The abbot's voice turned warm and fatherly. "From the first I knew that she was evil. Look at the garish show of wealth in which she is swathed, and her unusually tall stature. And remember how outspoken and willful she became last night?"

CC pulled at her bottom lip, sorry she hadn't kept a better hold on her temper the night before.

"And I simply thought of her as exotic and beautiful."

Even though CC didn't love the knight, she felt stung at the betrayal in his words.

"The heathen mean to entice us to forget ourselves," came the priest's answer.

"Then my time here has been wasted, and my quest to find a wife who could dower Caer Llion back to its original state of glory has failed."

CC blinked in shock. Andras was on a wife hunt and her jewels and her title had made Undine look like the perfect prey. She shook her head in self disgust. Why should she be so surprised? Noblemen had been allying themselves with wealth and land for centuries. Actually, arranged marriages were probably the norm for ancient Wales. What would be unusual would be to marry for love. And she had to admit she did feel a sense of relief. The knight didn't love her. Sure, he desired her body, but at least she didn't have to feel guilty for breaking his heart.

"Let us not discard the princess's possibilities too hastily," continued Abbot William.

"You would have me ally Caer Llion with Norsemen?"

"Perhaps." CC could hear Andras begin to sputter a response, but the abbot interrupted. "True, the Wyking are heathen murderers, thieves and blackguards, but they have wealth. Caer Llion is far enough inland that you need not worry that her family could appear at your gate, so the alliance would be tenuous at best."

In other words, CC thought angrily, Andras should just take the money and the girl and run.

"Remember, once she is your wife, she is your property to do with as you so desire." The abbot's voice was sly. "And she would be beyond the reach of her heathen people. Of course, you would immediately have to correct her willful spirit and be sure that her religious training is completed."

"I had already decided that if she became my wife she would have to curb her tongue and end her unacceptable behavior." He made a sarcastic scoffing sound. "Walking alone at night is not the behavior of a good Christian wife!"

"Just remember the Rule of Thumb, my son." The priest's voice sounded pleased. "You may not strike her with anything thicker than your thumb, no matter how much she vexes you, or how deserving she is of harsher discipline."

CC's mouth dropped open in shock.

"It would not please me to strike her at all, but I do understand that it is my duty," Andras said.

"I have no doubt that you would do your duty."

CC thought the abbot sounded almost giddy at the prospect, but his tone shifted and became more serious as he continued.

"There is one thing that concerns me very much. I am not certain that her walking alone at night is entirely innocent."

CC tried to still her heart from beating as she strained to catch every word.

"She may have been attempting to contact her people."

CC blinked in surprise. How was she supposed to have done that?

"How could she, Abbot?" Andras echoed her question.

"For all of her supposed ties to the Holy Mother, I believe that she is heathen, and perhaps even a sorceress."

She clearly heard the knight's sharp intake of breath.

"She could have been casting a spell in an attempt to contact the Norsemen. Did you not notice how mysteriously the fog suddenly surrounded Caldei? It could have been her conjuration in an attempt to cover her use of the black arts. Since Undine's arrival, Caldei has been filled with a sense of unease." The abbot paused, and neither man spoke for several breaths.

"I, too, have felt something." Andras's voice was almost a whisper, but it carried to CC's listening ears like a church bell. "I have not wanted to speak of it, but I have felt discord within these good walls."

"I cannot help but agree with you, my son. The woman's presence here in some way is causing evil."

CC thought that the abbot sounded more pleased than upset at the prospect.

"And knowing this, you still think I should consider marriage with her?"

"The Rule of Thumb, my son. Do not forget the Rule of Thumb. And do not underestimate the power of a strong, God-fearing husband. I believe once she is away from the sea, and the possibility of contact with other heathen, she will be able to be controlled. Of course, you may choose not to marry her at all."

"Then what of Caer Llion?" Andras asked.

"The princess could be ransomed. True, a dowry would probably be more profitable than a single ransom payment, and the Wykings are notoriously difficult traders, but then you would be free of the problems she could create, and you would have at least a portion of the money needed for Caer Llion."

The priest sounded like he was considering trading an animal or buying a piece of property.

"I shall decide upon my course with the princess soon. It is not honorable to give the impression of courting her, when I am, in truth, only willing to ransom her."

CC was pleased to hear that the knight did sound sincere in his desire not to mislead her. He wasn't evil; he was just a man of his times.

"Do not fret, my son. There is no need for a hasty decision. If her powers were great enough to truly call forth the heathen, she certainly would not have allowed herself to be lost at all, and it will take some time for your squires to spread the news of her rescue so that it can reach her people. Perhaps their response will illuminate the path you need to take."

"As always, Father, I look to you for guidance."

"You were wise as a child, and you have grown into a fine man." The priest's voice was wistful. "I often wished that you were not your father's firstborn son, so that you could have entered the priesthood. But Caer Llion needs you, and my desire was not to be."

CC's eyebrows raised. She thought she knew just exactly what Abbot William's true desire was for the knight, even if Andras refused to read between William's very suggestive lines.

"You flatter me, Abbot."

"And you please me, my son . . ."

CC's mouth twisted in a grimace as she silently retraced her steps. She didn't need to listen to the conversation deteriorate into a "You're so great—No, *you're* so great" contest. And anyway, she'd heard what she needed. They believed that she was a heathen Viking who had magical powers.

Well, she thought, her grimace changing into a grin, one out of three wasn't too bad. She had magic. That she knew for sure. She also knew that she wasn't going to be anyone's chattel, whether that anyone was Andras or Sarpedon.

She walked several yards back down the hall before she turned and began making her way very nosily to the entrance to the dining room. Smiling, she began to loudly hum the USAF theme song, hearing the *"Off we go, into the wild blue yonder . . ."* singing in her head. She pretended not to notice the knight and the abbot until Andras cleared his throat, then she jumped and giggled girlishly.

"Oh, you frightened me! I didn't realize anyone else was in the room. Good morning Andras, Abbot Williams. Isn't dawn a lovely time?"

"Good morning, Undine." The knight's voice sounded strained and unnatural.

"I am surprised by your attire, Princess Undine." The priest fluttered his fingers at the monastic robe she was wearing. "I would have thought our simple robes much too plain for your august tastes."

CC sighed and painted her face with a long-suffering expression. "So many people believe that princesses have to be constantly swathed in jewels and silk. It's simply not true. How would we get any work done?"

The priest raised a single, haughty eyebrow at her. "And what work could there be here for you to do, Princess?"

"I pledged that I would restore the statue of the Holy Mother," she admonished him. "It surprises me that you have forgotten such an important task."

For once the priest didn't have a glib comment waiting. CC realized that he really had forgotten and pressed her advantage, heading quickly for the servant's exit.

"I'll just go to the kitchen and have the servants lend me some cleaning supplies."

Andras finally found his tongue. Speaking quickly he said, "Undine, I can help you with collecting and carrying your supplies."

"No, Andras, this is something I need to do alone. I feel a special connection with the Virgin Mother, and I think it is important to her that she is cared for by another woman, but thank you. You always seem to be looking out for my welfare. I do appreciate your consideration very much." She smiled warmly at him and was pleased to see the knight shift guiltily in his seat.

"Princess Undine, will we be seeing you at evening mass today?" the abbot asked.

"Yes, Abbot William, I am pleased to say that you will be seeing a lot of me in the chapel. The statue of the Blessed Mother is in a sad state of disrepair, and it will take much work to be restored," she said over her shoulder as she disappeared into the servants' hall.

Ugh, what an awful man!

Chapter Seventeen

The hall did open into the kitchen area, which was a huge room, immaculately clean and lively. Hanging from the low-beamed ceiling were dozens of different types of herbs, many of which CC was pleased that she recognized. The walls of the kitchen were lined with hearths, both big and small. Isabel and three women whom CC had not seen before were busy preparing what would probably be the midmorning meal. None of them noticed CC in the shadowed doorway, and she took the opportunity to study them. It was easy to see a trend in the women chosen to be servants at the monastery. Each of them was old and in some way disfigured. The right side of the face of the woman kneading an impressive mound of bread dough was drooped and slack, giving her a partially melted appearance. The woman who was chopping potatoes and onions did so with one hand, holding her uselessly curled left hand tightly against her body. The third woman, who was plucking the feathers from a fat hen, did so hunched at an awkward angle caused by a large hump on her back.

CC felt the slow burn of anger in the back of her throat. The abbot might as well have had a huge sign hung around each woman's neck which read: I'M ALLOWED HERE BECAUSE MEN DON'T FIND ME ATTRACTIVE. No wonder Isabel had disliked her on sight.

Over one low-burning fire was suspended a huge blackened kettle in which Isabel, her back to CC, was slowly adding crushed garlic and leaves of basil.

"It smells wonderful," CC said. Each woman jumped in surprise at the sound of her voice. CC smiled warmly at Isabel. "I didn't know you made the stew. If I had, I would have told you sooner how delicious it is. You're a magnificent cook."

CC couldn't be sure, but she thought the sudden flush on Isabel's shriveled cheeks might have been from pleasure at the unexpected compliment. She turned and included the other women in her smile.

"Good morning! It's sure nice to see female faces. I've felt kind of outnumbered lately." She nodded her head back toward the rest of the monastery. When the women didn't speak, but continued to stare, she just widened her smile. "My name is Undine."

This seemed to thaw them to action, and the three women dropped quick, awkward curtseys and mumbled hellos in her general direction. Isabel limped to her side.

"Princess, are you lost?"

"No, I came looking for the kitchen."

"I did not think you would awaken this early or I would have been there to help you dress."

"Oh, that's not why I was looking for the kitchen. I need to get some cleaning supplies to take to the chapel. I thought the kitchen would be a good place to find a bucket and some rags, as well as soap and water. Did I guess right?"

"Yes, Princess, but all you need do is to tell me what you wish cleaned; you need not supervise the details." The shock of CC's sudden appearance had passed and Isabel's tone had returned to being edged with thinly veiled sarcasm.

"Oh, I don't want you to do the cleaning—I will." CC was pleased when Isabel's eyes widened in surprise. "All I need is for you to show me where I can get the supplies." She looked at each woman as she continued speaking. "Did you know that there is a beautiful statue of the Virgin Mother in the chapel?" All of the women remained silent, but CC nodded her head at the group as if they had answered her. "Apparently, no one knew about it. It's such a tragedy. It's obviously been ignored and neglected for years. I found it yesterday during mass and I pledged to the Mother that I would restore it." She turned her smile back on Isabel, who was staring at her like she had totally lost her mind.

"You will clean it yourself?" Isabel asked, unsure she had heard CC correctly.

"Yes. I'm not afraid to get my hands wet," CC said, loving her own little private joke. "So, if you'll just point me to a bucket and some soap, I'll get to work."

Numbly, Isabel pointed to an area next to the humpbacked woman who had been plucking the chicken.

"Thank you!" CC said. Purposefully, she walked across the room and picked up an empty bucket.

"There is water in the barrel and rags and soap there, Princess." The humpbacked woman pointed to a cupboard near one of the smaller, oven-looking hearths.

CC smiled her thanks and grabbed a bucket. There was a large ladle hanging from the side of the freshwater barrel, and CC quickly filled her bucket, then she picked several clean rags and a crude bar of pungent-smelling soap from the cupboard.

"Which way to the chapel?" she asked Isabel.

"That hallway will take you to the gardens. Can you find your way from there, Princess?"

CC nodded. The bucket was heavy, and she was glad that Undine's body was tall and strong. Before she left the room she turned, speaking to all four women.

"I appreciate your help. And, please, you don't need to call me Princess. My name is Undine—and I'm just another woman in a place filled with men."

Pleased with her parting comment, her smile didn't waver even as she struggled her way across the perfect gardens, occasionally sloshing water onto her robes and pointedly ignoring the shocked stares from monks already busy with their morning chores.

"They act like they've never seen a woman work before," she mumbled. Climbing the steps up to the chapel she tried not to look at the horrific renditions of hell carved around the entrance, but her eyes couldn't help lingering on them. For some reason they were even more disturbing the second time she saw them, even though this time she was ready for them. She hesitated, searching the stone for some glimpse of hope or salvation, but every scene mirrored only desperation and despair—eternal damnation and pain.

"It's like an awful car wreck I can't look away from," she whispered. Shaking herself, she forced her eyes away from the macabre artwork and entered the dim, incense-saturated building. Even the soft gray light of dawn was bright compared to the darkness within, and CC stood still for a moment, blinking to accustom herself to the gloom.

The chapel was deserted except for two monks who knelt before the mound of flickering candles that were to the right of the nave. When they glanced back at her, she smiled a greeting to them. They acknowledged her with brief nods before returning to their monotonous chanting.

As if a magnet was drawing her, CC made her way along the rear of the chapel to the deeply shadowed left side. Two brightly burning candles beckoned her back to the forgotten statue. She paused in front of it, taking a moment after setting down the bucket to catch her breath. She hadn't been wrong. The lovely statue had Gaea's unmistakable face.

First, she thought, she must have more light. Without hesitation she strode to the table at the front of the nave. It was laden with unlit candles and long, dry pieces of twig that were obviously used for lighting them. Gathering as many as her voluminous robe could hold, she clanked her way back to the statue. Then she worked at placing the candles all around the statue and lighting them. As her little corner of the chapel blazed with light, she felt the eyes of the monks on her back. Glancing quickly over her shoulder she caught them looking at her.

"Brothers, please add to your prayers those for the renovation of the Virgin's statue. It is long overdue." Without waiting for their answer she turned back to the job before her.

It was worse than she had realized the day before. The statue was flaky and filthy, but that wasn't all. That entire side of the chapel appeared to have been ignored. Filth and spiders ruled supreme. When CC dipped the first cloth into the bucket she was sure she heard something slither into the shadows.

Gritting her teeth, she swiped the bar of soap against the damp cloth, telling herself over and over again that crawly things were more afraid of her than she was of them—even though she sincerely didn't know how that could possibly be true.

While she worked she thought and prayed. She asked Gaea for guidance and tried to sort through the tangle of her own feelings. It didn't take long for her to realize that understanding she was in love wasn't the answer to everything—instead it was the beginning of many more questions.

Soon she fell into a cleaning rhythm. She had always been fond of keeping things neat and in their proper places—that was one of the reasons the air force had been such a nice fit for her. Military clean was a good thing, not passionless and contrived like the gardens of the monastery; just everything in the place in which it belonged and everything in the best shape possible. CC tore one of the rags in half horizontally and used it to tie her thick hair back out of her way. Three times she made the trek through the garden to the kitchen for clean water. The women still didn't speak to her unless she spoke to them first, but Isabel had a mug of herbal tea and a hunk of bread ready for her after the second trip, and on her last trip the woman with the shriveled hand smiled shyly at her.

She did notice that the sun was well overhead and that the day was pleasantly warm, but she was too busy cleaning to pay attention to much else—until she straightened up, groaning and rubbing at a kink in her back. Stretching, she stepped back and studied her work.

"Oh!" she gasped, struck by the sudden beauty of the statue. The newly cleansed Virgin seemed to glow with life. The warm light of the many candles illuminated the blue of her dress and the deep gold of her hair, and it seemed like she was surrounded with a halo of soft color.

"You are doing a wonderful job, Daughter." Gaea's voice came from behind her, and CC turned to find the goddess perched on the edge of a nearby pew. Today she was wearing a gown made of silk so white and ethereal that it looked like the goddess had found a way to capture a cloud and wrap herself within it.

CC glanced around the chapel. She had no idea when the two monks had left, but she was relieved to see that the building was deserted.

"I'm glad you think so." She wiped her wet hands on the dirt-smudged robe and walked over to Gaea. With a sigh she sank down to the floor at the goddess's feet. Leaning against the pew, she smiled up at Gaea. "It's tiring work, cleaning all that gunk away."

Gaea's eyes drifted back to the statue. "She has been forgotten for years. I want you to know that you are washing away more than simple dirt. You are washing away hatred and neglect."

"How could I do that? I don't understand."

"You will, Daughter. You will." The goddess reached out and smoothed a strand of hair back from CC's face. At her touch, CC felt some of the weariness leave her. "Now, I sense that you have come to a decision. Are you ready to tell me?"

CC nodded. Looking into the goddess's eyes she said, "I'm in love with Dylan, and I want to spend my life with him."

For an instant CC thought she saw an incredible sadness pass over Gaea's face, but the emotion was gone so quickly that she wondered if it had just been her imagination.

"Dylan is a wise choice," Gaea said, touching CC's cheek in a motherly caress.

"You mean except for the fact that I can't live in the sea without Sarpedon killing him and raping me?" CC put her chin in her hands and rested her elbows on her drawn-up knees.

"I must simply petition Lir on your behalf."

CC glanced sideways at her, not fooled by the lightness in the goddess's voice.

"If it was really that simple you would have done it before now," CC said.

"You did not know you loved Dylan until now," Gaea countered.

"Do you think Lir will listen to you?" CC asked tentatively, almost afraid to hope.

Gaea's smile was one of a seductress. "He has before. You are proof of that."

CC almost rolled her eyes and said she didn't want to hear the details, but she caught herself in time. Then she looked up to see the goddess watching her with sparkling eyes, and they both began to laugh.

"There are some things all daughters do not want to know," Gaea said, wiping mirthful tears from her eyes.

"You're right about that," CC said, then added, "Actually, you're right about most things. So, I'd like to know, do you think I'm making the right decision in choosing Dylan?"

"Before I answer you, I would like you to answer one question for me, Daughter. And do not ponder your answer; I want to know the first thought that comes to your mind." The question shot out. "What do you love most about the merman?"

Without hesitation CC answered, "His kindness."

"Ah," the goddess breathed. "I see. Then, yes, I believe you have made a wise choice, for when the thrill of his body fades or changes, and the difficulties of pledging yourself to only one person surface, kindness will be the balm that soothes the wounds of life."

"Thank you, Mother," CC said softly, her eyes filled with tears.

Unexpectedly, Gaea found that she, too, had to blink back tears, and she cleared her throat delicately before she could speak again.

"I will call to Lir tonight. Perhaps I will have news for you as soon as tomorrow night."

CC felt her heart skip. "Then maybe I won't have to change back into human form at all!"

Gaea returned the young woman's smile, careful to keep any sadness from showing on her face. "Perhaps," she repeated. "But remember, child, the immortals have their own timetable, and gods, particularly, do not like to be rushed. Lir may take some persuading." Gaea waggled her eyebrows suggestively.

CC pulled a face at her, and they sat together in compatible silence, each woman lost in dreams of the future, as the goddess slowly stroked her daughter's hair.

After several minutes CC said, "You know, it's not just the statue that is in bad shape over here." With a flick of her wrist she gestured, encompassing that entire side of the chapel. "This whole area is a mess. It's like someone purposely wanted this part of the chapel to repel people. You wouldn't believe all the filth I've found, and all I've focused on so far has been the statue." She pointed into the thickly shadowed corners. "I haven't started cleaning over there, yet, but it smells like some animal has used this place as a toilet. It's disgusting."

Gaea shook her head sadly. "It is what William has allowed, even encouraged. Having the statue of the Mother forgotten was not enough for him. He wanted it fouled and desecrated."

"Why? What's wrong with him?" CC asked.

"William is a complicated soul, and an excellent example of what happens to a man when he embraces all the negative aspects of power. He controls through fear and manipulation, preying on the weakness of others so that his own weaknesses will not be discovered. That is a particularly dangerous path for a man who has chosen the priesthood. Instead of embracing love, he encourages his followers to turn to fear and denial for salvation. In truth, he is a very passionate man, who at one time had a great deal of love to give." Gaea sighed. "Now he is a sad, twisted man. I pity him, but I am relieved that you will not have to stay near him for much longer." The goddess shook back her hair like she was flinging away a bad habit. "Enough of such morose thoughts! I must ready myself to call Lir, but first I believe I should give my hardworking daughter a little aid with her task."

The goddess approached the statue. Surprised, CC stood and followed her. Gaea stopped in front of the newly cleaned Virgin.

"Yes, I remember well that the devoted young sculptor wanted to add a little something to the hair, but the abbot who commissioned the work could not afford it. . . ." Gaea's words faded as she smiled secretly to herself.

"You knew the man who sculpted this?" CC asked, intrigued with the idea.

"Of course! How do you think he copied my features so well?" She smiled mischievously at CC. "I pretended to be a shepherdess who just happened to cross his path as he was praying for inspiration for the Virgin's statue. It was a pleasure to grant the prayers of such a talented artist." Her playful smile widened. "I have always believed art should not be controlled by one's purse. Do you agree, Daughter?"

Grinning, CC nodded.

"Good! Then I shall complete the sculptor's work."

CC watched as the goddess held open her left hand, palm up. With her right hand she swirled the air above her palm until CC could clearly see a little tornado of sparkles that looked like floating gold dust. Speaking to the swirling dust, the goddess intoned, *"Complete what the artist began. So have I spoken; so shall it be."* Then she blew gently on the little spiral and it burst apart. In a shower of golden waterfall, it rained down on the statue, settling like a fairy cloud into Mary's hair. For an instant more it twinkled and glistened magically, then Gaea made a little clucking sound, tongue against teeth.

"Not so brightly, beautiful ones," she said, and the twinkling died to the more earthly shine of plain, pressed gold.

"It's so lovely!" CC exclaimed, then she sobered. "But won't this cause Abbot William to ask me a lot of difficult-to-answer questions, like 'How did you cast a spell on the statue, Princess?'" CC scowled, imitating the abbot's simpering tone.

Gaea laughed lightly. "No, child, then he would have to admit that he knew what the holy statue looked like in its glory, thus proving that he purposefully allowed it to be forgotten and misused." She shook her head. "That would open too many difficult-to-answer questions for him. There are still good people left at Caldei, people who would be upset by the intentional desecration of the Virgin's image. William does not want to do anything to awaken them from their apathy." She took her daughter's hand. "But know that even though he will not mention its gilding, he will recognize that it has been added to the statue, and he will know that you are responsible. Beware of him, especially tonight and tomorrow when I may be otherwise occupied and unable to come quickly if you have need of me."

"I'll be care—" she started to say, but the sound of someone entering the chapel interrupted them.

CC glanced at the doors to see the distinctive shape of Isabel's limping body framed against the outside light. Suddenly the goddess was gone. CC sighed, but put on a happy face as Isabel approached.

Isabel looked around the sanctuary. "I thought I heard you talking to someone, Princess."

"I was just talking to the Holy Mother, telling her how wonderful she looks."

The old woman turned her questioning gaze to the statue and her eyes widened, instantly filling with tears. Trembling, she approached the Virgin and dropped to her knees in front of her with a grace that surprised CC.

"Look at her! I have never seen anything so beautiful. It is as if the Holy Mother glows with life." Isabel bowed her head and clasped her hands. When she was finished praying she genuflected and rose unsteadily to her feet. Then she turned to face CC.

"You did this. You brought her back to life. Thank you," Isabel said simply.

"There's no need to thank me, Isabel. And anyway, in a place filled with men, women need to stick together. Don't you think so?"

"Yes, Princess."

This time when Isabel used the title she did so with a smile, changing it from a formality to a term of endearment. CC could hardly believe how that genuine smile transformed the old woman's face. For the first time CC glimpsed the more youthful Isabel that hid behind the old woman's mask of bitterness.

"You must be hungry, Undine. You have worked through the day. It is almost time for vespers."

CC was surprised that so much time had passed. "It seems like it shouldn't even be midday yet." She looked down at her grimy robe. "Much as I would like to stay and watch the monks' reactions when they first see our statue, I don't think I'm dressed appropriately for vespers."

Isabel's face had split into another happy grin when CC used the word *our*, to describe the statue, and CC felt a rush of pleasure at the old woman's obvious joy.

"Let us change this soiled robe for clean clothes," Isabel said.

"Clean clothes sound wonderful," CC said.

She emptied the bucket of filthy water outside, and she and Isabel walked slowly through the garden, chattering about what cleaning supplies CC would need the next morning to continue the renovation.

They took a little turn in the path and walked through an area of the gardens that CC didn't recognize. That part of the gardens lacked flowers, but on either side of the path were sectioned off row after row of small, neat-looking plants. CC paused to take a closer look at the greenery.

"Oh!" she said with a delighted gasp. "Herbs! Isabel, look." CC tiptoed carefully between the rows, then she bent and brushed her hand over the nearest plant. It had dark green leaves with slightly jagged edges. She inhaled deeply the wonderful scent. "Mint." Her gaze shifted and she caressed other leaves. "And basil, cilantro and parsley." She laughed. "No, I mean parsley and cilantro. It's easy to get the two mixed up." She smiled up at Isabel who was staring at her in open surprise.

"You have knowledge of herbs?"

CC nodded. "Not as much as I wish I did, but I've always grown things. I love digging in the dirt and knowing that it was from my own efforts that the mint in my tea tastes so wonderful. Actually," she paused, choosing her words carefully so that she wouldn't offend the old woman. "Have you ever thought about adding mint to your amazing stew? I think it would compliment the mutton very well."

The old woman blinked owlishly.

"I didn't mean to offend you," CC said quickly, worried at Isabel's silence. "Your stew is already the best I've ever tasted."

"You have not offended me. You have surprised me. I believe I have been mistaken in my judgment of you, Undine, and when I am mistaken I do not dawdle about making corrections. I must ask that you forgive me."

"There's nothing to forgive." CC's smile reflected her pleasure at the old woman's words. "You didn't know me, and I didn't know you. Let's just call it a misunderstanding."

"A misunderstanding," the old woman repeated. "I like that. I also like your idea for adding mint to my stew. Shall we harvest some?"

"Together." CC grinned.

"Yes. Together." Isabel returned the grin and the two women began breaking off the tops of the fragrant herb.

Isabel's apron was filled with mint, and she and CC were talking amiably about the many uses of cilantro when they entered the kitchen. The other three women looked up, surprise clearly showing on their aged faces.

Isabel dumped the mint on the nearest counter. Several tendrils of silver hair had escaped from her bun and they curled wildly around her face. She pushed them behind her ears and grinned, suddenly reminding CC of a young girl.

"Undine has given me a wonderful idea for the evening stew." Isabel looked at each of the other women. "The princess is wise in the way of herbs."

"Well, I wouldn't call it wise. I just like working with plants, and I like to use them in my own cooking," CC said, a little embarrassed at Isabel's unexpectedly effusive praise.

"It is a wise woman who understands the ways of herbs," the humpbacked lady spoke softly.

CC smiled at the old woman. "I like to work with my hands. It makes me feel good when I've finished something, and I know that it's a job well done."

"Oh, you must see the Holy Mother!" Isabel exclaimed. "It is a miracle!"

"It is not a miracle," the woman with the shriveled hand grumped. "It is plain to see that the princess simply took the filth from the Mother and placed it on herself!" Then she cackled uproariously at her own joke.

The other women were silent, looking at CC to see if she took offense.

"I still think it can still be classified as a miracle," CC said seriously. "Have you ever known any reason for a *princess* to get this dirty, I mean, unless she was terribly clumsy and she fell off her knight's charger as he was whisking her away to their golden castle." She placed the back of her mint-stained hand against her smudged forehead and attempted her own rendition of a princessly swoon.

Isabel chuckled. "Princess, I think you need to practice your swoon. It does not seem very . . ." She searched for a word.

". . . believable." The slack-faced woman finished for her, slurring the word slightly.

"Not believable!" CC pretended offense, pressing her hand against her heart. "You've wounded me!"

"Oh, posh," the woman with the shriveled hand said. "You are too tough to be wounded so easily."

CC smiled at them. "Well, perhaps the four of you would care to demonstrate for me a believable swoon?"

Four pairs of sparkling eyes looked at her, then at one another. Then mayhem broke loose as each old woman, amidst much laughter and sighing, staggered around the kitchen, demonstrating her own version of a believable swoon.

CC couldn't remember when she'd laughed so hard. She'd just fallen into a chair, holding her side and begging the women to stop, when a monk CC recognized as Brother Peter burst into the kitchen.

"What is happening in this room?" he yelled. Then he came to an abrupt halt when he noticed CC.

The women sobered instantly, and CC clearly saw fear flash in their eyes.

She stood quickly, addressing the monk in what she hoped was the snotty, imperious tone of royal command. "You are Brother Peter, aren't you?"

The monk nodded. "Yes, Princess."

"As you can see by the filthy state of my garment, I have been cleaning the Virgin Mother's statue all day. It is tiresome, tedious work, and I needed some levity. Of course I didn't want to trouble any of the Holy Brothers, so I came looking for Isabel. I commanded that she and these other servants amuse me." She wafted her hand absently in the direction of the frozen women. "I am finished being amused now." She smiled graciously at the confused-looking monk. "Thank you for coming to check on me. Please give the abbot my regrets that I must miss mass this evening, but as you can see I am not dressed for vespers." She turned her back on him dismissively.

"Yes, Princess," he said and hurried from the room.

When she was sure he was gone she said to the women. "The monks don't have much fun, do they?"

The women slowly thawed, making scoffing sounds in their throats.

"It doesn't mean we can't," CC said. The women threw her doubtful looks.

"Abbot William says mirth is sinful," Isabel said, only this time her voice didn't sound smug, as it had the other times she had repeated the abbot's dictums to CC; this time she sounded tired and sad.

"How about what Jesus said?" CC asked, and all four pairs of eyes were instantly attentive. "He said, 'Suffer the little children to come unto me.' Well, children, especially little children, laugh and play and have fun all the time. You'd think if happiness was some big sin, then Christ would have said something like, 'Suffer the little children to shut up or I'll beat them and oppress them into heaven.' Wouldn't he?"

"You make an excellent point, Undine," the woman with the shriveled handed said.

"What is your name?" Undine asked her.

"Lynelle," she answered with a bright smile, showing lots of big, yellow teeth.

"And yours?" Undine asked the woman with the partially paralyzed face.

"Bronwyn," she slurred.

"My name is Gwenyth," the lady with the humpback volunteered before CC could ask.

"Ladies, it is a great honor to meet you. I am the Princess Undine Who Can't Remember Anymore Than Her Name," CC said in her best imitation of a British queen. Her audience cackled appreciatively. Then she dropped into the bow of a prima ballerina—and almost fell face first onto the floor when her back foot caught in the hem of her robe.

Laughing, Isabel caught her. "Perhaps I should help you out of this robe."

CC smiled at her. "And into something more queenly?"

"Of course," Isabel said, mimicking CC's royal imitation. "After you, my lady."

Both of them backed from the kitchen, waving royally at their laughing "subjects."

"Is there any possible way I could take a bath?" CC asked as they made their way through the deserted dining room.

Isabel patted her hand. "Go to your room. I will get the tub. If you stand in it, I will pour the water over you."

"Can I be naked?"

Isabel tried unsuccessfully to stifle a smile. "If you insist."

"I insist," CC said firmly.

"I do not actually leave my chemise on while I bathe," the old woman admitted.

"I knew that," CC said.

Isabel wrinkled her heavily lined forehead in surprise. "How did you know?"

CC sniffed in her direction. "You don't smell bad."

CC could hear the old woman's chuckles long after she disappeared to fetch the tub.

Chapter Eighteen

CC's stomach let out a very unladylike growl as Isabel finished lacing up her outer gown.

"Forgotten to eat, have you?" Isabel laughed.

"Please tell me there's some of your wonderful stew left."

"For you, yes. After all, you are the one who thought of adding the mint."

"It was good?"

"It was wonderful. I think Bronwyn was so impressed that she may even have saved you a loaf of her excellent bread."

"That sounds great," CC said as they hurried down the hall. "Do you think the monks will still be at evening mass? I'm really tired, and I'd rather not have to make conversation with the abbot and Andras." The hard physical labor of cleaning and scrubbing all day coupled with the ever-present ache for the water had exhausted her, and the last thing CC needed was to spar with the abbot or fend off Andras's attempts at courtship.

CC could feel Isabel's gaze. When she spoke, the old woman's voice sounded wise. "It is obvious that you and the abbot dislike one another, which is certainly no surprise. Abbot William disapproves of beauty, and you are beauty personified. Even I judged you harshly because of your appearance."

CC started to say something, but Isabel shook her head, not wanting to be interrupted. "No, do not excuse me. I am old enough to recognize when my behavior is foolish. So that explains why you would have hard feelings for the abbot, but I do not understand why you are not pleased by the attentions of Sir Andras. It seemed at first as if you enjoyed his company, but I have been observing the two of you. Of late it appears you are more often annoyed or distracted when you are with him than not."

"I didn't think I was being so obvious."

"It is only apparent when you are very tired." Isabel smiled at her. "And perhaps only then to another woman."

They began walking across the courtyard, and CC chewed her bottom lip, not sure how much she should admit to Isabel. She glanced at the silent well, but it looked like an ordinary pile of stone. Well, she thought, at least she's not asking me about that.

"Forgive me, Undine, if I have asked too personal a question," Isabel said.

"No," CC assured her. "I don't mind that you asked. I was just trying to figure out how best to answer you." She sighed, and decided on telling her the truth—or at least as much of the truth as she could. Liars didn't make good friends, and CC very much wanted to be the old woman's friend. "You're right. At first I thought I might be able to care about him, maybe even love him. He seemed nice, and he's certainly handsome enough."

Isabel made an appreciative noise and nodded.

"But the more time I've spent with him, and the better I've come to know him, the more obvious it is that he's not the man for me. It's not that he's a horrible guy or anything like that. It's not even really his fault. The truth is that he and I are mismatched." CC bent her head to Isabel's and lowered her voice. "And this morning I overheard him talking to the abbot about me. They were discussing whether or not he should marry me and it sounded like they were considering buying a brood mare or a piece of property."

Isabel raised her eyebrows. "And this surprised you, Undine?"

"Not really." CC sighed. "But I would never marry a man who thought of me as his property."

Isabel blinked slowly at her. "You must be from a land far away."

"That's one thing we know for certain," CC said firmly. "Another thing is that I'm sure that not all males think of women as property. Some of them are kind and respectful and consider us partners in life." CC's voice softened as she thought of Dylan.

"So you love another?" The old woman's eyes twinkled, and CC couldn't help but smile in return.

"Whore!" The word hissed through the air behind them.

Both women gasped and spun around to face Andras. The knight was wide-eyed and so unnaturally pale that he looked ghostly. His blond hair was in wild disarray, and his eyes flamed with an ominous silver light.

"Whore!" he hissed. *"Do not think you have fooled us. We know what you really are. We know you are not pure. You have whored yourself and you will pay the price for your betrayal!"*

CC shivered at the eerie sound of his words. They echoed from his mouth with an otherworldly force. *We?* Who was he talking about? Her thoughts raced through her mind as she glanced at the well. Hovering above it CC could see inky waves, like heat rising from the top of a sun-baked blacktop road.

"Go get help!" CC whispered frantically to Isabel.

"No! I will not leave you," she whispered back. Then she made a shooing gesture at the knight and spoke sharply in the confident voice of an irritated grandmother, "Go on, Sir Andras, leave the Princess be. If the two of you have had a misunderstanding, there are other ways to solve it. I do not think the abbot would approve of your ungentlemanly words."

The knight's eyes slitted as he answered Isabel. *"Yes, we have had a misunderstanding."* Snakelike, his glowing eyes shifted to Undine. *"One that can only be righted when we have been joined together. I will have what is mine by right!"*

Before CC could move, Andras lunged forward and grabbed her wrist in a vicelike grip.

At his touch, the amulet of the goddess began to radiate heat. CC could feel its power building swiftly.

"Stop this foolish charade," the disembodied voice whispered hot words into her ear. *"You cannot alter the ending. You will be mine."*

She met the silver eyes and spoke directly to the spirit which possessed the knight. "Never! I will never be yours, Sarpedon." CC concentrated on the power of the goddess that burned within the stone hanging between her breasts. She could feel it like she felt the ebb and flow of the tide. The power was fluid, and she knew it was hers to claim. In a blindingly swift motion, CC cast the power of the amulet down her and struck the knight a stinging blow across his cheek.

Andras shrieked as the might of the goddess knocked him away from CC. He doubled over and fell to his knees. From where she stood, CC watched the dark fumes dissolve down into the well.

Except for the sounds of the knight's ragged breathing, the courtyard was silent. CC felt weak, like the blow she had delivered had drained her of all her strength. She stumbled back a little, and Isabel rushed to give her a steadying hand.

"My son! What is it?"

The abbot strode into the courtyard, his red robe flapping behind him like a crimson flag. Several monks hurried after him, looking like confused white mice. The priest closed the space between them and helped Andras to his feet.

"Abbot William, the knight—" Isabel began with a shaking voice, but CC cut her off.

"He must have fainted." CC finished for her, squeezing her hand to keep her quiet. "Isabel was escorting me to dinner, and we found Andras lying here in the courtyard. He wasn't moving. It was quite a shock."

"Yes," Isabel added. "I would have gone immediately for help, but the princess was so distraught that I didn't feel I could leave her."

CC sent her a grateful look.

"Then Andras started to move, which is when you came into the courtyard."

Everyone turned to the knight. The glow in his eyes had completely extinguished, and his features had returned to normal. His expression was dazed. Sweat plastered his hair to his head and darkened wet circles under his tunic.

"I-I remember hearing Undine's voice." He shook his head in an attempt to clear the confusion from his mind. "And the amulet. I remember the amulet." He raked a trembling hand through his wet hair. "Then I remember nothing more until I heard your voice, Father."

"Do not fear, my son. We will discover what it is that has clouded your mind." His voice was gentle and fatherly. "Since its influence fled from my presence, whatever has affected you must be of the darkness because it flees the light of God."

The priest wasn't looking at the knight as he spoke; instead he studied CC. She could feel it when his gaze found the amber teardrop that hung on its long, silver chain. In the evening light it looked darker than its usual golden brown. Automatically, CC touched the amulet. The warmth that still radiated there comforted her. The abbot stepped closer to CC, narrowing his eyes as he peered at the pendant.

"What is this heathen talisman?" His voice lost its gentle charm when he addressed CC. "Take it off and let me examine it."

CC shook her head. "It is not heathen, and I can't take it off. It's a gift from my mother."

The priest's eyes were slits. "Now you have memory of a mother?"

"I remember her love and I remember her gift," CC said defiantly.

"I shall examine this gift," he sneered.

He walked toward her in slow motion, and all CC could think was that she knew the amulet *would* burn him. It had not failed to turn negative energy away from her, and the priest was one large ball of negative energy. His little piglike eyes glared at her, and she felt like she was going to hyperventilate.

That's it! she thought. And with a sigh that would have made Lynelle, Bronwyn and Gwenyth proud, CC swooned dramatically.

Thankfully, Isabel's strong arms were there to catch her, and both women tumbled to the ground. CC lay half in the servant's lap as Isabel rocked her like a child. Gulping air, she fluttered her eyelashes, pretending partial consciousness.

"Poor thing!" Isabel said. "She has had almost nothing to eat today. The child has been toiling since dawn for the Holy Mother." Out of the corner of her vision, CC could see several of the monks cross themselves reverently at the mention of the statue. "Here!" CC felt a tug as Isabel grasped the amulet firmly in her callused palm. "It does not burn. It is but a gift from a loving mother. Sir Andras has had an unfortunate apoplectic attack. The good knight is not in his right mind. He obviously needs your aid, as the princess needs mine." Isabel spoke with a firmness that appeared to shock the abbot into silence.

"Oh, Isabel, I feel so weak," CC gasped. "What happened?"

Isabel smoothed back CC's hair. "Hush, lamb, all is well. You will recover when you have eaten."

Struggling to her feet, the old woman pulled CC up with her. "Now I beg you to excuse us, Abbot. I will see that the princess is cared for and then retires for the night."

Isabel began limping towards the door to the dining room, one arm wrapped protectively around CC's waist. The sea of silent monks parted for them.

"Until we understand exactly what caused the attack on Sir Andras, I will post one of the Brothers outside the princess's door—to keep her from *harm*." The whiplike sound of the abbot's voice caused the women to pause.

CC kept a tight hold on Isabel as she half-turned to face the priest. He had moved back to the knight's side and his hand was resting protectively on Andras's shoulder.

"Thank you for your concern for my safety," CC said, allowing her voice to sound weak and shaky.

"I have concern for all of the lost . . ." The abbot's voice drifted after them as the women left the courtyard.

"I don't want to eat in the dining room," CC whispered to Isabel in the hall. Isabel nodded in understanding, and they headed for the servant's entrance to the kitchen.

Lynelle was the first to notice them. Her look of welcome shifted instantly to one of concern.

"Sir Andras attacked her," Isabel said grimly, leading CC over to a roughly carved stool that sat near the center workstation. "She needs food and drink."

The four women went to work like a well-oiled machine, and soon CC was eating a steaming bowl of Isabel's excellent mint-flavored stew and taking turns sipping from a mug of herbal tea and a goblet of rich red wine.

"Drink all of the tea," Bronwyn slurred as she and the other women hovered henlike around CC. "It is chamomile and rosehips. It will help to soothe your upset stomach."

"And drink all of the wine," Lynelle rasped in her grumpy voice. "It will help with everything else."

CC smiled weakly at the old women.

Isabel offered her a second helping of the stew, which CC enthusiastically accepted. As Isabel placed the steaming bowl in front of her, she asked, "Have you recovered enough to explain?"

The other women paused in their chores, their interest piqued. CC nodded slowly.

"The knight was not himself?"

"No, he wasn't," CC answered, meeting Isabel's gaze squarely.

"He seemed to be possessed," Isabel said.

CC heard the shocked gasps from the old women, but she kept her eyes on Isabel.

"Yes. Andras was possessed by a creature named Sarpedon. I was escaping from him when the knight found me washed up on the shore."

Isabel nodded. "I knew it. I could clearly see the change in the knight, and that was the name you used when you spoke to him." The old woman took a deep breath before she asked her next question. "You did not want the abbot to touch your amulet. Why?"

The room fell silent waiting for the answer.

"Because I didn't know what he would feel if he touched it. What did you feel?"

"Warmth," Isabel said simply.

CC nodded. "Because you don't wish me harm. Sarpedon did, and the amulet protects me. I think the abbot wishes me harm, too. I didn't know what would happen if he touched it."

"Are you a sorceress?" Isabel asked.

Still meeting her eyes, CC shook her head. "No, I'm not."

"But how do you know?" Gwenyth broke in breathlessly. "You cannot remember your past."

"I remember more about my past than I can admit to you right now, and I'm sorry about that. I can assure you, though, that I am not a sorceress." CC looked at each woman as she spoke. "But I do believe that women have magic. I don't mean anything dark and sinful. I just mean that I think that there is something special inside of us, and it's a part of what makes us women. I don't think you have to be young or beautiful or a princess to have it—you just have to be female and willing to listen within and to believe."

The room was silent as CC continued eating, but the silence didn't feel tense, instead it felt thoughtful.

"I had no idea I would be putting to use what you taught me this afternoon so quickly," CC said, breaking the silence with a smile.

CC was surrounded by looks of confusion until Isabel threw back her head and laughed.

"It was a ruse! The swoon was a ruse," Isabel said gleefully, nudging the two women nearest her. "You should have seen our princess. Like a delicate flower folding, she crumpled into my arms." Isabel did a rough imitation of CC's faint and the women cackled happily.

"Probably not as believable as my swoon," Lynelle grumbled before winking at CC and refilling her wine.

CC drank the last of the wine, grateful for the warm buzz in her stomach that helped offset the ache within her that seemed to be getting stronger by the minute. Now that work or talk wasn't distracting her, desire for the sea rolled through her and coupled with the longing she felt for Dylan, almost caused her to wince with the pain. Tomorrow night, she reminded herself. Then maybe she would never have to leave the water or Dylan again.

"You are tired, Undine. Come, let me take you to your chamber." Isabel said gently.

"Thank you, ladies. I appreciate all of you. Dinner was delicious—almost as good as the company. And thank you for trusting me."

A medley of "Sleep well, Princess" followed CC and Isabel from the room.

In the middle of the dining room, CC paused. "I don't want to walk back through the courtyard. Can we go the other way?"

"Certainly," Isabel said, changing direction for the doorway at the far end of the room through which CC had entered that morning.

"The creature's spirit comes from the well, doesn't it?" Isabel asked in a low voice.

CC glanced at the old woman. Then she nodded. "He is using the well to enter the monastery."

Isabel looked sharply at CC. "Can this thing harm you?"

CC shook her head slowly. "Not directly, but he can cause all kinds of problems for me, like he did this evening. And I worry what would happen if the abbot or even Sir Andras realize what is happening." CC turned to Isabel and grasped the old woman's gnarled hands. "Thank you so much for not betraying me to the abbot."

Isabel's smile was motherly. "As you have already said, women must stick together."

"And we certainly did stick together."

The women shared a satisfied smile that was decidedly feminine. They continued down the dim hall, swinging their joined hands.

"I am relieved to hear that the evil spirit cannot harm you. But I would also be relieved to know . . ." Isabel said haltingly.

"No, I don't think he is able to possess you and the other ladies." CC cocked her head to the side and grinned at her. "That is unless any of you are harboring hidden lusts for my body."

Isabel cackled and it took several moments for her to answer CC. "I feel confident that I speak truly for the other women when I say we feel no such desires for you."

"I'm glad to hear it."

Isabel snorted, and CC laughed.

They walked on a little way before CC spoke again. "I have to stay at the monastery for a little while longer."

Isabel flashed her a look of understanding. "You are safe here."

"Yes, and my family is helping me."

"As is the Holy Mother," Isabel said with certainty.

CC squeezed her hand. "Yes, the Great Mother is helping me."

They turned the corner. A plump little monk knelt near the door to CC's room. He appeared to be deep in prayer.

"Your guard," Isabel whispered.

"More like a jailer," CC whispered back.

The women exchanged grim looks as they entered CC's room, ignoring the kneeling monk.

Chapter Nineteen

CC warred with herself. She wanted to climb through the window, rush down the path to the sea and hurl herself into its wet comfort. She missed Dylan, and, of course, she worried for him, too. She knew he waited for her, just as surely as she knew Sarpedon hunted for a way to possess her.

Her skin crawled at the memory of his glowing eyes and the touch of his hand on her skin. Gaea had told her not to be afraid of the merman's spirit, but Andras's use of the word *we* had frightened her. He had said *we* know that you are not pure. Did that mean Sarpedon knew she loved Dylan? Or was he talking about an imagined affair with Andras? If Sarpedon had access to Andras's mind when he possessed the knight, he would know that Andras and Undine were not lovers, which gave the *we* an ominous meaning. He probably knew about Dylan. Wouldn't she just endanger Dylan if she went to him again?

And then, of course, she had to worry about the abbot. Before the incident in the courtyard, he already believed Undine was a Viking witch. The events of the day had done nothing but support his belief, and that definitely made CC uneasy.

Tossing fretfully in her narrow bed she wanted desperately to call to Gaea, but she knew she couldn't. Gaea would be busy with Lir, and CC couldn't interrupt her just to ask her a string of self-serving questions. CC sighed. She needed Dylan. She ached to have the comfort of his arms wash away the poison of Sarpedon's lust, and the pain of being separated from the sea, but tonight the answer had to be that she stay safely in her room and try to sleep. She closed her eyes. She'd dreamed of Dylan once before, maybe tonight she would again. . . .

DYLAN swam restlessly back and forth along the shore. He could feel Christine's need as clearly as he had felt her fear earlier that night—a fear that had to have been caused by Sarpedon. The merman must have found her in the monastery and discovered some way to accost her. Dylan's jaw clenched. He could feel it when she used the power of the goddess to thwart Sarpedon's attack. If only he could be there beside her!

A school of giant angelfish fled from his path as his rage caused the surrounding waters to froth and boil. He felt another surge of frustration as Christine struggled alone on land against her need.

"By Lir's trident, there must be something I can do!" Dylan raged.

"To begin with, you could change your curses. Evoking the power of Lir will not aid you at all if what you desire is on land." Gaea's lilting voice was a song as it carried clearly over the waves.

"Gaea!" Dylan exclaimed.

With powerful strokes, he propelled himself to the shoreline. The goddess was sitting on an old piece of driftwood, dangling her feet in the surf. She was clothed in a dress the color of night, but it shimmered with the reflection of the water as if it was made of liquid velvet.

"Your daughter needs me, Great Mother," Dylan said respectfully. His chest heaved as he tried to catch his breath.

The goddess's gaze was sharp. "Are you saying that you feel her need, merman?"

Dylan's fist closed over his heart. "As if it were my own."

Gaea's eyes warmed. "Yes, I can see that. You and Christine are linked. Your souls have found their match. It is a rare and wondrous thing, but it is a double-edged sword. Her pain is yours, as yours is hers."

"I would have it no other way."

"What is it you wish of me, Dylan?" she asked so softly that the merman had to strain to hear her.

"Grant me human form!" he said in a rush of words. "Allow me to go to her and comfort her."

Gaea tapped one slender finger against the driftwood as she considered the merman's request.

"My father was of the land. That must bind me to you in some way," Dylan beseeched. "I ask only for a temporary form. Allow me the remainder of this one brief night as a human man."

"It is true that you have a tie to the Earth. But this bond is mortal, as was your father. If I gift you with the form of a human, it will strengthen the part of you that is mortal. The cost could be high, Dylan. You may age. You certainly will become more vulnerable to injury, especially if you are wounded by an immortal." Gaea's beautiful voice was sad.

"Christine needs me."

The goddess sought and held the merman's steady gaze. She read clearly there his love for Christine. And she could feel Christine's soul, too, as it yearned for the respite only her lover's arms could provide.

"I am ever weak when faced with true love." Gaea spoke more to herself than to Dylan, but her words made his face blaze with joy. The goddess held up her hand in a gesture of restraint. "Listen well, Dylan. The spell will last only a short length of time. You must return to the waters before the light of the new day touches the land. If you do not,"—she added power to her words which raised the hair on the nape of Dylan's neck—"you will be trapped. You will belong to neither realm—the land or the sea. You will perish, and your soul will roam without rest for eternity."

The merman nodded gravely. "I will not forget, Great Goddess."

"See that you do not. My daughter would be most displeased."

Dylan smiled. "As would I."

Gaea tried unsuccessfully to keep her lips from turning up. "I am beginning to understand why my daughter chose you, merman."

"She simply showed the discerning wisdom of her Great Mother." Dylan bowed gallantly.

The goddess's laughter glittered around her as she motioned for the merman to swim closer so that she could begin casting her spell.

CC decided the night was never going to end. Her body ached and her mind wouldn't shut up.

"Wine," she said to the silent room as she lit the candle next to her bed. "That monk outside my room has to be good for something. I'll just act all regal and send him off to get me some wine." She spoke to the sputtering wick. "A couple cups of that thick red stuff I had the other night should do the trick."

Isabel had left her a fresh woolen robe, and CC wrapped it around her like a cloak. Satisfied the transparent chemise was well covered she walked quickly to the door, wincing at the cold of the stone floor against her bare feet. Mentally she made a note to stoke the fire to take the chill from the room.

She opened the door slowly, not wanting to startle the Brother. He was sitting with his back resting against the wall beside her door. His cowl was pulled up, and she couldn't see his face.

CC cleared her throat.

The monk didn't move.

"Um, excuse me, Brother," she said.

"He sleeps." The deep voice came from the shadows. The sound of it made her heart leap in response.

"Who's there?" CC asked.

"Do you need to ask, my love?" Dylan said as he stepped toward her.

"Oh!" CC pressed her hand against her mouth, sure that she was hallucinating, or that Sarpedon was playing a horrible trick on her.

Dylan touched her face. "Am I so very different, Christine?"

Her eyes darted from the strong lines of his familiar face down his body. He was wearing a monk's robe, but peeking from beneath it were two very human, very bare feet.

"I . . . you . . . but how?" Had she dreamed him?

"Let us call it a gift from a goddess."

His smile convinced her. He couldn't be a trick. Sarpedon wasn't capable of using such joy as a masquerade. She grabbed his hand and pulled him into her room, closing the door carefully behind them.

"The monk will not awaken. Gaea has seen to that." Dylan's eyes were sparkling. Then he looked around with open curiosity. "This is where you spend your days?"

"Well, not exactly," she said, surprised at her sudden nervousness. "I mean, I change my clothes here, and I sleep here, but I spend most of my day out there." She jerked her thumb in the direction of the door and ordered her mouth to quit babbling.

"It is . . ." Dylan hesitated. ". . . very gray," he finally concluded. Then he nodded at the narrow bed. "And that is where you rest your body at night?"

"In theory," CC sighed. "I don't seem to be having much success with resting lately."

Dylan turned to her and took her face in his hands. He noticed the dark circles under her eyes and the sallow tinge of her skin. He kissed her forehead and then gently kissed her lips. Her eyes fluttered shut.

"I have come to help you rest," he said.

Keeping her eyes closed, she leaned into him. "Now that you're here, I'm not tired at all."

She could feel the chuckle rumble through his chest.

"Then perhaps you would be willing to teach me something of this human body. It is an odd thing to have legs."

His kiss cut off her laughter. When they broke apart Dylan's eyes had darkened with desire. CC took his hand and led him to her bed. First, she dropped the robe from around her shoulders. Then she let the chemise fall from her body. She tugged on his robe, and he bent so that she could pull the rough woolen fabric over his head.

"Look at you," she said breathlessly. He was tall and had the build of an athlete. "Thank you, Gaea."

Dylan smiled. "I make an adequate man?"

CC raised one eyebrow as her gaze flicked down to the flesh that already stood erect between his long, muscular legs.

Her face warmed as her cheeks flushed pink. "Oh, yes. You make more than an adequate man."

Dylan pulled her into his arms. "Teach me how to love you as a human man loves a woman."

CC looked up at him and felt the restless pain within her loosen its stranglehold. "It's the same, my love. In any form you and I were made to fit perfectly together."

They sank down onto the bed, lost in one another.

Dylan knew that he hadn't banished the ache within her, but he had soothed it and made it bearable. She had needed him, and he had responded. No price was too great to pay to be with her. They would belong to each other for an eternity.

CHAPTER TWENTY

THE screech of a seagull woke him. It was such a normal sound, a sound he heard every day of his life. He had almost drifted back to sleep when the gull screeched again.

"Make it go away," CC mumbled, and snuggled more securely against his chest.

Dylan's eyes shot open, and he was instantly awake. His heart pounded painfully in his chest until his mind registered that the room was still cast in the darkness of predawn. He forced his panic to subside.

The gull screeched again.

CC's eyes cracked open. The bird was perched on the window ledge.

"What is it doing?" she grumbled. Then she kissed Dylan's chest and nuzzled him.

"I believe it is a messenger from your mother, reminding me that my time is limited."

"Do you have to go?" she asked sleepily.

Dylan kissed the top of her head. "If I do not, I will not live," he said simply.

"What?" CC's eyes sprang open. She read the truth on her lover's face. "You should have told me!" She lunged out of bed, pulling him after her. "When do you have to return?"

"Before light touches the land."

CC ran to the window. Dylan moved behind her, looking over her shoulder. Predawn was already beginning to gray the night-darkened ocean. His stomach contracted.

"You can't take the time to leave through the monastery." Her eyes darted to his masculine body, gauging his size. "I think you can fit if you squeeze."

He lifted his brows in a question.

"Through the window," she said, pointing. "The cliffside is right outside there. Hurry!"

Dylan nodded and bent to kiss her quickly. Then he hoisted his naked body up to the windowsill. It was a tight fit, and rock scraped his skin painfully, but it took him only a moment to pop through like a cork to the surface of a pool of water. On her toes, CC peered out the window. His smile flashed in the darkness.

"I have enjoyed being a man, Christine." His grin was endearingly male.

Even through her worry, CC smiled. "Hurry, silly."

"I will wait for you tonight," Dylan said. "And for all of eternity."

Then he turned and sprinted towards the cliff. CC's mouth opened in a soundless scream when she saw his naked muscles bunch powerfully. Before she could shout a warning, he reached the edge of the cliff and leapt from its impossibly steep side. His body arched in a spectacular dive, and in the moment before the sun touched the land CC saw the flash of fire that signaled his change from human to merman. She stood at the window for a very long time, struggling against the painful desire to follow him.

Dawn had shifted from gray to mauve when she finally turned from the window. All sight of Dylan was gone. Slowly, with movements that might have belonged to a woman Isabel's age, she pulled on her robe and belted it. Rolling up the sleeves she pushed open the door, almost causing the monk who knelt outside in the hall to fall over.

"Good morning, I didn't mean to startle you," CC said.

The monk stood. CC noticed that his face was flushed and he looked woozy, like he had just awakened from a delicious, goddess-induced dream.

"The abbot asked that I bring you to him upon your waking." The monk's voice cracked with sleep.

CC shook her head. Dylan's absence was a raw wound, and it left her in no mood to deal with Abbot William's sly questioning. "Please tell the abbot that I am honored by his invitation, but that I must get to work immediately on my restoration of the Holy Mother."

The monk's mouth opened and closed compulsively. CC thought it made him look like a bizarre species of land flounder.

"I'm sure the abbot will understand. He, of all people, knows the importance of honoring the Holy Mother. Have a blessed day, Brother, and thank you for watching over me last night."

CC hurried down the hall. When she glanced over her shoulder at the monk, he was still standing in front of her door. And his mouth was still open.

The way through the dining room which led to the servant's entrance to the kitchen felt like a familiar friend, and CC's leather slippers made soft little padding noises as she circumvented the courtyard and the silently watching well. Peeking into the dining room she let out a relieved breath. It was empty except for Isabel, who was clearing the last of the dishes from one of the tables.

"Good morning," CC said.

"That stubborn look tells me that no matter how weary you are, you will still be about the Virgin's business," Isabel stated with frustrated concern.

"Stubborn? I'm not stubborn."

Isabel's answer was a rude noise in the back of her throat, which almost made CC laugh.

They both headed into the kitchen, which was a wonderful mixture of busy women and delicious smells. Each woman greeted CC with a smile and a warm hello.

"Already had your bucket and such taken to the chapel," Lynelle said in her gruff voice.

"Thank you, but you didn't need to go to any trouble for me. You already have enough to do," CC said.

"We did not do it," Gwenyth said. "We asked some of the Brothers to gather and carry the things."

CC blinked in surprise.

"There are those among the Brothers who are pleased that the Holy Mother is being restored," Isabel explained.

"And a little water fetching does not take them long from tending their precious sheep and gardens," Lynelle grumbled.

"I made this for you," Bronwyn slurred softly, handing CC a mug of warm tea.

"Eat this on the way to the chapel. You must not allow yourself to weaken. The Holy Mother needs you strong and healthy." Gwenyth gave her a hard roll with a hunk of cheese and meat inside of it.

"You have no idea how much this means to me this morning," CC said, suddenly feeling near tears. "Thank you. I appreciate all of you."

The four women made scoffing noises, waving off her thanks, but CC could see the pleasure that flushed their wizened faces.

"Go on with you," Isabel said. "Today we will make certain that you eat."

On impulse, CC leaned down and kissed the old woman's cheek before hurrying out the door.

It must have rained sometime during the night, because the gardens were still wet and sparkling. CC breathed deeply, enjoying the damp smells of grass and flower as they mixed with the ever-present salt tang of the nearby ocean. Chewing the last of the breakfast roll, she strolled slowly through the twisting paths, taking the long way to the chapel. She passed several monks already busy pruning and weeding and was pleasantly surprised when two of them met her gaze and nodded shy good mornings.

The chapel was dim and still filled with an oppressive layer of incense from dawn mass, but as CC made her way to the Virgin's statue, she felt her spirit lighten. The Blessed Mother was lit by dozens of white candles, and the statue glowed like a golden beacon of hope. Yesterday, CC had left six candles burning around the base of the statue. Someone, perhaps even several someones, had already begun visiting the Virgin.

Placed in a neat row to one side of the niche that held the statue were three buckets of clean water, a hunk of soap, a pile of clean rags and a large straw broom.

"Time to get to work," she told Gaea's serene face.

"UGH!" CC scooped up another pile of rancid-smelling mess while she muttered to herself. "I have no way of being certain, but I think that this is poo from a giant squirrel."

"Actually, it is from a raccoon, but a giant squirrel is an excellent guess." Gaea had materialized in front of the statue, her blue and gold silk wrap mirroring the soft colors in the Virgin's robes.

"I should have known that even a giant squirrel wouldn't be giant enough to make this nasty mess." CC smiled at the goddess. "Good morning, it's nice to see a clean face."

"Good *afternoon* to you, daughter. You have worked the morning away." Gaea returned her smile and clicked her fingers. In a shower of silver sparks a wet towel appeared in one hand and a goblet appeared in the other. She gestured for CC to join her.

"Come, sit and refresh yourself. I have news."

CC sat next to the goddess and gratefully accepted the damp towel, wiping the dirt from her face and hands with a sigh of pleasure. When she was at least semiclean, Gaea handed her the goblet. It was filled with a thick, honey-colored liquid. CC sipped.

"Yum! This is delicious. What is it?"

With a gentle wave of her wrist Gaea produced her own goblet.

"It is Viking mead. I thought it the appropriate drink since you have been mistaken for a Norse sorceress."

"Very appropriate," she agreed. "I want to thank you for the gift you gave Dylan and me last night." She felt heat spring to her cheeks as Gaea's sparkling eyes smiled knowingly at her.

"He did make a spectacular man," the goddess said wistfully.

"As usual, you are correct. Last night was . . ." She sighed dreamily. ". . . exactly what I needed. Thank you, Mother."

Gaea nodded graciously and sipped her mead. She would not share with her daughter the cost of last night's passion. It had been Dylan's choice, and he had made it willingly. She would not taint his sacrifice by telling Christine news that would surely cause her guilt and pain. And, if fate was kind, the price Dylan would have to pay would be no more than a few wrinkles or an attractive graying of his ebony-colored hair.

Gaea cleared her throat. Without preamble she said, "Lir is preoccupied. I called to him from our private cove, and he sent a selkie as his messenger." The goddess flipped back her thick hair and crossed her legs, obviously annoyed. "There is some problem with Pele, the Hawaiian fire goddess. Mano is causing some mischief with her local priestesses, and Pele has threatened to erupt an underwater volcano in retribution. Mano has appealed to Lir. And, of course, Lir has never minded interceding when the passion of a goddess is involved."

"Who is Mano?"

"The Hawaiian shark god—and a rather nasty fellow." Gaea shook her head in disgust. "Island immortals are all so petty. Too little land to ground them and to provide them the depth they need for real wisdom."

"So you didn't get to talk to Lir at all?"

"No, his message said he would come to me as soon as he has resolved the Hawaiian problem."

"And he didn't say when that would be."

"No, but I will not allow him to put me off for long. I am a goddess and I will not be trifled with." Gaea's eyes flashed with suppressed power.

"Speaking of being trifled with, Sarpedon has become more annoying," CC said. "Yesterday he possessed Andras again. Your amulet reminded him that wasn't a smart move, but while he was possessed Andras made some comments about knowing that I'm not pure."

Gaea's eyes narrowed. "The merman is troublesome, but now that he has found you it seems that he is focusing his attention on the monastery. I know from your dolphin friends that he has been distinctly absent from the waters near Caldei." Gaea's expression lightened and she smiled playfully at CC. "That is especially fortunate because the dolphins report news of another merman, who is spending all of his time in the waters surrounding this island."

"Dylan?"

"Of course it is Dylan. Who else?"

CC smiled sheepishly. "I know it's silly, but I just wanted to hear you say it."

"This silliness, as you call it, is part of the magic of love. And remember love is the strongest magic in the world. It even has the ability to tame a goddess."

"I want to be with him, Mother. Always."

Gaea smoothed back CC's hair. "I know, Daughter, and tonight you shall be with your lover again. Feign exhaustion and retire early to your bed. I will summon storm clouds to obscure the sun so that you need not wait for full dark to go to Dylan." Gaea's look turned sly. "It is my turn to use Sarpedon's connection with the young knight. I will whisper dreams to Andras in which you figure predominately. Sarpedon will be kept very busy tonight trying to decide what is real, and what is fantasy. He will be much too busy chasing the ghosts of dreams to haunt the waters looking for you."

CC hugged Gaea in gratitude, and the goddess's laughter filled the chapel.

"All will be well, Daughter. With just a little more patience, all will be well. Do not forget, you must return to the monastery when the bell tolls for morning mass."

"I won't forget. Will you be at the shore tonight?" CC asked.

"Tonight I will leave you to your lover. You see, I, too, will be concentrating on calling a lover. Lir will not long be able to resist."

CC wondered how Lir could resist the goddess at all. Even in the dimness of the chapel, Gaea's beauty was awe-inspiring, and when she mentioned her lover the light that always shone within her intensified until CC almost felt the need to avert her eyes.

CC grinned at Gaea. "Lir's a goner, and he doesn't even know it—yet."

"Oh, he knows, Daughter. He knows."

The cheery yellow glow of the candles that surrounded Mary's statue blinked and quivered in response to the women's laughter, filling CC with a sense of well-being. How could anything go wrong as long as Gaea was beside her?

Suddenly, the expression on Gaea's face sobered and before CC could speak the goddess's body dissipated into hundreds of tiny golden lights, which pulsed once and then faded. Her disappearance was followed by the sound of a deep, male voice.

"Good afternoon, Undine," Andras said.

CC looked warily at the knight, half expecting his eyes to begin to glow, but there was no sign of anything unusual in his appearance.

"Hello, Andras." She took a breath and decided there was no way she could avoid the subject. "You look like you feel better today. Did you and the abbot figure out what happened yesterday in the courtyard?"

The knight's welcoming expression flattened. "Abbot William is diligently praying about the event. He remains confident that an answer will be found."

"Well, I'm just glad to see that you've recovered. I'm sure the abbot's prayers will be helpful." She kept her voice light.

Instead of meeting her eyes, the knight's gaze slid away and lit on the statue. "You have done an excellent job here. It is good to see that you are taking such an interest in religion. A woman needs to be grounded in the structure of the church so that she can know her proper place as wife and mother."

His face had relaxed and his smile was genuine, even if the words were patronizing.

"I'm not restoring the Holy Mother's statue out of religious zealousness or piety; I'm restoring it out of love," she said, reminding herself that it wasn't his fault that he was a medieval man. He probably thought he had just paid her an enormous compliment.

"Exactly." Andras sounded pleased. "Love of the church."

"No," she automatically corrected him. "Love of the Mother."

Confusion spread over his face. "Is there a difference?"

"I think so. I think there is a world of difference between devotion to man and devotion to the divine."

"Do you not believe that man can be divine?" Andras's chuckle said that he found it amusing that he was discussing theology with a woman.

"Truthfully, I haven't found much evidence of it."

Andras squinted his eyes at her, as if he wasn't sure he'd heard her correctly. Then he smiled indulgently. "Undine, I find your sense of humor refreshing, but the reason I need to speak with you requires us to be serious. My squires have relayed to me several reports of an unusual nature."

"Unusual reports?" she prompted when he just stared at her and didn't continue speaking.

"Creatures have been seen in the waters off the coast."

She forced her expression to be one of mild curiosity.

"Creatures? You mean like whales and dolphins? That doesn't seem very unusual to me. You and I saw a dolphin very close to shore just a couple of days ago."

"I do not mean creatures that were fashioned by God. The fishermen talk of abnormal beings, half man and half fish, that have been seen inhabiting the waters surrounding this island."

"And you believed the fantasies of those poor people? That surprises me, Andras. They are, after all, peasants." She hoped that she was using the right buzz words. Andras was a knight, which meant he was a part of the nobility. Hadn't he been raised to look down on the working classes? At that moment she fervently hoped so.

"You are correct. They are peasants. I simply find their sightings interesting, especially because they seem to coincide with your appearance on our shores."

CC laughed. "Are you saying that you think that I am half fish?"

"Of course not."

"Then what are you saying?" she asked. At the mention of the sea, the longing within her sprang painfully alive, wearing away at her ability to be cordial to the overbearing knight.

"I know of your love for the sea. I am saying that you should be content with observing it from afar, and save excursions to the shoreline for quieter times."

CC squeezed a tight smile on her lips. "As always, I appreciate the concern you show for my welfare, but I'm sure it is nothing but foolish superstitions worrying the fishermen. After all, I was blown ashore by a storm. It's only logical that other sea creatures were blown off course, too."

"Other sea creatures?" Andras pounced. "You sound like you are saying you are a creature of the sea, too."

"Do I look like a creature of the sea?" she asked with a teasing smile.

"I ask that you give me your word that you will not walk by the shoreline alone again."

Andras's voice had an unmistakably hard edge to it, and CC's ability to be polite was rapidly unraveling when Isabel's grainy voice quivered across the chapel.

"It is well after midday and you have forgotten to eat again, Undine." The old woman limped toward them. She paused when she neared the statue of Mary, crossed herself and curtseyed reverently. Then she nodded respectfully to the knight.

"Thank you for reminding me, Isabel. Now that I think of it, I am very hungry."

"The mutton stew that will be served for this evening's meal is ready. Just this morning I harvested a fresh crop of mint," Isabel croaked happily.

"I promised to meet with the abbot and share with him the news I received from my men, but if you can wait I would be pleased to have an early evening meal with you, Undine," Andras said.

"I wish I could wait, but I think I should hurry and eat so that I can get back to work before the chapel is needed for vespers. I wouldn't want to create an inconvenience for the abbot."

Before he could argue Isabel chimed in. "Princess, I think it wise that you eat immediately." She shared a conspirators' look with Andras. "We must be certain the princess takes care with her health."

"Of course I would not put the princess's health in jeopardy. Perhaps we can take in the air this evening, Undine?"

Andras reached for her hand to kiss. Laughing nervously CC pulled it out of his reach.

"Oh, you don't want to do that. My hand is filthy." She made a big show of wiping her hands on her dirty robe. "A walk would be nice, if I'm not too tired."

"I will come to your chamber this evening after vespers, where I will pray that you are not too tired." His look was intense.

CC felt her face flush. Could he not just leave her alone? Thankfully, Isabel spoke up.

"Sir Andras, you need not trouble yourself. I know how you enjoy your chess games with the abbot. If the princess is not too fatigued, I will come with word from her." She looked quickly at CC. "If that is agreeable to the princess."

CC hurried over to Isabel. "Yes! There's no need for you to interrupt your time with Abbot William if I'm asleep on my feet. Thank you, Isabel. That was a wonderfully considerate idea." She linked her arm through the servant's and began walking with her toward the door. "I hope you have a good evening, Andras, and if I don't see you tonight I'm sure we'll be able to spend some time together tomorrow."

Andras stood silently in the shadowy church, watching the women disappear into the gardens. His expression was introspective and his full lips were turned down in irritation. Had she begun to avoid him, or was it only maidenly shyness coupled with her newly discovered devotion to the Holy Mother that seemed to be keeping her from him? The knight felt a stirring of anger as he pondered the question. His anger coupled with something else, something that whispered hypnotically deep within his mind. Andras's hands trembled, and he balled them into fists. Images flashed through his mind. Undine naked and slick with sweat . . . Undine on her knees before him . . . Undine crying his name aloud as his seed exploded within her . . .

Overwhelmed by the visions, Andras felt himself harden. His breath was ragged. He raked a hand through his hair. What was happening to him? He had never before experienced anything like his growing obsession with the princess. Perhaps the abbot was correct. His eyes narrowed so that the silver glow that stained them was almost undetectable. Sorceress or not, she was only a woman. When she belonged to him, he would purge the pagan taint from her soul, then he would satisfy his desire for her. She had no choice.

"THANK you," CC whispered as soon as they were out of range of Andras's hearing. "He doesn't seem to be able to take no for an answer."

"You are most welcome, but you must realize that few women would tell Sir Andras no," Isabel whispered back. "Are you quite certain that is your desire?"

"Absolutely. I don't want a husband who has to rule over and control me."

"So you have said before, but I still believe that there are few men of any other kind." Isabel looked closely at her. "At least not in this world."

"If there's not, I won't have any husband at all. I'm a human being, not a piece of property."

"So young and headstrong," Isabel clucked.

"Where I'm from we call it having good sense and a backbone."

Isabel's look was clearly disbelieving.

They were halfway across the voluminous gardens before CC noticed how murky the day had become.

"Is it really that late? It looks like the sun is setting already."

"It is late for your midday meal, but the sun is not yet setting. There is a storm coming." Isabel squinted up at the rolling clouds. "It is odd, normally my leg warns me of a storm long before I see clouds. Today it did not. It is almost as if the change of weather was suddenly conjured."

Not wanting to travel down that line of thinking, CC asked, "What happened to your leg?"

Isabel looked surprised at the question, but she answered without hesitation. "I was born with a twisted limb. My father wanted to dispose of me on the hillside, but I was the only girl child my mother had born, and she was quite old. She would not part with me."

CC was shocked at the matter-of-fact way Isabel spoke of something so horrifying.

"That's awful."

"A girl child with a twisted limb is of no use. My father knew no man would marry me." Isabel shrugged. "It is a blessing that I have a certain skill with cooking. When my youngest brother's beautiful wife gave birth to their fifth healthy child, she said there was no room for a crippled sister in their home. My other brothers felt the same. It was fortuitous that the monastery needed a cook. They took me in. I have been here since."

"Do you ever see your family?"

Isabel shook her head. "My mother and father are long dead, and my brothers do not visit. My family is here."

"The monks?" CC asked.

Isabel cackled and patted her hand. "Goodness no! The other women. We are all each other's only family now."

"I don't really have any family here, either," CC said.

Isabel paused on the threshold to the kitchen, where homey smells and sounds enveloped them. She turned to CC and smiled warmly at the younger woman.

"You do now, Princess."

CC paced and paced and paced. She had already pulled the dresser under the window. For what felt like the zillionth time she hitched up her chemise and climbed on top of it. She studied the fading evening. Gaea's clouds were rolling in from the west, directly over the tumultuous ocean. They were low-hanging and reminded CC of a giant gray comforter being pulled over the sky. The setting sun was certainly obscured, but was it dark enough yet? She didn't think so. She could still see most of the way down the side of the cliff, which meant if anyone happened to be looking seaward, they would be able to see her if she was making her way down the side of that cliff. And she couldn't be sure that Andras wouldn't be looking seaward after the fishermen had aroused suspicion in him.

CC sighed and rubbed her temples. It seemed her heart pounded there in time with the distant crashing of the surf. Her body was a throbbing shell of need; she ached for the waters and for her lover. *Dylan*. Just thinking his name sent a shiver of anticipation low in her stomach.

Patience, she told herself firmly. Just a few more minutes and it'll be dark enough. She turned and sat on top of the dresser, resting her head against the windowsill. She'd lasted this long, she could certainly wait a little longer.

At first the day had felt like it would never end, so CC had been shocked when the Brothers began filling the chapel for vespers, and she realized that it must be late evening. Quietly, she had piled her cleaning supplies in a shadowed corner, wiped her hands on her very grimy robes and slipped out the side entrance before Abbot William or Andras could accost her.

She had stopped at the kitchen long enough to grab another bowl of Isabel's excellent stew and a goblet of wine. The ladies were at their busiest, cleaning up the evening meal and beginning preparations for the next day. It took some doing, but she persuaded Isabel that she really didn't need any help bathing and undressing. The old woman obviously didn't like it, but when CC promised that she really just wanted to get out of her dirty clothes and crawl into bed, Isabel acquiesced, assuring CC that she would make her excuses to Andras.

CC knew that the circles under her eyes had darkened to bruises; the need inside her was making her feel weak and nauseous. But after she had washed the filth from her body, she forced herself to eat all of the stew and drink the entire goblet of wine. The wrenching ache was still there, but a full stomach made her feel less nauseous and dizzy.

A sound turned her attention back to the view outside the window. CC smiled. "Thank you, Gaea," she said.

Rain was falling in the comforting patter of a gentle mist, swallowing the last of the evening light. Quickly, CC sat on the windowsill, found her toehold, and dropped quietly to the soft grass below the window. Gaea's rain was a cool caress against her feverish skin, and for a moment she stood on the edge of the cliff with her arms held straight out and her head thrown back, letting the water of the goddess soothe her body and soul. Keeping the image of Dylan's dive from the side of the cliff in her mind, she balled up her chemise with one hand so that her long legs were free to run, then she moved with unerring certainty down the winding sheep path.

Dylan! She used all of her mental strength to call to him. *I'm coming! Please be there!*

Rocky ground gave way to sand and she ran to her familiar log, pulling off her shift with shaking hands. She kicked off her slippers and hurried to the shoreline. When her feet touched the water she paused, suddenly unsure.

"Do not make me wait, my love." Dylan's voice carried over the waves, surreal and disembodied.

"I can't see you." At the sound of his voice, CC's breath caught and her stomach tightened.

"But I can see you. You are a white goddess of beauty, fashioned of long, curving lines and softness. Come to me, my goddess," Dylan said.

With two quick steps CC ran and leapt, diving into the surf. Before her outstretched hands touched the water she felt the exquisite burning begin at her waist and shoot down through her legs. A rush of power followed the burning as the inhuman strength of her tail propelled her forward and then up. She broke the surface laughing.

The merman materialized out of the mist in front of her. Tonight his long, dark hair was free, and it fell in a thick, damp wave around his shoulders. Dylan's exotic beauty and the erotic sense of maleness that surrounded him struck her, and she felt a thrill of excitement at his nearness. He drifted close.

"I have missed you, Christine."

"You were just with me last night," she teased.

"I have discovered that the more I am near you, the more I want you. You belong at my side, and I at yours." His voice reminded her of dark chocolate—rich and sensual.

She reached up and wound her arms around his neck, loving the way his boyish smile made his lips curve when he took her in his arms.

"I don't think I could have stayed away from you another second," she said as his face tilted down to hers.

Their lips touched in a gentle kiss as they became reacquainted with the taste and touch of one another.

"Not a moment went by today when I did not wish that you were here beside me," Dylan said as he rested his forehead against hers while his hands caressed the long, smooth line of her back.

"I tried not to think about you. I was afraid if I thought about you too much, I would throw myself off the side of the cliff and into the ocean like you did." She snuggled against him, wanting to get as close as possible.

CC could feel the tremor of emotion that ran down his body. Then the merman tightened his grip on her and she opened her mouth to him. Their tongues met and teased. CC couldn't stop the hum of desire that escaped from the back of her throat. She felt Dylan's muscles quiver in response and the kiss deepened. CC ran her hands down his shoulders, skimming over his firmly muscled arms and chest. He was slick and warm, soft skin and hard muscle all wrapped enticingly together.

CC pressed her body against his and jerked back in surprise when she felt their tails entwine.

Dylan looked down at her questioningly.

"I . . ." CC hesitated, feeling a little foolish. She cleared her throat.

"I've never . . ." She trailed off, pointing down at the part of their bodies that was submerged under the water.

Understanding cleared Dylan's questioning look. He touched her face. "Remember last night? I was afraid, too."

"You were afraid?" she asked, incredulous. "It certainly didn't seem like it."

His smile was gentle. "Making love to you as a human man was an experience I will remember always."

CC pressed her face into his palm. "I want you now as badly as I did in my human body. I'm just nervous." She took a breath and met his eyes. "The truth is, even though I said that we fit together perfectly in any form, I'm really not sure what to do."

He smiled at her and brushed her lips lightly with his. "Will you trust me tonight, as I trusted you last night, Christine?"

Without hesitation she nodded.

"Then let me teach you."

This time she was able to smile at him. "Well, I already know you're an excellent teacher."

He took her hand in his. "Then let me teach you how mer-folk make love."

CC nodded again, this time breathlessly.

Dylan pulled her under the waves and they swam side by side into deeper water. Before they surfaced, the merman stopped and turned to her, but, instead of taking her in his arms, he held her out, almost half an arm's length away from his body. First, he kissed the palm of her hand. Then he touched her cheek, letting his hand slide down her long neck to her shoulder, then on down to gently cup her breast. Teasingly, he ran his palm over her nipple, which puckered under his caress. But his hand didn't stay at her breast, instead it moved down over her rib cage to the curve of her waist. When his hand met her mer-flesh, his caress changed. Instead of his palm, he used his fingertips to touch her with featherlike strokes, which swirled enticingly down and around her hips.

His fingers were fire. Dylan's touch was like nothing she had ever experienced—it was so incredibly different from having her legs caressed by a man. When he stroked that soft, glowing skin, his touch was magnified. It carried through every part of her mer-body, like his fingertips were superconductors for erotic sensation, and she was his conduit. As the newness of unexplored sensations surged the length of her body, CC felt weak and powerful at the same time. She closed her eyes, overwhelmed by the intensity of the feeling.

No, Christine. Dylan's voice came gently into her mind. *Do not close your eyes. Watch me touching you. Look how incredibly beautiful you are.*

CC opened her eyes. Dylan kissed her gently again, then he let his body drift down, so that his hands and his mouth could explore the rest of her. His mouth traveled from her breasts to the softness of her belly. When the warm heat of his mouth slid to her mer-flesh she had to hold tightly to his shoulders to steady herself.

Amazed, she felt herself open to him as his tongue moved down her body, coaxing and teasing alive sensations that she hadn't even imagined possible. She watched him love her and the last of her trepidation died under the heat of his touch. She gazed at her body and at the astonishing creature who held her so intimately, and she realized that it truly didn't matter what form their bodies reflected—it was love that anchored her to him, not a body or a time or place.

Dylan's mouth and hands continued to work their magic, and CC's ability for rational thought splintered. All she could do was to hold tightly to Dylan and experience the sensations that surged through her body. His touch merged with the soft pressure of the water that surrounded them until it seemed to CC that even the ocean was making love to her. Suddenly, her mind fragmented as an orgasmic rush of electricity rippled through her body.

Dylan cradled her within his arms and pulled her to the surface. He kissed her deeply. CC felt so liquid that she almost believed that her body could dissipate and become a part of the seas, and only Dylan's touch kept her connected to the physical world. They drifted in the ocean, hidden by the loving caress of the goddess's rain.

"Did that please you, my love?" he whispered against her lips.

"You please me, Dylan, more than I could ever tell you. It was a good thing that we were underwater; I think if air had touched me I might have combusted."

Dylan laughed. "Your nervousness must be gone."

"Forever." She grinned, then playfully took his bottom lip between her teeth and pulled gently. His moan of response brought to her a rush of new pleasure. "Now I want to please you," CC said.

She reached between them and took his already hard flesh in her hand. Stroking his shaft, she felt him throb and pulse with need. His breathing deepened sharply and his eyes closed.

"No," she said, her voice thick with the power of seduction. "Don't close your eyes. I want you to watch me touch you, too."

Dylan's gaze was hot as he watched her hand slide up and down his length. She kissed him again, then let her body drift down under the water until she took his golden flesh in her mouth. She felt him quiver as she let her tongue and lips work together. When she took him deeply into her mouth, his gasp of pleasure sent a thrill of desire through her. She loved the taste of him. He was salt and sea and the musky tang of an aroused man. And he was beautiful.

Abruptly, she felt him tug at her shoulders and she allowed him to pull her up. She found his mouth, and heat exploded within her at the ragged intensity of their kiss. She felt his hardness against her. Instinctively, she reached down to guide him within her, but Dylan stopped her.

"Wait, love. There is more," he said between broken breaths as she kissed the firm line of his jaw and slid her tongue teasingly down his neck.

"How could there be more than this?" She pressed against him.

"Watch," he said, his eyes dark with passion and promise.

Dylan unwound one hand from where it had been buried in her hair. Raising his arm he drew a circle in the air above them. CC's eyes widened in surprise as the ocean around them started to swirl in response.

"I command a bed in which to love our princess!"

Dylan's voice was filled with power, and it echoed against the misty night. As he spoke the seething water changed. It bubbled and frothed and somehow hardened until the two mer-creatures were buoyed up on a bed of aqua sea foam where they lay in each other's arms. It was as if they were resting inside a crested wave where Dylan had somehow halted time and the elements.

"You have magic," CC gasped.

"My magic is you, Christine."

Dylan kissed her, letting his hands move down her body to cup her breasts and then stroke her glowing flesh until CC moaned in response.

"Now, please," she panted. "Don't make me wait anymore."

Dylan shifted his weight until he lay over her, holding himself up on his forearms. When she reached down to guide him into her, he was powerless to resist.

"Christine!" he gasped her name as her heat tightened slickly around him.

They moved together easily, finding a rhythm that was at first slow and gentle. CC marveled at how well they fit. His body pressed against hers, and everywhere they touched sparks of sensation tingled through her skin. She ran her hands over the taut muscles of his arms, amazed at his power and how he trembled under her touch. Then their rhythm quickened, and CC strained upward to meet his thrusts. Her hands found the hard ridges of his back, and she let her fingernails tease, before she locked her arms around him, pressing him more firmly against her.

"I cannot wait," Dylan moaned.

"Then don't. Please, Dylan!" she urged.

With a last, powerful thrust CC felt Dylan begin to throb within her, and when he shouted her name she felt her own body explode in response. As her sense of reality fragmented into the realm of sensation she held tightly to Dylan, trusting him to bring her safely back to earth.

Chapter Twenty-one

"I love you, Christine."

She must have fallen asleep, because Dylan's voice woke her. At first CC thought they were still lying on the bed of sea foam, but the sound of waves breaking against the shore around them and the velvet feel of sand under her hip made her realize that she and Dylan had drifted to shore. She was still nestled against his chest and he lay semireclining, with his back against one of the many smooth rocks that peppered the shore.

"I'm so glad," she said and stretched languidly. Then she laughed.

"What?" he asked.

"I was just thinking that I feel like a satisfied cat, which seemed kind of funny under the circumstances." She gestured at their entwined tails. Then she raised her eyebrows at him. "You do know what a cat is, don't you?"

He tugged a wet strand of her hair playfully. "It is a feline creature that is closely allied to human women." He looked introspective for a moment, like he was remembering something, then he added, "They are fond of eating fish." His face split, and he laughed, too.

"Not that we're fish," CC said between giggles.

"Certainly not. You are Goddess of the Seas," he amended good-naturedly.

"That must make you," she finished with a flourish, "God of the Seas!"

Dylan's face instantly changed. It took on a guarded expression that caused CC a pang of anxiety. He hesitated before he spoke, and when he did his words sounded heavy, as if they were weighed down by the sadness of painful memories.

"No, Christine. We are different. My mother was a simple water nymph who preferred rivers and streams to the ocean. My father was a human. When my mother became pregnant she went to Lir and asked that she be granted a human form so that she could spend her life with her human lover. Lir agreed, but when my mother left the waters my father rejected her." Dylan's jaw tightened, and he looked away from her. "He already had a wife and a family. He had no use for a sea creature and her bastard offspring. My mother returned to the waters, which is where I was born. But she never found contentment. She was forever returning to the river where she had met and mated with my father. When he failed to return she killed herself. Lir allowed me to stay in his crystal palace while I was young out of love for Undine, who was my playmate. When I grew to adulthood he granted me the responsibility of overseeing the waters where they merged, river and sea. I think the great sea god hoped that under my watchfulness no other river nymphs would be lost to the lust of humans. But I am not the son of immortals; I am not as you are. Perhaps you did not realize that. Forgive me for not explaining our differences to you earlier." He wouldn't meet her eyes.

"Dylan." She took his chin in her hand, forcing him to look at her. His face was tight and withdrawn, but she could see the pain reflected in his eyes. "I'm sorry about your mother, and it makes me sad about your father, but it could never change what I feel for you. How could you believe that could matter to me?"

"You are Goddess of the Sea. I do not have even a palace or a realm to offer you."

"Yeah, I know all about being offered a realm—Sarpedon already did that," she said fiercely. "And I'm not interested." She nodded her head toward the monastery. "And there's a knight up there who has a castle to offer me," she scoffed. "I'd rather be trapped on land than accept their kind of love. Or, better yet, I'd rather have no lover at all than what they offer."

At the mention of the other two males Dylan's jaw clenched, and she could feel his body tense against her.

"I want what you offer me," she said.

"But I have nothing to offer you," he said miserably.

CC splayed her open hand on his chest over his heart. "You have this."

"No," Dylan's voice was thick with emotion. "I do not even have a heart. It was lost to you lifetimes ago."

"Don't ever think it's lost, Dylan. I'll keep it safe. Always." She pulled him down to her and their kiss was filled with the tenderness of true love.

"For an eternity," he said.

"Yes, for eternity," she agreed. "And I want to stay with you. Here, in the water, in this form, forever."

Dylan's look of joy was quickly shadowed by worry. When he spoke his voice was calm and filled with the hardness of purpose.

"I will protect you from Sarpedon," he said. "I will not allow him to harm you."

Remembering the raging, insane power of the gigantic merman, CC felt a stab of fear. "No! You won't have to. Gaea is going to Lir. She'll work everything out; she just asks that we be a little patient. She said Lir has some problem with another goddess who's taking his attention right now."

"I am not God of the Sea, but I do have some power of my own, Christine." Dylan's expression had darkened, and CC felt the deep, constant strength that rested beneath the merman's kind exterior.

"I know you do! But Sarpedon is crazy, and he's getting more and more bizarre. He scares me, Dylan. Please let Gaea handle it. I couldn't bear it if anything happened to you."

Dylan opened his mouth to argue, but CC silenced him by pressing a finger against his lips.

"Promise me you'll stay away from him."

When he didn't answer her, the stab of fear turned to panic. Her mind whirred while she searched for something she could say to convince him. Then she knew.

"If something happened to you I would be forced to marry the knight so that I could stay on land, away from Sarpedon's realm," she said simply. She hated that her words caused the flash of pain that crossed the merman's face, but fear for his life overrode her desire to protect his feelings.

"I promise you I will not seek out Sarpedon. But I also promise you I will not allow him to take you from me."

She smiled at him, trying to lighten his mood. "Do you really think it would be so easy to take me?"

Begrudgingly, Dylan's face relaxed, and he smiled back at her.

"No, I believe you would be very difficult to capture." He kissed her quickly. "You must have been a goddess in your old world, too."

CC's laughter sparkled.

"Well, I was a sergeant. I guess that's pretty close to a goddess, at least in some circles."

"What is this, *ser-geant?*" He pronounced the foreign word slowly, which made CC want to laugh again. "Where was your realm?"

"The Comm Center." She grinned. Then she sighed at his confused expression and tried to explain. "I was in the USAF, the United States Air Force. My, uh, I guess you'd call it my realm, was the United States. The air force is a branch of the armed forces that protects my realm's freedoms. I worked in the communications part of the USAF—making sure different people and countries got the information they needed to make wise decisions."

Dylan nodded his head. "A messenger goddess protecting her realm. Yes, that suites you. I would have guessed as much."

CC opened her mouth to try and explain that there really were no goddesses in the USAF, but she sighed again and stayed silent. Hadn't she just been trying to convince Isabel that there was magic inside of each woman? So why couldn't she take that belief one step further and claim the goddess within every woman?

A wonderful thrill swept through her as her thoughts touched upon a belief so ancient that she could feel the depths of her soul leap in response. That was it! Each woman must hold some part of the Divine Feminine deep within her. CC wanted to shout with the discovery.

"Yes," she said joyously. "You're right. I am a goddess."

Dylan didn't look surprised at all. "I wish I could visit your realm of the United States Air Force."

CC almost choked as a mental image of Dylan in Oklahoma flashed into her mind.

"Well," she said quickly. "It's in the middle of a land that's far from the ocean. There's really no way to swim there." Even if we were in the same century, she finished the sentence silently.

"I would have to have legs again," Dylan said thoughtfully. "Having legs was such an unusual experience."

CC tried not to laugh.

"I do not think we can ever go back," Dylan said.

CC shook her head. "I seriously doubt it."

The merman studied her. "Will you miss it? What of your family there?"

CC took a deep breath. She had been avoiding thinking about her parents. Now homesickness filled her. Yes. She would miss them. She loved them. But . . . her gaze traveled out over the fog-covered water. The soft fingers of the surf caressed her body.

The realization came swiftly to her mind. She belonged here.

She had left home when she was so young because she had never felt like she really belonged, and she had been traveling all of her adult life trying to find someplace where she truly fit in. The air force had been satisfying, she realized, not just because she enjoyed her work, but because she never stayed in one place long enough to begin to feel the discomfort of not belonging. While her peers were settling down, getting married and having children, she had been living the nomadic life of a woman searching for home. Deep within her she knew she had finally found that home.

She touched Dylan's cheek. "Yes, I'll miss my parents, but it's time for me to grow up and move on." She remembered their Silver Cruise schedule with a poignant smile. "They'll be fine. They have each other. And this is where I belong."

The monastery bells began their lazy morning toll. CC felt each clang as if it was a physical thing.

"I wish you would stay," Dylan said, his voice sounding strained.

CC pressed her head against his chest. "There's nothing I want more." Except to keep you safe, she thought. "But I promised Gaea that I would be patient and wait for her to fix things with Lir."

"You must keep your word to the goddess." Dylan's voice was muffled as he buried his face in her hair.

"It can't be too much longer. You should have seen Gaea today; she was magnificent. There's just no way Lir will be able to resist her. Soon she'll come to me and tell me that everything's fine, and I'll run down that cliff and swim to you, and whatever human is watching can just go straight to hell if they don't like it!"

"Do not place yourself in danger," Dylan said sharply. "You are right. We can be patient."

CC kissed the corner of his mouth. "You'll be waiting here in case I can slip away?"

Dylan cupped her chin in his hand. "For an eternity, Christine. I will wait for you for an eternity. Never forget that."

"I couldn't, Dylan," she whispered.

They kissed—a long, gentle kiss that held the sweet promise of more to come.

"I have to go." When she spoke the words aloud she felt the morphing burn begin at her waist, and in an instant the sand gave way under her naked legs.

Dylan smiled sadly and ran a hand caressingly down the length of one of her newly re-formed legs.

"You know I do love to touch your legs."

"Apparently men don't change much, no matter their form." She smiled, trying to keep her tone light. She kissed him quickly before she stood.

"I love you, Dylan," CC said. Then she turned and walked slowly to the log that held her clothes.

"And I love you, Christine. Always." Dylan's voice echoed around her. She heard the wet slap of his body against the water as the ocean reclaimed him.

The goddess's rain had finally stopped, and the lightening of the sky told CC that she should hurry, but her steps were slow and leaden. Her feet felt awkward after the powerful grace of her mermaid body. And each step took her away from Dylan. She forced herself to navigate the final twists of the path. As she climbed up onto the grassy space outside the monastery wall, she spoke a prayer aloud to her goddess.

"Please hurry. I can't stand this separation much longer."

"The abbot was wise when he told me to beware your beauty. I see now that it clouded my mind into believing you were simply an innocent maid." Andras's voice was hard and angry as he and his two squires stepped from the shadows of the monastery wall.

CC jumped, and her hands automatically splayed to cover her breasts, which were clearly visible through the sheer, damp chemise.

"Andras! You startled me," CC blurted, her heart pounding painfully.

"Yes, I imagine being caught would startle you."

"Caught?" She straightened her spin, irritated at the arrogant tone of his voice. The way the three men leered at her overrode her rush of fear at the possibility of arousing the spirit of Sarpedon. "At what do you think you've caught me?"

"Innocent maidens do not cavort at night naked and alone."

She noticed that his eyes maintained their normal color, but he squinted and peered around her like he expected to discover a busload of sailors she had been entertaining.

"Cavort? I was climbing up from the cliffside path. There was very little cavorting involved. And I'm certainly not naked."

"It is improper for you to be seen in your chemise, and it is obvious from the state of your chamber that you escaped through your window," Andras challenged.

"I didn't want to ruin my dress," CC said reasonably. "And I didn't *escape*. I used my window because I didn't want to wake any of the Brothers."

"Enough talk!" Andras snapped, grabbing her arm painfully. "You shall return to your chamber now. We will speak of this with the abbot after he has completed morning mass and when you are properly clothed." He started to pull her toward the front entrance of the monastery.

CC dug in her heels and wrenched her arm back. Andras whirled to face her. His face was flushed with anger and the hand that didn't hold her arm was closed in a fist as if he wanted to strike her. CC swallowed her fear and pulled strength from deep within her. As she spoke she felt the protective warmth of the amber amulet against her breast.

"Don't ever touch me without my permission. I am still a princess and even though this is not my realm I am not totally without power here. I will not tolerate such treatment," she hissed at him. Her body felt hot and her head tingled like energy was rushing into her from above.

The fierce look on the knight's face faltered as he watched Undine transform. Seconds before she had been a wet, nearly naked woman, who looked scared and alone. Now she stood with her back straight and her chin held high. Her drying hair crackled around her and she seemed to glow with radiant power. Unexpectedly, a little shiver of foreboding crawled the length of his spine. *Sorceress!* The word whispered through his mind and he loosened her arm as if it burned his hand.

"That's better," she said. "Now I will be pleased to return to my chamber; I was already on my way there when you interrupted me." CC turned and strode confidently down the path to the monastery gate. The three men followed silently behind her.

The gate was unbarred, and CC pushed it open without waiting for the knight. Expecting the courtyard to be deserted, she was surprised to see Isabel, Lynelle, Bronwyn and Gwenyth huddled nervously against the wall near the gate.

"Oh, Undine!" Isabel's words came out in a rush of air.

But before she could say any more, Andras broke in. "You were right to report her absence. Your diligence and loyalty will be rewarded."

His words stabbed her heart. Isabel had betrayed her? She remembered how cold and judgmental Isabel had been when they had first met, but CC had thought those days were over, that Isabel and the other women had begun to care for her as she had them. She forced her face to remain expressionless as she continued woodenly across the courtyard to the entrance of the hallway that led to her room. She wanted to rush back to the group of women and yell, *Why? I thought we were friends—family even!* But she refused to give Andras the satisfaction of seeing her pain.

At the door to her room Andras spoke belligerently to her. "The abbot will expect to see you as soon as mass is finished. I will send for you then." He paused before adding, "I assume you will not be making any further lone trips today, but for your own safety my men will see that you remain in your chamber until you are summoned."

CC met his eyes with her own hard gaze. "For my protection, is it? It sounds to me like you're appointing jailers."

Without waiting for a reply, she entered her room, giving the door a resounding slam behind her.

Chapter Twenty-two

CC sat on her narrow cot and hugged her legs against her chest. Her anger was gone, and it had taken with it most of her princessly bravado. Andras had stationed one of his men outside her door and another outside her window.

"It's a jail," she muttered, fighting down a sudden sense of panic. What would happen if she was still being watched this closely in three days? Her stomach fluttered nervously. Gaea had said if she didn't return to her mermaid form that she would die, and after experiencing the throbbing ache that filled her body every third day as she waited impatiently to change, she knew all too well the truth of the goddess's warning. Trapped, alone in this room, she would die a horrid, painful death. And she would never see Dylan again. She shuddered. No wonder the monks called it a cell.

A hesitant knock sounded against her door, and before CC could call out, the guard opened it for Isabel. The old woman was carrying a tray that held a goblet of wine and a hunk of fresh bread and fragrant white cheese. She nodded to the surly guard, who gave CC a sharp look before backing from the room and closing the door. Isabel limped to the dresser, where she placed the tray.

In an abnormally loud voice she said, "Princess, I brought you something to break your fast. And it is time you readied yourself to meet with the good abbot." Isabel brought the goblet over to CC, who took it and drank the sweet white liquid, grateful for the soothing effect it had on her throat and her nerves.

"I did not mean to betray you, Undine," Isabel whispered urgently, almost causing CC to choke on a swallow of wine. The old woman leaned closer to CC, her voice low and soft. "I was worried about you—you looked so tired and wan yesterday. When my duties in the kitchen were complete, I came to check on you. I knocked, and when there was no answer I was afraid that you were not simply sleeping deeply, but that you were truly ill. When I found the room empty I could only think that you were somewhere alone and perhaps you were very sick. I rushed from your room to check the chapel, hoping that you had returned to the Virgin Mother's statue for comfort, but on the way there Sir Andras discovered me. He saw that I was troubled, and asked if he could aid me." Isabel tightened her lips and shook her head in obvious disgust. "I should have remembered your misgivings about the knight. Instead, I explained my worry. When you were not in the chapel, he became incensed. His anger was terrible." Isabel's eyes were bright with unshed tears. "Forgive me, Undine."

CC took one of the old woman's gnarled hands. "There's nothing to forgive," she whispered. "It's my fault. I should have confided in you, then you would have known not to worry."

The sound of a man's sudden cough from outside her window caused both women to narrow their eyes.

"Here now, eat some of this bread and cheese while I comb through your hair, Princess," Isabel croaked, raising her voice so that it carried easily through the window.

"Please do," CC said in a loud, imperious tone. "I expected you some time ago. I have been sitting here waiting. It seems I am to be treated with disrespect, even by servants." CC curled her nose and made a face at the window. Isabel covered her mouth to stifle a laugh.

"Disrespect was not my intention, Princess," Isabel blared.

"Oh, do stop speaking. I want to enjoy my breakfast and my coiffure in silence!" CC commanded.

"As you wish, Princess," Isabel shouted.

The two women rolled their eyes at each other.

CC chewed the bread and cheese as Isabel brushed gently through the tangles in her long hair. She felt relieved at the knowledge that Isabel and the other women had not betrayed her, and her mind whirled with possibilities. Abruptly, she turned her head, interrupting Isabel's grooming. The old woman looked questioningly at the princess.

"Do you think that I am evil, Isabel?" CC asked, being careful to keep her voice low enough that it wouldn't be overheard by her guards.

Isabel's furrowed brow raised. "No," she answered quietly. "Some of your beliefs are rather odd, but your heart is kind and your love for the Mother is true."

CC nodded. "If I asked you to trust me, even if what I tell you will seem unbelievable and maybe even a little frightening, would you?"

Isabel's eyes widened until she looked like an ancient bird, but she nodded her head and whispered a single word. "Yes."

"Then listen, and I'll tell you everything."

CC began with the night of her birthday and worked forward from there. She was amused to hear that Isabel found the idea of an inanimate creation that flew through the skies more disturbing than learning about Sarpedon or the fact that CC was really Undine who was really a mermaid, although CC told her she agreed completely with her terrified reaction to the airplane. When CC described her love for Dylan, Isabel nodded and smiled thoughtfully. The only thing CC was not completely honest about was Gaea. She was afraid that the old woman would not be able to accept the goddess. CC didn't leave her out of the story, she simply changed the goddess's name. When she spoke of Gaea, she called her the Holy Mother. Isabel believed totally in the power of the Virgin, and she didn't question CC's bond with her.

"So you must claim sanctuary here until the Holy Mother can be certain that Sarpedon is no longer a threat. Then you can be united with your Dylan," Isabel said after CC had finally stopped talking. The old woman's hands were clasped firmly together in her lap as if to keep them from trembling, but her gaze was bright and steady.

"And I have to have the freedom to be able to get to the ocean," CC added.

"I think the other women and I can aid you with your freedom," Isabel said thoughtfully. She smiled mischievously at CC. "The men are much too busy and important to spend their time watching a lowly woman, even if she is a princess. It is a task better performed by women."

CC felt a rush of gratitude and relief. "Thank you, Isabel. I know how difficult this must be for you to believe. It means so much that you trust me."

Isabel squeezed the young woman's shoulder. "Do not think on it. Women must help one another." Then her face twisted with worry. "But I am concerned about your safety."

"Sarpedon can't hurt me as long as I'm on land, well, at least not directly."

Isabel shook her head. "It is not his evil spirit that I fear most. I have heard rumors. Some of the Brothers are saying that you are a sorceress, and that it is your connection with the devil that caused Sir Andras's apoplexy. Now that you can no longer trust the protection of the knight, I am afraid of what could happen if the abbot thinks he has enough evidence to take you to trial for witchcraft."

A chill moved down CC's spine, and she searched frantically through her memory. Did they burn supposed witches in A.D. 1014? Isabel's grim expression said that it was very likely that they did. CC swallowed hard.

"Evidence?" CC's whisper came out as a croak.

"Yesterday he sent several Brothers to scour the surrounding countryside to see if there have been any unexplained illnesses or deaths."

CC's eyes widened in horror. "I don't mean any offense to your time, Isabel, but aren't most illnesses or deaths hard to explain or linked with superstitious beliefs?"

"Yes, and it does not end there. The Brothers are also to look for evidence of cows or goats that have gone dry, babies that will not stop crying once the sun sets, and the appearance of more than three black cats."

"But any of those things would be easy to find—or easy to fabricate." CC felt the blood leave her face.

"Then we must fabricate evidence that says you must not be harmed," Isabel said firmly.

CC chewed her bottom lip. Think! she told herself. She was an intelligent, independent woman from the modern world. Surely she could figure out a way to stay safe. She just needed to think of it as a puzzle that had to be solved—then put the pieces together . . .

And a wonderfully simple plan came to her. She sat up straight and smiled at the confused-looking Isabel.

"Isabel, what do you know about the Wykings?"

Chapter Twenty-three

A hard fist knocked brusquely on the door.

"The abbot summons Princess Undine," the guard's voice rasped from the hall.

CC and Isabel looked at each other. Isabel nodded.

"Tell him I am coming," CC snapped. Then she whispered to Isabel. "Isn't it ironic? I'm supposed to be royalty, yet he's summoning me. Talk about princess envy."

"You are a princess." Isabel smoothed an invisible wrinkle from the front of CC's dress. "I do not think I have ever told you how lovely you are, and that loveliness comes from more than these jewels or your beautiful gown."

CC felt her eyes fill. "Thank you, Isabel." She hugged the old woman, breathing in her comforting scent, which was a mixture of stew and freshly baked bread. "Your friendship means so much to me."

"As yours does to me, child. You have breathed life into this dreary place, and into me again; do not ever forget that."

CC nodded at her. "Let's get this over with. It's show time."

Isabel looked confused.

"It means it's time for us to start performing." CC grinned, and almost told her to "break a leg," too, but she didn't think they had time for more explanations.

Isabel's face hardened with resolve. "Show time," she whispered in perfect agreement, and both women stepped into the hall.

"Follow me to the abbot," said the stone-faced squire. "He and Sir Andras will receive you in his antechamber."

CC had no idea what an antechamber was, but she gave the man a curt nod and followed him. Isabel limped behind them. The squire led them through a maze of halls that threaded through a part of the monastery on the opposite side from which CC's little room was located. Just when she was thinking how hopelessly lost she was, the squire stopped in front of a large wooden door. He knocked quickly twice.

"Enter!" The abbot's high-pitched voice carried easily through the door.

CC hesitated only a moment, and then she strode into the room. It was a large chamber, and CC was surprised by how comfortable it appeared at first glance. A fire was burning cheerfully in a hearth that was large enough that four or five men could have stood at full height inside of it. There were several metal candleholders scattered around the room, mostly between groupings of well-upholstered chairs and polished side tables. Something about the walls of the room caught her attention and CC's gaze slid to them, then her eyes widened in disgust. Carved into the rock walls around the circumference of the room were intricate scenes of suffering, much like the carvings that decorated the exterior walls of the chapel. CC forced her eyes from them.

"You may approach, Princess Undine." The abbot made a delicate gesture with one hand.

He sat on a dais in an ornate chair, thronelike in its intricate design. It was placed at the far side of the room, so that it faced the other chairs and the entryway. Andras stood at his right hand, smug and silent. To his left were four monks. Only Abbot William met her eyes.

Ready for battle, CC walked purposefully forward. Isabel stayed inside the room, near the door.

"I was just admiring your lovely furnishings." CC swept a graceful finger at the chairs and sconces. "It pleases me to see such sumptuous things, even if it is a surprise to see them in a monastery."

The abbot's spine straightened at CC's words, and his pale cheeks flushed suddenly red, reflecting the crimson of his robe.

"They are gifts from my benefactor, and though I would be comfortable with less opulent furnishings, it would be rude to refuse them."

"Benefac*tor*?" CC's brows came together in confusion. "I understood that this monastery belonged to Sir Andras's mother, so wouldn't that make her a benefac*tress*?"

The knight spoke up quickly. "The monastery belonged to my mother's family and passed through her to my father at the time of their marriage." His handsome face twisted into a superior sneer. "Women cannot own property. What is a wife's is, by right and by law, always her husband's."

"How very convenient for the husband," CC said without glancing at Andras.

"We are not here to discuss the role of husbands and wives, no matter how badly you are in need of such instruction." Abbot William's voice was sharp. "We are here to solve the problem of your behavior, Princess Undine."

"Then this will be a short visit. I know of no problem with my behavior." CC inclined her head regally. "I hope you have a nice day, Abbot William."

But before she could turn to leave the abbot's voice shot out. The hatred in it chilled CC's blood.

"You will not leave until you have my permission to do so!"

CC froze, her eyes riveted on the abbot's florid face. She thought she could actually see the veins at his temples throbbing in anger. When he continued to speak, he did so through clenched teeth.

"Your behavior has been indiscreet and inappropriate. I believe evidence will come to light that you are a danger to this monastery and to those within it."

"How could that be? By your own standards, I am nothing more than a woman, and even though I am a princess, my function ultimately will be to belong to a man. What possible danger could I represent?" CC spoke quickly, her heart hammering so loudly that she was sure everyone could hear it.

The abbot smiled slyly, like she had just unknowingly stepped into the loop of a trap.

"You are correct that alone a woman is a helpless creature, fashioned only to serve man and to bear his body and his children. But it is that very weak and seductive nature that man must guard against. Remember, it was Eve's original sin that destroyed the paradise that God had created for man!" His voice had risen until the word *man* came out as a shriek. The monks at his side began to glance nervously around the room, as if looking for an escape or a hiding place. Andras was nodding his head in agreement, completely ignoring his mentor's crazed tone.

The outrage that had been simmering inside of CC for days finally boiled, and she slipped the noose of cordiality, allowing herself to truly speak her mind.

"Where I come from many of us look a little deeper into that particular Biblical story. If I remember correctly, Lucifer, who was described as God's most beautiful creation, tempted Eve. She resisted, but eventually gave in." CC shrugged her shoulders nonchalantly, but her eyes challenged the priest. "I think even the strongest among us has something by which he can be tempted, don't you Abbot? Anyway, Eve gave in to Lucifer's temptation. Then she went to Adam and offered him the fruit. And Adam basically said, *'Okay!'* He chose the forbidden—with no supernatural temptation, and without much resistance; he just automatically did what a woman told him to do. When you look at it logically, as I would think a *man* would, you come up with a much different conclusion about who committed the greater sin. At least I think most—"

"Silence!" The priest's shriek echoed off the disfigured stone walls. This time the monks literally cringed, and even Andras's eyes widened in surprise at the abbot's loss of control.

"You will not dare to speak such blasphemy in my presence. Your words are proof that you are in league with the Evil One. Since you first passed through our gates, you have brought darkness within. You shall be purged from this holy place, and by thus purging you from our midst, evil will be defeated once more." He pointed a shaking finger at the squire who hovered behind her. "Take her to her room to await her punishment."

Terror turned her stomach, but she held her chin high and in her most imperious voice she spoke for the first time directly to the knight.

"Sir Andras, please explain to the abbot that harming me would not be your most profitable course of action."

When the abbot started to speak, Andras lay a calming hand on his arm.

"Father," he soothed. "Let us hear her out."

"I have remembered my birthright. Harm me and know that you trifle with the only daughter of King Canute, conqueror and Lord of Vikings." Her voice was strong and filled with pride.

At her proclamation, Andras's body went very still, and the florid color of the abbot's face drained away like dripping wax.

CC's smile was arrogant. "I have already sent my own message to him. The fishermen were right in part of their reports; it's too bad that they were so clouded by superstition that they did not recognize that what they sighted were my people searching for the daughter of their beloved king. Last night they found me, and it was then that my memory returned. You know yourself that you accosted me as I finished my climb from the beach." Her laughter was sharp. "Why else would I be so drawn to the waters? They are my birthright. Soon my father will come for me." The anger in CC's voice filled the room. "If you harm me, he will loose his Berserkirs and they will destroy you."

The room was silent. Andras and the abbot exchanged furtive glances.

"If your father is King Canute and his men did come for you last night, why is it you remain here?" Andras shot the question at her.

CC scoffed indignantly. "A Viking princess does not steal away in the night like a lowly servant. I sent word to my father that I had been rescued and was uninjured. I knew he would want to come for me himself so that he could reward those who treated me well."

And punish those who did not . . .

The unspoken words seemed to hang powerfully in the electric air around CC.

"If you don't believe me your solution is simple. Just wait. If I'm telling the truth, my father will appear to claim me, and you will be rewarded. If I'm lying, and I don't have a powerful family, no one will come for me and you can *punish* me to your heart's content." CC raised one eyebrow at the knight. "And something tells me that you very much need my father's reward money."

The knight and the abbot exchanged another look, and CC was relieved to observe that the priest seemed to have brought himself under control.

"We would, of course, not wish to harm the daughter of a king," Abbot William said. He glanced again at Sir Andras, who nodded briefly. "We will continue to provide you sanctuary for the amount of time it should require your father to come for you."

"No more than a fortnight," Sir Andras added.

The abbot nodded solemnly. "A fortnight it is. If King Canute has not claimed you as his own within that time, I will have no choice but to put you on trial for heresy and witchcraft."

"I agree," CC retorted.

"Until King Canute comes to Caldei, you will remain in your chamber under guard. We must be certain that no harm befalls such a *valuable* lady," the priest said.

CC felt panic like a brand. She was going to be locked in her room? Her heart skittered in her chest.

She met the abbot's reptilian gaze. "I am a Viking princess—I demand more freedom than that. If you lock me in my room I will tell my father that you treated me like a prisoner and not a guest. He does not reward jailers."

"Undine." Andras's tone had lost its anger and had returned to being patronizing. "Surely you will agree that your safety is of the utmost concern to us, especially in light of the proclamation of your noble blood."

"Yes—"

Andras cut her off. "Good. Then you will understand that if you choose to leave your chamber you will be accompanied at all times by an armed guard."

CC raised her chin. "Am I so dangerous?"

"You are so protected."

"Oh, do not think that I'm without protection." She narrowed her eyes to slits and was pleased to see Andras's eyes widen in response.

"Enough, witch!" the priest spat. "We may have to tolerate your presence until your heathen father claims you, but we will not tolerate your blasphemous threats."

CC shook her head slowly side to side and gave the abbot a pitying look. "Why do you automatically assume a strong woman is evil? What happened to you to twist you into this?"

Abbot William held up a shaking hand, palm forward like he could ward off her words. "Escort the princess back to her chamber. Now!" he snarled.

Without waiting for the squire, CC turned and strode across the room. As she neared the door, Isabel made a spectacular show of cringing away from her and crossing herself. CC scoffed and made a dismissive wave in her direction. As the squire closed the door behind them, CC could hear Isabel's distinctive voice croaking, "Evil! I knew it from the first day I laid eyes on her! Evil!"

Isabel's performance made CC bite the inside of her cheek to keep from laughing as the nervous young squire led the way back to her chamber.

Chapter Twenty-four

CC wrenched open her door, startling the squire who stood guard outside.

"I want to go to the chapel, and I need help changing my clothes. Get that old servant, whatever her name is."

The squire blinked balefully at her, suddenly reminding her of a calf. She sighed. "Now! I don't have all the rest of the day to waste!" She slammed the door in his face.

"This princess stuff just gets easier and easier," she muttered to herself. His boots clinked smartly against the stone floor as he hurried down the hall, rushing to obey her command.

She paced while she waited for Isabel. She had been back in her room for hours, alone, under guard, with absolutely nothing to do except worry. She couldn't stand it anymore. Maybe if she spent time cleaning the chapel she could work off some of her tension, and if she got really lucky Gaea might even show up. The goddess certainly had been quiet lately, which was making CC more than a little uneasy.

Two theatrically hesitant knocks sounded on her door.

"Come in!" CC didn't have to pretend the frustration in her voice.

"You summoned me, Princess?" Isabel said as she limped with obvious reluctance into the room.

"Yes, yes, yes," CC said. "Hurry up and close the door. I'm going to go work in the chapel, and I need help changing."

CC saw the old woman give the squire a frightened look before she closed the door.

As soon as they were alone Isabel hurried over to her and the women embraced.

"You were spectacular!" Isabel spoke into CC's ear as she worked loose the intricate set of laces at the back of CC's outer garment.

"You weren't half bad yourself," CC whispered back, and the two women shared a grin. "But I can't sit here any longer. I have to stay busy, and cleaning the chapel will definitely keep me busy."

"I will bring your food to the chapel. It is well past midday." Isabel shook CC's shoulders. "You have missed another meal. How will you stay strong for your lover if you do not eat?"

"You're always so wise," CC said.

"And well it is that you remember it," Isabel scolded her fondly.

"What happened after I left?" CC whispered.

Isabel's hands stilled for a moment as she collected her thoughts. "The abbot wants to destroy you. That has not changed," she spoke grimly. "It is only the knight's influence, and the fear of retribution from the Vikings that keeps him from harming you."

"It seemed like Andras believed my story."

CC could feel the old woman's nod. "He covets King Canute's money, and he still desires you, but he is not a fool. He is sending for reinforcements from Caer Llion. He worries that even if you are returned safely to the Vikings, the king will decide to sack the monastery."

"Doesn't seem that there's much here to sack," CC muttered.

"Oh, you are wrong, Undine. The monks are well known for their fine wool and their fat, tasty lamb. Also, Abbot William has several ancient manuscripts that Brothers, specially chosen by him, meticulously copy."

"I didn't realize all that," CC said thoughtfully.

"The knight is acting wisely."

"Well, I never thought Andras was stupid, just narrow-minded."

"I agree with you," Isabel said.

"It's about time."

The old woman snorted.

"DO you *have* to follow me into the chapel, too?" CC asked the guard, who was walking a little behind her, carrying two buckets brimming with clean water. "I'm going to be in there working."

"I must stay with you at all times, Princess," the squire said mechanically.

"While I work I like to pray. Your presence will be interfering with my prayer time." She shot him a knowing look. "Are you married?"

Caught off guard by her question, he was too surprised not to answer. "Yes."

"Do you have any children?"

"Not yet, Princess."

"Well, in my country there is a belief that the Holy Mother can gift couples with children and can make men especially potent." She paused pointedly and let her glance drift briefly down his body before continuing. "*If* they please her. And, of course, she can do the opposite if they don't. I can't believe that the Holy Mother will be very pleased by you interrupting my prayer time."

"I would never want to interfere with the piety of one so devout. I will await you outside this door." The squire suddenly looked very pale.

"Thank you. I'm sure your sensitivity will be rewarded," CC said sweetly. Taking the buckets from him, she entered the dim sanctuary and breathed a sigh of relief when the door closed firmly behind her.

The laughter of the goddess greeted her.

"Oh, Daughter! Threatening that poor man with impotency. Really, I think that was somewhat harsh."

Gaea lounged on the floor in front of her statue, looking radiant in a long gown of sheer, sparkling silk the color of ripe green olives. Her hair curled around her waist and seemed to pool in a glistening carpet all around her.

The enormous sense of relief CC felt at the sight of the goddess didn't stop the sharp edge in her voice.

"I'm tired of being followed and watched and kept under guard."

Instantly, the weight of the buckets disappeared as invisible hands took them from her. They floated inches off the floor until they came to rest just where CC would have placed them herself. She smiled her gratitude at Gaea and felt her mood lighten, too.

"Thank you, Mother. That helps. And I'm sorry I snapped at you."

"It is understandable, young one," Gaea said indulgently. "So the abbot has you under guard? What has happened?"

Quickly, CC brought Gaea up-to-date on the events of the day. By the time she finished speaking the goddess's eyes were glowing with pride.

"You have done well, Daughter. You have found your way by using your own wits. I am pleased with you."

CC felt a wonderful rush of warmth at the goddess's praise.

"And I have news for you. Lir will be in these waters on the third night. There he will hear your petition and render judgment."

"But how did he sound? Did you tell him about Sarpedon and Dylan?"

"I have not spoken with the God of the Seas." Gaea tossed her hair back in irritation. "He is still embroiled in the problems of the Hawaiian deities."

"Then how do you know he's coming?" CC asked.

"I sent my messenger to him with my request that he come to us. His own messenger brought his reply just this morning." A shadow passed over the goddess's face, clouding her lovely features.

"But something's bothering you. Are you worried about what he'll decide?" CC asked nervously.

"No," Gaea said quickly. "I do not fear his judgment. Lir's wish has always been for Undine to love the waters and for her to choose to live there happily. Now he will have his wish. I do not believe that your rejection of Sarpedon's suit will change his feelings, especially after he understands that you have my full support."

"So you think Lir will keep Sarpedon from going after Dylan?"

Gaea patted her hand reassuringly. "Lir knows Dylan. He knows that the merman is honorable and kind. I believe that he will honor your choice. It will, undeniably, be an uncomfortable scene when he explains to Sarpedon that you have chosen another, but the word of the God of the Seas will be obeyed—and there are many willing nymphs from which young Sarpedon may choose."

"Then why the worried look?" CC pushed.

"You begin to know me too well, Daughter," Gaea said affectionately. Then she squinted her eyes thoughtfully. "Lir's choice of messenger was unusual. I have never known him to use any messenger but one of his handpicked dolphins or selkies, and this time he chose to send a sea eel. The creature did not even appear to be very intelligent." Gaea shrugged her shoulders. "Perhaps the trouble with those barbarous island gods has been more of a strain on him than I imagined."

"So it wasn't meant as a slight to us or a sign that he's mad or anything?"

"The Lord of the Seas would not slight the Mother of the Earth or her daughter." Gaea's eyes sparkled.

"I should have known better," CC said, giving the goddess a knowing look.

"Yes, you should have." Gaea winked back at her. Then her voice sobered. "In two days this part of your life will be over, and you will forever be a creature of the sea, mated with a merman. I will only ask you once more, Daughter. Are you certain of your choice? You need not think that the only human from which you have to choose is the knight. If you ask me to intercede, I will send forth a call that many men will answer. You could have your pick of them."

CC spoke slowly when she answered the goddess, but her words were firm and her decision was clear. "I know it should seem scary to me to leave the land forever, but the water calls me, Gaea. And, yes, I know that a lot of that is because this body's true form is not human, so it continually longs for the water." CC gazed steadily into Gaea's eyes, willing her to understand. "But I don't want to give that up. I love who and what I am when I'm a mermaid. And I love Dylan. It's like I've finally found the perfect mixture of magic in my life." CC pointed in the direction of the sea. "And it's out there."

The goddess's smile was bittersweet. "I will honor your choice, my daughter, as well as take pride in your strength."

"But, it's not like I'll be gone forever. I'll still get to see you!" CC exclaimed.

"Yes, Daughter. My cove will be waiting to welcome you, and I will always answer your call." She raised one brow and smiled mischievously. "Perhaps one day you will gift me with a land-loving granddaughter."

"How about several of them?" CC laughed.

Before Gaea could answer they were interrupted by Isabel's distinctly gravelly voice coming from the entrance of the chapel.

"Yes! If I need your protection from her witchcraft, I shall certainly call. But I must bring her food. If she weakens and dies it will not go well for us when her father, the king, appears." Isabel's gruff voice easily traveled the length of the chapel. She sighed theatrically before the guard closed the door behind her.

CC giggled and winked at Gaea. "She really should have been an actress; she's enjoying this a little too much."

Expecting the goddess to disappear as usual, CC turned to greet the old woman and took several steps toward her, intending to take the heavy tray from her. Isabel was limping down the side aisle, scanning all of the pews to be certain they were alone. When she saw there were no monks lurking around praying, her disgruntled expression shifted into a wide grin.

"I brought you a new kind of st—" The old woman stopped speaking. She was staring at something behind CC.

Confused, CC glanced over her shoulder to see what had startled Isabel. There stood Gaea, next to the statue of Mary. And yet it wasn't Gaea. The woman was very pretty, but she was most definitely mortal. Delicate wrinkles gave her face a comfortable, lived-in look, and laugh lines betrayed her good humor. She was clothed in simple robes of undyed linen. A brown shawl was draped over her head, hiding most of her coffee-colored hair, but what escaped the shawl was just beginning to show a fine weaving of silver. Despite the evidence of age, her face had a timeless look. She could have been twenty or forty, it was impossible to tell. She smiled at Isabel.

"Excuse me, Princess Undine. I did not realize that you were not alone." Isabel set the tray on a nearby pew and turned hastily to leave.

"Please, there is no need for you to go." Gaea's voice was melodic and accented much like Andras's. "My name is Galena. I came to Caldei to barter ewes for my father's flock. I heard word of the restoration of the Holy Mother, and I could not leave without visiting her shrine."

Isabel was studying Gaea with an intent expression of open curiosity. "Forgive me for saying so, but it is unusual that a father would allow a daughter to tend to his business."

"My father has no sons, and I have no husband. In his old age he is wise enough to trust me."

"See, I told you some men respect women," CC said, recovering her voice.

"You are correct, Princess, some men do," Gaea said with a soft smile. "But no matter the beliefs of men, women will always have a special power within themselves." Her gaze touched the gleaming statue. "I believe Mary would agree with me."

"You sound much like the princess," Isabel said.

Gaea's smile widened. "What a lovely coincidence, as is my visit today."

Isabel's eyes hadn't left Gaea's face. Suddenly, they widened in discovery. "Forgive me for staring, but you bear a striking resemblance to the statue of the Holy Mother."

Gaea's laughter was a musical sound. CC hoped that Isabel wouldn't notice that the flames of the candles surrounding the statue leapt and danced in response.

"Is that so surprising?" the goddess said. "Do you not believe that every woman carries the spark of the Divine Feminine within her?"

"I . . ." Isabel cleared her throat. "I have never heard it spoken so."

Gaea's voice was filled with compassion. "Come close. I have something to show the two of you."

On unsure feet Isabel let CC lead her to the disguised goddess's side.

Gaea held one hand out in front of her, palm down. "Place your hands beside mine."

Without hesitation, CC put her hand next to Gaea's, and Isabel followed suit.

"Look at how amazing we are, we three, as we reflect the three aspects of the Divine Feminine," Gaea said. She pointed to each of the women's hands in turn, beginning with CC's, which were shapely and unlined. "The maiden, lovely and young, with her life stretching before her, magical and new. She is vibrant and fresh, drawing the power of springtime to her."

Then she pointed at her own hand. It was stronger and the knuckles were already beginning to show lines. It was a hand that could do a full day's work and then comfort a sick child. "The mother, full and ripe, filled with the power of summer and autumn. She is life-giver and nurturer. She is the heart of her hearth and home. Without honoring the mother, the family cannot thrive."

Then, with an infinitely gentle gesture, she touched Isabel's gnarled hand. "And the crone, although I prefer her matriarchal title, the wise woman. She is rich with wisdom and experience, a leader to those who will someday take her place when she is gone, and a comfort to those who are at the end of their life's journey. Her power is of great depth. It is that of the experience of ages forged with the strength of winter." Gaea spoke solemnly, clasping their hands in hers. "Alone, each is important and unique. But joined together, they form a three-fold link that is soldered by the Divine Feminine. We need each other—that is how we are fashioned. To deny this is to live a life less than fulfilled."

"Women need to stick together," CC agreed. "Even if we are different."

"Isn't that what woman is, a magical, complex blending of differences?" Gaea said.

"I am ashamed that it has taken me a lifetime to know this," Isabel said.

Gaea's smile was filled with unending love. "So you see, it should be of no surprise when you recognize the reflection of the divine within another woman."

"You are very wise, Galena," Isabel said, still holding Gaea's hand.

"I am a shepherdess who has had long hours of solitude in which to think and pray," she said simply. Then she squeezed Isabel's and CC's hands before slipping loose from them. "And now I can hear my flock calling me. They are impatient for my return. I must bid you good day, ladies."

"May the blessing of the Holy Mother go with you," Isabel said.

"Yes, have a safe journey home," CC added quickly.

Gaea nodded to each of them, then she bowed briefly before the statue of the Holy Virgin. When she raised her head, CC caught the sparkle in her eyes. The disguised goddess called a farewell to them as she walked toward the chapel's exit. The ever-present mist of incense seemed to swallow her as she faded into the shadows.

"A very interesting woman," Isabel said thoughtfully.

"She sure is."

"I will consider her words. They are new thoughts for me, but they touched my heart in a way that I have never before felt . . ." Her words faded as the squire threw open the door.

"Is all well here?" he asked, blinking quickly like a nervous bird as his eyes became accustomed to the dark. "I heard something odd."

"Everything is fine. I'm just going to keep this old woman in here to help me with the rest of the heavy cleaning. You should probably send word to the kitchen that she's going to be busy for the remainder of the afternoon." CC made a shooing gesture at him.

He looked doubtful, but CC's impotency threat still weighed heavily on his mind. "I am only a short distance away," he told the silent Isabel as he backed out the door.

CC and Isabel looked at each other.

"I thought maybe you'd want to stay here for a while," CC said simply.

"Thank you. I would like nothing more than to aid you in restoring the Mother's chapel. And I do so enjoy spending time with you."

CC grinned. "I like it, too."

Isabel took a deep breath and asked the question that had been haunting her mind. "When must you leave us?"

CC felt a pang of regret. "I must leave on the third night. But it doesn't have to be forever. I'll still be here—I'll just, well, live in the water and look a little different, that is, from my waist down."

Isabel blinked in surprise. "Then we could still visit with one another?"

"If I wouldn't frighten you," CC said slowly.

Isabel touched her cheek in an infinitely tender gesture. "You could never frighten me, my dear friend. Differences do not matter between us."

Relief flooded through CC. "I'm so glad, Isabel."

"As am I, sweet girl." Then she squared her shoulders and began rolling up her sleeves. "If we only have two more days, we had better get to work."

"My thoughts exactly," CC said.

Isabel took the closest broom and began attacking a nest of spider webs in a dark corner. "You know, you may be a wise woman yourself some day," she said.

"Make that a wise mer-woman, and I'll take you up on it."

As they worked together to restore what was rightfully the Mother's, their laughter joined and painted the walls with the joy of women working together in perfect harmony.

Chapter Twenty-five

Isabel had just finished combing through CC's thick hair when a sharp knock interrupted their quiet conversation. She limped to the door and cracked it open.

"I have come to see the princess," Andras's deep voice commanded.

"Please tell Sir Andras that I have already dressed for bed. The events of the day have tired me so much that I have to retire early." CC let her voice carry to the listening knight.

"Sir Andras, the princess—" Isabel began, but the knight cut her off.

"Perhaps the princess would not be so fatigued if she had not felt the need to cavort about the countryside last night."

CC sighed and yanked a robe over her head. Ignoring Isabel's silent look that counseled temperance she shoved open the door. Andras stood with his hands planted on his waist, face flushed with irritation. He had obviously taken great care with his appearance. He was freshly scrubbed and wearing the same dashing outfit he had worn the first day she had met him. Appalled, CC realized that he must have come to her door to court her.

Wasn't she his prisoner and possibly a dangerous witch?

Then CC understood and blinked in surprise. Andras had told the abbot that he would make his decision soon about whether he was going to marry or ransom her. Obviously, he had decided on marriage, so he was simply behaving honorably and beginning his courtship in earnest. It seemed the Rule of Thumb had outweighed her heathen tendencies and her outspoken mouth. CC supposed she should have been flattered. Instead she was annoyed. He didn't want her, he wanted a medieval Barbie doll.

"Sir Andras, I am exhausted because over the course of one short day I have remembered my birthright, defended myself against a charge of witchcraft and worked hard to restore a chapel that looks like it has been neglected for decades. I think that even a man would find a day like that tiring," she finished, trying to keep the sarcasm out of her voice.

Almost as if he couldn't help himself, Andras's eyes studied her face, lingering on the high, graceful planes of her cheeks and the full, sensual sweep of her lips. Then they traveled down her long, shapely neck and stared hotly at the glimpse of skin where the chemise gaped open. He wet his lips.

CC watched him closely. Just how far had Sarpedon's influence spread? His eyes appeared normal, and his facial features were his own, but his look was one of raw desire, and that was unusual for the knight. Until Sarpedon began possessing him, Andras had treated her carefully—he had not seemed like the kind of man who would think it was proper behavior to leer at the lady he was trying to woo.

"True, Undine, you have had a difficult day. But I remember that not long ago you proclaimed that you found the exercise of walking especially gratifying, even when you are fatigued," he persuaded. "I ask that you walk with me, Princess Undine." He held a muscular arm out to her as if he expected no other response than for her to happily accept his proposal.

"Not tonight, but thank you for asking."

Isabel stirred restlessly at her side as Andras's face darkened with anger at her rejection.

"I ask as a knight and a gentleman that you come walking with me, and you spurn me?" he said incredulously.

"I was under the impression that when a lady is asked a question, she has the right to answer yes *or* no," CC said impatiently. She hadn't been lying to the knight. She was tired and wanted nothing more than to finish her glass of wine and to fall into bed. "I didn't spurn you, I simply exercised my right."

"Then as a gentleman I choose to exercise my right to protect you from your own excesses so that you will be less exhausted and able to walk with me. Tonight and every night hereafter there will be a guard stationed at your door and your window to insure that you do not exhaust yourself with further needless forays to the shore," he said with cruel finality. "Tomorrow, then, Princess Undine. May I find you in more lively spirits, or perhaps I will have to be assured of your health and rest by confining you to your room for the daylight hours, too."

He closed the door with a solid slam.

"I should have just walked with him." CC sighed.

Isabel nodded her head. "I was afraid your refusal would bait the knight. His behavior has been unusual of late."

"Yes, I can see that now, and we both know why."

"Sarpedon," Isabel whispered the name.

CC nodded, rubbing her face wearily. "All this time I've been more worried about Abbot William. I guess I underestimated Sarpedon's effect on Andras."

"You underestimated the effect of your beauty," Isabel said as she helped CC off with the robe.

CC laughed sardonically. "I'm not used to it. My other body was nothing like this one. Men pretty much ignored me."

Isabel gave her a skeptical look and made a rude noise in her throat.

"What?" CC asked.

"Did you not tell me that a woman's beauty is more complex than her physical appearance? That applies to you as well as to me."

When CC started to argue Isabel held her hand up to silence her.

"Take this wise woman's words for truth. There is more to you than physical beauty. The knight knows that and desires to possess you—all of you. Sarpedon's evil influence has simply intensified that desire." Isabel turned down the covers of the narrow bed and gestured for CC to climb in. "Rest, Undine. Your eyes have that dark, haunted look. Sleep will strengthen you."

CC pulled the coarse blanket up under her arms and leaned against the hard wooden headboard as she watched Isabel tidy the small room. Outside her window she could hear the sounds of a guard settling in for the night. What would happen in two nights? How would she get out of her room? Her stomach churned. Isabel's weight caused the bed to sag.

"Do not fear," she whispered reassuringly while she fussed with CC's bed sheets. "Remember, we are one, the maiden, the mother and the wise woman. Together we will find a way to return you to the seas."

"And to Dylan," CC murmured, her eyes suddenly bright with tears.

Isabel cupped CC's chin gently. "And to your lover. We are stronger than they know. All will be well."

CC curled onto her side and Isabel stroked her hair, soothing her into a deep sleep by humming a lilting lullaby that somehow reminded CC of the sound of waves.

Chapter Twenty-six

The next day, flanked by two guards, CC managed to stay unavailable to Andras through a hasty breakfast in the kitchen, and a midday meal, even though it took her only a few crowning polishes to complete her work in the chapel. To avoid the knight, she kept herself busy weeding the herb garden and harvesting a long list of fresh plants for Isabel. She was pleasantly surprised when, from time to time, a passing monk would stop to compliment her on the beauty of Mary's restoration. She had just returned to her room to scrub something sticky from her hands and change her soiled robe for a new one when a knock sounded against her door.

She cracked the door. The knight was dressed as he had been the evening before, and his expression was strained.

"Good afternoon, Sir Andras," CC said formally, feeling especially uncomfortable without Isabel at her side.

Andras inclined his head. "Princess Undine, I trust today you are recovered and able to walk with me."

"I would be happy to, but as you can see I'm really not dressed for it." She pointed at her dirty robe.

"I will send for the servant, Isabel, to aid you. I await you in the courtyard," he said firmly, then executed an abrupt military about-face and strode away.

CC sighed and closed the door. She didn't have to wait long for Isabel to arrive.

"Come, let me help you into your beautiful gown," she said, lifting the shining material from where it was draped across the bed.

"I don't want to walk with him," CC said.

"You must, or you chance being locked away."

At that reminder, CC shivered in fear.

"Smile at Sir Andras. Stroke his ego," Isabel said.

"I'm worried about what Sarpedon could make him do." CC chewed her bottom lip.

Isabel frowned. "You must take care not to arouse the knight's anger, then perhaps the evil spirit's influence will sleep. Think of Andras as the dashing knight who rushed to rescue you from the seas. And remember, this is the last night you will spend as a human. Tomorrow you return to the water. Can you not play the pretty princess for such a short time?" Isabel finished lacing her outer garment and began clasping the long strands of jewels around CC's neck. "Perhaps you can persuade the knight to walk with you by the sea. Could you not tolerate him in exchange for the chance at a glimpse of your Dylan?"

"I hadn't even thought of that!" CC said, her heart racing.

As had become her habit during the time that she could not spend with him, CC had tried to stay busy and not think too much of Dylan. She had found that if she dwelled on how much she missed him, the ache of her longing for him and for the sea merged into one painful force, which came dangerously close to overwhelming her. Now she felt herself tremble with suppressed desire as thoughts of her lover filled her mind.

"Hurry!" she told Isabel.

"Child,"—the old woman took CC's shoulders in her hands, forcing her to look into her eyes—"you may catch sight of him, but you must control your reaction to his nearness. Do not display your emotions and reveal yourself to the knight. Remember, you must wait on the timing of the Holy Mother. Promise me you will use caution."

"Yes, yes! I promise," she said quickly, wanting to reassure Isabel and bolt from the room. But the old woman wouldn't release her.

"Remember Sarpedon. Do not put yourself or your lover in danger because you mistakenly allow passion to rule your actions."

At the mention of Sarpedon, CC felt her head clear. "You're right. I promise to be careful."

"Go, child. And luck be with you as well as the blessings of the Holy Virgin."

CC turned in the doorway. "Thank you, my wise friend." Then she hurried to the courtyard.

Andras was pacing restlessly back and forth in front of the arched entryway that led from the hall. His two squires were flanking him a little way inside the courtyard.

"I'm ready for our walk," CC said.

The three men looked at her, and the heat of their stares was a tangible force against CC's body. Their eyes seemed to bore into her, and she felt the exposed skin on her chest, neck, face and arms burn with an electric shock of discomfort.

Her hand went automatically to her neck. "Is something wrong?" she asked.

Andras blinked and pulled his gaze from her body to meet her eyes. He approached her with a feral glide that reminded CC of an animal stalking its prey. When he reached her side he took her unresponsive hand and raised it to his lips. CC wanted to pull her hand from his possessive grasp and bolt back down the hallway.

"I had forgotten how lovely you are in your gown. It is unfortunate that you have been spending so much time in the coarse robes of the Brothers." He slid her hand through his arm proprietarily and together they moved across the courtyard. "A woman of your beauty and breeding should spend all of her time in glittering gowns surrounded by luxurious things."

With an effort, CC didn't sigh. "Then I would be no more than a pretty doll or a piece of art. Those things are nice to look at, but they have no real purpose."

The knight's laugh was condescending. "Is not a woman's purpose in life to be a thing of grace and beauty, a true asset to her husband and family?"

"As I am not yet a wife, I believe I am being an asset to my family by working to restore the area of the chapel that is devoted to Mary. Do you not agree that my work for the Great Mother is important?"

Andras nodded quickly. "Of course—piety is always important, especially in a woman."

CC ground her teeth together to keep her retort inside her mouth.

Just then they passed the well, and CC felt her attention and her gaze drawn to it. During the past few days, she had successfully avoided coming near this area of the courtyard. Until now. At the sight of the well her stomach fluttered nervously. The stone structure stood silently in the middle of the courtyard, looking perfectly normal. There was no vapor escaping from it, no ghostly shape hovering above it. CC didn't even detect any of the feelings of dread she had experienced around the time Sarpedon began manifesting.

CC wasn't sure why, but her lack of any reaction to the well made her feel very uneasy.

"How have you been feeling lately?" she asked abruptly.

"Much improved," Andras said.

"No more"—she struggled for an appropriate word—"dizziness, or falling or anything?"

"None. During the midday meal Abbot William even mentioned how pleased he is that I have recovered and returned to myself. His prayers on my behalf were obviously successful."

"And no one else has been acting, um, *strangely*?" CC asked.

"No." His voice had a suspicious edge to it. "Why do you ask?"

She shrugged nonchalantly. "No reason in particular." She could feel that the knight was still studying her, so she added what she thought he wanted to hear. "The whole thing scared me. It's a relief to know that you are well."

Andras patted her hand indulgently. "Of course it would frighten you, but you may rest easy. I am fully recovered, and you must know that under my protection you have nothing to fear."

CC gave him a tight grimace masquerading as a smile, and he patted her hand again. At least he seemed to be acting like himself.

They exited through the monastery gates, and it was then that CC noticed that the squires were following them. And they, like Andras, were well armed.

Raising her eyebrows at the knight she asked, "Is there something out here that you're afraid of?"

"Of course not," Andras said, drawing himself up to his full, imposing height, blond mane shimmering in the early afternoon sunlight.

He really was incredibly handsome, the perfect knight in shining armor.

"Oh, then those guards must be for me." She fluttered her eyelashes at him coquettishly. "Silly me, I thought I just heard you say that I didn't need to be afraid of anything while I was under your protection. Or is that just while we're within the walls of the monastery?"

The knight's jaw tightened. "Marten! Gilbert! Remain here. I will escort the princess alone."

The two squires sent hot looks in CC's direction, but they did as they were ordered.

"Come," Andras said, his voice gentled from the tone of command he used with his men. "We shall walk down the road. It branches not far from here and the eastern fork winds through a rather nice meadow. I thought that you should visit some of the *inland* parts of Caldei," he said, putting an emphasis on the word.

CC wanted to tell him that she could care less about what was inland—she just wanted to go to the seashore! Instead she swallowed her frustration and strolled casually beside him, careful to keep her expression neutral.

"Anywhere you would like to go is fine with me. You were right; I do enjoy the exercise."

Andras smiled at her compliment, and CC couldn't help returning his smile. He did seem to have shaken Sarpedon's influence and was his usual, macho self again. The thought made her smile turn into a grin, and even though they weren't near the water, CC found that she was actually enjoying the walk. Soon they came to what CC recognized as the little path that branched from the road and meandered down to the shore. CC pointed to the trail.

"Isn't that the path that we took before?" she asked.

"Yes."

CC sighed dramatically.

"Are you well, Undine? Perhaps you would like to rest before we continue?" Andras asked.

"No, I'm fine. I was just remembering what a wonderful lunch you had packed for us and what a nice time we had that day."

Andras's eyes widened. "I am pleased to hear you say so, Undine."

CC took a deep breath, steeling herself. Then she turned to face the knight. "Andras, I have been thinking about us." She paused, letting the word *us* linger in the air between them. "We have had some unfortunate misunderstandings, and I am sorry for that. After all, you did save me, and I should be more appreciative than I have been." Purposefully she looked down at her feet, pretending maidenly shyness. Then, glancing up at him through thick lashes she said, "Maybe we could start over."

CC watched a fierce look of triumph pass quickly over the knight's face.

"Yes, let us begin anew," he said passionately.

CC plastered a wide smile on her face. When the knight began to lean toward her as if he wanted to kiss her, she pulled her hand from his arm and clapped girlishly.

"Oh, good!" CC chirped, waggling her fingers in the direction of the trail and brightening her face, as if an idea had just occurred to her. "And what better way to start over than for us to follow the same path we did before all of our misunderstandings started!"

The knight hesitated only a moment before responding. "If it would make you happy, Undine."

CC sighed in relief as they stepped off the road and began following the twisting trail. It took very little time for them to break through the trees and come to the sandy shoreline. CC breathed deeply, washing herself in the aroma of the salt breeze. Her spirit, dressed in her human body, quivered and strained with its desire to rejoin the waters. The ocean was sweet-laughter blue, and the whimsical waves played tag with the shore, calling to her in a voice that echoed through her blood.

"You always become even more beautiful when you are near the sea." Andras's voice was raw with lust. "I wonder why that is."

CC wrenched her thoughts from the water to focus on the knight. His features were tight, locked in the intense expression of a man determined to possess a woman. CC felt a shiver of apprehension. She had been a fool to believe that Sarpedon's influence could be so easily shaken. She realized that she had to distract him. Struggling to calm the fear within her, she formed her lips into a friendly smile.

"Well, it must be because I love the sea so much. Being near it makes me feel like I'm home." She took another deep breath, schooling her face into an aspect of polite interest. "But enough about me. You've hardly told me anything about your childhood. I would love to hear about Caer Llion."

The mention of his home seemed to break through his fog of lust, and Andras blinked like a man surfacing after a long dive.

"Caer Llion is a place of great beauty," he said solemnly. "It is not wild, as is this coastline. It is well-ordered and civilized." Andras stepped closer to her. "You could find there everything your heart desires."

CC summoned up a delighted laugh and skipped a step away from him, as if she could hardly contain her glee at the thought of learning more about his home.

"Oh, it sounds wonderful! Please, tell me more," she said as she wandered girlishly down the shoreline, picking up an occasional seashell or piece of discarded coral, while she moved ever closer to the water.

"Well," Andras said thoughtfully as he followed CC. "The first thing you should know about Caer Llion is that it is a well-ordered castle . . ."

Andras loved his home, and his voice was warm and animated as he enumerated the wonders of Caer Llion. All CC had to do was to make an occasional, interested noise and smile encouragingly. He was so intent on his description of Caer Llion's stables that he didn't even notice when CC slipped off her shoes. It was only when she hiked up her skirts and actually stepped into the water that he paused in his recitation.

"You should have care. The water can cause a chill."

CC noticed that his gaze was riveted on the glimpse of knee and calf she was exposing.

"I'll be careful," she said, cheerfully ignoring the heat in his eyes. "Go on, you haven't described the main hall of the castle yet."

CC breathed a sigh of relief as he continued his dissertation. Nodding and smiling, she half turned away from him and continued walking down the shoreline. Hungrily, her eyes scanned the water. There was no flash of orange and gold, no sign of Dylan's sleek body.

She wanted to call to Dylan. She had planned to—until she had stepped onto the beach. What would Dylan think when he saw her with Andras? Would he trust her, or would he be angry and jealous? Or worse, would he feel hurt and betrayed? Questions filled her mind as she made polite noises at the knight to keep him talking.

The shoreline bent to the east, then it curved back abruptly to the west. In the middle of the bend was formed a shallow cove that was littered with large, smooth rocks. The water there was more tamed than the wild waves that jarred the shore beneath the monastery. CC pulled her skirts up a little higher and walked out into the cove, climbing easily up on the rounded top of the nearest rock.

"Undine, those rocks are slick with sea water," Andras said.

"Oh, they're really not very slick. See?" She tapped the sand-colored rock with her toe. "The tide is out and the top is dry." She smiled at him. "Andras, would you say that the stones from which Caer Llion was constructed are the same color as this rock, or do they look more like the gray stones of the monastery?"

Andras rubbed his chin, pondering rock colors and shades of his beloved Caer Llion. CC stepped to the next rock. By skipping from rock to rock she had traveled well out into the cove and was four stony mounds away from the knight before he finished the description of the wall surrounding Caer Llion.

"Undine, perhaps you should return to shore now."

CC glanced over her shoulder at him. He had walked closer to the waves and was nervously watching the water. This time CC didn't stifle her grin.

"Andras, can't you swim?" she asked.

The knight stuck out his well-defined chin. "No. I cannot."

CC's laughter danced across the water. "You really should learn—it's a lot of fun, not to mention excellent exercise."

"I have no desire to engage in such barbaric behavior." He took one step closer to the water. "You should return now, Undine."

Before she could answer him, a flash of brilliance caught the corner of her gaze. Her heart thumped wildly as she saw a familiar golden shadow just below the surface of the water. It was gliding toward her rock.

"I think I'll sit out here a little while," CC said quickly. Gathering her skirts she sat on the smooth, cool surface of the rock. Her legs dangled down into the water, which covered her feet and calves. "I think I am a little tired. I should rest before I try to climb back to shore." She gave him an apologetic look. "I guess you were right, again."

"I will come to you." Andras's voice was curt as he put one booted foot into the edge of the waterline.

"No!" she shouted. The knight paused, and CC continued in a more controlled voice. "I'll be fine in a few minutes, and I wouldn't want you to fall into the water. I'm pretty sure that it's well over your head out here."

Andras gave the waves a distasteful look.

A few yards from her rock the water flashed golden.

"I'll just sit here," she said. Then she looked down at her legs. Widening her eyes, as if noticing for the first time that she was showing so much skin, she squeaked a little gasp of shock. With what she hoped was maidenly modesty, CC shifted her seat until her legs were facing seaward, their partial nudity hidden by the bulk of the rock. She twisted at the waist to look back at the knight. "How foolish of me to get into this situation. And I certainly didn't realize I was being so immodest."

"It is just the two of us, Undine." Andras's voice deepened suggestively.

"And what a relief that is to me!" CC said, filling her voice with naiveté. "I'd be mortified if anyone else knew. I hope I can trust you not to mention this to my father."

"Your honor is safe with me, Undine." The look Andras sent her was long and intimate.

"Thank you. Now, I'm going to sit here and rest for a little while. Why don't you continue with your description of Caer Llion? You haven't told me yet about your personal chambers."

"I would rather that you visited those chambers yourself someday, Undine," Andras said.

"Why don't you whet my curiosity with a description?" she said quickly.

As Andras launched into another lengthy description, Dylan's head broke the surface of the water near her feet. His body was shadowed by the rock, and as long as he remained on the seaward side of it he would be shielded from the knight's vision.

"Is all well, Christine?" The merman's whisper was strained and his eyes were dark with worry.

"Yes. But don't let him know you're here." CC glanced nervously over her shoulder and nodded attentively at the knight's description of the tapestries that covered the walls of his bedchamber.

He holds you prisoner? Even inside her head the words sounded fierce.

Not really. He is just escorting me on a walk. CC sent her thoughts to him, pouring all the love she felt for him through her eyes. *Lir has sent word to Gaea that he will be in these waters tomorrow night. She is sure that he will bless our union and tell Sarpedon to back off. Tomorrow night I can return to the water and to you. Forever.*

Dylan reached out and with one strong hand he stroked her right calf with a slow, sensuous touch. CC shivered at the current of desire that traveled up her leg to nestle, pulsing with heat, deep within her.

It seems an eternity from now till then. Within her mind his voice was a seductive lure.

You did say you would wait for me for an eternity, she teased.

And I shall, Christine. I shall, my love.

"Undine, have you recovered your strength enough yet?" Andras's voice cut into their thoughts.

Dylan's jaw clenched.

He is nothing to us. CC sent the thought to Dylan before calling over her shoulder to the knight.

"Almost. Just another few minutes. Your chamber sounds lovely. Why don't you tell me what a normal day is like at Caer Llion."

"For whom? Caer Llion and its grounds are home for hundreds of people," he said with easy arrogance.

When CC turned her head and answered the knight her face was a mask of innocent curiosity. "Start by telling me what you do. Then I would love to hear what the ladies of the castle do to keep themselves busy during the day."

Andras's chest swelled. "Being the eldest son, my duties are extensive and they begin at daybreak . . ."

"The warrior wants you to belong to him." The softness of Dylan's voice did nothing to disguise his anger.

"It doesn't matter what he wants. I could never belong to him," she whispered urgently. "Please believe me, Dylan. I want no one except you."

"Did you say something, Undine?" Andras shouted.

CC swiveled at the waist. "I was just commenting on how interesting all this is becoming to me. I'm sorry to interrupt, please continue." She turned back to Dylan as Andras resumed his description of castle life.

I hate that you must endure him. Dylan's thought entered her mind.

He's really not that bad; he's just not the man for me. And anyway, it won't be much longer now.

One moment without you is too long, my love. The merman pulled her leg to him and gently kissed her calf. *Your legs are such soft, wonderful things*. With light kisses his mouth moved down the shapely swell of her calf, burning a trail of erotic heat. *I admit that I shall miss them.*

His lips found the delicate arch of her instep. While his mouth possessed her, his hands caressed the sensitive area behind her knees, then moved down to her ankle and back. When he moved to her other leg CC couldn't hold back the moan of pleasure that escaped her parted lips.

"Undine! What is it?" CC could hear the splash of the knight's boots as he plodded awkwardly into the water.

"Nothing! Nothing!" she yelled, looking back in time to see him floundering up to his knees in the surf. "No need to come out. I'm rested and ready to leave. Just let me make sure that I am presentable," she said, fussing with her skirt.

She turned back to Dylan, sending her thoughts to him. *Tomorrow night, my love. Wait for me tomorrow night.*

Reluctantly, the merman took his hands from her leg and began to sink beneath the shimmering surface.

For an eternity, Christine. I will wait for you for an eternity

Then he was gone. CC swallowed hard, fighting against an almost overwhelming desire to leap into the water and swim after him.

No, she told herself firmly. I have to wait on the timing of the goddess. I've come too far to mess it up now. It's just one more day.

But as she stood and began her rock-skipping trip back to the restlessly waiting knight she felt empty, like her soul had followed Dylan out to sea, and she had been left with only the shell of her body.

Reacting to the bereft expression on her face, and her sad, lethargic movements, Andras began his lecture as soon as he had helped her down from the last rock.

"Perhaps next time you will remember that it is wise to listen to me, especially in matters of your safety."

Dylan's absence filled her with sadness, and her shoulders slumped as she muttered a quick, "You're right, next time I'll be more careful."

Andras gave her a self-satisfied smile. "I am pleased to hear you say so, Undine. I understand that you are a princess, but even a princess must take counsel from those who are wiser and more experienced. But please, there is no need for you to look so sad. I am here for you."

Andras took a step closer to her. Before she could protest, he took her hand in his and raised it to his lips. Thankfully, the kiss was short, but he didn't let go of her hand when he had finished. Instead he stepped even closer to her and placed his hands on her shoulders. They were rough and heavy, and CC felt their weight as if they were shackles. A tremor of fear mixed with loathing traveled through her, and she tried to pull away from him.

"Do not be frightened." His voice was husky. "You must know my intentions are honorable. I plan on speaking to your father as soon as he arrives."

"About my ransom?" she asked, still trying to pull away.

"It is little wonder you tremble if that is what you believe!" Andras said heatedly. "You may be assured, Undine, that I am not the type of man who would use a maiden lady and then send her back to her father soiled. Your honor is safe with me."

"So are you saying you'd only use a woman who you didn't consider a lady?"

Andras's brow furrowed as if he couldn't decide if her question was naive or impertinent. Remembering her reaction to discovering she was displaying an immodest glimpse of her legs, the knight realized that Undine must have meant the question in simple naiveté. He smiled indulgently at her, and his voice took on a fatherly tone.

"What I am saying, my beautiful one, is that I intend to ask your father for your hand in marriage."

"But I thought you said that beauty needs to be guarded against," she blurted, scanning his face for the telltale signs of Sarpedon.

Believing her breathlessness was a result of joy at his announced intentions, Andras freed one of her shoulders so that he could cup her chin within his hand.

"Not if the beauty has proper guidance. As your husband, I will provide you with that guidance." His voice deepened and his eyes gleamed with a light that caused her stomach to clench. "Consider us betrothed, my beauty. You belong to me."

The knight's grip on her tightened, and he bent his head down to her. CC couldn't breath. She was trapped, overwhelmed by his size and strength. What would happen if he kissed her lips? Intuition told her Sarpedon's influence would flare to an uncontrollable level. She had to do something that would break his desire for her without making him angry. Fighting panic, she forced herself to think rationally. And a single idea came to her, ironically born from something Andras had said. Suddenly she wanted to laugh aloud in glee.

Instead she drew in a deep breath, as if she was readying herself for an underwater dive, and the instant before Andras's lips touched hers, CC sneezed. Violently.

The knight jerked back from her.

"Oh, my goodness!" CC covered her nose with her hands and sniffed. "I'm so sorry."

When she lowered her hands from her face, Andras took her forcefully back into his arms.

"It is of no matter, my beauty," he murmured, bending again to her lips.

"*Ahhh, chew!*" This time CC opened her mouth and managed to actually rain spittle onto the knight's face.

He let loose of her so quickly that she staggered forward, causing him to back away from her.

"*Ahhh, ahhh . . .*" CC gasped, waving her hands in front of her face. "*Chew!*"

CC rubbed at her nose. She was pleased to feel it getting hot and red under her rough handling. Andras was looking at her as if he was afraid she might begin to indiscriminately release any number of bodily functions. All traces of glowing silver had left his eyes.

"It looks like you were right, again," she said, giving her voice a nasally twinge. "I must have caught a chill out there on that wet rock."

"We should return," Andras said.

"You are so wise," CC said, ending her sentence in a barking cough.

As she followed the knight up the path that led from the beach, CC was sure she heard Dylan's deep, male laughter mixed with the rhythmic music of the surf. She disguised her answering giggle in a phlegmy cough.

REENTERING the monastery grounds, CC was relieved to see Isabel's silhouette in a nearby hall, obviously keeping watch for CC's return.

CC coughed and sneezed almost simultaneously.

"You, there!" Andras yelled at Isabel. "The princess has taken a chill. What herbal remedies have you?"

Isabel hurried over to the knight, clucking her tongue like a ruffled hen.

"It seems I should have listened to Sir Andras's advice. He warned that I could catch a chill from the water, and I think I—*ha . . . ha . . . ha . . . chew!*—have," CC said wetly.

Isabel took the shawl from her shoulders and wrapped it around CC while she muttered under her breath about foolish young women and ushered her toward the hall that led to her bedchamber. Andras began to follow them, then he stopped, looking as if he wasn't sure what he should do.

"Sir Andras, I will care for the princess. It would be wise if you had one of the servants pour you a strong draft of the Brothers' special vintage. We certainly would not want you to become ill, too." She lowered her voice ominously, then said, "The princess may be contagious."

The knight's eyes widened, and he automatically backed a step farther away from CC.

"I will be in the dining hall if you have need of me, Undine." Andras gave her a neat little bow. Then he told Isabel, "Care for my betrothed well. I hold you personally responsible for her health." The knight turned and retreated quickly across the courtyard.

"Betrothed?" Isabel whispered as they hurried down the hall to CC's room.

CC grimaced and whispered back. "Somehow Andras managed to get engaged to me today without me saying yes." CC paused to add a sneeze and a couple of loud coughs, just in case any of the Brothers were lurking around.

The door to her room looked like a sanctuary. As soon as it was firmly closed behind them CC nodded to the window and asked in a low voice. "Is the guard still out there?"

"No," Isabel answered in a normal voice. "The squires are busy scanning the coast for any sign of Vikings." Isabel looked closely at her. "This illness is only a pretense?"

CC nodded and grinned. "Absolutely. Do you honestly believe that water could make *me* sick?"

As her laughter joined Isabel's, CC felt her spirits lift, and she sent a silent thank-you to the goddess for the gift of the old woman's friendship.

"It is a ruse to keep the knight away from you?" Isabel asked.

CC nodded. "He scared me out there. It's like Sarpedon is with him all the time, even when Andras appears perfectly himself, but any little thing I do or say can cause him to surface."

"Little wonder you looked ill," Isabel said.

"I'm glad this will be over soon. I don't know how much longer I can avoid Andras."

"The chapel is certainly clean, and the kitchen has become a forest of drying herbs," Isabel said.

"I can promise you that there are no weeds in the herb garden."

"Then it is best if an illness renders you indisposed," Isabel said thoughtfully.

CC grinned mischievously. "So what kind of remedies do you have in mind for me?"

"Oh, I think we should begin with mulled wine laced with healing herbs, and perhaps a mustard poultice for your chest to relieve that raking cough."

CC wrinkled her nose, and Isabel laughed.

"I'm fine with the wine, but the poultice sounds kind of scary. What are you going to put in it? Frog poop and lizard tongues?"

"Would you rather have Andras or a poultice on your chest?"

"I'll take the frog poop," CC assured her.

Isabel cackled cheerfully as she gathered up the pitcher and cup from CC's dresser. "It will be necessary to make you as aromatic as possible to ensure that the knight will want to stay well away from you."

"I suppose that means that I'll have to stay confined to my room tonight and tomorrow," CC sighed.

"I imagine that if you appear well enough to walk about, Andras will devote himself to personally overseeing his betrothed's recovery."

"*Ugh*," CC groaned.

"Exactly," Isabel said, walking to the door. "I shall prepare your remedies and return shortly."

"Don't be gone too long."

"Only as long as it takes to gather the frogs and lizards." The door closed on Isabel's cackling laughter.

Chapter Twenty-seven

"Uck! I thought you were kidding about the frog poop. That stuff smells horrible. What the heck is in it?" CC asked, backing away from Isabel who was holding a jar that she had just uncovered. CC could almost see the waves of stench emanating from its open mouth.

"Ground mustard, garlic, lard and sheep urine," Isabel said, smiling evilly. "It is an ancient remedy for a wet cough."

"I don't have a wet cough," CC said, being sure to keep her bed between the two of them.

"The knight needs to believe you do."

"Can't we just smear it around the door? I'm sure he'll be able to smell it even through six inches of wood."

Isabel laughed. "I suppose we could dab it on some rags and waft them about. That should keep the knight away."

"It'll keep Andras, his friends, the Brothers and every creature known to man away," CC said, glancing nervously at the jar even after Isabel placed it on the dresser. "And do you think you could wait to start the wafting until after I've eaten my dinner?"

"You are very demanding for a woman who is supposed to be so ill," Isabel teased.

"Well, I am a princess."

"Obviously."

They grinned at each other, and CC nodded a grateful thank-you to Isabel, then began eating the thick stew with gusto.

"Funny that this illness hasn't affected my appetite," CC said through bites of fresh bread.

"I already considered that." Isabel pointed to the heavily laden tray she had carried into the chamber.

"Seems like a lot of jars of poultice. I don't think anyone can be *that* sick." CC scowled. "Not and still live."

"Yes, it would seem like I am rather overdoing it with the poultice, but it is understandable. I have never before treated a sick princess."

She lifted the cloth covering from one of the jars, and CC flinched, but instead of the rank odor of sheep urine, all she could smell was more of the wonderful stew.

Isabel grinned conspiratorially. "This, I believe, is more than even you can eat. I will refill your bowl, and it will appear that your appetite is suffering."

"You are a genius, Isabel."

"Just a wise woman, Princess," Isabel said smugly.

CC reached for her goblet of wine and hesitated. "Is there anything awful in the wine?"

"Just some mild herbs. Nothing that will do anything more than cause you to relax."

CC sniffed at the wine. "It doesn't smell bad."

Isabel took her own goblet and drank deeply.

CC smiled in relief and took a healthy drink. "It's good!"

"Do not be so surprised," Isabel grumped. "I made it."

"You made the poultice, too," CC pointed out.

"No, Bronwyn and Gwenyth made the poultice," Isabel said smugly. "They are renowned for their healing poultices. They send with it their love."

"Well, it's only their love and my loathing for Sarpedon that could get me to let that stuff anywhere near my body," CC said, giving the jar a squeamish glance.

Isabel cackled. "They are all too aware of that. You should have heard them preparing it. *Add a little more urine, shall we? The princess should only have the best.*" Isabel mimicked the two ladies voices so accurately that CC laughed so hard she almost spilled her wine.

"While I'm sequestered do you think there's any chance that the other women could visit?" CC asked. "It may be the last time . . ."

"They will come," Isabel said brusquely, pouring both of them more wine. "And that is quite enough of talk like that. We will see you again."

CC nodded firmly. "You're right, of course. It's not like I'm going back to my own time, I'm just going—well—some place wetter."

They smiled at each other and sipped their wine.

"Undine, would you tell me of your time?"

CC shrugged. "Sure." Then she realized she didn't have any idea how to start explaining the twenty-first century to a medieval woman who had never been more than a day's walk away from her home. "Is there something in particular you'd like to know?" CC asked, hoping for some direction.

"I would like to know how food is prepared in your time," Isabel said without hesitation.

CC grinned. "You'll love this. Wait till you hear about supermarkets and microwaves."

CC had just finished explaining to an open-mouthed Isabel about fast food restaurants, when two quick knocks sounded on the door.

CC barked several loud coughs before calling in a raspy voice, "Who is it?"

"Andras."

CC sneezed. "Just a moment."

Isabel was already unveiling the foul-smelling pot. "Time for wafting." She whispered and ladled a generous amount of the yellowish goop onto a linen rag, which she began waving around the room. CC added to the effect by coughing loudly.

Turning her head upside-down CC vigorously snarled her hair into a twisted mess and rubbed at her already much-abused nose. Then she wrapped the blanket from the bed around her shoulders and shuffled to the door.

"Wait!" Isabel whispered urgently. Before she could protest Isabel took the poultice-encrusted rag and hung it around her neck. CC gagged and didn't have to pretend the sneeze that rocked her body.

When CC cracked the door her nose was running. She smelled like a vat of old urine and she looked disheveled and pale. In the hall Andras and Abbot William had their heads bent together speaking in low voices. At the sound of the door opening they broke off their discussion and turned their attention to her. CC was pleased to see the shocked expression on Andras's face and the look of disgust on the abbot's. Emboldened, CC took a half step out into the hall. Both men moved quickly back.

"Andras! Abbot William!" CC said in a thick, nasally voice. "It's so nice to see both of you. Would you like to come in?"

"No!" the knight said hastily. "We would not think of tiring you."

"It would be most improper for Sir Andras to enter your bedchamber, even chaperoned by me," the priest said, fluttering his fingers effeminately in front of him, as if he was trying to ward off her contagion.

"Oh," CC said sadly. The poultice was causing her nose to run and she paused to wipe it on the back of her hand. "Are you sure? After all, Andras and I are betrothed."

"Not officially until your father arrives and blesses the union," Abbot William said. "That is what Andras and I have been discussing."

"I'm sure my father will—*ahh . . . ahh . . . ahhh . . . chew!*—approve," CC said, pleased beyond words that her latest sneeze had caused the two men to retreat another step from her.

"I, too, am certain of his approval," Andras spoke rapidly. "Now you must rest and regain your strength."

"Yes," Abbot William said, his nose curled in distaste as he caught another whiff of the foul poultice. "Have the servant Isabel bring you anything you wish." The two men were already moving away from her door. "We bid you good night and a hasty recovery."

"Pray for me," CC called after them. She could barely make out their mumbled replies.

As soon as the door was closed she took the stinking rag from around her neck. Laughing, she handed it back to Isabel.

"They didn't want to come in for a visit. Imagine that."

"It certainly does not seem very caring of them," Isabel said, and her cackles joined CC's melodic laughter.

"They did say you could bring me anything I wish." CC picked up her empty goblet and said dramatically. "I wish for more of this excellent wine. It's medicinal. And company. Do you think the other women would be willing to brave possible contagion to visit me?"

"Certainly. It is only right for a princess to have several nurses." Isabel performed a graceful curtsey that made CC laugh. "And I shall leap to obey you, my lady." Grabbing the empty pitcher, Isabel hurried to the door with the energy of a girl one-third her age.

Chapter Twenty-eight

SEVERAL hours later the four old women and CC lay in heaps around the floor amidst scattered bedding and pallets. Isabel had returned to CC's room accompanied by the three "nursemaids." On her trip from the kitchen, Isabel had interrupted Sir Andras and the abbot at their nightly game of chess. She had explained that the Princess needed more care than she alone could provide, and that she would need that care all during the night. The two men readily agreed, both visibly relieved that the responsibility for Undine's nursemaiding would not be their own. Isabel had mimicked the abbot's simpering voice as she repeated how he had ordered her and as many other women as were necessary to spend the night in the princess's chamber. Isabel had invited the men to look in on her patient during the night. The abbot had explained that his time would be better spent in prayer. Although Andras had appeared honestly concerned about her, he had hastily agreed that Undine must be allowed to rest, and that she certainly could not do so if he insisted on visiting her.

And, of course, the guards stationed outside the princess's door and window would not be needed. Even if the princess was well enough to sneak out—which Isabel assured them she was not—the all-night presence of the old women would ensure that she would have to stay in her chamber.

CC felt a wonderful sense of freedom as she sipped Isabel's excellent mulled wine. The five women had been laughing and talking well into the night. Isabel had confided in them the truth about CC, and the women couldn't seem to learn enough about modern customs and conveniences. Now their weathered faces were flushed with excitement as well as wine.

"I did so enjoy learning the Poultry Dance," Gwenyth said, waving a hand in front of her heated face.

"Chicken Dance," CC corrected with a giggle.

"Chicken Dance," Gwenyth repeated. The old woman's eyes sparkled.

CC grinned at her. "Just let me catch my breath, and I'll teach you another dance." CC waggled her eyebrows suggestively. "And how about a song to go with it?"

The four old women squealed in delight. It was like a slumber party, CC thought. The year didn't matter—the comradery of women joined together to celebrate life and friendship was eternal. While the women chattered excitedly about what they were going to learn next, CC hummed softly to herself, trying to remember all the words to Aretha Franklin's classic, "Respect." When they were cheerleaders, she and her best friend, Sandy, had made up a funky dance to the song for a high school pep rally, and she was pretty sure she could remember most of the moves. CC eyed her backup singers. They were going to love this one. . . .

"NO, Bronwyn, you have to flick the tips of your fingers on both hands in time with the words—just a . . . just a . . . just a—before you do the side-to-side head toss and sing the *just a little bit* part," CC explained again to the old woman.

"Undine, is it then that we begin thrusting our hips?" Gwenyth asked.

Isabel spoke up before she could answer. "Yes. We thrust our hips in time with our head tosses."

CC had to stifle her grin. The ladies had attacked learning the motions and words to "Respect" with a vengeance. And she had to admit the four old women had decent voices and natural senses of rhythm.

"Okay!" CC said, and the room fell to an attentive silence. "Think we're ready to try it again from the beginning?"

In the candlelight the four gray heads seemed to glow as they nodded enthusiastically in response.

"Bronwyn, you cannot dance with that wine goblet in your hand," Isabel pointed out.

Bronwyn's smile showed two missing teeth as she winked at CC before gulping the last drop from the goblet and sliding it out of the way on the floor.

"Backup singers take your places," CC said officially, and the women hurried to form a horizontal line behind her. "Are you ready?"

"Ready, Undine!" the four answered.

With a huge grin CC turned around and started shimmying and humming in time to the beat of an imaginary band, and with a *Whoop!* her backup singers joined her in a rousing medieval version of Aretha's classic, after which the five of them collapsed in breathless laughter across CC's bed.

"In your old world women must have such fun," Lynelle said wistfully.

"Yes, they do. But I can't remember a time when I was happier there then I am here, at this moment."

The women beamed smiles at one another. Bronwyn hiccupped a little drunkenly, and they all laughed.

"Tell us of your lover," Lynelle said.

CC blinked at her in surprise. Until then they had confined their questions to CC's past—her human life. She had assumed that the thought of her mermaid life made the women uncomfortable. Now Bronwyn and Gwenyth echoed Lynelle's request. Isabel nodded encouragingly. CC's heart swelled at their acceptance.

"Well," she said softly. "Dylan is different from the men here."

Lynelle snorted. "Of course he is, child."

"Yes," Bronwyn blurted. "He is a fish."

Isabel elbowed her and made a *shush*ing noise. Bronwyn looked chagrined.

"Actually," CC said, smiling at her, "he's a mammal, like a dolphin or a whale. But when I said he's different, I wasn't talking about his body." CC touched her temple with one finger. "He's different in here." Then she moved that finger to rest briefly on her breast over her heart. "And here. He is kind and good. He doesn't see me as a thing to be possessed or used. He sees me as his equal, as even more than his equal."

"He loves you," Lynelle said.

"Yes, and to him that doesn't mean that he has to control me or destroy what is unique about me so that he can remake me into some kind of twisted image of what he sees as female perfection."

"That would be Sir Andras," Isabel said.

"And many other men of our world," Bronwyn added. Isabel and Gwenyth nodded in agreement, but Lynelle looked thoughtful.

"My husband was not like Sir Andras. I believe his love was more like your merman's," Lynelle said.

CC's eyes widened in surprise and Lynelle's smile was bittersweet.

"No, I have not always been as such." Her good hand pointed at the shriveled appendage that she held limply against her side. "This happened shortly after we were married. He could have cast me aside, but he did not . . ." The old woman's eyes filled with tears and she took a gulp of wine and cleared her throat before she could continue speaking. "He was a good man. And it was my great joy to be his wife."

"And you will find joy in being Dylan's wife," Isabel said.

"To love!" Lynelle said brightly, raising her goblet.

"To love!" the women toasted, beaming at each other.

They drank in compatible silence, each lost in memories, until Lynelle's voice interrupted the stillness with another question.

"Does . . ." she hesitated and glanced quickly at the other women as if for support. Then she rushed on. "Does his touch please you?"

CC felt her cheeks growing warm from more than the wine. "His touch makes me feel like I'm on fire."

The four women sighed happily.

"Undine!" Lynelle's voice was filled with excitement. "Why don't you go to him tonight?"

"I have to wait until tomorrow. Then Sarpedon will be dealt with," CC said.

"Yes, to join him permanently you must wait until tomorrow," Lynelle said quickly. "But can you not visit him before then?"

CC felt a rush of exhilaration. "I-I think I can, but I would have to be very careful."

"We have taken care—neither the abbot nor the knight will be looking for you tonight," Isabel said.

"But the squires have been posted to watch for Vikings," Bronwyn reminded them.

"True," said Isabel. "But they will be looking out to sea for the invaders. They will not be watching for one fleet-footed girl who knows how to disappear into the waves."

"Will your merman be there tonight?" Gwenyth asked.

CC nodded. "All I have to do is call him."

Gwenyth's aged face crinkled with worry. "You must not call loudly."

CC laughed and stood up, spinning in a little improvised dance step of happiness. "I don't have to call him with my voice; I call him with my heart." An eternity, CC thought. He would answer for an eternity.

"Go to him," Lynelle said.

"Yes," Bronwyn and Gwenyth said together.

CC turned to Isabel.

With the gentle hands of a mother, the old woman brushed a blond curl from CC's face.

"We will be here. If the abbot or Sir Andras call for you, we will simply tell them that the drugged wine and the illness have left you senseless. Then we will waft more poultices under their noses. Go to your lover."

"Then help me pull that dresser under the window," CC said eagerly. "Could someone find my shoes?"

The room exploded into female motion. In one sweep the clutter was removed from the top of the dresser, the dresser was wrestled to its position under the window and CC's two doeskin slippers were located and placed quickly on her feet. She was already wearing only her chemise, so she didn't have to wait impatiently for Isabel to unlace her from the bondage of her ornate gown.

Before she climbed atop the dresser, she hugged each of the women.

"It is so romantic," Lynelle whispered into her ear.

"And wonderful," Bronwyn agreed.

"Exciting," Gwenyth added.

"Go with the blessing of the Holy Mother." Isabel's hug was strong.

CC kissed the old woman's cheek. "I'll be careful."

"You must return before dawn so that the lightening of the sky does not betray you to the knight's men."

"I will. Don't worry." She gave Isabel another quick hug and started to turn, then, changing her mind, she stopped. On a sudden impulse CC lifted the silver chain from around her neck. The amber teardrop swung lazily as she placed the pendant over the old woman's head.

"Keep it for me while I'm gone," she said to Isabel, whose eyes were filling with tears as her hand lovingly cupped the goddess's amber.

Unable to speak, the old woman nodded and watched as CC climbed nimbly up the dresser, using the partially opened drawers as stair steps.

Slowly, CC peered out the window. The night was dark; the richness of the late hour cloaked the monastery in a veil of black velvet. The moon was a thin, glowing scythe that cast just enough light to turn trees into shadows and paths into ribbons of pale light.

"Do you see any of the men?" Isabel's whisper carried in the still room.

CC shook her head.

"Then go quickly," Isabel urged.

Holding her breath, CC shifted her seat to the windowsill, then she turned, found her toehold and dropped silently to the soft ground. She heard a grunt from inside the room, followed by a glimpse of Isabel's face framed by the window. A flash of moonlight reflected off the silver chain.

"What are you doing?" CC hissed.

"Keeping watch for you." The old woman whispered. "Now go to your lover."

CC smiled and blew Isabel a kiss before scurrying across the little patch of ground that separated the monastery from the rocky cliff. With feet that felt light and swift, CC navigated the familiar path. Often she glanced up at the cliff's edge above her, worried that she would see the silhouetted shape of one of Andras's squires, but the cliff remained empty and soon her feet sank into the sand of the beach.

Dylan! Her heart called as she stepped out of her slippers and slid the chemise from her naked body. *I'm here! Please come to me.*

The cool fingers of the waves washing against her legs felt like a wonderful, erotic dream, and as she walked into the surf the almost uncontrollable desire to change into her mermaid form and disappear into its inviting depths tugged at her will. She forced the desire down, trembling with the effort it cost her.

Tomorrow, she promised herself. I only have to wait until tomorrow, then I will never have to be parted from my mermaid form.

Or from me. Dylan's voice sounded within her mind an instant before he surfaced a few feet in front of her.

"Have I dreamed you here, my love?" the merman asked.

"Well, let's see. If you touch me, and I can feel it, then it's not a dream," CC said.

Her feet ran out of firm ground, but before she could swim two full strokes, Dylan pulled her into the warmth of his arms. Greedily, their bodies met. CC felt a shiver of pleasure as she tasted his slick, hot mouth.

"Can you feel that?" Dylan's breath was warm against her parted lips.

"I can feel everything," CC said.

"Then I did not dream you here; I wished you here."

"I don't have long tonight." CC's breath caught as the merman's mouth explored the hollow of her neck. "Andras thinks I'm sick, so he's not looking for me, but his men are keeping watch for Vikings."

Dylan's laughter was muffled against her skin, and his teeth pulled playfully at her earlobe before he spoke.

"I did enjoy your performance on the beach."

"Well, I couldn't very well let him kiss me," CC said. She would not mention Sarpedon's possession of the knight to him. She would not spoil their short time together and cause him needless worry.

Dylan cupped her face in his hand. "No, you could not let him kiss you." And the merman pressed his lips to hers, effectively erasing the image of Andras's thwarted kiss from their minds.

"I'll have to leave before dawn this time," CC said, arching her body against his, loving the intensely erotic sensation of his exotic body pressed against hers.

"I want to feel myself within you." Dylan's voice was rough with passion.

"Yes!" CC said, pulling on his bottom lip with her teeth.

The merman moaned, and CC felt his hard shaft as it pulsed against the softness of her thigh. She shifted so that he could easily slide within her, but Dylan shook his head.

"Not here. Not like this. This is the last time you will make love as a human. It should not be something done in the haste of thoughtless passion. It should be savored."

CC nibbled on his neck. "I am savoring it."

Dylan's laughter mixed with a groan of desire. "Come with me, siren; I will teach you of savoring."

"Well, there's certainly no doubt that you're my favorite teacher," CC said as she settled against his chest, letting the powerful strokes of his tail propel them down the beach. CC closed her eyes, enjoying the mingled sensations of the water and her lover against her naked skin. When she felt sand against her body her eyes opened in surprise.

They were laying half out of the water in the little rock-dotted cove CC had found earlier that day. The curved moon cast a subdued, magical light, which reflected off the lazy water around them. Dylan's body pressed against hers, and he stroked the length of her with sea-slick hands.

CC felt hot and cold and liquid all at the same time.

"I think you're the siren," she said, caressing the flame-colored flesh that swelled erect against her.

Dylan made a choked noise and shifted his weight so that they were on their sides, facing each other, and she could touch him more easily.

"I cannot be. It is *I* who am under *your* spell," Dylan said.

The merman drew his hand up the length of her thigh, rubbing enticing circles over the silken skin of her legs. Then he bent to her and his mouth replaced his hand and he lavished her skin with kisses and teasing pretend bites until he found the wet center of her. There he devoured her, his tongue continuing his circular caresses, increasing in movement and rhythm until CC gripped his shoulders and shuddered with the intensity of her climax.

Again he shifted his weight and pulled her into his arms. She felt alive with sensation, and enfolded within his strength, CC explored his mouth, letting her hands roam down his body as if they had a will of their own.

"Your body amazes me," CC told him as her mouth and hands discovered new ridges of muscle.

Remembering the sensitivity of her own mer-body, she caressed his fiery flesh with teasing fingertips. Dylan's breath quickened and CC could feel the tension humming through his body, which was now slick with sweat as well as the salty water that lapped against him. When her mouth began tracing the line low on his torso where mer-flesh met human skin, his body trembled and he called her name between ragged breaths.

In one swift movement, he pulled her up. Then he was above her, resting his weight on his forearms. The night sky outlined his powerful body, and CC could see his dark eyes flash with unleashed desire. She opened herself to him, and, wrapping her legs around him, she arched, wordlessly urging him on. Dylan buried himself within her, and CC met his thrusts with equal intensity. He devoured her mouth and their tempo increased. CC felt the delicious tension build within her again, and when the merman's body began to shudder in orgasm, her own climax met his as the night fragmented into an explosion of sensation.

Afterward, CC nestled securely against Dylan's chest. The merman brushed sand from her shoulders with gentle hands that tended to linger at the long, graceful curve of her back.

"Now I see what you mean about savoring," she murmured.

Dylan's chest rumbled with his deep chuckle. "I would like to have attempted more savoring." CC felt him shrug his shoulders. "But I could not resist you, siren."

CC looked up at him. "Are sirens mermaids?"

His chuckle turned into laughter, and he hugged her. "No. Sirens are water nymphs."

"Not mermaids?"

"Definitely not mermaids." He kissed her forehead. "But they are alluring creatures filled with erotic intent." He gave her a meaningful look.

"Are you sure they're females? They sound a lot like you," CC teased.

Dylan smiled at her. "There are no male sirens."

"You could have fooled me," CC said, pulling his mouth down to hers. She kissed him, pressing her body so closely against his that she could feel his heartbeat increasing against her breast.

"If you keep kissing me like that, you will not be back at the monastery before dawn." Dylan's voice had already deepened with his growing desire.

CC sighed and nibbled at his full bottom lip. "One more day."

"One more day," he repeated, kissing her gently.

They didn't speak as they floated away from the shore and back toward the cliffs that held the monastery. CC rested against her lover's chest, watching the night sky begin to unveil its layers of darkness as it climbed steadily toward dawn. A thought tickled the edges of her mind as CC pulled her attention from the sky to look around her.

"You know, I haven't seen my dolphin friend the last couple times I've come to the water. Have you seen her?" she asked Dylan.

Dylan considered the question, then shook his head.

"No, I have not encountered the little creature."

"I guess I don't blame her for staying away, especially after Andras hit her with that rock," CC said.

"She never stays away from Undine for long. I am certain she is there,"—Dylan gestured out to sea—"awaiting the return of her princess."

"I'm sure you're right," CC said, trying not to worry.

The water around them became choppier and the sound of the waves crashing against the beach told her that they were near the monastery even before Dylan changed direction and swam slowly to the shore.

"You can stand now," Dylan said.

CC put her feet against the sandy bottom, but she kept her arms wrapped around the merman.

"The sky lightens," he said and kissed the top of her head.

"I wish it wouldn't," CC spoke into his chest.

Dylan cupped her face in his hands. "Then this last day would not pass. Remember, my love, with its passing comes the night."

"And that's when I'll come to you . . . forever," she finished for him.

Their kiss was a sweet promise. Before she began walking away from him she linked her fingers through his and said, "Tell me once more how long you would wait for me."

"For an eternity, Christine. I would wait for you for an eternity."

He brought her hand to his lips and kissed her palm. Reluctantly, he released her and she turned to the beach.

The lightening of the sky was becoming more pronounced and her discarded chemise was easy to find. She was shaking the sand from it when a sharp voice cut across the beach.

"Behold the whore!"

Chapter Twenty-nine

THE abbot stepped triumphantly from the cover of the trees that grew in dwarflike tufts at the base of the cliff. Several confused-looking monks milled nervously there, too. Andras stood beside the abbot, so close that in the dim light their bodies appeared to be joined. The knight's face was a pale disk broken only by his eyes, which were bright silver slits of hatred, and he was dragging with him a weeping Isabel.

"They broke into your room," Isabel sobbed. "We could not stop them. They said they must have proof that you were within."

Andras's voice echoed with Sarpedon's demonic amplification. *"I knew the whore was with her lover. I knew it! Take her."* His command was like ice, and one of the squires leapt to obey him.

CC felt as if their appearance had turned her to stone. She held the chemise to her chest, trying to cover her nakedness. She wanted to run back into the sea, but her feet would not obey her. The squire quickly covered the few yards that separated them and grabbed her arm, purposely digging his fingers into her delicate flesh.

"Maybe we will have a little fun before they burn you," he sneered, his eyes ravishing CC's naked body. The foul cloud of his rotting breath made her gag.

"Touch her again and you will not leave this island alive," Dylan's voice carried across the waves with such force that CC saw the squire cringe—then he stared open-mouthed at the sight of the merman.

Dylan had raised himself well out of the water, so that his powerful tail seemed to glisten and ripple as if he was on fire.

"The demon!" Abbot William's voice held an edge of hysteria. "The witch has a demon lover!"

"Kill it!" Sir Andras barked the order, and almost instantly the chilling sound of an arrow whistled from the other squire's position behind them on the beach.

As the arrow flew toward the water, CC felt a rush of power within her, and her body unfroze. The squire who held her arm was still gazing slack-jawed at the merman, and it was with surprising ease that CC rammed her knee into his groin and wrenched her arm from his grasp. Spinning around she ran for the waterline.

"Stop her, you fool!" Andras yelled.

"Quickly, Christine!" Dylan called, dodging another arrow.

She could hear the sounds of the squire as he grunted and scrambled to his feet behind her. She glanced over her shoulder to see Andras sprinting across the sand, longbow held forward and eyes flashing as he took aim at Dylan. As the arrow twanged free, CC reached the water. Thrusting her arms over her head as if she was an Olympic diver, she leapt forward, calling the power of her mermaid body alive. The delicious heat of transformation sizzled down her body, and she hit the water flying. CC's sleek mermaid form skimmed just below the surface, and then with one stroke of her tail she swam up, angling herself at Dylan's body. She broke through the waves like she had been shot from a cannon.

And the arrow meant for Dylan sliced neatly through the muscle of her left shoulder blade. The pain was white hot, and she crumbled forward into her lover's arms. Dylan's agonized cry was echoed on the shore. Through a haze of pain Christine looked back to the beach.

Andras was standing unnaturally still and straight. His mouth was stretched impossibly wide by a horrible shriek of rage.

"No!" The voice no longer made any pretense of belonging to the knight. *"Not her! You were not to harm her!"*

Andras fell to his knees, his body writhing grotesquely like there were hundreds of worms beneath his skin. Then, with a ripping sound a liquid cloud of darkness vomited from his mouth. It shimmered and pooled in hideous wetness and seemed to crawl toward the surf. When it touched the water the darkness shifted and reformed, drawing substance from the saltwater. With a roar, Sarpedon rose, fully formed and glistening with power.

He faced the humans, swollen with anger and disdain.

"Puny creatures. You dare to harm a child of Lir! Know that your fate has been sealed."

Sarpedon swirled one massive hand into the water next to him until it boiled and seethed with activity. In horror, the humans watched as a many-tentacled monster erupted from the sea. It engulfed the shrieking body of a monk who had drifted too close to the sea, and in one motion snapped his spine and hurled his lifeless body against the cliff. Then it turned its awful attention to the knight. Preparing for battle, Sir Andras planted his feet and brandished his sword. Shouting, his squires scrambled to reach his side.

Suddenly, a wall of flesh obscured CC's view of the battle, and Sarpedon towered above them.

"The game is ended, Undine. It is time you took your rightful place as my mate." Sarpedon's voice was deceptively calm.

CC felt light-headed. Dylan still held her within his arms, and CC noted with detached curiosity that the water surrounding them was tainted scarlet. That must be my blood, the thought played slowly through her mind and she struggled against the urge to close her eyes and sink beneath the waves.

"Stay away from her, Sarpedon," Dylan spoke with iron in his voice. He shifted his grip on CC so that he placed his body protectively between Sarpedon and the mermaid.

Sarpedon's laugher was a roar. "Does the son of a human believe he can stand against the power of the gods?"

Blinking to clear the bright spots from her vision, CC forced herself to move to Dylan's side.

"He and I stand together against you, Sarpedon. And when Lir gets here tonight he will stand with us, too." CC's voice surprised her by sounding strong and clear.

Sarpedon's lip curled in a sneer. "Oh, I seem to remember there was a message sent to our father. Tragic that the little dolphin messenger met with such an untimely end, *before* she could relay the Earth goddess's request. But, no matter. I was gracious enough to answer for our father. So you see that I stand ready to render judgment in his stead."

A tremor of fear passed through CC. "No. You can't."

The enormous merman moved closer to them. "You have been wrong about many things, Undine. And you are wrong yet again."

A scream from the beach interrupted them. Sarpedon turned, laughing evilly as the creature he had called to the surface squeezed the life out of the squire who had grabbed CC.

"See how I punish those who would do you harm?" Sarpedon said.

"Make it stop," CC cried. Her voice was hoarse with emotion.

Sarpedon's eyes widened in surprise. "But they would have killed you. Why would you ask to spare them?"

"Because to use your power like this is wrong."

"It is justice," Sarpedon scoffed.

"It's not justice—it's vengeance. Vengeance meted out by a creature bloated with his own imagined importance. You are a disgusting toad. I loathe you, and I will never belong to you."

Sarpedon seemed to swell with rage. "Never is a very long time. Perhaps you will change your mind when you see your pathetic human friend in my grasp." The merman shouted a command in a garbled language that CC was shocked to realize she could understand.

"Kill the old one!"

Instantly the sea monster snaked out a tentacle around Isabel's neck, but the amulet of the goddess sparked and glowed, causing the creature's grip to falter. As the old woman tried to scramble out of reach, Sarpedon shouted another command, and the monster wrapped a tentacle around her ankle. Isabel lost her balance and fell hard onto the sand. The creature began to pull her toward the water.

"No!" CC screamed.

"Never, you said!" Sarpedon bellowed. "We shall see how long never is as you watch your lover and your friend die!"

Sarpedon closed his hand around a froth of wave and instantly it solidified into the foam-colored blade of a stiletto. The huge merman lunged forward and CC struggled painfully not to slide under the surface as Dylan lost his protective hold on her and surged forward to meet the giant. The two mermen met with a sound that cracked and reverberated like thunder.

"Undine!" Isabel's voice was a sob of terror. The sea creature appeared to be toying with the old woman as it slowly pulled her to the edge of the water where its beak-shaped head glistened with daggerlike teeth. The remaining squire and Sir Andras sent arrow after arrow into its pulsating body, but the creature seemed impervious to their weapons.

The sound of wailing came from the cliff, and CC glanced up. Lynelle, Bronwyn and Gwenyth were clinging to each other and crying with terror. Around them milled several of the monks. Some of them were on their knees praying, but most of them stood in impotent silence. There was no sign of Abbot William.

Dylan hissed in pain, and CC's eyes snapped back to her lover as Sarpedon's blade sliced a trail down the muscles of his chest.

"That is just a taste of what is to come, son of a human. My Undine will watch as I carve you into pieces," Sarpedon said.

Dylan circled him warily. When he spoke his voice was calm. "You may kill me, Sarpedon, but you will not win her love. She will loathe you forever."

Sarpedon's laughter was sharp. "An eternity is a long time. She will forget you."

An eternity. The words echoed within CC's mind. It was Dylan's promise to her. And there was only one way she wanted to spend eternity—next to Dylan's side.

Ignoring the pain in her shoulder, she beat against the water with powerful strokes of her tail, so that she rose up, lifting her entire torso from the waves.

I am the daughter of a goddess, she told herself, and I claim my birthright. With a voice that filled the morning air, she called to her mother.

"Gaea! Your daughter needs you! Help me, Mother!"

Then, using the sea magic that sang within her true mermaid body, CC reached out and cupped some of the bubblelike foam that surrounded her.

"Make me a weapon," she commanded the waters. Instantly, the handle of a knife formed against her palm. Her blade wasn't the color of foam—it was the crimson of her newly shed blood.

"Dylan!" she called to her lover, and both mermen paused in their battle to turn to her. "Catch," she said and tossed him the dagger.

Dylan caught the knife deftly and sent her a tight smile of thanks. Then his attention shifted back to Sarpedon.

"That will not help you," Sarpedon snarled, and they continued circling each other, blades flashing in the morning light.

CC felt the change in the air the moment before the goddess materialized. She strode from the foliage at the base of the cliff. Her anger was terrible; the air around her crackled and sparked with it. The knight and the squire dropped their weapons and cringed before her on the beach. She spared no glance for them. Her attention was riveted on the sea monster that had dragged Isabel to within inches of its gaping maw.

The goddess stretched out her hand and in a burst of green light a leaf-colored spear appeared. Gaea plucked it from the air and hurled it straight into the monster's open mouth. The force of the spear was so great that it traveled through the creature's body and exploded out the rear of it, followed by a slick fountain of blood and entrails.

"Return to the dark depths from whence you were born!" Gaea commanded.

The monster writhed spasmodically. Losing its grip on Isabel, it sank below the surface in a muddy cloud. Isabel scrambled to her feet, but she wasn't able to walk and she stumbled, falling in a heap at Gaea's feet. The goddess knelt and passed her shining hands over the old woman's body.

"There, the pain is gone, my Isabel."

Isabel's eyes widened in recognition as she gazed upon Gaea. The old woman crossed herself reverently.

"Thank you, Holy Mother!"

Gaea touched Isabel gently. Then she stood, facing the sea. Her silver cloak billowed behind her and the white silk of her transparent gown shimmered with the goddess's might. She walked to the water's edge, and the sand surged forward, hardening under her delicate feet until she stood on a bridge of earth that jutted out into the sea.

Mere feet from the goddess, the mermen were locked together in silent combat, each straining to end the battle with a killing slash. Dylan was bleeding heavily from several gaping wounds. His body looked like it was clothed in scarlet.

"ENOUGH!"

The power of the word was a tangible thing, lifting the hairs on CC's neck and ringing through her blood. A wall of white light exploded between the mermen, knocking them apart. CC swam quickly to Dylan's side.

Sarpedon spun on the goddess, raising himself out of the water until he levitated over her bridge.

"This is not your battle, Land Goddess," he spat. "I preside here in my father's absence."

"Foolish child," the goddess's voice held pity. "I have tolerated your interference out of love for your father. But your hatred has gone too far."

Gaea lifted her graceful arms to the sky, crossing them at the wrist. Above her materialized a cloud of power that spun and sparked like the dust of diamonds.

"LIR! THE EARTH DEMANDS YOUR PRESENCE AS SHE RENDERS JUDGMENT UPON YOUR SON!"

As Gaea spoke the command she brought her arms down in a sweeping arch, fingers pointing at the surrounding water. Like fireworks, the cloud exploded, raining power and energy, and the echo of the goddess's words into the sea.

Sarpedon's face had paled, but when he spoke his voice was still filled with arrogance.

"My father will not answer your summons. He is not an Earth child to jump at your bidding." His laughter sounded hollow and forced. "And he is much too busy presiding over the problems of the islands. The Shark God and I have made quite certain of that."

Gaea shook her head sadly at the merman. "Lir's absence stank of your interference. I knew it, and I should have interceded. The deaths that have happened today were needless. Your hatred caused them, son of Lir, but I could have prevented them. That guilt will be my sadness to bear. But with or without the presence of your father, I will cast judgment upon you—and fulfill your punishment."

"You have no right to punish me, Earth creature!" Sarpedon growled. "I am a sea god. In the realm of water my desires are fulfilled, and my commands obeyed. I will have Undine as my mate, and the rest of these pathetic creatures will stand aside or face my wrath!"

Before the goddess could respond, the water surrounding them began to seethe and bubble. Then a pillar of brilliant seawater geysered into the sky. The thick column swirled, morphing in color from the clarity of glass to the turquoise of shallow water, which refracted and changed in shade to the blue-black of the ocean's depths. The center of the pillar suddenly split, as if a bolt of lightning had cleft it apart, and from within that split appeared a giant of a man, carrying a massive trident made of deadly looking ebony. On his head was a crown of golden shells speckled with the iridescent white of perfect pearls. His silver hair was the color of moonlight on water and it curled in a thick cascade around his shoulders, mingling with the luxurious length of his beard. His togalike robe, the exact color of waves, was draped across his body. It left much of his powerful chest exposed, and as he stepped free of the pillar and strode to Gaea, walking as if the water was solid ground, CC couldn't help but marvel at his majesty.

Gaea spoke first, offering him one slender hand, which the giant took and bowed over, kissing it with an easy intimacy.

"Lir, the Earth welcomes you." The goddess's voice was warm and intimate.

"The sea responds in kind," the giant said. "It has been much too long since we two have met." Lir spoke with obvious affection. Then his attention shifted to the scene surrounding them and a frown creased his brow. "What have we here, Earth Mother—errant children?"

"Father, this Earth goddess interferes in matters of the sea. There is no trouble here that is not of her making," Sarpedon blurted.

"Sarpedon, your tone is offensive. Gaea does not meddle in the affairs of others. Be wary that you do not make the Earth your enemy." Lir's face tightened and though his voice remained calm, his reprimand was sharp. He glanced around the restless water and the sea god's eyes narrowed in anger as he noticed Undine's injury.

"Who dared to harm my child?"

The waves trembled at Lir's words, and CC's tongue felt thick and awkward. But Dylan's answer was swift, and he met the sea god's eyes unflinchingly.

"The arrow that wounded your daughter was meant for me. Although Sarpedon did not loose the arrow, it was his jealousy that caused the humans to try and destroy me."

"Undine." Lir turned to her. "What has happened here?"

CC took a deep breath, swallowing her fear and the pain that radiated in cruel fingers from her shoulder. When she spoke her voice sounded tinny and strange, like it belonged to someone else.

"First of all, you need to know that I'm not really Undine. My soul is human. Your daughter and I exchanged places because she hated it here and because—"

Lir's roar stopped her words. "Deceit and deception!" He whirled on Gaea. "Did you do this?"

Calmly, Gaea touched the sea god's arm. "Allow the child to finish, Lir. Her soul may not have been born as your daughter, but she is tied to you through her body and, unlike Undine, she has a deep, abiding love of the sea."

Lir narrowed his eyes, but he nodded tightly and turned his attention back to the mermaid.

"I will listen."

CC tried to smile her appreciation, but her lips could only form a brief grimace of pain. Then Dylan's hand linked with hers. She clung to him and drew strength from his touch.

"Undine's desire to exchange places with a human wasn't just because she longed for the land; a big part of it was because she wanted to escape from Sarpedon."

"She lies, Father!" Sarpedon shouted.

"Silence!" Lir commanded his son. Then he gentled his voice and said, "Continue, child."

"I know all too well what Undine felt. The first thing that happened to me when I found myself in her body was that I had to escape from an attempted rape—by him." CC tossed her head in Sarpedon's direction.

"More lies, Father!" Sarpedon exploded. "There was no need to force myself on her; she wanted me. Then she decided to dally with this pathetic son of a human, and I have simply tired of waiting for her to finish her little game. Now I claim what has always been mine."

"Love is not something that can be possessed and ordered," Gaea broke in, her voice filled with scorn. "And the only lies spoken here have come from your mouth, Sarpedon." Gaea raised her hand, palm up, and drew a glistening oval in the air before them. "Behold the truth, God of the Seas." The goddess pursed her shapely lips and blew a delicate breath of air onto the shining mirror. Instantly, images flashed across its surface like a movie playing in a darkened theater.

First there was an image of the plane wreck, and CC watched herself being pulled beneath the waves and exchanging souls with the beautiful mermaid. Then the scene flashed to Sarpedon's attempted rape, and CC's magical transformation into a temporarily human body. The mirror showed Dylan's rescue of her and Andras's subsequent discovery of her as he pulled her from the sea. Glimpses of scenes from CC's days at the monastery included Gaea's various calls for Lir's aid, and the death of the loyal dolphin messenger at the hands of Sarpedon.

Included in the images was the discovery of the Mother's statue in the chapel and her growing friendship with the women, as well as her hard treatment at the hands of Abbot William.

Then the images shifted again, and Sarpedon's presence was clearly seen drifting, oil-like, out of the well. The mirror reflected the events that unfolded when the merman inhabited the knight's body, and it clearly displayed the havoc Sarpedon's influence caused among the humans.

CC felt her head spin as she watched the mirror's image of herself being shown the wonders of the sea by Dylan. She experienced again the magic of their love as it was born and reveled in hearing the mirror image of her lover repeat his promise of waiting an eternity for her.

Again, the scene changed to show the humans' discovery of CC and her lover, and Sarpedon's materialization from the body of Andras. The last vision exposed through the glassy surface was of Gaea calling forth Lir to preside over the punishment of his son. Then the glistening surface went blank, and Gaea blew on it again, causing it to dissipate into a puff of shining smoke, leaving a shroud of silence that hung over the water.

Lir spoke first to the goddess. "I did not hear any of your calls." He shook his head sadly. "Sarpedon should not have been able to keep them from me. I allowed myself to be distracted."

Gaea nodded in understanding. "I knew Sarpedon was involved in your absence, but I was loath to act against your child. We share the responsibility of our errors."

"Yes. And too many have paid for them in our stead." The sea god faced the beach.

Andras and his squire were still crouched in the sand, eyes glassy with shock at what they were witnessing. Bronwyn, Lynelle and Gwenyth had joined Isabel on the beach and the four women stood together, their hands linked. Most of the monks had fled from the cliffside, but the few who remained were kneeling as if in prayer. The abbot was nowhere to be seen.

Lir glanced at Gaea and asked, "Are you willing to exchange roles, so that justice will truly be served?"

The goddess lifted her brows questioningly. "What do you propose?"

"I propose that I render judgment in your realm, as you will in mine."

Gaea hesitated only a moment. "Agreed."

Lir turned his attention to the humans on shore. First he focused his hard gaze on Andras and his man. "My judgment is thus—the knight and his squire shall return to their kingdom of land unharmed." Lir paused, and his eyes took on a sly glint, then he added, "Sir Andras, you shall learn the value of women. Henceforth you will be able to father only daughters, and your daughters will bear only female children. You would be wise to remember that the goddess of the Earth will be watching closely that you treat your daughters well." The knight's face drained of all its color, and he seemed to shrink in upon himself; then the two men scurried off the beach.

Lir spoke to the women next. "Wise women, because I am grateful for the friendship you have shown my daughter, I gift you with this monastery." Lir swept his arm in a grand gesture that encompassed the rocky walls above them, and suddenly the bland, gray color was washed away, replaced by stones that seemed to shine with the color of pearls. The four women on the beach gasped in pleasure.

"You will find I have made some *changes* within, too, as is befitting your new home." Lir smiled fondly at the women. Then he raised his head and his voice carried to the few monks who were still kneeling on the cliff. "You males may stay, but know that these women are no longer your servants. Live and worship peacefully with them, as equals, or flee their island and the wrath of the God of the Seas."

Then Lir's sharp gaze searched the beach until he found a quivering mound of flesh hiding behind a fallen log.

"Abbot! You cannot hide from the gods. Stand and receive your judgment."

Trembling, Abbot William raised his head and struggled to his feet. His face was streaked with tears and vomit soaked the front of his blood-colored robe.

Gaea touched Lir's arm again. Her voice was gentle. "Perhaps we should judge him together. He is, after all, our child."

The abbot's eyes widened in horror, and he shook his head from side to side in jerky, panic-filled denial.

Lir scowled. "Stop sniveling, William. *Remember!*" he commanded as he flicked his wrist, raining a spray of seawater across the beach and onto the abbot.

Instantly, a change came over William's face, and he blinked several times, rubbing his eyes as if he was just awakening from a bad dream.

"I told you we should have left him with his memories," Gaea said.

Lir sighed. "He always was our most difficult child. He could not abide the seas, yet he did not belong on the land. What do you propose we do with him now?"

Gaea tapped her chin thoughtfully with one slim finger. Then her eyes widened, and her smile was glorious. "I propose he spend the next century with Cernunnos helping him guard the Gateway to the Underworld. Perhaps one hundred years with the dead will teach our son to appreciate the beauty of life, and to be more accepting of himself and of others."

"Excellent!" Lir said, and he struck his trident three times against the water. At the third strike the beach at William's feet split open and swallowed him, closing quickly on his high-pitched cry for help.

"Now it is your turn, Earth Mother," Lir said.

"I will try to be as wise and just as the Lord of the Seas," the goddess said with a magnanimous smile.

Gaea and Lir faced the mer-beings. Gaea turned first to the two lovers. When she spoke, the goddess's words were filled with the warmth of a mother.

"Undine and Dylan—your love is strong and true. Though it causes me sadness to have my favorite daughter live apart from the land, your union brings me great joy. I bless your lives and smile upon your joining. May an eternity not diminish your love."

CC felt the goddess's blessing settle over her, and her soul swelled with happiness as Dylan took her gently into his battered arms.

Then she faced Sarpedon, whose face had already darkened in a rage of disbelief, and her expression hardened. His eyes flicked nervously from Lir to Gaea, as if he expected his father to step in and prevent the goddess from continuing.

"Sarpedon, you have been an overindulged child, and your punishment is long overdue. Since you misused the well that nourished the monastery, and you thought that through violence and entrapment you could cage love, your punishment shall reflect your misdeeds. I sentence you to be trapped within a well for the next century. And your jail will not be near the seas so that you can draw power from them to cause evil among those who would use your well. You will be caged far inland, deep in the center of a castle known for its well-ordered discipline. In the land of Caer Llion, the people banished magic decades ago. There you will neither be acknowledged nor feared. My wish for you is that this punishment teaches you to appreciate your freedom enough to allow others their own."

Gaea raised her hand to call forth her judgment, but with a snakelike movement Sarpedon's arm struck out, and he used his supernatural strength to shatter the bridge of land on which the goddess stood. The sand dissolved under her feet and, with a cry of shocked surprise, Gaea fell into the water. Whipping his thick tail, Sarpedon caused the water to whirlpool and boil as it closed over the goddess's head.

Roaring in disbelief, Lir parted the seething blue liquid and grasped Gaea's hand, pulling her up into his arms.

Quickly, Sarpedon spread his hands out into the water, as if he was searching for a hidden treasure within the waves. His voice was the sound of madness.

"If I cannot have her, no one will have her!"

The crazed merman raised his mighty arm from the waves. In his fist he clutched the spear Gaea had fashioned to kill the sea monster. In a movement blurred with speed, Sarpedon hurled the spear at CC.

Dylan saw the spear coming and the world seemed to slow around him. He could not let Sarpedon kill her. She needed him; the cost did not matter.

An instant before the weapon would have penetrated CC's body, Dylan twisted, throwing himself in front of the mermaid. CC felt her lover spasm as the spear embedded itself in his back, and she watched in horror as its tip blossomed out of the merman's chest like a terrible crimson flower.

Her cry of despair joined with Lir's roar of rage. The sea god's reaction was swift. He hurled his trident at his son, striking him full in the chest. Sarpedon's eyes widened in shock an instant before his lifeless body began to liquefy and lose substance, until he no longer held the form of a merman, but became part of the waters from which he had been born.

In two enormous strides the sea god was at Dylan's side. He barked a word of command and the water hardened so that it held Gaea aloft, above its frothing wetness. Both deities knelt before the wounded merman.

Dylan focused his remaining power and sent one simple thought to Gaea.

Do not let her know. It is a cost I willingly paid.

Gaea knew that his transformation into a human had weakened him too much. Now, not even the power of the Gods could save him. The goddess closed her eyes on tears and nodded.

My daughter shall not know.

Dylan's body slumped in CC's arms. His eyes were closed and his breathing was shallow and rapid. Blood poured from the flesh that gaped around the spearhead. Lir grasped the handle of the spear protruding from the merman's back, as if to pull it from Dylan's body, but Gaea's restraining hand halted him.

"It will only cause him more pain." The goddess's words were rich with sorrow.

"What do you mean?" CC's voice was tinged with growing hysteria. "Of course you have to pull it out! How else are you going to save him?"

In a gesture infinitely gentle, Gaea touched the mermaid's tear-drenched cheek.

"I cannot save him, Christine."

"You have to!" CC sobbed. "You're a goddess. You have to be able to save him."

The goddess's eyes filled with tears. As she spoke they spilled down her cheeks, leaving trails of glistening diamonds in their wake.

"He has been pierced with my own spear, a weapon fashioned by my hand as a device of destruction. I cannot heal a wound caused by my own hand."

"But you didn't throw it!"

"I wrought it, and that is enough. I did not have to wield it, too," Gaea said sadly.

CC looked desperately at Lir. "Then you save him. You're a god."

The sea god exchanged a look with Gaea. When he spoke, his voice held the weight of centuries. "I cannot undo the destruction brought about by the Earth goddess. Even gods and goddesses are bound by the rules of the universe."

"Then turn back time! Do something!" CC screamed.

"Christine," Dylan's voice was a choked whisper. His body twitched as he struggled to turn his face up to hers. "They cannot help me." He coughed and blood gushed in a new torrent from his wound.

"*Shhh*," CC pressed her hand to his lips. "Don't talk. Save your strength. We'll figure out something."

With an almost imperceptible movement, Dylan shook his head. "I knew the choice I was making when I moved within the path of the spear. I made it freely"—he paused to pant for breath—"and I would make it again." The merman closed his eyes, struggling against a wave of pain.

"Dylan, no!" CC kissed him frantically. "You can't die. You can't leave me. Remember," she sobbed, "you promised me an eternity."

The merman's lips tilted briefly in a smile, and he opened his eyes. "I still await you. For an eternity, Christine."

In one last heave, the merman's chest rose and his shaking hand brushed CC's tear-soaked cheek.

"For an eternity . . ."

With those last words, Dylan's life fled his body, and CC was left clutching the shell of her beloved until it, like Sarpedon's body, began to fade and liquefy, returning to the water of his creation.

As if sifting sand through a colander, CC's hands tried to recapture the scattered brilliance of the colors of flame that floated briefly atop the water.

"Come, child," Gaea said, grasping CC's hands so that their frantic motion was stilled.

Gaea opened her arms to her daughter, but even the embrace of a goddess could not soothe the pain of loss within CC, and the mermaid sobbed so desperately that she felt as if her soul had dissolved around her like Dylan's body.

Then other arms joined the goddess. They were softer, more aged arms, arms that were weathered and worn and had born witness to a lifetime of hardship and sorrows.

"I know, child. I know."

CC looked up into Isabel's tear-stained face. Then she felt more arms around her. Standing chest deep in water, Lynelle, Bronwyn and Gwenyth had joined Isabel. The four women completed the circle around CC, lending her their strength and filling her with their love. CC sobbed out her pain and loss, secure in the knowledge that the women who held her would not let her go.

In the midst of despair, Gaea reached her hand out to her daughter, motioning to the path that the arrow had carved through the mermaid's flesh.

"Let me heal you of this wound, Daughter," Gaea said. But before the goddess touched the bloody furrow, she hesitated. Slowly she withdrew her hand. "I must wait. The judgment is not complete." Gaea looked at Lir. "Events have changed, and so must my judgment."

Wearily, the sea god nodded.

"This judgment will differ from those of the past, because today's events have forever changed me." Gaea's audience was hushed, even Lir seemed to be holding his breath in anticipation of the goddess's next words. "For the bravery and loyalty you have shown, my beloved daughter, my judgment is that you may choose your future path." CC's tear-ravaged face brightened, and Gaea was quick to continue. "I cannot change your lover's death, and for that I will be eternally sorry, but I can offer you two choices."

"What are they?" CC asked in a voice that shook.

"You may choose to stay here, in this world and this time, either as a mermaid and Goddess of the Seas, or as Earth's beloved daughter and a goddess in my realm. You will reign beside either parent, and your days will be filled with the duties of a deity."

"Forever?" CC asked.

"Forever," Gaea assured her.

"What is my other choice?"

"I will return you to your old world and your old time—to the site of your accident, the moment before the wreckage pulled you under the waves. You will survive the accident and continue with your human life."

"But what will happen to Undine if I choose to return to my world?" CC asked.

Lir's voice sounded ancient with grief. "My son exists no more. That is as unchanging as the death of Dylan. If Undine returns to me, she will be allowed her own choice. Whether she decides to remain in the seas with me, or joins her mother on land, she has my blessing. I shall no longer try to control the lives of my children."

"There is one more thing you should know before you make your choice," Gaea spoke into the silence that surrounded the god's words. "It is within our power"—here she glanced at Lir and he nodded slowly in agreement—"to wipe clean the slate of your memory."

"You mean you can send me back to the instant that I was being pulled under by the wreckage, and you can make me forget everything that has happened here? It'd be like I was never gone, like Undine and I had never changed places?" CC asked.

"Yes," the goddess said.

CC felt herself become very still. She closed her eyes and, against the background of her darkened lids, she replayed the days and nights she had spent on Caldei. And her eyes snapped open.

"I know what I want," she said firmly.

"Tell me daughter; complete your own judgment."

"I have loved being in this world; I thought that I had finally found a place where I could belong, a place I could call my true home. But I understand now that a sense of belonging is not physical. We can't find it by changing where we live or what we do. We have to carry it within us." CC took a deep breath. "Forgive me, Mother." Her gaze included both Gaea and Isabel. "I can't spend an eternity without him, even if it is as a goddess. And I've learned that I carry my true home within me. So I want to be sent back to my old world. And I want to remember—all of you and him." Her words ended in a whisper.

"Very well," the goddess said.

"We will miss you, Undine." Isabel spoke for the women, who nodded and wiped tears from their streaming eyes.

CC hugged each of them.

"Take care of each other and other women, too," CC said through her tears.

"Take this back with you." Isabel tried to return to her the amber amulet, but CC shook her head.

"No, keep it and remember me."

"We will never forget," Isabel promised.

Then CC turned to Lir. She touched his arm gently, in a gesture that mimicked that of the goddess.

"I would have liked to have known you."

"As I would have you, child." His voice rumbled with feeling. "You no longer have your mother's amulet. Allow me to gift you with one of my own." The sea god reached into the waves and when he pulled his hand up, a delicate golden chain glittered from one of his fingers. From the end of the chain hung an exquisite baroque pearl, gleaming all the colors of sunrise. He placed it around her neck and kissed her lightly on her forehead. "Remember me," he said sadly. "And know that if you ever desire solace, all you need do is to find the water. In any world it will welcome you with a father's embrace."

At last CC faced the goddess. With the loss of Dylan she had thought her heart unable to ache anymore, but as Gaea smoothed back her hair and wiped the tears from her face, CC felt a new wound open within her.

"No, child." Gaea cupped CC's face in her hands. "Do not let this parting cause you more grief; I could not bear it. You must know that even in your distant world, I will be watching you. You can find me in the trees and flowers and plants you so love. And whenever the moon is at its most full, look there and you will see the reflection of my face."

CC choked back a sob, wondering if she would die of sadness.

As if reading her mind the goddess spoke quickly with knowing finality. "You will survive. You are child of my spirit and your strength is great."

CC nodded, feeling fresh tears warm her cheeks.

Gaea kissed her gently on the lips. "Go with my blessing, Daughter. Always remember that you are much loved by a goddess, and that you hold within you the magic of the Divine Feminine."

Then Lir moved to stand beside Gaea and, as one, the immortals raised their arms to the sky.

"I call upon the power at my command. I am Earth, body and soul." Gaea's voice was filled with strength. In response to her call, the air around the goddess began to shimmer with energy.

"I call upon the power at my command. I am sea, breath and life." Lir's voice followed Gaea's and as he spoke the water around them began to glow.

"Once we joined to create a child," Gaea intoned.

"Now we join to send a child back whence she came," Lir continued.

"Return to the world of man," Gaea said.

"Carrying blessings from the world of gods," Lir said.

"SO HAVE WE SPOKEN; SO SHALL IT BE."

The immortals intoned the final command together, and CC felt a great funnel of power settle over her, as if she had been swallowed by a current of electricity. Blinding light engulfed her, and she squeezed her eyes shut. Her body was being pulled backward with such force that she was unable to breathe. On and on the sensation went, like she was caught on a giant roller coaster that only ran in reverse. Panicking, CC wrenched open her mouth to scream, and it filled with saltwater as her head broke through the surface of the water, and she choked and sputtered, struggling to breathe and stay afloat.

She heard two quick splashes, and, in an instant, a head broke the surface not far from her, along with a lifeless body clad in a flight suit and strapped within a life jacket.

The sense of déjà vu was so overwhelming that she had to struggle to concentrate past blinding dizziness.

"There."

Blinking wildly, CC watched as the colonel pointed at the fluorescent orange life raft that drifted about forty feet in front of them.

"Swim! We have to get away from the plane." He set off, sidestroking and kicking hard as he dragged the lifeless body with him.

CC's numbed thoughts told her that those were the same words the colonel had spoken to her before. And the body was Sean. Another man who had died for her. She choked again, this time on a sob instead of seawater. Her mind felt stuck in a labyrinth of pain and remembrance.

A horrendously familiar explosion burst behind her, and she spun around in the water in time to bear witness a second time to the death of the plane. It was an enormous, gaping beast, and, in its death throes, it eerily reminded her of Sarpedon's sea monster.

With a sense of increasing detachment CC realized the same thing she had understood all those days before—the sinking plane was too close to her.

And this time she didn't care. There had been so much death. Why shouldn't she just relax and give in to it? At least this time she wouldn't be filled with fear of the water. She felt cold and unbearably tired. CC closed her eyes and quit struggling as she waited for the mechanical tentacle to wrap around her ankle.

When she felt the first bump against her body she was mildly surprised. She hadn't remembered getting thrown around before the thing had dragged her under.

The bump turned into an insistent, jetlike force, and soon she was sputtering, gasping for air, and flailing her arms desperately around for balance as she was firmly propelled up and forward by two somethings that felt slick and muscular and very familiar against her swiftly moving body.

This isn't happening, she thought. It can't be real.

"I'll be! Will you look at that?" A dark-haired captain holding a flat yellow paddle pointed in her direction.

Even the colonel, who was dragging Sean's lifeless body aboard the raft, paused to stare.

The pressure against CC released, and she came to a halt as she knocked against the side of the orange raft. The pointing captain grabbed her arm and pulled her aboard. At the rough handling, newly awakened pain raked through her body, and CC shivered violently as a warm rush of blood poured from her wounded shoulder.

"It's the same shoulder," she said, looking down at the red stain that was blending with the desert brown of her sodden fatigue shirt. "Different body, but same shoulder." The words were coming out of her mouth, but CC didn't feel very connected to them, just as she didn't feel very connected to her body. Somewhere through the layers of grief and shock, the laughter of hysteria began to bubble inside her throat.

"Shit, yes, your shoulder's hurt. We know that. But what the hell were those things?" the master sergeant asked, pointing at the sleek gray shapes that were streaking away from them.

"Dolphins," CC said, erupting into uncontrollable giggles. "They're dolphins."

"Well, kiss my ass and call me Santa Claus! I've never seen nothing like that. Those damn fish just saved your life," the Master Sergeant said, slapping his thick thigh.

"Actually, they're mammals, not fish," CC said between giggles and gulps for air. "And I guess they still think I'm a princess."

Except for her unnaturally shrill giggles, the raft was quiet while the men stared at her.

"Uh, sarg," the colonel said gently. "You better let me take a look at that shoulder."

The pain of having her shoulder handled killed CC's hysteria.

"This will hurt like hell," the colonel told her. "But I have to pack it and get the bleeding stopped or you're going to be in bad shape."

CC wanted to tell him that she didn't care, that she'd rather just die, but he had turned away and was busy searching through the first aid kit for packets of gauze.

"Looks like a fuckin' arrow sliced through her," the master sergeant said before the colonel told him to shut the hell up.

"Here, bite this." The colonel handed her a wooden tongue depressor, and she clamped her teeth down on it. "You try and think of someplace you'd rather be, and I'll try and be quick," he told her. "Ready?"

She nodded weakly and closed her eyes, thinking of a moonlit night when neon-colored fish were candles and the world was filled with the newness of love. She could see Dylan's face as he bent to kiss her and, for an instant, she could almost taste his wild, salty flavor.

Pain exploded, splintering her concentration as flecks of light dotted her closed lids. And then the sweetness of unconsciousness claimed her.

"HANG on, sarg! We've got ya!"

The steady *twap, twap, twap* of the helicopter and the pain in her shoulder wrenched CC back into screaming consciousness. She opened her eyes to find a Search and Rescue Trooper working over her, murmuring encouragement while he unsnapped the lid of a syringe filled with clear liquid and jabbed it into her thigh. The medicine's sharp burn was almost unnoticeable compared to the agony that was her shoulder.

"It'll be better now. Just relax, and we'll have you in the chopper in no time."

He spoke to her soothingly as he finished strapping her into the harness. Then he gave the thumb's up sign to the air above him, and CC felt a sickening lurch as she was lifted from the raft to the hovering helicopter.

She was the first to be rescued, but the others weren't far behind. CC watched through a morphine haze as Sean's body was pulled into the helicopter, followed quickly by the master sergeant, then the lieutenant, the captains, and finally the colonel.

As they flew away from the crash site, CC locked her gaze on the glimpse of sapphire water she could still see through the helicopter's open door. With all her soul she wished she would catch a flash of fiery orange streaking under the surface, shadowing the path of the aircraft and eternally waiting for her return.

Her vision of the glistening water blurred as her eyes filled and spilled over with tears.

"You'll be all right now, sarg," said the medic who was starting an IV in her arm. "We'll get you home and get you all fixed up."

CC opened her mouth to say that it would never be all right again, but a cry from the other side of the chopper bay interrupted her.

"Oh, shit! Johnson! Get over here; I need another set of hands! This man is alive."

The medic working on CC gave her IV sack a quick adjustment before he rushed to help his colleague.

Somewhere in the back of her mind CC understood that the frantically working medics were surrounding Sean's body, but her thoughts weren't working properly, and she couldn't seem to focus her mind.

And she thought she knew why. It had nothing to do with the loss of blood, or the pain, or the morphine. It was because even though her body was alive, her heart was dead. It died in another world and dissipated to nothingness within the seas.

The blue of the ocean crystallized through her tears, and then began to fade as gray unconsciousness folded over the edges of her vision, and, like a favorite blanket, lulled her into a deep, dreamless sleep.

Part Three

Chapter Thirty

Nine months later

"OH, please! That's nothing but a big pile of poo!" CC yelled and threw the book across the room, narrowly missing decapitating the lilac-colored orchid that was in magnificent bloom on her coffee table. "Hans Christian Andersen, T.S. Eliot, Lucretius, Tennyson, and now this horrible de la Motte Fouqué person. Uh! None of them were even close to getting it right!"

CC sighed and retrieved the book, all the more irritated that she had to reach under the couch for it. Finally grabbing it, she made straight for the wastebasket in the kitchen, rolling her eyes at the title.

"*Romantic Fairy Tales*," she scoffed, and lifted the lid of the wastebasket. But, as usual, she couldn't make herself actually throw the book away. Shaking her head and mumbling, she marched to her spare room.

"There's not one thing romantic about that stupid story. As usual, the mermaid doesn't even have a soul unless she can get some mule-headed guy to marry her. And in this particular version, he betrays her for another woman and she still pines away for him."

In her spare room she searched through her new bookshelves, trying to find a place for the slim book. Finally she slipped it between a lavishly illustrated copy of *Mermaids: Nymphs of the Sea*, and Oscar

Wilde's *The Fisherman and His Soul*. Then she put her hands on her hips and glared at her ever-expanding collection.

"All those words and you couldn't manage to capture more than a fraction of the truth. And none of you so much as hinted at the magic of his smile."

CC didn't say his name aloud; she didn't even think it. She couldn't. Even after nine months, she still felt too hollow and fragile. If she allowed herself to think too much about the empty place inside of her, she was sure that the shell of normalcy she had tried to glue together around her life would shatter. And then she didn't know how she would go on.

So instead, she haunted the bookstores and the Internet, always searching for everything and anything that pertained to mermaids. Then she devoured the pages as if they were her lifeline. Maybe they were. They kept her anger and frustration alive, which felt easier to live with than emptiness and despair.

She had gone on the Web and searched Amazon once using the term "merman." Two responses had popped up—an audio collection of Ethel Merman's greatest hits, and some kind of toy called Masters of the Universe Evil Enemies: Mer-men. After that, she had confined her searches to mer*maids* and mythology in general.

When she discovered her newest acquisition, the *Romantic Fairy Tales* book, she had been filled with an almost unbearable sense of anticipation as she opened its pages. The blurb on Amazon had said that de la Motte Fouqué's classic tale was written about the mermaid Undine. It proclaimed that the story was about "a water nymph who falls in love, acquires a soul and so discovers the reality of human suffering." But, as usual, her reading had left her disappointed and irritated.

"It was nothing but another preachy allegory written by some old dead white guy," CC said miserably.

Then she sighed again and rubbed at the pink, puckered scar that furrowed across her shoulder, cringing at the dull ache that radiated down her arm. CC glanced at her watch. It was almost 9:00 P.M. on a Friday night. Even on a hot August night, the opulent, Olympic-sized pool at her apartment complex would be deserted, which was just the way she liked it.

As she changed into her one-piece racing style Speedo and hastily pulled her shoulder length brown curls up into a tight ponytail she could almost hear her mother's voice echoing through her apartment.

"Dear, a pretty girl like you shouldn't be alone on a Friday night. It's just not good for the soul."

The bathroom light glinted on the golden chain that always hung around her neck, and CC's lips curved into a bittersweet smile. With one finger she stroked the smooth, iridescent surface of the huge pearl. Then she looked at herself in the mirror, pretending she was speaking to her mother.

"My soul's fine, Mom. It's just not all here."

Imagining the shocked reaction on her mother's face made her lips tighten. She didn't like to think about the pain her accident had caused her parents. They had never left her side throughout her month-long hospital stay, and when CC was released to return to Tinker AFB, her mom had come with her and had stayed another two months, helping her with the painful rehabilitation exercise routine. She certainly would never say anything to her mother that would make her worry any more about her than she already did, which meant she could never tell her mother that she longed to be in another world and another time.

CC shook her head. No, she wouldn't let depression win—she refused to live as a morose shadow. She felt like she had spent the past nine months trying to give birth to a new self, and she had to keep reminding herself that the birthing process always involved pain. It was just another part of life.

CC forced herself to smile as she pulled on her terrycloth cover-up, grabbed a towel and her swim bag and hurried out her apartment door. The water would make her feel better. It always did.

Mrs. Runyan was just coming up the stairs, and she waved a cheerful greeting.

"Going for your nightly swim, dear?" she asked.

"Yes, ma'am." CC smiled warmly at her. CC and her neighbor had grown very close in the months of her recovery. She felt honored to have been gifted with the friendship of another wise woman.

"Well, it's a lovely night for it. The moon is full and the sky is clear."

CC glanced up in surprise. The butter-colored moon was just rising, full and lustrous, over the greenbelt that backed their apartment complex.

"You're right. I hadn't remembered that it would be a full moon tonight."

At work CC had been preparing for another of the Communication Center's endless inspections. She had only been back full-time for three months, and she was so busy that she had completely lost track of the phases of the moon. Now she felt an unexpected rush of pleasure at the thought of swimming her laps beneath the beauty of the full moon.

Mrs. Runyan smiled mischievously at CC and tapped her on the nose. "Better keep your eyes open tonight. Wonderful things happen during the full moon."

"I'll remember, Mrs. Runyan. And I'll also remember our date tomorrow night to watch *An Affair to Remember*," CC said as she hurried past her friend.

"You had better, young lady. You're bringing the champagne!" the old woman called good-naturedly after her.

CC was still smiling as she swung through the wrought-iron gate to the pool. She sighed happily. As she had hoped, the pool was totally unoccupied. It never failed to surprise CC how quickly the residents of the pricey complex lost interest in their beautiful facility.

The pool was magnificent. It was a huge rectangle made of aqua-colored tile, hand painted around the rim with images of frolicking fish. To one side of the pool was a built-in Jacuzzi, complete with a fountain and cascading waterfall. Expensive deck chairs were clustered in neat circles around glass-topped, canopied tables. Thickly cushioned lounge chairs dotted the edge of the pool.

CC shrugged off her cover-up and fished her goggles out of the bag, then she left both bag and wrap in a heap on the nearest lounge chair. Eagerly, she approached the deep end of the pool.

Tonight the turquoise water was illuminated from above as well as below. Like hidden lanterns, the recessed lighting cast a magical turquoise glow through the calm water, while on its surface the moonlight danced and played, breathing life into the water's stillness and temporarily lending it the appearance of ocean waves.

The last time she had seen the moonlight reflecting off the ocean she had been in the arms of . . .

CC's breath caught in her throat, and hastily she reined in her thoughts. She hadn't been prepared for the sudden powerful image or for the painful memory it had evoked. In the past nine months she had discovered that memory was a tricky thing, and to keep from being dragged into its vortex of pain she had to stay vigilant, only allowing certain memories to sift into her consciousness, one at a time, and only when she was well prepared for them. Tonight she hadn't been prepared, and her desire for Dylan was a sharp yearning.

CC rubbed at her eyes, reminding herself firmly that she was finished crying. She was getting on with her life. Then she turned her face up to the moon.

"I hope you can see me," she said. "You were right; I did make it. I am strong."

A little breeze whispered around CC's body, ruffling the fine hairs on the back of her neck before it blew across the pool, causing the surface of the water to ripple in response.

CC smiled. "Thank you, Mother, for not allowing me to forget the magic that I still hold within me."

Feeling her soul lighten, CC fitted the goggles on her face and took several deep breaths. Then she sprang in a graceful arc into the water. Kicking, she angled to the surface where she started the steady, measured strokes that would carry her lap after lap across the pool.

As she counted laps, CC thought about what a shock her sudden love of swimming had been to her friends and family. Her first real request as she was recovering from her shoulder injury was to be taken to the water—any water—and allowed to swim.

"But dear, you've never liked the water," CC's mother had said, clearly confused by her daughter's unusual request.

"You aren't even a very good swimmer," her dad had added.

But CC had insisted, and, along with the blessing of her doctor, she had begun working in a pool with her physical therapist.

Now CC could say with confidence that she was an excellent swimmer, as a matter-of-fact; her physical therapist had said she showed a special aptitude for swimming. That had made CC laugh, and then, much later when she had been alone in her bed, it had made her cry.

Continuing to count laps as she kicked away from the side of the pool, she felt the tension in her body begin to relax. In the water, CC always felt secure. Lir had been right; it welcomed her with a father's touch—even if it she was only swimming in a man-made pool. And she ached for the sanctuary the water provided. The C-130 crash had been big news, especially after word of CC's dolphin saviors and Sean's resurrection had leaked to the civilian media. To CC's horror, reporters from all over the world had descended on her, all vying for a "personal angle to the tragedy." Apparently, *leave me alone* was a phrase that was not taught in journalism school.

CC only hoped that they hadn't been as tenacious about bothering Sean. She hadn't seen him since the rescue helicopter. She had been taken to the military hospital at Navy Siganella in Italy and rushed into surgery. Sean had ended up in Ramstein Air Base, Germany. She had only heard snatches of reports about him, but from them she had discovered that he had recovered, and that the doctors were calling it a miracle.

All she knew for sure was that she had nearly been responsible for his death, and that was a guilt she carried around with her every day. She had sent him a card—once. She'd addressed it to him in care of his fighter unit in Tulsa. She still cringed when she remembered her bumbling attempt at thanking him for exchanging places with her and her inept apology. He hadn't replied—and she hadn't expected him to.

Her stroke faltered, and she pushed thoughts of the accident from her mind. The moon was full, and she was alone, surrounded by the security of the water. All she had to do tonight was to stroke, kick and breathe—stroke, kick and breathe.

When she tilted her head up for her next breath, she thought she saw a shape pass over the moon. Clouds, she thought, and disappointment washed through her. She hadn't remembered the weatherman saying there was a chance of rain, but Oklahoma in the summer meant changing weather. With a burst of energy, she redoubled her efforts. If she was going to have to cut her swim short, at least she would be sure she got in a decent workout.

The shout came through the waves of water as more vibration than sound, and at first CC ignored it, thinking it was just the distant rumble of approaching thunder. At her next breath, though, the vibration turned into words.

"Sergeant Canady!"

CC ground her teeth together and came to an abrupt halt, treading water near the edge of the lap end of the pool. A man was standing several yards away from her. Through the blur of her goggles he looked tall and lean, but indistinct. She didn't bother to remove them.

"What?" she snapped.

"Are you Sergeant Canady? Sergeant Christine Canady?"

The man's voice was vaguely familiar, which told CC that he was probably one of the reporters who had been calling her for the past several months, whining for a story.

"Look, you shouldn't be here."

"I only ask if you are Christine Canady. The Christine Canady who was in the accident."

Irritation sliced through CC. She pulled her goggles off her face and brushed her escaping curls from her eyes.

"I don't want to talk to—"

Her words stopped as her vision cleared and she got a good look at him. She had been right, he was tall and lean, almost too thin. He was wearing faded jeans and a polo-style shirt. Over the upper right chest pocket of the shirt there was an embroidered emblem. The moonlight touched it, illuminating clearly the head of an Indian chieftain in the distinct pattern that was the well-known logo of Tulsa's F-16 Unit.

CC's eyes snapped to the man's face. His hair was military short, and he was clean-shaven. The raised pink ridge of scar tissue ran from the hairline over his left eye and down, marking a path over his well-defined cheekbone before disappearing into the shadows behind his ear.

"Sean?" CC's stomach heaved in a nauseating flutter.

His brow furrowed, and he hesitated before answering. CC thought that he looked nervous.

"Yes, but I . . ." Here he gestured abstractly and sighed, as if at a loss for words.

CC stared at him, and then, ashamed of herself she looked quickly away. He'd had part of his head sliced off. It was a miracle that he was walking and talking, so it shouldn't be surprising that he got words mixed up, or that he seemed confused about what he was trying to say. When CC met his gaze again she gave him a tentative smile.

"How about I get out of this pool so we can talk?"

Sean nodded and CC swam away from him to the ladder. As she started to climb out of the water she called to him over her shoulder.

"Can you wait a second while I get my cover-up and dry off a little?"

"I would wait an eternity for you, Christine."

Sean's words filled the night.

Like she had been hit in the stomach, CC's body jerked in response. She missed the next rung of the ladder and tumbled back into the water. Gasping, she kicked for surface, but, before she reached air, strong hands grabbed her arms and pulled, lifting her up to the side of the pool where she sat in a heap, coughing the water she'd swallowed and staring at the pale man who crouched beside her.

"I would never let you drown," he said softly.

"Why?" CC shook her head, pulling back from him. "Why are you saying these things?"

"Christine, I . . ." Sean reached for her and she lunged away from him.

"Please stop!" Her whisper sounded like a hiss of angry steam. "I know you've been hurt, and I know I'm responsible. But you have to stop talking like this."

Sean's face twisted in sadness. When he spoke, he kept his tone kind, like he was trying to reason with an upset child. "I told you once that I made my choice freely, and that I would make it again. That has not changed. You did not cause it, my love."

"There!" CC exploded to her feet. She wrapped her arms around herself as if she was afraid she would break into pieces. "That's what I mean. Stop staying those things."

Sean stood slowly and took a tentative half step toward her, but when she backed away from him, he stopped, holding his hand out like a peace offering.

"I cannot stop speaking thus to you. My words are truth," he said.

"Why are you doing this? *How* are you doing this?" She felt herself begin to shake uncontrollably.

"Christine, do you not know me?" he asked gently.

"I know who you sound like, but he's dead. I watched him die in another world." CC covered her face with her hands and sobbed.

Sean crossed the space between them and took her into his arms. At first she struggled, but soon she just stood there, rigid with pain in the cocoon of his unfamiliar embrace.

"I see that I must convince you." She felt the warmth of his breath against her wet hair. "Then let me describe for you a place. It is a place you would easily recognize, for there is none other like it. A ring of stone stands proudly in the middle of clear waters; its dome is open to the sky."

As he spoke, CC lifted her face so that she could look into the hazel depths of his eyes.

"The waters there are lit by luminous fish and filled with the magic of sea horses moving together in a dance of mating." He smiled tenderly at her. "It was there that you first loved me, but I believe that I have loved you forever—that you were a part of me even before we met in the storm that was your mother's creation. And I will continue to love you for an eternity, Christine."

Hesitantly, as if she were afraid he would disappear if she moved too quickly, Christine reached up and touched his cheek.

"How?" she asked.

He turned his head so he could kiss her palm. "I do not know, but I like to think of it as a gift from a goddess. I am sorry it took me so long to come to you. Being human is a very odd thing." He paused and laughed with a sound so familiar that CC's heart quivered in response. "When they die their bodies do not return to water. They stay intact, as if waiting for another's soul to fill them, but this body was . . ." He paused, shrugging his wide shoulders. "It was very badly damaged, and it has taken me longer to heal than I would have thought possible. Many said I would not heal at all, but they did not know the promise I had to fulfill."

"Dylan." CC breathed the word.

"Yes, my love," Dylan said.

CC felt the pain within her shatter and dissolve. In its place she was filled with an overwhelming sense of joy. Then her eyes widened in wonder.

"It's the opposite of all those mermaid stories that humans have written!" she exclaimed.

He gave her a quizzical look.

"In those stories the mermaid is saved by the love of a human man—and if he doesn't love her, she dies."

Dylan's smile mirrored her own. "It appears the humans had it wrong. It is the *woman's* love that saves the *merman's* soul."

"Or maybe they just save each other," she said.

"And so we shall, Christine."

"For an eternity."

"For an eternity," he assured her.

And as he claimed her lips, their ears were filled with the magical sound of a goddess's delighted laughter.

Turn the page to read an excerpt
from the next book in
P. C. Cast's Goddess Summoning series

Goddess of Spring

Prologue

"EVEN amidst the lovely Dryads your daughter shines, my lady," Eirene said. She wasn't looking at me as she spoke. Instead she was smiling at Persephone in a proud, motherly fashion, and she did not notice that my lips tightened into a thin line at her words.

"She is spring personified and even the beauty of the nymphs cannot begin to compete with her splendor."

At the sound of my words Eirene's sharp gaze immediately shifted to my face. My faithful nursemaid had known me too long not to recognize my tone.

"The child troubles you, Demeter?" she asked gently.

"How could she not?" I snapped.

Only Eirene's silence betrayed her hurt. I shifted my golden scepter from my right hand to my left, and leaned forward so that I could touch her arm in a wordless apology. As usual, she stood near my throne, always ready to serve me. But she was, of course, much more to me than a simple nursemaid or servant. She was my confidante and one of my most loyal advisors. As such she deserved to be treated with respect, and it was a sign of how distracted I had become that I had spoken so harshly to her.

Her distinctive gray eyes softened with understanding at my touch. "Would you like wine, Great Goddess?" She asked.

"For us both." I did not smile; it was not my way. But she understood me and my moods so completely that often only a look or a word was needed between us.

I studied my daughter as Eirene called for wine. The little Nysaian meadow had been the perfect choice in which to spend the unseasonably warm afternoon. Persephone and her wood nymph companions complemented the beauty that surrounded us. Though the day was pleasant, the trees that ringed the meadow were already beginning to shed their summer clothes. I watched Persephone twirl gracefully under one ancient oak, making a game of trying to catch the brilliantly colored falling leaves. The nymphs aided the young goddess by dancing on the limbs to assure a steady waterfall of orange and scarlet and rust.

As usual, Eirene was correct. The woodland Dryads were ethereal and delicate. Each of them was a breathing masterpiece. It was easy to understand why mortals found them irresistible. But when compared with Persephone, their beauty turned mundane. In her presence they became common house slaves.

My daughter's hair shone with a rich mahogany luster, the color of which never ceased to amaze me because I am so fair. It does not curl, either, as do my grain-colored tresses. Instead her hair was a ripple of thick, brilliant waves that lapped around the soft curve of her waist.

Obviously feeling my scrutiny, she waved joyously at me before capturing another watercolored leaf. Her face tilted in my direction. It was a perfect heart. Enormous violet-colored eyes were framed by arched brows and thick, ebony lashes. Her lips were lush and inviting. Her body was lithe. I felt my own lips turn down.

"Your wine, my lady." Eirene offered me a golden goblet filled with chilled wine the color of the sun.

I sipped thoughtfully, speaking my thoughts aloud, secure that they were safe with Eirene. "Of course Persephone is supple and lovely. Why would she not be? She spends all her time frolicking with nymphs and picking flowers."

"She also creates glorious feasts."

I made a very ungoddess-like noise through my nose. "I am quite aware that she produces culinary masterpieces, and then lolls about feasting to all hours with—" I wafted my hand in the direction of the Dryads "—semi-deities."

"She is much beloved," Eirene reminded me patiently.

"She is frivolous," I countered.

Suddenly, I closed my eyes and cringed as another voice rose from the multitudes and rang with the insistence of a clarion bell throughout my mind. *Lovely, somber Goddess of the Fields and Fruits and Flowers, strong and just, please aid our mother's spirit as she roams restless through the Darkened Realm without the comfort of a goddess . . .*

"Demeter, are you well?" Eirene's concern broke through the supplication, effectively causing the voice to dissipate like windblown dust.

Opening my eyes, I met her gaze. "It has become never-ending." Even as I spoke more voices crowded my mind. *O Demeter, we do call upon thee, that our sister who has passed Beyond be accorded the comfort of a Goddess . . . and . . . O gracious Goddess who gives life through the harvest, I do ask your indulgence for my beloved wife who has passed through the Gates of the Underworld and dwells evermore beyond the comfort of a goddess . . .*

With a mighty effort I blocked the teeming throng from my mind.

"Something must be done about Hades." My voice was stone. "I understand the mortals. Their entreaties are valid. It is fact that there is no Goddess of the Underworld." I leapt up and began to pace back and forth in frustration. "But what am I to do? The Goddess of the Riches of the Field cannot abandon her realm and descend into the Land of the Dead."

"But the dead do require the touch of a goddess," Eirene agreed firmly.

"They need more than the touch of a goddess. They need light and care and . . ." My words faded away as Persephone's bright laughter filled the meadow. "They need a breath of spring."

Eirene's eyes widened. "You cannot mean your daughter!"

"And why can I not! Light and life follow the child. She is exactly what is needed within the shadowy realm."

"But she is so young."

I felt my gaze soften as I watched Persephone leap over a narrow stream, allowing her hand to trail over the dried remains of the season's last wildflowers. Instantly the stalks filled and straightened and burst into brilliant bloom. Despite her faults, she was so precious, so filled with the joy of life. There was no doubt that I loved her dearly. I often wondered if my fierce devotion had kept her from growing into a goddess of her own realm. I straightened my shoulders. It was past time that I taught my daughter to fly.

"She is a goddess."

"She will not like it."

I hardened my already firm jaw. "Persephone will obey my command."

Eirene opened her mouth as if she wished to speak, then seemed to change her mind and instead drank deeply of her wine.

I sighed. "You know you may speak your mind to me."

"I was just thinking that it would not be a matter of Persephone obeying your command, but rather . . ." She hesitated.

"Oh, come! Tell me your thoughts."

Eirene looked decidedly uncomfortable. "Demeter, you know that I love Persephone as if she were my own child."

I nodded impatiently. "Yes, yes. Of course."

"She is delightful and full of life, but she has little depth. I do not think she has enough maturity to be Goddess of the Underworld."

A hot retort came to my mind, but wisdom held my tongue. Eirene was correct. Persephone was a lovely young goddess, but her life had been too easy, too filled with cosseted pleasures. And I was at fault. My frivolous daughter was proof that even a goddess could make mistakes as a parent.

"I agree, my old friend. Before Persephone can become Goddess of the Underworld, she must mature."

"Perhaps she should spend some time with Athena," Eirene said.

"No, that would only teach her to pry into the affairs of others."

"Diana?" Eirene offered.

I scoffed, "I think not. I would some day like to be blessed with grandchildren." I narrowed my eyes. "No, my daughter must grow up and see that life is not always filled with Olympian pleasures and luxury. She needs to learn responsibility, but as long as she can draw upon the power of a goddess, as long as she can be recognized as my daughter, she will never learn—" And suddenly I knew what I must do.

"My lady?"

"There is only one place where Persephone will truly learn to be a goddess. It is a place where she must first learn to be a woman."

Eirene drew back, her face taking on a horrified expression as she began to understand.

"You will not send her there!"

"Oh yes. *There* is exactly where I shall send her."

"But they will not know her; they do not even know you." Eirene's deeply lined brow furrowed in agitation.

I felt my lips turning up in one of my rare smiles. "Exactly, my friend. Exactly."

Chapter One

Oklahoma, Present Day

"No, it's not that I don't 'get it,' it's that I don't understand how you could have let it happen." Lina spoke slowly and distinctly through gritted teeth.

"Ms. Santoro, I have already explained that we had no idea until the IRS contacted us yesterday that there had been any error at all."

"Did you not have any checks and balances? The reason I pay you to manage the taxes for my business is because I need an expert." I glanced down at the obscenely large number typed in neat, no-nonsense black and white across the bottom of the government form. "I understand accidents and mistakes, but I don't understand how something this *large* could have escaped your notice."

Frank Rayburn cleared his throat before answering. Lina had always thought he looked a little like a gangster wannabe. Today his black pinstriped suit and his slippery demeanor did nothing to dispel the image.

"Your bakery did very well last year, Ms. Santoro. Actually, you more than doubled your income from the previous year. When we're talking about a major increase in figures, it is easy for mistakes to happen. I think that what would be more productive for us now is to focus on how you can pay what you owe the government instead of casting blame." Before she could speak he hurried on. "I have drawn up several suggestions." He pulled out another sheet of paper filled with bulleted columns and numbers and handed it to her. "Suggestion number one is to borrow the money. Interests rates are very reasonable right now."

Lina felt her jaw clench. She hated the idea of borrowing money, especially that much money. She knew it would make her feel exposed and vulnerable until the loan was repaid. *If* the loan could be repaid. Yes, she had been doing well, but a bakery wasn't exactly a necessity to a community, and times were hard.

"What are your other suggestions?"

"Well, you could introduce a newer, more glitzy line of foods. Maybe add a little something for the lunch crowd, more than those . . ." he hesitated, making little circles in the air with his thick fingers, ". . . baby pizza things."

"Pizette Fiorentine." She bit the words at him. "They are mini-pizzas that originated in Florence, and they are not meant to be a meal, they are meant to be a mid-afternoon snack served with cheese and wine."

He shrugged. "Whatever. All I'm saying is that it doesn't draw you a very big lunch crowd."

"You mean like a fried chicken buffet would? Or maybe I could even crank up the grill and churn out some burgers and fries?"

"Now there's an idea," he said, totally missing the sarcasm in her tone. "Suggestion number three would be to cut your staff."

Lina drummed her fingers on the top of the conference table. "Go on," she said, keeping her voice deceptively amiable.

"Number four would be to consider bankruptcy." He held up a hand to stop her from speaking, even though she hadn't uttered a sound. "I know it sounds drastic, but after those expensive renovations you've just completed, you really don't have any reserves left to fall back on."

"I only commissioned those expensive renovations because you assured me that Pani Del Goddess could afford them." Lina's hands twitched with the desire to wrap themselves around his neck.

"Be that as it may, your reserves are gone," he said condescendingly. "But bankruptcy is only one option, and not the one I would recommend. Actually, I would recommend option number five—sell to that big chain that offered to buy you out a couple of months ago. They just wanted your name and location. Give it to 'em. You'll have enough money to pay your debt and start over with a new name and place."

"But I've spent twenty years building up the Pani Del Goddess name, and I have no desire to move." If Frank Rayburn had been even the least bit intuitive, he would have recognized the storm that brewed in Lina's expressive eyes, even though it had not yet reached her mouth.

Frank Rayburn was not intuitive.

"Well, I just tell ya the options." Frank leaned back in the plush chair and crossed his arms while he gave Lina what he liked to think of as his stern, fatherly look. "You're the boss; it's your job to decide from there."

"No, you're wrong." Lina's voice was still calm and soft, but it was edged in honed steel. "You see, I am not your boss anymore. You are fired. You have proven yourself to be as incompetent with my business as you are with your choice in attire. My lawyer will be in contact with you. I'll make sure that she has several *options* drawn up for you to consider. Maybe one of them will keep you out of court. Now, good day, Mr. Rayburn, and as my dear, sainted grandmother would say, *Io non mangio in questo merdai. Fongule e tuo capra!* Lina stood, smoothed her skirt and snapped shut her leather briefcase. "Oh, how rude of me. You don't speak Italian. Allow me to translate my grandmother's sage words. 'You are a common turd. Fuck you and your goat!' Arrivederci."

Lina turned and strode through the professionally decorated office grinning wickedly at the well-rouged receptionist.